THE MYSTERIOUS FLAME OF QUEEN LOANA

Umberto Eco is the author of five bestselling novels, *The Name of the Rose*, *Foucault's Pendulum*, *The Island of the Day Before*, *Baudolino* and, most recently, *The Mysterious Flame of Queen Loana*. His collections of essays include *Five Moral Pieces*, *Kant and the Platypus*, *Serendipities*, *Travels in Hyperreality*, *How to Travel with a Salmon and Other Essays*, *On Beauty* and *On Literature*. A Professor of Semiotics at the University of Bologna, Umberto Eco lives in Milan.

Geoffrey Brock is the acclaimed translator of Cesare Pavese and Roberto Calasso. His own poetry has appeared in the *Paris Review*, *Poetry*, *The Hudson Review*, *The Southern Review* and elsewhere. He lives in San Francisco.

ALSO BY UMBERTO ECO

Baudolino

The Island of the Day Before

Foucault's Pendulum

The Name of the Rose

On Literature

On Beauty

Five Moral Pieces

Kant and the Platypus

Serendipities

How to Travel with a Salmon

Travels in Hyperreality

UMBERTO ECO

The Mysterious Flame of Queen Loana

TRANSLATED FROM THE ITALIAN BY
Geoffrey Brock

VINTAGE BOOKS
London

Published by Vintage 2006

8 10 9 7

First published as *La Misteriosa Fiamma della Regina Loana* by RCS Libri S.p.A. in 2004

First published in Great Britain in 2005 by Secker & Warburg

Vintage
Random House, 20 Vauxhall Bridge Road,
London SW1V 2SA

The Random House Group Limited Reg. No. 954009

A CIP catalogue record for this book is available from the British Library

ISBN 9780099481379

Penguin Random House is committed to a sustainable future for our business, our readers and our planet. This book is made from Forest Stewardship Council® certified paper.

Printed and bound in Germany by
GGP Media GmbH, Pössneck

CONTENTS

Part One

THE INCIDENT

1. The Cruellest Month

"And what's your name?"
"Wait, it's on the tip of my tongue."

That is how it all began.

I felt as if I had awoken from a long sleep, and yet I was still suspended in a milky grey. Or else I was not awake, but dreaming. It was a strange dream, void of images, crowded with sounds. As if I could not see, but could hear voices that were telling me what I should have been seeing. And they were telling me that I could not see anything yet, only a haziness along the canals where the landscape dissolved. Bruges, I said to myself, I was in Bruges. Had I ever been to Bruges the Dead? *Where fog hovers between the towers like incense dreaming? A grey city, sad as a tombstone with chrysanthemums, where mist hangs over the façades like tapestries…*

My soul was wiping the tram windows so it could drown in the moving fog of the headlamps. Fog, my uncontaminated sister… A thick, opaque fog, which enveloped the noises and called up shapeless phantoms… Finally I came to a vast chasm and could see a colossal figure, wrapped in a shroud, its face the immaculate whiteness of snow. *My name is Arthur Gordon Pym.*

I was chewing fog. Phantoms were passing, brushing me, melting. Distant bulbs glimmered like will-o'-the-wisps in a graveyard...

Someone is walking by my side, noiselessly, as if in bare feet, walking without heels, without shoes, without sandals. A patch of fog grazes my cheek, a band of drunks is shouting down there, down by the ferry. The ferry? It is not me talking, it is the voices.

The fog comes on little cat feet... There was a fog that seemed to have taken the world away.

Yet every so often it was as if I had opened my eyes and were seeing flashes. I could hear voices: "Strictly speaking, Signora, it isn't a coma.... No, don't think about flat encephalograms, for heaven's sake.... There's reactivity...."

Someone was aiming a light into my eyes, but after the light it was dark again. I could feel the puncture of a needle, somewhere. "You see, there's withdrawal..."

Maigret plunges into a fog so dense that he can't even see where he's stepping.... The fog teems with human shapes, swarms with an intense, mysterious life. Maigret? Elementary, my dear Watson, there are ten little Indians, and the hound of the Baskervilles vanishes into the fog.

The grey vapour was gradually losing its greyness of tint, the heat of the water was extreme, and its milky hue was more evident than ever... And now we rushed into the embraces of the cataract, where a chasm threw itself open to receive us.

I heard people talking around me, wanted to shout to let them know I was there. There was a continuous drone, as though I were being devoured by celibate machines with whetted teeth. I was in the penal colony. I felt a weight on my head, as if they had slipped the iron mask onto my face. I thought I saw sky blue lights.

"There's asymmetry of the pupillary diameters."

I had fragments of thoughts, clearly I was waking up, but I could not move. If only I could stay awake. Was I sleeping again? Hours, days, centuries?

The fog was back, the voices in the fog, the voices about the fog. *Seltsam, im Nebel zu wandern!* What language is that? I seemed to be swimming in the sea, I felt I was near the beach but was unable to reach it. No one saw me, and the tide was carrying me away again.

Please tell me something, please touch me. I felt a hand on my forehead. Such relief. Another voice: "Signora, there are cases of patients who suddenly wake up and walk away under their own power."

Someone was disturbing me with an intermittent light, with the hum of a tuning fork. It was as if they had put a jar of mustard under my nose, then a clove of garlic. *The earth has the odour of mushrooms.*

Other voices, but these from within: *long laments of the steam engine, priests shapeless in the fog walking single file towards San Michele in Bosco.*

The sky is made of ash. Fog up the river, fog down the river, fog biting the hands of the little match girl. Chance people on the bridges to the Isle of Dogs look into a nether sky of fog, with fog all round them, as if they were up in a balloon and hanging under the brown fog... I had not thought death had undone so many. The odour of train station and soot.

Another light, softer. *I seem to hear, through the fog, the sound of bagpipes starting up again on the heath.*

Another long sleep, perhaps. Then a clearing, *like being in a glass of water and anisette...*

He was right in front of me, though I still saw him as a shadow. My head felt muddled, as if I were waking up after having drunk too much. I think I managed to murmur something weakly, as if I were in that moment beginning to talk for the first time: "*Posco reposco flagito*—do they take the future infinitive? *Cujus regio ejus religio*... is that the Peace of Augsburg or the Defenestration of Prague?" And then: "Fog too on the Apennine stretch of the

Autosole Highway, between Roncobilaccio and Barberino del Mugello..."

He smiled sympathetically. "But now open your eyes all the way and try to look around. Do you know where we are?" Now I could see him better. He was wearing a white—what is it called?—*coat.* I looked around and was even able to move my head: the room was sober and clean, a few small pieces of pale metal furniture, and I was in bed, with a tube stuck in my arm. From the window, through the lowered blinds, came a blade of sunlight, *spring on all sides shines in the air, and in the fields rejoices.* I whispered: "We are... in a hospital and you... you're a doctor. Was I sick?"

"Yes, you were sick. I'll explain later. But you've regained consciousness now. That's good. I'm Dr. Gratarolo. Forgive me if I ask you some questions. How many fingers am I holding up?"

"That's a hand and those are fingers. Four of them. Are there four?"

"That's right. And what's six times six?"

"Thirty-six, of course." Thoughts were rumbling through my head, but they came as if of their own accord. "The sum of the areas of the squares... built on the two legs... is equal to the area of the square built on the hypotenuse."

"Well done. I think that's the Pythagorean theorem, but I got a C in maths in high school..."

"Pythagoras of Samos. Euclid's elements. The desperate loneliness of parallel lines that never meet."

"Your memory seems to be in excellent condition. And by the way, what's your name?"

That is where I hesitated. And yet I did have it on the tip of my tongue. After a moment I offered the most obvious reply.

"My name is Arthur Gordon Pym."

"That isn't your name."

Of course, Pym was someone else. He did not come back again. I tried to come to terms with the doctor.

"Call me... Ishmael?"

"Your name is not Ishmael. Try harder."

A word. Like running into a wall. Saying *Euclid* or *Ishmael* was easy, like saying *Jack and Jill went up a hill.* Saying who I was, on the other hand, was like turning around and finding that wall. No, not a wall; I tried to explain. "It doesn't feel like something solid, it's like walking through fog."

"What's the fog like?" he asked.

"*The fog on the bristling hills climbs drizzling up the sky, and down below the mistral howls and whitens the sea*... What's the fog like?"

"You put me at a disadvantage—I'm only a doctor. And besides, this is April, I can't show you any fog. Today's the twenty-fifth of April."

"*April is the cruellest month.*"

"I'm not very well read, but I think that's a quotation. You could say that today's the Day of Liberation. Do you know what year this is?"

"It's definitely after the discovery of America..."

"You don't remember a date, any kind of date, before... your reawakening?"

"Any date? Nineteen hundred and forty-five, end of World War Two."

"Not close enough. No, today is the twenty-fifth of April, 1991. You were born, I believe, at the end of 1931, all of which means you're pushing sixty."

"Fifty-nine and a half. Not even."

"Your calculative faculties are in excellent shape. But you have had, how shall I say, an incident. You've come through it alive, and I congratulate you on that. But clearly something is still wrong. A slight case of retrograde amnesia. Not to worry, they sometimes don't last long. But please be so kind as to answer a few more questions. Are you married?"

"You tell me."

"Yes, you're married, to an extremely likeable lady named Paola, who has been by your side night and day. Just yesterday evening I insisted she go home, otherwise she would have collapsed. Now that you're awake, I'll call her. But I'll have to prepare her, and before that we need to do a few more tests."

"What if I mistake her for a hat?"

"Excuse me?"

"There was a man who mistook his wife for a hat."

"Oh, the Sacks book. A classic case. I see you're up on your reading. But you don't have his problem, otherwise you'd have already mistaken me for a stove. Don't worry, you may not recognize her, but you won't mistake her for a hat. But back to you. Now then, your name is Giambattista Bodoni. Does that tell you anything?"

Now my memory was soaring like a glider among mountains and valleys, towards a limitless horizon. "Giambattista Bodoni was a famous typographer. But I'm sure that's not me. I could as easily be Napoleon as Bodoni."

"Why did you say Napoleon?"

"Because Bodoni was from the Napoleonic era, more or less. Napoleon Bonaparte, born in Corsica, first consul, marries Josephine, becomes emperor, conquers half of Europe, loses at Waterloo, dies on St. Helena, May 5, 1821, *he was as if unmoving*."

"I'll have to bring my encyclopaedia next time, but from what I remember, your memory is good. Except you don't remember who you are."

"Is that serious?"

"To be honest, it's not so good. But you aren't the first person something like this has happened to, and we'll get through it."

He asked me to raise my right hand, then to touch my nose. I understood perfectly what my right hand was, and my nose. Bull's-eye. But the sensation was absolutely new. Touching your nose is like having an eye on the tip of your index finger, looking you in the face. I have a nose. Gratarolo thumped me on the knee and then here and there on my legs and feet with some kind of little hammer. Doctors measure reflexes. It seemed that my reflexes were good. By the end I felt exhausted, and I think I went back to sleep.

I woke up in a place and murmured that it resembled the cabin of a spaceship, like in movies. (What movies, Gratarolo asked; all of them, I said, in general; then I named *Star Trek*.) They did things to me I did not understand, using machines I had never seen. I think they were looking inside my head, but I let them, not thinking, lulled by humming sounds, and now and then I dozed again.

Later (or the next day?), when Gratarolo returned, I was exploring the bed. I was feeling the sheets: light, smooth, pleasing to the touch. Less so the cover, which was a little prickly against my fingertips. I turned over and pounded my hand into the pillow, enjoying the fact that it sank into it. I was going *whack whack* and having a great time. Gratarolo asked me if I thought I could get out of bed. With the help of a nurse, I managed to stand up, though my head was still spinning. I felt my feet pressing against the ground, and my head was up in the air. That is how you stand up. On a tightrope. Like the Little Mermaid.

"Good. Now try going to the bathroom and brushing your teeth. Your wife's toothbrush should be in there." I told him one should never brush one's teeth with a stranger's toothbrush, and he remarked that a wife is not a stranger. In the bathroom, I saw myself in the mirror. At least I was fairly sure it was me, because mirrors, *as everyone knows,* reflect what is in front of them. A white, hollow face, a long beard, and two sunken eyes. This is great: I do not know who I am but I find out I am a monster. I would not want to meet me on a deserted road at night. Mr. Hyde. I have identified two objects: one is definitely called *toothpaste,* the other *toothbrush.* You have to start with the toothpaste and squeeze the tube. Exquisite sensation, I ought to do it frequently. But at a certain point you have to quit—that white paste at first pops, like a bubble, but then it all comes out like *le serpent qui danse.* Don't keep squeezing, otherwise you'll be like Broglio with the stracchini. Who's Broglio?

The paste has an excellent flavour. *Excellent, said the Duke.* That is a Wellerism. These, then, are flavours: things that caress the tongue and also the palate, though it seems to be the tongue that detects the flavours. Mint flavour—*y la hierbabuena, a las cinco de la tarde*...I made up my mind and did what everyone does in such cases, quickly and without thinking much about it: first I brushed up and down, then from left to right, then around the whole set. It's interesting to feel bristles going between two teeth, from now on I think I will brush my teeth every day, it feels nice. I also ran the bristles over my tongue. You feel a sort of shudder, but in the end if you don't press down too hard it's okay. That was a good idea, because my mouth was quite pasty. Now, I said to myself, you rinse. I ran some water from the tap into a glass and swirled it around in my mouth, happily amazed at the sound it made. And it gets even better if you toss your head back and make it—gurgle? Gurgling is good. I puffed up my cheeks, and then it all came out. I spat it out. *Sfroosh*...a cataract. You can do anything with lips, they are extremely flexible. I turned around, Gratarolo was standing there watching me *like I was a circus freak,* and I asked him if it was going well.

Perfectly, he said. My automatisms, he explained, were in good shape.

"It seems we have an almost normal person on our hands," I remarked, "except that he might not be me."

"Very witty, and that's a good sign too. Now lie back down—here, I'll help you. Tell me: what did you just do?"

"I brushed my teeth; you asked me to."

"Absolutely, and before you brushed your teeth?"

"I was in this bed and you were talking to me. You said it's April 1991."

"Right. Your short-term memory is working. Tell me, do you by any chance recall the brand of the toothpaste?"

"No. Should I?"

"Not at all. You certainly saw the brand when you picked up the tube, but if we had to record and store all the stimuli we encounter, our memory would be a bedlam. So we choose, we filter. You did what we all do. But now try to remember the most significant thing that happened while you were brushing your teeth."

"When I ran the brush over my tongue."

"Why?"

"Because my mouth was pasty, and after I did that I felt better."

"You see? You recorded the element most directly associated with your emotions, your desires, your goals. You have emotions again."

"It's a nice emotion, brushing your tongue. But I don't recall having ever brushed it before."

"We'll get there. Now, Signor Bodoni, I'll try to explain all this in plain language, but it's clear that the incident has affected certain regions of your brain. And even though a new study comes out every day, we don't yet know as much as we'd like to know about cerebral localizations, especially as regards the various forms of memory. I'd dare say that if what has happened to you had happened ten years from now, we'd have a better idea how to manage the situation. Don't interrupt, I understand, if it had happened to you a hundred years ago you'd already be in a madhouse, end of story. We know more today than we did then, but not enough. For example, if you were unable to talk, I could tell you exactly which area had been affected. . . ."

"Broca's area."

"Bravo. But we've known about Broca's area for more than a hundred years. Where the brain stores memories, however, is still a matter of debate, and more than one area is certainly involved. I don't want to bore you with scientific terms, which in any case might add to the confusion you feel—you know how, when the dentist has done something to one of your teeth, for a few days afterwards you keep touching it with your tongue? Well, if I were to say, just for instance, that I'm not as concerned about your hippocampus as I am about your frontal lobes, and perhaps the right orbital frontal cortex, you would try to touch yourself there, and it's not like exploring your mouth with your tongue. Endless frustration. So forget what I just said. And besides, every brain is different from every other, and all brains have extraordinary plasticity, so that over the course of time yours may be able to assign the tasks that the injured area can no longer perform to some other area. Do you follow, am I being clear enough?"

"Crystal clear, keep going. But first are you going to tell me that I'm the Collegno amnesiac?"

"You see? You remember the Collegno amnesiac, which is a classic case. It's only your own, which isn't classic, that you don't remember."

"I'd rather have forgotten about Collegno and remembered where I was born."

"That would be more unusual. You see, you identified the toothpaste tube immediately, but you don't recall being married—and indeed, remembering your own wedding and identifying the toothpaste tube depend on two different cerebral networks. We have different types of memory. One is called implicit, and it allows us to do with ease various things we've learned, like brushing our teeth, turning on the radio, or tying a tie. After the toothbrushing experiment, I'm willing to bet that you know how to write, perhaps even how to drive a car. When our implicit memory is assisting us, we're not even conscious of remembering, we act automatically. And then there's something called explicit memory, by which we remember things and know we're remembering them. But this explicit memory is twofold. One part tends nowadays to be called semantic memory, or public memory—the one that tells us a swallow is a kind of bird, and that birds fly and have feathers, but also that Napoleon died in... whenever you said. And this type seems to be working fine in your case. Indeed, I might even say too well, since all I have to do is give you a single input and you begin stringing together memories that I would describe as scholastic, or else you fall back on stock phrases. But this is the first type to form even in children. The child quickly learns to recognize a car or a dog, and to form general categories, so that if he once saw a German shepherd and was told it was a dog, then he'll also say 'dog' when he sees a Labrador. It takes the child longer, however, to develop the second type of explicit memory, which we call episodic, or autobiographical. He isn't immediately capable of remembering, when he sees a dog, say, that a month earlier he saw a dog in his grandmother's yard, and that he's the person who has had both experiences. It's episodic memory that establishes a link between who we are today and who we have been, and without it, when we say *I,* we're referring only to what we're feeling now, not to what we felt before, which gets lost, as you say, in the fog. You haven't lost your semantic memory, you've lost your episodic memory, which is to say the episodes of your life. In short, I'd say you know all the things other people know, and I imagine that if I were to ask you to tell me the capital of Japan..."

"Tokyo. Atom bomb on Hiroshima. General MacArthur..."

"Whoa, whoa. It's as though you remember all the things you read in a book somewhere, or were told, but not the things associated with your direct experience. You know that Napoleon was defeated at Waterloo, but try to tell me the name of your mother."

"*You only have one mother, your mother is still your mother*... But as for my mine, I don't remember her. I suppose I had a mother, since I know it's a law of the species, but... here again... the fog. I'm sick, doctor. It's horrible. I want something to help me go back to sleep."

"I'll give you something in a moment, I've already asked too much of you. Just lie back now, good.... To repeat, these things happen, but people get better. With a great deal of patience. I'll have them bring you something to drink, perhaps some tea. Do you like tea?"

"*Maybe I do and maybe I don't.*"

They brought me tea. The nurse had me sit up against my pillows and placed a tray in front of me. She poured some steaming water into a cup with a little bag in it. Go slow, she said, it burns.

What do you mean, slow? I sniffed the cup and detected the odour, I wanted to say, of smoke. I wanted to see what tea was like, so I took the cup and swallowed. Dreadful. A fire, a flame, a slap in the mouth. So this is boiling tea. It is probably the same with coffee, or camomile, which everyone talks about. Now I know what it means to burn yourself. Everybody knows you are not supposed to touch fire, but I did not know at what point you could touch hot water. I must learn to recognize the threshold, the moment when before you couldn't and after you can. I blew mechanically on the liquid, then stirred it some more with the spoon, until I decided I could try again. Now the tea was warm and it was good to drink. I was not sure which taste was the tea and which the sugar; one must have been *bitter* and the other *sweet*, but which was the sweet and which the bitter? In any case, I liked the combination. I will always drink my tea with sugar. But not boiling.

The tea made me feel peaceful and relaxed, and I went to sleep.

I woke again. Perhaps because in my sleep I was scratching my groin and scrotum. I was sweating under the covers. *Bedsores?* My groin is damp, and when I rub my hands over it too energetically, after an initial sensation of violent pleasure, the friction feels very unpleasant. It's nicer with the scrotum. You take it between your fingers—gently I might add, without going so far as to squeeze the testicles—and you feel something granular and slightly hairy: it's nice to scratch your scrotum. The itching does not go away immediately, in fact it gets worse, but then it feels even better to continue. *Pleasure is the cessation of pain,* but itching is not pain, it is an invitation to give yourself pleasure. *The titillation of the flesh.* By indulging in it you commit a sin. The provident young man sleeps on his back with his hands clasped on his chest so as not to commit impure acts in his sleep. A strange business, itching. And my balls... *You're a ballbuster. That guy's got balls.*

I opened my eyes. A woman was standing there. She was not all that young, over fifty I would guess, with fine lines around her eyes. But her face was luminous, still youthful. A few little streaks of white hair, barely noticeable, as though she had had them lightened on purpose, coquettishly, as if to say, I'm not trying to pass for a girl, but I wear my years well. She was lovely, but when she was young she must have been stunning. She was caressing my forehead.

"Yambo," she said.

"Iambo who, Signora?"

"You're Yambo. That's what everyone calls you. And I'm Paola, your wife. Recognize me?"

"No, Signora—I mean, no, Paola. I'm very sorry, the doctor must have explained."

"He explained. You no longer know what's happened to you, but you still know perfectly well what's happened to others. Since I'm part of your personal history, you no longer know that we've been married, my dear Yambo, for more than thirty years. And we have two daughters, Carla and Nicoletta, and three wonderful grandchildren. Carla married young and had two children, Alessandro who's five and Luca who's three. Nicoletta's son, Giangiacomo, Giangio for short, is also three. Twin cousins, you used to say. And you were... you are... you will still be a wonderful grandfather. You were a good father, too."

"And... am I a good husband?"

Paola rolled her eyes skywards: "We're still here, aren't we? Let's say that over the course of thirty years there have been ups and downs. You were always considered a good-looking man..."

"This morning, yesterday, ten years ago, I saw a horrible face in the mirror."

"After what's happened to you, that's the least you'd expect. But you were, you still are, a good-looking man, you have an irresistible smile, and some women didn't resist. Nor did you—you always said you could resist anything but temptation."

"I ask your forgiveness."

"Well, that's a bit like the guys dropping smart bombs on Baghdad and then apologizing when a few civilians die."

"Bombs on Baghdad? There aren't any in *A Thousand and One Nights.*"

"There was a war, the Gulf War. It's over now. Or maybe not. Iraq invaded Kuwait, the Western nations intervened. You don't recall any of it?"

"The doctor said that episodic memory—the kind that seems to have gone tilt—is tied to the emotions. Maybe the bombing of Baghdad was something I felt strongly about."

"I'll say. You've always been a devout pacifist, and you agonized over this war. Almost two hundred years ago Maine de Biran identified three types of memory: ideas, feelings, and habits. You remember ideas and habits but not feelings, which are of course the most personal."

"How is it you know all this good stuff?"

"I'm a psychologist, that's my job. But wait a second: you just said that your episodic memory had gone tilt. Why did you use that phrase?"

"It's an expression."

"Yes, but it's a thing that happens in pinball and you are... you were fanatical about pinball, like a little kid."

"I know what pinball is. But I don't know who I am, you see? There's fog in Val Padana. By the way, where are we?"

"In Val Padana. We live in Milan. In the winter months you can see the fog in the park from our house. You live in Milan and you're an antiquarian book dealer. You have a studio full of old books."

"The curse of the pharaoh. If I was a Bodoni and they baptized me Giambattista, things couldn't have turned out any other way."

"They turned out well. You're considered very good at what you do, and we're not billionaires but we live well. I'll help you, and you'll recover a little at a time. God, if I think about it, you might have not woken up at all. These doctors have been excellent, they got to you in time. My love, can I welcome you back? You act as if you're meeting me for the first time. Fine, if I were to meet you now, for the first time, I'd marry you just the same. Okay?"

"You're very sweet. I need you. You're the only one who can tell me about the last thirty years."

"Thirty-five. We met in college, in Turin. You were about to graduate and I was the lost freshman, roaming the halls of Palazzo Campana. I asked you where a certain classroom was, and you hooked me immediately, you seduced a defenceless high-school girl. Then one thing and another—I was too young, you went off to spend three years abroad. Afterwards, we got together—as a trial, we said, but I ended up getting pregnant, and you married me because you were a gentleman. No, sorry, also because we loved each other, we really did, and because you liked the idea of becoming a father. Don't worry, Papà, I'll help you remember everything, you'll see."

"Unless this is all a conspiracy, and my name is really Jimmy Picklock and I'm a burglar, and everything you and Gratarolo are telling me is a pack of lies, maybe, for instance, you're secret agents, and you need to supply me with a false identity in order to send me out to spy on the other side of the Berlin Wall, *The Ipcress File,* and..."

"The Berlin Wall isn't there any more. They tore it down, and the Soviet empire is falling to pieces..."

"Christ, you turn your back for a second and look what they get up to. Okay, I'm kidding, I trust you. What are stracchini?"

"Huh? Stracchino is a kind of soft cheese, but that's what it's called in Piedmont, here in Milan it's called crescenza. What makes you bring up stracchini?"

"It was when I was squeezing the toothpaste tube. Hang on. There was a painter named Broglio, who couldn't make a living off of his paintings, but he didn't want to work because he said he had a nervous condition. It seemed to be an excuse to get his sister to support him. Eventually his friends found him a job with a company that made or sold cheeses. He was walking past a big pile of stracchini, each one wrapped in a packet of semitransparent wax paper, and because of his condition, or so he said, he couldn't resist the temptation: he took them one by one and *whack,* he smashed them, making the cheese shoot out of the package. He destroyed a hundred or so stracchini before he was fired. All because of his condition. Apparently smacking stracchini, or as he said, *sgnaché i strachèn,* was a turn-on. My God, Paola, this must be a childhood memory! Didn't I lose all memory of my past experiences?"

Paola started laughing: "I'm sorry, I remember now. You're right, it is something you heard about as a kid. But you told that story often—it became part of your repertoire, so to speak. You were always making your dinner companions laugh with the story of the painter and his stracchini, and they in turn told others. You're not remembering your own experience, unfortunately—it's just a story you've told on numerous occasions and that for you has, how shall I say?, entered the public domain, like the story of Little Red Riding Hood."

"You're already proving indispensable to me. I'm happy to have you as my wife. I thank you for existing, Paola."

"Good Lord, just a month ago you would have called that expression soap-opera schmaltz..."

"You'll have to forgive me. I can't seem to say anything that comes from the heart. I don't have feelings, I only have memorable sayings."

"Poor dear."

"That sounds like a stock phrase, too."

"Bastard."

This Paola really loves me.

I had a peaceful night—who knows what Gratarolo put in my veins. I woke gradually, and my eyes must still have been closed, because I heard Paola whispering, so as not to wake me: "But couldn't it be psychogenic amnesia?"

"We can't rule that out," Gratarolo replied. "There may always be unfathomable tensions at the root of these incidents. But you saw his file, the lesions are real."

I opened my eyes and said good morning. Two young women and three children were also present. I had never seen them before, but I guessed who they were. It was terrible, because a wife is one thing, but daughters, my God, they are blood of your blood, and grandchildren too. The eyes of those two young women were shining with happiness, and the kids wanted to get up on the bed. They took me by the hand and said Hi, Grandpa. And nothing. It was not even fog, it was more like apathy. Or is it ataraxia? Like watching animals at the zoo—they could have been little monkeys or giraffes. Of course I smiled and said kind words, but inside I was empty. I suddenly thought of the word *sgurato,* but I did not know what it meant. I asked Paola. It is a Piedmontese word that means when you wash a pot thoroughly and then scrub it out with that metal wool stuff, so that it looks new again, as shiny and clean as can be. That was it, I felt thoroughly *sgurato.* Gratarolo, Paola, and the girls were cramming a thousand details of my life into my head, but they were like dry beans: when you moved the pot, they slid around in there but stayed raw, not soaking up any broth or cream—nothing to titillate the taste buds, nothing you would care to taste *again.* I was listening to things that happened to me as though they had happened to someone else.

I stroked the children and could smell their odour, without being able to define it except to say that it was tender. All that came to mind was *there are perfumes as fresh as a child's flesh.* And indeed my head was not empty, it was a maelstrom of memories that were not mine: the marchioness went out at five o'clock in the middle of the journey of our life, Abraham begat Isaac and Isaac begat Jacob and Jacob begat the man of La Mancha, and that was when I saw the pendulum betwixt a smile and tear, on the branch of Lake Como where late the sweet birds sang, the snows of yesteryear softly falling into the dark mutinous Shannon waves, *messieurs les Anglais je me suis couché de bonne heure,* though words cannot heal the women come and go, here we shall make Italy or a kiss is just a kiss, *tu quoque alea,* a man without qualities fights and runs away, brothers of Italy ask not what you can do for your country, the plough that makes the furrow will live to fight another day, I mean a Nose by any other name, Italy is made now the rest is commentary, *mi espíritu se purifica en Paris con aguacero,* don't ask us for the word crazed with light, we'll have our battle in the shade and suddenly it's evening, around my heart three ladies' arms I sing, oh Valentino Valentino wherefore art thou, happy families are all alike said the bridegroom to the bride, Guido I wish that mother died today, I recognized the trembling of man's first disobedience, *de la musique où marchent des colombes,* go little book to where the lemons blossom, once upon a time there lived Achilles son of Peleus, and the earth was without form and too much with us, *Licht mehr licht über alles,* Contessa, what oh what is life? and Jill came tumbling after. Names, names, names: Angelo Dall'Oca Bianca, Lord Brummell, Pindar, Flaubert, Disraeli, Remigio Zena, Jurassic, Fattori, Straparola and the pleasant nights, de Pompadour, Smith and Wesson, Rosa Luxemburg, Zeno Cosini, Palma the Elder, Archaeopteryx, Ciceruacchio, Matthew Mark Luke John, Pinocchio, Justine, Maria Goretti, Thaïs the whore with the shitty fingernails, Osteoporosis, Saint Honoré, Bactria Ecbatana Persepolis Susa Arbela, Alexander and the Gordian knot.

The encyclopaedia was tumbling down on me, its pages loose, and I felt like waving my hands the way one does amid a swarm of bees. Meanwhile the children were calling me Grandpa, I knew I was supposed to love them more than myself, and yet I could not tell which was Giangio, which was Alessandro, which was Luca. I knew all about Alexander the Great, but nothing about Alessandro the tiny, the mine.

I said I was feeling weak and wanted to sleep. They left, and I cried. Tears are salty. So, I still had feelings. Yes, but made fresh daily. Whatever feelings I once had were no longer mine. I wondered whether I had ever been religious; it was clear, whatever the answer, that I had lost my soul.

The next morning, with Paola there, Gratarolo had me sit at a table where he showed me a series of little coloured squares, lots of them. He would hand me one and ask me what colour it was. *A-tisket, a-tasket, a green and yellow basket... Was it red? Was it brown? Was it blue? No! Just a little yellow basket.* The first five or six I recognized without any trouble: red, yellow, green, and so on. Naturally I said that *A noir, E blanc, I rouge, U vert, O bleu, voyelles, je dirais quelque jour vos naissances latentes.* But I realized that the poet or whoever was lying. What does it mean to say A is black? Rather it was as if I were discovering colours for the first time: red was quite cheerful, *fire red,* but perhaps too strong. No, maybe yellow was stronger, like a light suddenly switched on and pointed at my eyes. Green made me feel peaceful. The difficulties arose with the other little squares. What's this? Green, I said. But Gratarolo pressed me: what type of green, how is it different from this one? Shrug. Paola explained that one was emerald green and the other was pea green. Emeralds are gems, I said, and peas are vegetables that you eat. They are round and they come in a long, lumpy pod. But I had never seen either emeralds or peas. Don't worry, Gratarola said, in English they have more than three thousand terms for different colours, yet most people can name eight at best. The average person can recognize the colours of the rainbow: red, orange, yellow, green, blue, indigo, and violet—though people already begin to have trouble with indigo and violet. It takes a lot of experience to learn to distinguish and name the various shades, and a painter is better at it than, say, a taxi driver, who just has to know the colours of traffic lights.

Gratarolo gave me a pen and paper. Write, he said. "What the hell am I supposed to write?" was what I wrote, and it felt as if I had never done anything but write. The pen was sleek and glided smoothly over the paper. "Write whatever comes to mind," Gratarolo said.

Mind? I wrote: love that within my mind discourses with me, the love that moves the sun and the other stars, stars hide your fires, if I were fire I would burn the world, I've got the world on a string, there are strings in the human heart, the heart does not take orders, who would hear me among the angels' orders, fools rush in where angels fear to tread, tread lightly she is near, lie lightly on her, a beautiful lie, touched with the wonder of mortal beauty, wonder is the poet's aim.

"Write something about your life," Paola said. "What did you do when you were twenty?" I wrote: "I was twenty. I won't let anyone say that's the best time of a person's life." The doctor asked me what first came to mind when I woke up. I wrote: "When Gregor Samsa woke one morning, he found himself transformed in his bed into an enormous insect."

"Maybe that's enough, Doctor," Paola said. "Don't let him go on too long with these associative chains, or he might go crazy on me."

"Right, because I seem sane to you now?"

All at once Gratarolo barked: "Now sign your name, without thinking, as if it were a cheque."

Without thinking. I traced "GBBodoni", with a flourish at the end and a round dot on the *i*.

"You see? Your head doesn't know who you are, but your hand does. That was to be expected. Let's try something else. You mentioned Napoleon. What did he look like?"

"I can't conjure up an image of him. Just words."

Gratarolo asked Paola if I knew how to draw. Apparently I'm no artist, but I manage to doodle things. He asked me to draw Napoleon. I did something of the sort.

"Not bad," Gratarolo remarked. "You drew your mental scheme of Napoleon—the tricorne, the hand in the waistcoat. Now I'll show you a series of images. First series, works of art."

I performed well: the Mona Lisa, Manet's *Olympia,* this one is a Picasso, that one is a good imitation.

"See how well you recognize them? Now let's try some contemporary figures."

Another series of photographs, and here too, with the exception of one or two faces that meant nothing to me, my answers were on target: Greta Garbo, Einstein, Totò, Kennedy, Moravia, and who they were. Gratarolo asked me what they had in common. They were famous? Not enough, there's something else. I balked.

"They're all dead now," Gratarolo said.

"What, even Kennedy and Moravia?"

"Moravia died at the end of last year. Kennedy was assassinated in Dallas in 1963."

"Oh, those poor guys. I'm sorry."

"That you wouldn't remember about Moravia is almost normal, he just died recently, and your semantic memory didn't have much time to absorb the event. Kennedy, on the other hand, baffles me—that's old news, the stuff of encyclopaedias."

"He was deeply affected by the Kennedy affair," Paola said. "Maybe Kennedy got lumped with his personal memories."

Gratarolo pulled out some other photographs. One showed

two men: the first was certainly me, except well groomed and well dressed, and with that irresistible smile Paola had mentioned. The other man had a friendly face, too, but I did not know him.

"That's Gianni Laivelli, your best friend," Paola said. "He was your desk mate from primary school through high school."

"Who are these?" asked Gratarolo, bringing out another image. It was an old photograph. The woman had a thirties-style hairdo, a white, moderately low-cut dress, and a teeny-tiny little button nose. The man had perfectly parted hair, maybe a little brilliantine, a pronounced nose, and a broad, open smile. I did not recognize them. (Artists? No, it was not glamorous or stagy enough. Maybe newlyweds.) But I felt a tug in the pit of my stomach and—I do not know what to call it—a gentle swoon.

Paola noticed it: "Yambo, that's your parents on their wedding day."

"Are they still alive?" I asked.

"No, they died a while ago. In a car accident."

"You got worked up looking at that photo," Gratarolo said. "Certain images spark something inside you. That's a start."

"But what kind of start is it, if I can't even find papà and mamma in that damn hellhole," I shouted. "You tell me that these two were my parents, so now I know, but it's a memory that you've given me. I'll remember the photo from now on, but not them."

"Who knows how many times over the past thirty years you were reminded of them because you kept seeing this photo? You can't think of memory as a warehouse where you deposit past events and retrieve them later just as they were when you put them there," Gratarolo said. "I don't want to get too technical, but when you remember something, you're constructing a new profile of neuronal excitation. Let's suppose that in a certain place you had some unpleasant experience. When afterwards you remember that place, you reactivate that initial pattern of neuronal excitation with a profile of excitation that's similar to but not the same as that which was originally stimulated. Remembering will therefore produce a feeling of unease. In short, to remember is to reconstruct, in part on the basis of what we have learned or said since. That's normal, that's how we remember. I tell you this to encourage you to reactivate some of these profiles of excitation, instead of simply digging obsessively in an effort to find something that's already there, as shiny and new as you imagine it was when you first set it aside. The image of your parents in this photo is the one we've shown you and the one we see ourselves. You have to start from this image to rebuild something else, and only that will be yours. Remembering is a labour, not a luxury."

"These mournful and enduring memories," I recited, "this trail of death we leave alive..."

"Memory can also be beautiful," Gratarolo said. "Someone said that it acts like a convergent lens in a camera obscura: it focuses everything, and the image that results from it is much more beautiful than the original."

"I want a cigarette."

"That's a sign that your organism is recovering at a normal pace. But it's better if you don't smoke. And when you go back home, alcohol in moderation: not more than a glass per meal. You have blood-pressure problems. Otherwise I won't allow you to leave tomorrow."

"You're letting him leave?" Paola said, a little scared.

"Let's take stock, Signora. From a physical standpoint your husband can get by pretty well on his own. It's not as though he'll fall down the stairs if you leave him alone. If we keep him here, we'll exhaust him with endless tests, all of them artificial experiences, and we already know what they'll tell us. I think it would do him good to return to his environment. Sometimes the most helpful thing is the taste of familiar food, a smell—who knows? On these matters, literature has taught us more than neurology."

It is not that I wanted to play the pedant, but if all I had left was that damned semantic memory, I might as well use it: "Proust's madeleine," I said. "The taste of the linden-blossom tea and that little cake give him a jolt. He feels a violent joy. And an image of Sundays at Combray with his Aunt Léonie comes back to him... *It seems there must be an involuntary memory of the limbs, our legs and arms are full of torpid memories*... And who was that other voice? *Nothing compels memories to manifest themselves as much as smells and flame.*"

"So you know what I mean. Even scientists sometimes believe writers more than their machines. And as for you, Signora, it's practically your field—you're not a neurologist, but you are a psychologist. I'll give you a few books to read, a few famous accounts of clinical cases, and you'll understand the nature of your husband's problems immediately. I think that being around you and your daughters and going back to work will help him more than staying here. Just be sure to visit me once a week so we can track your progress. Go home, Signor Bodoni. Look around, touch things, smell them, read newspapers, watch TV, go hunting for images."

"I'll try, but I don't remember images, or smells, or flavours. I only remember words."

"That could change. Keep a diary of your reactions. We'll work on that."

I began to keep a diary.

I packed my bags the next day. I went down with Paola. It was clear that they must have air-conditioning in hospitals: suddenly I understood, for the first time, what the heat of the sun was. The warmth of a still raw spring sun. And the light: I had to squint. You can't look at the sun: *Soleil, soleil, faute éclatante*...

When we got to the car (never seen it before) Paola told me to give it a try. "Get in, put it in neutral first, then start it. While it's still in neutral, press the accelerator." I immediately knew where to put my hands and feet, as if I'd never done anything else. Paola sat next to me and told me to put it in first, then to remove my foot from the clutch while ever so slightly pressing the accelerator, just enough to move a metre or two forward, then to brake and turn the engine off. That way, if I did something wrong, the worst I could do was run into a bush. It went well. I was quite proud. I defiantly backed up a little too. Then I got out, left the driving to Paola, and off we went.

"How does the world look?" she asked me.

"I don't know. They say that a cat, if it falls from a window and hits its nose, can lose its sense of smell and then, because cats live by their ability to smell, it can no longer recognize things. I'm a cat that hit its nose. I see things, I understand what sort of things they are, of course—those are stores over there, here's a bicycle going by, there are some trees, but... but they don't quite fit somehow, as if I were trying to put on someone else's jacket."

"A cat putting on someone else's jacket with its nose. Your metaphors must still be loose. We'll have to tell Gratarolo, but I'm sure it will pass."

The car continued on. I looked around, discovering the colours and shapes of an unknown city.

2. The Murmur of Mulberry Leaves

"Where are we going now, Paola?"

"Home. Our home."

"And then?"

"Then we'll go inside, and you'll get comfortable."

"And then?"

"Then you'll take a nice long shower, you'll shave, put on some decent clothes. And then we'll eat. And then—what would you like to do?"

"That's just what I don't know. I remember everything that's happened since my reawakening, I know all about Julius Caesar, but I can't imagine what comes next. Until this morning I wasn't worried about any next—only about the before that I wasn't able to remember. But now that we're going... somewhere, I see fog ahead of me, too, not just behind me. No, it isn't fog ahead—it's as if my legs were slack and I couldn't walk. It's like jumping."

"Jumping?"

"Yes, to jump you have to make a leap forward, but to do that you have to get a running start, so you have to back up first. If you don't back up, you won't go forward. So I have the feeling that in order to say what I'll do next, I need to know a lot about what I did before. You get ready to do a thing by changing something that was there before. Now, if you tell me I need to shave, I can see why: I rub my hand over my chin, it feels bristly, I should get rid of this hair. It's the same if you tell me I should eat, I recall that the last time I ate was last night, broth, prosciutto, and stewed pear. But it's one thing to say I'll shave or I'll eat, and something else to say what I'll do next, in the long run, I mean. I can't grasp what the long run means, because I'm missing the long run that was there before. Does that make sense?"

"You're saying you no longer live in time. We are the time we live in. You used to love Augustine's passages about time. He was the most intelligent man who ever lived, you always said. We psychologists can learn a lot from him still. We live in the three moments of expectation, attention, and memory, and none of them can exist without the others. You can't stretch towards the future because you've lost your past. And knowing what Julius Caesar did doesn't help you figure out what you yourself should do."

Paola saw my jaw tightening and changed the subject. "Do you recognize Milan?"

"Never seen it before." But when the road widened I said: "Castello Sforzesco. And then the Duomo. And the *Last Supper,* and the Brera Art Gallery."

"And Venice?"

"In Venice there's the Grand Canal, the Rialto bridge, San Marco, the gondolas. I know what's in the guidebooks. It may be that I've never been to Venice and have lived in Milan for thirty years, but for me Milan's the same as Venice. Or Vienna: the Kunsthistorisches Museum, the third man. Harry Lime up on that Ferris wheel at the Prater saying the Swiss invented cuckoo clocks. He lied: cuckoo clocks are Bavarian."

We got home and went inside. A lovely apartment, with balconies overlooking the park. I really saw *an expanse of trees.* Nature is as beautiful as they say. Antique furniture—apparently I am well-off. I do not know how to get around, where the living room is, or the kitchen. Paola introduces me to Anita, the Peruvian woman who helps around the house. The poor thing does not know whether to celebrate my return or greet me like a visitor. She runs back and forth, shows me the door to the bathroom, keeps saying, "*Pobrecito el Señor Yambo, ay Jesusmaría,* here are the clean towels, Signor Yambo."

After the commotion of my departure from the hospital, my first encounter with the sun, and the trip home, I felt sweaty. I decided to sniff my armpits: the odour of my sweat did not bother me—I do not think it was very strong—but it made me feel like a living animal. Three days before returning to Paris, Napoleon sent a message to Josephine telling her not to wash. Did I ever wash before making love? I do not dare ask Paola, and who knows, maybe I did with her and did not with other women—or vice versa. I had myself a good shower, soaped my face and shaved slowly, found some aftershave with a light, fresh scent, and combed my hair. I look more civil already. Paola showed me my wardrobe: apparently I like corduroy pants, slightly coarse jackets, wool ties in pale colours (pea green, emerald, chartreuse? I know the names, but not how to apply them yet), checkered shirts. It seems I also have a dark suit for weddings and funerals. "Just as handsome as before," Paola said, when I had put on something casual.

She led me down a long hallway lined with shelves full of books. I looked at the spines and recognized most of them. That is to say I recognized the titles—*The Betrothed, Orlando Furioso, The Catcher in the Rye.* For the first time, I had the impression of being in a place where I felt at ease. I pulled a volume from the shelf, but even before looking at the cover I held the back of it in my right hand and with my left thumb flipped quickly through the pages in reverse. I liked the noise, did it several times, then asked Paola whether I should see a soccer player kicking a ball. She laughed; apparently there were little books that made the rounds when we were children, a kind of poor man's movie, where the soccer player changed position on each page, so that if you flipped the pages rapidly you saw him move. I made sure that this was something everyone knew: I thought as much, it was not a memory, just a notion.

The book was *Père Goriot,* Balzac. Without opening it I said: "Goriot sacrificed himself for his daughters. One was named Delphine, I think. Along come Vautrin alias Collin and the ambitious Rastignac—just the two of us now, Paris. Did I read much?"

"You're a tireless reader. With an iron memory. You know stacks of poems by heart."

"Did I write?"

"Nothing of your own. I'm a sterile genius, you used to say; in this world you either read or write, and writers write out of contempt for their colleagues, out of a desire to have something good to read once in a while."

"I have so many books. Sorry, we do."

"Five thousand here. And there's always some imbecile who comes over and says, my how many books you have, have you read them all?"

"And what do I say?"

"Usually you say: Not one, why else would I be keeping them here? Do you by chance keep the tins of meat after you've emptied them? As for the five thousand I've already read, I gave them away to prisons and hospitals. And the imbecile reels."

"I see a lot of foreign books. I think I know several languages." Verses came to me unbidden: "*Le brouillard indolent de l'automne est épars... Unreal city, / under the brown fog of a winter dawn, / a crowd flowed over London Bridge, so many, / I had not thought death had undone so many... Spätherbstnebel, kalte Träume, / überfloren Berg und Tal, / Sturm entblättert schon die Bäume, / und sie schaun gespenstig kahl... Mas el doctor no sabía,*" I concluded, "*que hoy es siempre todavía...*"

"That's curious, out of four poems, three are about fog."

"You know, I feel surrounded by fog. It's just that I can't see it. I know how others have seen it: *At a turn, an ephemeral sun brightens: a cluster of mimosas in the pure white fog.*"

"You were fascinated by fog. You used to say you were born in it. For years now, whenever you came across a description of fog in a book you made a note in the margin. Then one by one you had the pages photocopied at your studio. I think you'll find your fog dossier there. And in any case, all you have to do is wait: the fog will be back. Though it's no longer what it used to be—there's too much light in Milan, too many shop windows lit up even at night; the fog slips away along the walls."

"*The yellow fog that rubs its back upon the window-panes, the yellow smoke that rubs its muzzle on the window-panes, licked its tongue into the corners of the evening, lingered upon the pools that stand in drains, let fall upon its back the soot that falls from chimneys, curled once about the house and fell asleep.*"

"Even I knew that one. You used to complain that the fogs of your youth weren't around any more."

"My youth. Is there someplace here where I keep the books I had when I was a kid?"

"Not here. They must be in Solara, at the country house."

And so I learned the story of the Solara house, and of my family. I was born there, accidentally, during the Christmas holidays of 1931. Like Baby Jesus. Maternal grandparents dead before I was born, paternal grandmother passed away when I was five. My father's father remained, and we were all he had left. My grandfather was a strange character. In the city where I grew up, he had a shop, almost a warehouse, of old books. Not valuable, antiquarian books, like mine, just used books, and lots of nineteenth-century stuff. In addition, he liked to travel and went abroad often. In that era, abroad meant Lugano, or at the very most Paris or Munich. And in such places he collected things from street vendors: not only books but also movie posters, figurines, postcards, old magazines. Back then we did not have all the memorabilia collectors we have today,

Paola said, but he had a few regular customers, or maybe he collected for his own pleasure. He never made much, but he enjoyed himself. Then in the twenties he inherited the Solara house from a great-uncle. An immense house, if you could see it, Yambo, the attics alone look like the Postojna caves. There was a lot of land around it, which was farmed by tenants, and your grandfather derived enough from that to live on, without having to work too hard at selling books.

Apparently that was where I spent all my childhood summers, Christmas and Easter vacations, and many other religious holidays, as well as two full years, from 1943 to 1945, after the bombings had begun in the city. That is where all my grandfather's things must be, along with all my schoolbooks and toys.

"I don't know where they are; it was as if you didn't want to see them any more. Your relationship with that house has always been bizarre. Your grandfather died of a heart attack after your parents were lost in that car accident, around the time you were finishing high school..."

"What did my parents do?"

"Your father worked for an import business, eventually becoming the manager. Your mother stayed home, as respectable ladies did. Your father eventually managed to buy himself a car—a Lancia no less—and what happened happened. You were never very explicit on that score. You were about to go off to university and you and your sister Ada lost your whole family in a single blow."

"I have a sister?"

"Younger than you. She was taken in by your mother's brother and sister-in-law, who had become your legal guardians. But Ada got married young, at eighteen, to a guy who whisked her off to live in Australia. You don't see each other often. She makes it to Italy about as often as the pope dies. Your aunt and uncle sold the family house in the city, and almost all the Solara land. Thanks to the proceeds, you were able to continue your studies, but you quickly gained your independence from them by winning a university scholarship, and you went to live in Turin. From that point on you seemed to forget Solara. I insisted, after Carla and Nicoletta were born, that we go there for summers. That air is good for the kids. I sweated blood to get the wing that we stay in livable. And you went against your will. The girls love it, it's their childhood, even now they spend all the time they can there, with the little ones. You'd go back for their sake, stay two or three days, but you never set foot in the places you called the sanctums: your old bedroom, your parents' and grandparents' rooms, the attics... On the other hand, there's still enough space left that three families can live there and never see each other. You'd take a few walks in the hills and then there would always be something urgent that required you to return to Milan. It's understandable, your parents' deaths basically split your life into two parts, before and after. Perhaps the Solara house represented for you a world that had vanished for ever, and you made a clean break. I always tried to respect your discomfort, though sometimes jealousy made me think it was just an excuse—that you were going back to Milan alone for other reasons. *Mais glissons.*"

"The irresistible smile. So what made you marry the laughing man?"

"You laughed well, and you made me laugh. When I was a girl I always talked about a schoolmate of mine—it was Luigino this and Luigino that. Every day I came home from school talking about something Luigino had done. My mother suspected I was sweet on him, and one day she asked me why I liked Luigino so much. And I said, Because he makes me laugh."

Experiences can be recovered in a hurry. I tested the flavours of different foods—the hospital fare had all tasted the same. Mustard on boiled meat is quite appetizing. But meat is stringy and gets between your teeth. I discovered (rediscovered?) toothpicks. If only I could work one into my frontal lobe, get the dross out... Paola had me taste two wines, and I said the second was incomparably better. It ought to be, she said; the first is cooking wine, good for a stew at best, the second is Brunello. Well, I said, no matter what shape my head is in, at least my palate is working.

I spent the afternoon testing things, feeling the pressure of my hand on a cognac glass, watching how the coffee rises in the coffee-maker, tasting two varieties of honey and three kinds of marmalade (I like apricot best), rubbing the living-room curtains, squeezing a lemon, plunging my hands into a sack of semolina. Then Paola took me for a short walk in the park; I felt the barks of the trees, I heard *the murmur of mulberry leaves in the hand.* We passed a flower seller in Largo Cairoli, and Paola had him put together, against his better judgement, a bouquet that looked like a harlequin. Back at home I tried to distinguish the scents of different flowers and herbs. *And he saw that everything was very good,* I said, cheered. Paola asked me if I felt like God. I replied that I was quoting just for the sake of quoting, but I was certainly an Adam discovering his Garden of Eden. And an Adam who learns quickly, it seems: I saw, on a shelf, some bottles and boxes of cleansers, and I knew at once not to touch the tree of good and evil.

After dinner I sat down in the living room. Instinctively I went over to the rocking chair and sank into it. "You always did that," Paola said. "It's where you had your evening scotch. I think Gratarolo would permit you that." She brought me a bottle, Laphroaig, and poured me a good amount, no ice. I rolled the liquid around in my mouth before swallowing. "Exquisite. It tastes a little like kerosene, though." Paola was excited: "You know, after the war, in the early fifties—it was only then that people started drinking whisky. Maybe the Fascist higher-ups drank it before that, who knows, but normal people didn't. And we started drinking it when we were about twenty. Not often, because it was expensive, but it was a rite of passage. And our folks all looked at us and said, how can you drink that stuff, it tastes like kerosene."

"Well, tastes aren't conjuring up any Combray for me."

"It depends on the taste. Keep on living and you'll find the right one."

On the little side table there was a pack of Gitanes, *papier maïs*. I lit one, inhaled greedily, and coughed. I took a few more puffs and put it out.

I let myself rock gently until I began to feel sleepy. The tolling of a grandfather clock woke me, and I almost spilled my scotch. The clock was behind me, but before I could identify it, the tolling stopped, and I said, "It's nine o'clock." Then, to Paola, "You know what just happened? I was dozing, and the clock woke me. I didn't hear the first few chimes distinctly, that is to say, I didn't count them. But as soon as I decided to count I realized that there had already been three, so I was able to count four, five, and so on. I understood that I could say four and then wait for the fifth, because one, two, and three had passed, and I somehow knew that. If the fourth chime had been the first I was conscious of, I would have thought it was six o'clock. I think our lives are like that—you can only anticipate the future if you can call the past to mind. I can't count the chimes of my life because I don't know how many came before. On the other hand, I dozed off because the chair had been rocking for a while. And I dozed off in a certain moment because that moment had been preceded by other moments, and because I was relaxing while awaiting the subsequent moment. But if the first moments hadn't put me in the right frame of mind, if I had begun rocking in any old moment, I wouldn't have expected what had to come. I would have remained awake. You need memory even to fall asleep. Or no?"

"The snowball effect. The avalanche slides towards the valley, gaining speed as it goes, because little by little it gets larger, carrying with it the weight of all it has been before. Otherwise there is no avalanche—just a little snowball that never rolls down."

"Yesterday evening... in the hospital, I was bored, and I started humming a tune to myself. It was automatic, like brushing my teeth... I tried to figure out how I knew it. I started to sing it again, but once I began thinking about it, the song no longer came of its own accord, and I stopped on a single note. I held it a long time, at least five seconds, as if it were an alarm or a dirge. I no longer knew how to go forward, and I didn't know how to go forward because I had lost what came before. That's it, that's how I am. I'm holding a long note, like a stuck record, and since I can't remember the opening notes, I can't finish the song. I wonder what it is I'm supposed to finish, and why. While I was singing without thinking I was actually myself for the duration of my memory, which in that case was what you might call throat memory, with the befores and afters linked together, and I was the complete song, and every time I began it my vocal cords were already preparing to vibrate the sounds to come. I think a pianist works that way, too: even as he plays one note he's readying his fingers to strike the keys that come next. Without the first notes, we won't make it to the last ones, we'll come untuned, and we'll succeed in getting from start to finish only if we somehow contain the entire song within us. I don't know the whole song any more. I'm like... a burning log. The log burns, but it has no awareness of having once been part of a whole trunk nor any way to find out that it has been, or to know when it caught fire. So it burns up and that's all. I'm living in pure loss."

"Let's not go overboard with the philosophy," Paola whispered.

"No, let's. Where do I keep my copy of Augustine's *Confessions?*"

"In the bookcase with the encyclopaedias, the Bible, the Koran, Lao Tzu, and the philosophy books."

I went to pick out the *Confessions* and looked in the index for the passages on memory. I must have read them because they were all underlined: *I come then to the fields and the vast chambers of memory.... When I enter there, I summon whatever images I wish. Some appear at once, but others must be sought at length, dragged forth as it were from hidden nooks.... Memory gathers all this in its vast cavern, in its hidden and ineffable recesses.... In the enormous palace of my memory, heaven, earth, and sea are present to me... I find myself there also.... Great is the power of memory, O my God, and awe-inspiring its infinite, profound complexity. And that is the mind, and that is myself.... Behold the fields and caves, the measureless caverns of memory, immeasurably full of immeasurable things.... I pass among them all, I fly from here to there, and nowhere is there any end....* "You see, Paola," I said, "you've told me about my grandfather and the country house, everyone's trying to give me all this information, but when I receive it in this way, in order really to populate these caverns I'd have to put into them every one of the sixty years I've lived till now. No, this is not the way to do it. I have to go into the cavern alone. Like Tom Sawyer."

I do not know what Paola said to that, because I was still making the chair rock and I dozed again.

Briefly, I think, because I heard the doorbell, and it was Gianni Laivelli. We had been desk mates, the two Dioscuri. He embraced me like a brother, emotional, already knowing how to treat me. Don't worry, he said, I know more about your life than you do. I'll tell you every last detail. No thanks, I told him, Paola already explained our history to me. Together from elementary school through high school. Then I went off to college in Turin while he studied economics and business in Milan. But apparently we never lost touch. I sell antiquarian books, he helps people pay their taxes—or not pay them—and by all rights we should have each gone our separate ways, but instead we're like family: his two grandchildren play with mine, and we always celebrate Christmas and New Year's together.

No thanks, I had said, but Gianni could not keep his mouth shut. And since he remembered, he seemed unable to grasp that I did not. Remember, he would say, the day we brought a mouse to class to scare the maths teacher, and the time we took a trip to Asti to see the Alfieri play and when we got back we learned that the plane carrying the Turin team had gone down, and the time that..."

"No, I don't remember, Gianni, but you're such a good storyteller that it's as if I did. Which one of us was smarter?"

"Naturally, in Italian and philosophy you were, and in maths I was. You see how we turned out."

"By the way, Paola, what did I major in?"

"In letters, with a thesis on *Hypnerotomachia Poliphili*. Unreadable, at least to me. Then you went off to Germany to specialize in the history of ancient books. You said that because of the name you'd been stuck with you couldn't have done anything else. And then there was your grandfather's example, a life among papers. When you came back, you set up your rare book studio, at first in a little room, using the little capital you had left. After that, things went well for you."

"Are you aware that you sell books that cost more than a Porsche?" Gianni said. "They're gorgeous, and to pick them up and realize they're five hundred years old, and the pages still as snappy beneath your fingers as if they'd just come off the press..."

"Take it easy," Paola said, "we can start talking about his work in the next few days. Let's give him a chance to get used to his home first. How about a scotch, kerosene-flavoured?"

"Kerosene?"

"It's just something between me and Yambo, Gianni. We're starting to have secrets again."

When I escorted Gianni to the door, he took me by the arm and whispered to me in a complicit tone, "And so you haven't yet seen the beautiful Sibilla..."

Sibilla who?

Yesterday Carla and Nicoletta came with their whole families, even their husbands, who are friendly. I spent the afternoon with the children. They are sweet, I am beginning to get attached to them. But it is embarrassing; at a certain point I realized that I was smothering them with kisses, pulling them to me, and I could smell them—soap, milk, and talcum powder. And I asked myself what I was doing with those strange children. Am I some kind of paedophile? I kept them at a distance and we played some games. They asked me to be a bear—who knows what a grandfather bear does. So I got on all fours, going *awrr roarr roarr,* and they all jumped on my back. Take it easy, I'm not young any more, my back aches.

Luca zapped me with a water pistol, and I thought it wise to die, belly up. I risked throwing my back out, but it was a success. I was still weak, and as I got back up my head was spinning. "You shouldn't do that," Nicoletta said, "you know you have orthostatic pressure." Then she corrected herself: "I'm sorry, you didn't know. Well, now you know again." A new chapter for my future autobiography. Written by someone else.

My life as an encyclopaedia continues. I speak as if I were up against a wall and could never turn around. My memories have the depth of a few weeks. Other people's stretch back centuries. A few evenings ago I tasted a small nut. I said: *The distinctive scent of bitter almond.* In the park I saw two policemen on horseback: *If wishes were horses, beggars would ride.*

I knocked my hand against a sharp corner, and as I was sucking the little scratch and trying to see what my blood tasted like, I said: *Often have I encountered the evil of living.*

There was a downpour and when it ended I exulted: *For lo, the rain is over and gone.*

I usually go to bed early and remark: *Longtemps je me suis couché de bonne heure.*

I do fine with traffic lights, but the other day I stepped into the street at a moment that seemed safe, and Paola managed to grab my arm just in time, because a car was coming. "I had it timed," I said. "I would have made it."

"No, you wouldn't have made it. That car was going fast."

"Come on, I'm not an idiot. I know perfectly well that cars run over pedestrians, and chickens too, and to avoid them they hit the brakes and black smoke comes out and they have to get out to start the car again with the crank. Two men in dustcoats with big black goggles, and me with mile-long ears that look like wings." Where did that image come from?

Paola looked at me. "What's the fastest you think a car can go?"

"Oh," I said, "up to eighty kilometres per hour..." Apparently they go quite a bit faster now. My ideas on the subject seemed to come from the period when I got my licence.

I was astonished that, as we made our way across Largo Cairoli, every few steps we passed a Negro who wanted to sell me a lighter. Paola brought me for a bike ride in the park (I have no trouble riding a bike), and I was astonished again to see a group of Negroes playing drums around a pond. "Where are we," I said, "New York? Since when have there been so many Negroes in Milan?"

"For some time now," Paola replied. "But we don't say Negroes any more, we say blacks."

"What difference does it make? They sell lighters, they come here to play their drums because they probably don't have a lira to go to a café, or maybe they're not wanted there. It looks to me as if these blacks are as badly off as the Negroes."

"Still, that's what one says now. You did, too."

Paola observed that when I try to speak English I make mistakes, but I do not when I speak German or French. "That doesn't surprise me," she said. "You must have absorbed French as a child, and it's still in your tongue the way bicycles are still in your legs. You learned German from textbooks in college, and you remember everything from books. But English, on the other hand, you learned during your travels, later. It belongs to your personal experiences of the past thirty years, and only bits of it have stuck to your tongue."

I still feel a little weak. I can focus on something for half an hour, an hour at the most; then I go and lie down for a while. Paola takes me to the pharmacist every day to have my blood pressure checked. And I have to pay attention to my diet, avoid salt.

I have begun watching television; it is the thing that tires me least. I see unfamiliar gentlemen who are called president and prime minister. I see the king of Spain (was it not Franco?) and ex-terrorists (terrorists?) who have repented. I do not always understand what they are talking about, but I learn a great deal. I remember Aldo Moro, the parallel convergences, but who killed him? Or was he in the plane that crashed into the Banca dell'Agricoltura in Ustica? I see some singers with rings through their earlobes. And they are male. I like the TV series about family tragedies in Texas, the old films of John Wayne. Action movies upset me, because with one blast of their tommy guns they blow up rooms, they make cars flip over and explode, a guy in an undershirt throws a punch and another guy smashes through a plate-glass window and plummets into the sea—all of it, the room, the car, the window, in a few seconds. Too fast, my head spins. And why so much noise?

The other night Paola took me to a restaurant. "Don't worry, they know you. Just ask for the usual." Much ado: How are you Dottore Bodoni, we haven't seen you for a long time, what will we be having this evening? The usual. There's a man who knows what he likes, the owner crooned. Spaghetti with clam sauce, grilled seafood plate, Sauvignon Blanc, then an apple tart.

Paola had to intervene to prevent me from asking for seconds on the fish. "Why not, if I like it?" I asked. "I think we can afford it, it doesn't cost a fortune." Paola looked at me abstractedly for a few seconds, then took my hand and said: "Listen, Yambo, you've retained all your automatisms, and you have no problems using a knife and fork or filling a glass. But there's something we acquire through personal experience, gradually, as we become adults. A child wants to eat everything that tastes good, even if it will give him a stomach-ache later. His mother explains over time that he must control his impulses, just as he must when he needs to pee. And so the child, who if it were left up to him would continue to poop in his nappies and to eat enough Nutella to land him in the hospital, learns to recognize the moment when, even if he doesn't feel full, he should stop eating. As we become adults, we learn to stop, for example, after the second or third glass of wine, because we remember that when we drank a whole bottle we didn't sleep well. What you have to do, then, is re-establish a proper relationship with food. If you give it some thought, you'll figure it out in a few days. In short, no seconds."

"And a calvados, I presume," said the owner as he brought the tart. I waited for a nod from Paola, then replied, "*Calva sans dire.*" I could tell he was familiar with my wordplay, because he repeated, "*Calva sans dire.*" Paola asked me what calvados called to mind, and I replied that it was good, but that was all I knew.

"And yet you got drunk on it during that Normandy trip... Don't worry, it takes time. In any case, *the usual* is a good phrase, and there are lots of places around here where you can go in and say *the usual,* and that should help you feel comfortable."

"It's clear by now that you know how to deal with traffic lights," Paola said, "and you've learned how fast cars go. You should try taking a walk by yourself, around the Castello and then into Largo Cairoli. There's a gelateria on the corner; you love gelato and they practically live off you. Try asking for the usual."

I did not even have to say it—the man behind the counter immediately filled a cone with stracciatella: Here's your usual, Dottore. If stracciatella was my favourite, I can see why: it is excellent. Discovering stracciatella at sixty is quite pleasant. What was that joke Gianni told me about Alzheimer's? The great thing about it is that you're always getting to meet new people.

New people. I had just finished the gelato, throwing away the last part of the cone without eating it—why? Paola later explained that it was an old habit; my mother had taught me as a child that you shouldn't eat the tip because that's where the vendor, back in the days when they sold gelato from carts, held it with his dirty fingers—when I saw a woman approaching. She was elegant, around forty or so, with a slightly brazen demeanour. The *Lady with an Ermine* came to mind. She was already smiling at me from a distance, and I got a nice smile ready too, since Paola had told me my smile was irresistible.

She came up to me and took hold of both my arms: "Yambo, what a surprise!" But she must have noticed something vague in my expression; the smile was not enough. "Yambo, don't you recognize me? Do I look that much older? Vanna, Vanna..."

"Vanna! You're more beautiful than ever. It's only that I've just been to the eye doctor, and he put something in my eyes to dilate my pupils. My vision will be blurry for a few hours. How are you, Lady with an Ermine?" I must have said that to her before, because I had the impression that she got a little misty-eyed.

"Yambo, Yambo," she whispered, caressing my face. I could smell her perfume. "Yambo, we lost touch. I always wanted to see you again, to tell you that it might have been brief—perhaps that was my fault—but I'll always have the fondest memories. It was... lovely."

"It was beautiful," I said, with some feeling, with the air of a man recalling his garden of delights. Superb acting. She kissed me on the cheek, whispered that her number had not changed, and left. Vanna. Apparently a temptation I had been unable to resist. *What scoundrels men are!* With De Sica. But goddamn, what good is it to have had an affair if later you cannot even—I am not talking about telling your friends, but should you not at least be able to savour it now and then, as you lie snug beneath your covers on a stormy night?

Since the first night, as we lay beneath the covers, Paola had lulled me to sleep by stroking my hair. I liked feeling her beside me. Was that desire? Eventually I overcame my embarrassment and asked her if we still made love. "In moderation, mostly out of habit," she said. "Do you feel the urge?"

"I don't know. As you know, I still don't have many urges. But I wonder..."

"Don't wonder, try to get some sleep. You're still weak. And besides, I certainly don't want you making love with a woman you've just met."

"Affair on the Orient Express."

"Yikes, this isn't a Dekobra novel."

3. Someone May Pluck Your Flower

I know how to get around outside, have even learned how to act when people greet me: you gauge your smile, your gestures of surprise, your delight or courtesy by observing the other person's smiles, gestures, and courtesies. I tried it out on neighbours, in the elevator. Which proves that social life is mere fiction, I said to Carla when she congratulated me. She said this incident is making me cynical. Of course, if you didn't start thinking it was all play-acting, you might shoot yourself.

Now then, Paola said, it's time you went back to the office. Go by yourself, visit with Sibilla, and see what feelings your place of work inspires. Gianni's whisper about the beautiful Sibilla came back to me.

"Who's Sibilla?"

"She's your assistant, your girl Friday. She's fantastic and has kept the studio running these past few weeks. I called her today and she was quite proud of having made some amazing sale or other. Sibilla—don't ask me her last name because nobody can pronounce it. A Polish girl. She was majoring in library science in Warsaw, and when the regime there began to crumble, even before the fall of the Berlin Wall, she managed to get a permit to come and study in

Rome. She's sweet, maybe too sweet, she must have figured out how to win some bigwig's sympathy. In any case, once she got here she started looking for a job and never went back. She found you, or you found her, and she's been your assistant for nearly four years now. She's expecting you today, and she knows what happened and how she should behave."

She gave me the address and phone number of my office. After Largo Cairoli feeds into Via Dante and before you get to the Loggia dei Mercanti—you can tell it's a loggia from a distance—you turn left and you're there. "If you have trouble, go into a café and call her, or me, and we'll send a team of firemen, but I don't think it will come to that. Oh, bear in mind that you started off speaking French with Sibilla, before she learned Italian, and you never stopped. A little game between the two of you."

So many people in Via Dante. It feels good to pass by a series of strangers without being obliged to greet them, it gives you confidence, makes you realize that seven out of ten people are in the same condition you are. After all, I could be someone who is new to the city, who feels a little alone but is getting his bearings. Except that I am new to the planet. Some man waved hello from a café door, no call for theatrical recognition, I waved back and it went smoothly.

I found the street and my studio like the boy scout who wins the treasure hunt: a sober plaque on the ground floor said STUDIO BIBLIO. I must not have much imagination, though I suppose the name sounds serious—what was I supposed to call it, Roman Holiday? I rang, went up the stairs, saw a door that was already open, and Sibilla on the threshold.

"Bonjour, Monsieur Yambo... pardon, Monsieur Bodoni..." As if it were she who had lost her memory. She was indeed quite beautiful. Long, straight blond hair that *framed the perfect oval of her face*. Not a trace of make-up, except perhaps for a slight touch of something around the eyes. The only adjective that came to mind was *darling*. (I am dealing in stereotypes, I know, but it is thanks to them that I have been getting by.) She was wearing a pair of jeans and one of those T-shirts with an English message on it, SMILE or something like that, which emphasized, modestly, two adolescent breasts.

We were both embarrassed. "Mademoiselle Sibilla?" I asked.

"*Oui,*" she answered, then quickly: "*ohui, houi.* Entrez."

Like a delicate hiccup. The first "*oui*", uttered almost normally, was quickly followed by the second, which caught briefly in her throat as she was breathing in, then the third, as she exhaled again, with the faintest quizzical tone. The overall effect was of childish embarrassment and at the same time a sensual timidity. She stepped aside to let me come in. I noted a tasteful perfume.

If I had had to explain what a book studio was, I would have described something much like what I now saw. Bookcases of dark wood, filled with antique volumes, and more old books on the heavy, square table. A little desk in a corner, with a computer. Two colourful maps on either side of a window with opaque glass. Soft light, broad green lampshades. Through a door, a long narrow storage room—it seemed to be a workroom for packing and shipping books.

"So you must be Sibilla? Or should I say Mademoiselle something—I'm told you have an unpronounceable last name."

"Sibilla Jasnorzewska, yes, here in Italy it causes some problems. But you've always just called me Sibilla." I saw her smile for the first time. I told her I wanted to get my bearings, wanted to see our prize books. That wall in the back, she said, and she went over to show me the correct bookcase. She walked silently, brushing the floor with her tennis shoes. But maybe it was the moquette that muted her steps. *There hangs, adolescent virgin, a sacred shadow over you,* I was about to say aloud. Instead I said: "Who wrote that, Cardarelli?"

"What?" she said, turning her head, her hair twirling. "Nothing," I said. "Let's see what we have."

Lovely volumes with an ancient air. Not all of them had a title label on the spine. I took one from the shelf. Instinctively I opened it to look for the title page, but I did not find one. "Incunabulum, then. Sixteenth-century blind-tooled pigskin binding." I ran my hands over the sides, feeling a tactile pleasure. "Headcaps slightly worn." I flipped through the pages, touching them to see whether they squeaked, as Gianni had said. They did. "Wide, clean margins. Ah, minor marginal staining on the endpapers, the last signature is wormed, but it doesn't affect the text. Lovely copy." I turned to the colophon, knowing it was called that, and slowly sounded out: "Venetiis mense Septembri... fourteen hundred ninety-seven. Could it be..." I turned to the first page: *Iamblichus de mysteriis Aegyptiorum*... It's the first edition of Ficino's *Iamblichus,* isn't it?"

"It's the first... Monsieur Bodoni. You recognize it?"

"No, I don't recognize anything, you'll have to learn that, Sibilla. It's just that I know that the first *Iamblichus* translated by Ficino is from 1497."

"Forgive me, I'm trying to get used to it. It's just that you were so proud of that copy, it's really splendid. And you said that for now you weren't going to sell it, there are so few around—we'd wait for one to appear in some American catalogue, since they're so good at jacking up prices, and then list ours."

"So I'm a canny businessman, then."

"I always said it was an excuse, that you wanted to keep it to yourself awhile, so you could look at it now and then. But since you did decide to sacrifice the Ortelius, I have some good news."

"Ortelius? Which one?"

"The 1606 Plantin, with 166 colour tables and the Parergon. Period binding. You were so pleased to have discovered it when you bought Commendatore Gambi's entire library on the cheap. You finally decided to put it in the catalogue. And while you... while you weren't well, I managed to sell it to a client, a new one. He didn't seem like a real bibliophile to me, more like someone who buys as an investment because he's heard that antiquarian books appreciate quickly."

"Too bad, a wasted copy. And...how much?"

She seemed afraid to say the amount; she got a form and showed it to me. "In the catalogue we put 'price on request', and you were prepared to deal. I immediately named the highest price, and he didn't even try to bargain, just signed a cheque and was off. 'On the nail,' as they say in Milan."

"We've reached these levels now..." I didn't have a sense of current prices. "Well done, Sibilla. How much did it cost us?"

"Basically nothing. That is, with the rest of the books from the Gambi library we'll easily make back, little by little, the lump sum we paid for the whole lot. I took care of depositing the cheque in the bank. And since there was no price listed in the catalogue, I think that with Mr. Laivelli's help we'll come out quite well on the financial side."

"So I'm one of those who don't pay their taxes?"

"No, Monsieur Bodoni, you just do what your fellow dealers do. For the most part, you have to pay the full amount, but with certain fortunate deals you might, how do you say, round down. But you're ninety-five per cent honest as a taxpayer."

"After this deal it'll be fifty per cent. I read somewhere that citizens should pay every penny of their taxes." She looked humiliated. "Don't worry about it, though," I said paternally. "I'll talk it over with Gianni." Paternally? Then I said, almost brusquely, "Now let me take a look at some of the other books." She turned around and went to sit at her computer, silent.

I looked at the books, flipped through their pages: Bernardino Benali's 1491 *Commedia,* a 1477 edition of Scot's *Liber Phisionomiae,* a 1484 edition of Ptolemy's *Quadripartite,* a 1482 *Calendarium* by Regiomontanus. Nor was I exactly lacking when it came to later centuries: there was a fine first edition of Zonca's *Novo teatro,* and a marvellous Ramelli...I was familiar with each of these works, like every antiquarian who knows the great catalogues by heart. But I did not know I owned copies of them.

Paternally? I was pulling out books and putting them back, but in fact I was thinking about Sibilla. Gianni had given me that hint, clearly mischievous, and Paola had delayed telling me about her until the last minute, and had used certain phrases that were almost sarcastic, even if her tone was neutral—"maybe too sweet", "a little game between the two of you"—nothing particularly rancorous, but she seemed a hair's breadth away from calling her a slyboots.

Could I have had an affair with Sibilla? The lost maiden newly arrived from the East, wide-eyed and curious, meets an older gentleman (though I was four years younger when she got here) and falls under his spell, after all he is the boss and knows more about books than she does, and she learns, hangs on his every word, admires him; and he has found his ideal pupil—beautiful, smart, with that hiccupped *oui oui oui*—and they begin working together, all day every day, alone in this studio, partners in so many *trouvailles* great and small; and one day they brush against each other by the door and in that instant the story of their affair begins. But me, at my age? You're just a girl, go and find a boy your own age for God's sake, don't take me so seriously. And she: No, I've never felt anything like this before, Yambo. Was I summarizing some movie everyone knows? And it goes on like a movie, or a romance novel: I love you, Yambo, but I can't go on looking your wife in the eye, she's so dear and kind, and you have two daughters and you're a grandfather—Thanks for reminding me that there's a whiff of the corpse about me already—No, don't talk that way, you're more . . . more . . . more than any man I've ever met, boys my age make me laugh, but maybe it's right that I should leave—Wait, we can still be good friends, just seeing each other every day will be enough—But don't you see, that's just it, if we see each other every day we could never remain friends—Sibilla, don't say that, let's think this through. . . . One day she stops coming to the studio, I call her and say I'm going to kill myself, and she says don't be infantile, *tout passe*, then later she is the one who comes back, unable to stay away. And it goes on like that for four years. Or does it end?

I seem to know all the clichés, but not how to put them together in a believable way. Or else these stories are terrible and grandiose precisely because all the clichés intertwine in an unrealistic way and you can't disentangle them. But when you actually live a cliché, it feels brand-new, and you are unashamed.

Would it be a realistic story? In recent days I felt that I no longer had desires, but as soon as I saw her I learned what desire is. I mean, someone I just met for the first time. Imagine being around her every day, following her, seeing her glide around you as if she were walking on water. Of course this is mere speculation; I would never start something, in the state I am in now, something like that, and besides, with Paola, I would really be the prize swine. For me, this girl might as well be the Immaculate Virgin, I cannot even think it. Great. But for her?

She might still be in mid-affair, maybe she wanted to greet me with *tu* and my first name; fortunately in French you can use *vous* even when you are sleeping together. Maybe she wanted to throw her arms around my neck—who knows how much she too might have suffered in recent weeks—and here she sees me come along, pretty as you please, saying how do you do Mademoiselle Sibilla, and now won't you leave me to my books, very kind of you thanks. And she understands that she can never tell me the truth. Perhaps it is better like this, time she found herself a boy. And me?

That I am not quite all here is a matter of clinical record. What am I brooding on about? With me sharing my office with a beautiful girl, of course Paola would play the part of a jealous wife—that is just a game old married couples play. And Gianni? It was Gianni who spoke of the beautiful Sibilla, maybe he is the one who has fallen for her, maybe he drops by my office all the time with some tax excuse, then hangs around pretending to be enchanted by the squeaking pages. He is the one with the crush, I have nothing to do with it. It is Gianni, old enough to smell a little like a corpse himself, he is trying to steal away, has stolen away, the woman of my dreams. Here we go again: the woman of my dreams?

I thought I was going to be able to handle living with so many people I do not recognize, but this is the greatest hurdle yet, ever since those senile fantasies entered my head. What pains me is that I might cause her pain. So you see, then... No, it is natural for a man not to want to hurt his own adoptive daughter. Daughter? The other day I felt like a paedophile and now I discover I am incestuous?

And after all, my God, who said we ever slept together? Maybe it was just a kiss, a single kiss, or a platonic attraction, each understanding what the other felt but neither ever speaking of it. Round Table lovers, we slept for four years with a sword between us.

Oh, I also have a *Stultifera Navis,* though it does not look like a first edition and in any case is not a first-rate copy. And this *De Proprietatibus rerum* by Bartholomaeus Anglicus? Completely rubricated from top to bottom—too bad the binding is modern, antique style. We can talk business. "Sibilla, the *Stultifera Navis* isn't a first edition, is it?"

"Unfortunately no, Monsieur Bodoni. Ours is the 1497 Olpe. The first is also Olpe, Basel, but from 1494, and in German, *Das Narren Schyff.* The first Latin edition, like ours, appears in '97, but in March, and ours, if you look at the colophon, is from August, and in between there were also April and June editions. But it isn't so much the date, it's the copy; as you can see, it's not terribly appealing. I won't say it's a reading copy, but it's nothing to ring the bells about."

"You know so much, Sibilla, what would I do without you?"

"You were the one who taught me. To get out of Warsaw I passed myself off as a *grande savante,* but if I hadn't met you I'd be just as stupid as when I arrived."

Admiration, devotion. Is she trying to tell me something? I murmur, "*Les amoureux fervents et les savants austères...*" I anticipate her: "Nothing, nothing, a poem popped into my head. Sibilla, we should be clear about something. Perhaps as we go forward I'll seem almost normal to you, but I'm not. Everything that happened to me before, and I mean everything, you understand, is like a blackboard that's been sponged clean. I am immaculately black, if you'll pardon the contradiction. You should understand that, and not despair, and...stand by me." Did I say the right thing? It felt perfect, it could be understood in two ways.

"Don't worry, Monsieur Bodoni, I completely understand. I'm here and I'm not going anywhere. I'll wait..."

Are you really a slyboots? Are you saying that you are waiting for me to get back on my feet, as of course everyone is doing, or that you are waiting for me to remember a certain thing? And if the latter, what will you do, in the coming days, to remind me? Or do you want with all your heart for me to remember, but will not do anything, because you are not a slyboots but a woman in love, and you are holding your tongue to avoid upsetting me? Are you suffering, not letting it show because you are the marvellous creature you are, yet telling yourself that this is finally the right time for the two of us to come to our senses? You will sacrifice yourself, never doing anything to make me remember, not trying to touch my hand some evening as if in passing so that I might taste my madeleine—you who with the pride of all lovers know that although no one else can make me smell the scents that will be my Open Sesame, you could do so at will, simply by letting your hair brush my cheek as you lean over to hand me a form. Or by speaking again, as if casually, that banal phrase you spoke the first time, which we spent four years embroidering, quoting like a magic word whose meaning and power only we knew, we whom our secret set apart? Like: *Et mon bureau?* But that was Rimbaud.

Let us try at least to get one thing clear. "Sibilla, perhaps you're calling me Monsieur Bodoni because it's as if today I were meeting you for the first time, even though after working together we may have begun to use *tu* with each other, as often happens in such cases. What did you call me before?"

She blushed, emitting again that modulated, tender hiccup: "*Oui, oui, oui,* in fact I called you Yambo. You tried to make me feel at ease from the start."

Her eyes glittered with happiness, as if a weight had been lifted from her heart. But using *tu* does not mean anything: even

Gianni—Paola and I went to his office with him the other day—uses *tu* with his secretary.

"Well then!" I said cheerfully, "we'll pick up exactly where we left off. You know that in general picking up where I left off may be helpful to me."

How did she take that? What did picking up where we left off mean to her?

Back home I spent a sleepless night, and Paola stroked my hair. I felt like an adulterer, yet I had done nothing. On the other hand, I was not troubled for Paola's sake, but for my own. The best part of having loved, I told myself, is the memory of having loved. Some people live on a single memory. Eugénie Grandet, for example. But to think you have loved, yet not be able to recall it? Or worse still, you may have loved, you cannot remember it, and you suspect you have not loved. Or another possibility, which in my vanity I had not considered: Madly in love, I made an advance, and she put me in my place, kindly, gently, firmly. She stayed because I was a gentleman and behaved from that day on as if nothing had happened, in the end she enjoyed working there, or could not afford to lose a good job, maybe was flattered by my move; indeed, her feminine vanity, without her realizing it, had been touched, and although she has never admitted it even to herself, she is aware of having a certain power over me. An *allumeuse.* Or worse: This slyboots took me for a ton of money, made me do whatever she wanted—clearly I had left her in charge of everything, including the revenue and the deposits and maybe even the withdrawals, I sang *cock-a-doodle-doo* like Professor Rath, I was a broken man, I stopped going out.... Maybe this lucky disaster will allow me to get out of it, every cloud has a silver lining. How wretched I am, how I sully everything I touch, she might be still a virgin and here I am making a whore of her. Whatever the case, even the mere suspicion, disavowed, makes things worse: If you cannot remember having loved, you will never know whether the one you loved was worthy of your love. That Vanna I met a few mornings ago, that was a clear case—a flirtation, a night or two, then perhaps a few days of disappointment and that was all. But here four years of my life are at stake. Yambo, could it be that you are falling in love with her today, when maybe nothing existed before, and are now rushing towards your ruin? All because you imagine you were damned then and want to rediscover your paradise? And to think that there are lunatics who drink to forget, or take drugs. Oh, if only I could forget it all, they say. I alone know the truth: Forgetting is dreadful. Are there drugs for remembering?

Maybe Sibilla...

Here I go again. *If I spy you passing at such regal distance, with your hair loose and your whole bearing august, vertigo carries me off.*

The next morning, I took a taxi to Gianni's office. I asked him straight out what he knew about Sibilla and me. He seemed floored.

"Yambo, we're all a bit infatuated with Sibilla—myself, your fellow dealers, lots of your clients. There are people who come to you just to see her. But it's all a joke, schoolboy stuff. We all take turns kidding each other about it, and we often kidded you: I have a feeling there's something between you and the lovely Sibilla, we'd say. And you'd laugh, and sometimes you'd play along, as if to imply outrageous things, and sometimes you'd tell us to lay off it, that she could be your daughter. Games. That's why I asked you about Sibilla that evening: I thought you'd already seen her and I wanted to know what impression she'd made."

"So I never told you anything about me and Sibilla?"

"Why, was there something to tell?"

"Don't joke about this, you know I'm an amnesiac. I'm here to ask you if I ever told you anything."

"Nothing. And you always told me about your affairs, perhaps to make me envious. You told me about Cavassi, about Vanna, about the American at the London book fair, about the beautiful

Dutch girl you made three special trips to Amsterdam to see, about Silvana..."

"Come on, how many affairs did I have?"

"A lot. Too many, I thought, but I've always been monogamous. About Sibilla, I swear to you, you never said a thing. What's got into you? You saw her yesterday, she smiled at you, and you thought it would have been impossible to be around her and not think about it. You're human; I certainly wouldn't have expected you to say, Who's this hag...And besides, none of us ever managed to find out whether Sibilla had a life of her own. Always relaxed, eager to help anyone as if she were doing him a special favour—sometimes a girl can be provocative precisely because she doesn't flirt. The ice sphinx." Gianni was probably telling the truth, but that meant nothing. If something had happened and Sibilla had become more important to me than all the others, if she were The One, I certainly would not have told even Gianni about it. It would have had to remain a delicious conspiracy between Sibilla and me.

Or not. The ice sphinx, in her off-hours, has her own life, perhaps she already has a man, keeps it to herself, is perfect, does not mix her work and her private life. I am stung by jealousy of an unknown rival. *And someone will pluck your flower, mouth of the wellspring, someone who won't even know, a fisher of sponges will take this rare pearl.*

"I have a widow for you, Yambo," said Sibilla with a wink. She is gaining confidence, how nice. "A widow?" I asked. She explained that antiquarian book dealers of my stature have certain methods of procuring books. There is the fellow who shows up at the studio asking whether his book is worth something, and how much it is worth depends on how honest you are, though in any case you try to make a profit. Or the guy is a collector hard up for cash, he knows the value of what he is offering, and the most you can do is haggle a little over the price. Another technique is shopping the international auctions, where you can get a bargain if you are the only one to realize a book's worth, but your competitors are not fools. Thus the margin is minimal, and things get interesting only if you can set a very high price for your find. Then too you buy from your colleagues: one might have a book that is of little interest to his sort of client, so his price is low, but you know a collector who is lusting after it. Then there is the vulture method. You identify the great families in decline, with the old palazzos and the ancient libraries, and you wait for a father to die, a husband, an uncle, at which point the heirs already have their hands full selling the furniture and the jewels, and they have no idea how to appraise that hoard of books they have never examined. "Widow" is just a manner of speaking: it could be a grandson who wants to turn a quick buck, and if he has problems with women, or drugs, so much the better. Then you go and look at the books, spend two or three days in those great shadowy rooms, and formulate your strategy.

This time it actually was a widow. Sibilla had received a tip from someone (my little secret, she said with a pleased, mischievous air), and it seems I have a way with widows. I asked Sibilla to come along, since by myself I ran the risk of not recognizing *the* book. What a lovely house, Signora, why thank you, yes, perhaps a cognac. Then off to browse, *bouquiner, hojear*... Sibilla was whispering the rules of the game. Typically you find two or three hundred volumes of no value: you immediately spot the various pandects and theological dissertations, and these will end up in the stalls of the Sant'Ambrogio market, or else the eighteenth-century duodecimos of *The Adventures of Telemachus* or the utopian journeys, all bound identically, perfect for interior decorators, who will buy them by the metre. Then lots of sixteenth-century small-format stuff, Ciceros and rhetorics for Herennius, cheap junk that ends up in the stalls of Piazza Fontanella Borghese in Rome, where people pay twice what it is worth just so they can say they have a sixteenth-century book. But we look and we look, and there—even I noticed it—a Cicero, true, but in Aldine italics, and no less than a *Nuremberg Chronicle* in perfect condition, and a Rolewinck, and Kircher's *Ars Magna*

Lucis et Umbrae, with its splendid engravings and only a few pages browned—rare for paper of that time, and even a delicious Rabelais by Jean-Frédéric Bernard, 1741, three quarto volumes with illustrations by Picart, splendid red morocco bindings, gold-stamped covers, gilt bands and decorations on the spines, green silk doublures with gilt dentelles—the deceased had kindly covered the volumes in light-blue paper to protect them, so they made no impression at first glance. It's certainly not the *Nuremberg Chronicle,* Sibilla murmured, the binding is modern, but collectible, signed Rivière & Son. Fossati would snap it up—I'll tell you about him later, he collects bindings.

By the end we had identified ten volumes that at good prices would have netted us, conservatively speaking, at least a hundred million lire: the *Chronicle* alone would fetch an absolute minimum of fifty million. Who knows how they got there—the deceased was a notary, his library was a status symbol, and he apparently had been a miser, buying only books that didn't cost him much. He must have acquired the good ones by accident forty years earlier, in the days when people would throw them at you. Sibilla told me how we handle these situations, I called the signora over, and it was as if I had always done this job. I said there was a lot of stuff here, but none of it was worth much. I slapped the least felicitous examples onto the table: foxed pages, moisture stains, weak joints, morocco bindings that looked as though they had been sanded, pages wormed to lace. Look at this one, Dottore, Sibilla said. Once they're warped like this you can never get them back to normal, even with a press. I mentioned the Sant'Ambrogio market. "I don't know if I can even place them all, Signora, and you realize that if they remain in stock our storage costs skyrocket. I'll offer fifty million for the lot."

"You call it a *lot*?!" Oh, no, fifty million for that splendid library, her husband spent a lifetime assembling it, it was an offence to his memory. On to phase two of our strategy: "Well, Signora, look, the only ones really of interest to us are these ten. I'll tell you what, I'll offer you thirty million just for them." The signora does the maths: fifty million for an immense library is an offence to the sacred memory of the departed, but thirty million for just ten books is a coup; she'll find another book dealer who is less picky and more munificent to look at the rest. Sold.

We came back to the studio as gleeful as kids who had just played a practical joke. "Is it dishonest?" I asked.

"Of course not, Yambo, *così fan tutti.*" She quotes too, like me. "She would've got even less from one of your colleagues. And besides, did you see the furniture and the paintings and the silver? Those people are filthy rich, and books mean nothing to them. We work for people who truly love books."

How would I manage without Sibilla? Tough and gentle, wise as a dove. The fantasies began to haunt me again, and I re-entered the terrible spiral of the day before.

Luckily, the visit to the widow had completely worn me out. I went straight home. Paola remarked that I seemed more unfocused than usual, I must be working too hard. Better to go into the office only every other day.

I tried to think of other things: "Sibilla, my wife says that I collected writings about fog. Where are they?"

"They were horrible photocopies, little by little I transferred them to the computer. Don't thank me, it was fun. Watch, I'll find you the folder."

I knew computers existed (just as I knew aeroplanes existed), but of course I was now touching one for the first time. It was like riding a bicycle: I put my hands on it, and my fingertips remembered on their own.

I had gathered at least a hundred and fifty pages of quotes about fog. I must truly have taken the subject to heart. Here was Abbott's *Flatland,* a country of just two dimensions, inhabited only by planar figures: triangles, squares, polygons. And how do they recognize each other if they cannot see each other from above and so perceive only lines? Thanks to fog: "Wherever there is a rich supply of Fog, objects that are at a distance, say of three feet, are appreciably dimmer than those at the distance of two feet eleven inches; and the result is that by careful and constant experimental observation of comparative dimness and clearness, we are enabled to infer with great exactness the configuration of the object observed." Blessed are these triangles who wander in the mist and can see things—here a hexagon, there a parallelogram. Two-dimensional, but luckier than I.

I found I could finish most of the quotations from memory.

"How is that possible," I asked Paola, "if I've forgotten everything that has to do with me? I made this collection myself, with a personal investment."

"It isn't that you remember them because you collected them," she said, "you collected them because you remembered them. They're part of the encyclopaedia, like the other poems you recited to me on your first day back home."

In any case, I recognized them on sight. Beginning with Dante:

Just as the gaze commences to rebuild,
as soon as the fog first begins to clear,
all that the mist that filled the air concealed,
so I, piercing that dense, dark atmosphere...

D'Annunzio has some lovely pages on fog in *Nocturne:* "Someone walking by my side, noiselessly, as if in bare feet.... The fog enters my mouth, fills my lungs. Towards the Canalazzo it hovers and gathers. The stranger becomes greyer, fainter, turns to shadow.... Beneath the house of the antiquarian, he suddenly disappears." Here the antiquarian is a black hole: what falls in never comes out.

Then Dickens, the classic opening of *Bleak House:* "Fog everywhere. Fog up the river, where it flows among green aits and meadows; fog down the river, where it rolls defiled among the tiers of shipping and the waterside pollutions of a great (and dirty) city..." And Dickinson: "Let us go in; the fog is rising."

"I didn't know Pascoli," Sibilla said. "Listen to how lovely it is..." Now she had come quite close so she could see the screen; she could have brushed my cheek with her hair. But she did not. She pronounced the verses with a soft Slavic cadence:

Motionless in the haze
the trees; the long laments
of the steam engine rise...

O pallid impalpable fog,
hide what is far away;
O vapour climbing the sky
of a new day...

She balked at the third quotation: "Fog...per*co*lates?"

"*Per*colates."

"Ah." She seemed excited to have learned a new word:

Fog percolates, a puff of wind
filling the gully with strident leaves;
lightly through the barren stand
the robin dives;
beneath the fog the cane field pales,
giving voice to a fevered tremor;
above the fog there rise the bells
of the far tower.

Good fog in Pirandello, and to think he was Sicilian: "You could slice the fog....Around every streetlamp a halo yawned." But Savinio's Milan is even better: "The fog is cosy. It transforms the city into an enormous candy box, and its inhabitants into pieces of sugar candy....Women and girls pass hooded in the fog. A light vapour huffs around their nostrils and at their half-open mouths.... You find yourself in a parlour stretched by mirrors... you embrace, each still fragrant with fog, as the fog outside—discreet, silent, protective—presses against the window like a curtain..."

The Milanese fogs of Vittorio Sereni:

The doors flung vainly open onto evening fog
no one getting on or off except
a gust of smog the cry of the newsboy—
paradoxical—the Tempo di Milano the alibi
and the benefit of fog things hidden
walk under cover move towards me
veer away from me past like history past
like memory: twenty thirteen thirty-three
years like tramcar numbers...

I collected everything. Here is *King Lear:* "Infect her beauty, you fen-sucked fogs, drawn by the powerful sun." And Campana? "Through the breach in the red, fog-corroded ramparts, the long streets open silently. The awful vapour of the fog droops between the palazzos, veiling the tops of the towers, the long streets as silent and empty as if the city had been sacked."

Sibilla was enchanted by Flaubert: "A whitish day passed beyond the curtainless windows. She glimpsed treetops, and in the distance, the prairie, half-drowned in fog that smoked in the moonlight." And by Baudelaire: "The buildings sank into a sea of fog, / And deep in hospices the dying heaved..."

She was speaking other people's words, but for me it was as if they were rising up from a fountainhead. *Someone may pluck your flower, mouth of the wellspring...*

She was there, the fog was not. Others had seen it and distilled it into sounds. Perhaps one day I really could penetrate that fog, if Sibilla were to lead me by the hand.

I have already had several check-ups with Gratarolo, but in general he approves of what Paola has done. He likes the fact that I have now become almost self-sufficient, thus at least eliminating my initial frustrations.

I have spent a number of evenings with Gianni, Paola, and the girls playing Scrabble; they say it was my favourite game. I find words easily, especially esoteric ones like ACROSTIC (by adding on to TIC) or ZEUGMA. Later, incorporating an M and an H that were the first letters of two words going down, I start from the first red square in the top row and go all the way past the second, making AMPHIBOLY. Twenty-one times nine, plus the fifty-point bonus for playing all seven of my letters: two hundred and thirty-nine points in a single play. Gianni got mad. Thank God you're an amnesiac, he yelled. He said it to boost my confidence.

Not only am I an amnesiac, but I may be living out fictitious memories. Gratarolo mentioned the fact that in cases like mine, some people invent scraps of a past they never lived, just to have the sensation of remembering. Have I been using Sibilla as a pretext?

I have to get out of it somehow. Going to my studio has become torture. I said to Paola, "Pavese was right: Work's tiring. And I always see the same old part of Milan. Maybe it would do me good to take a trip; the studio runs fine without me, and Sibilla is already working on the new catalogue. We could go to Paris or somewhere."

"Paris is still too much for you, with travel and all. Let me give it some thought."

"Okay, not Paris. *To Moscow, to Moscow...*"

"To Moscow?"

"That's Chekhov. You know quotations are my only fog lights."

4. Alone through City Streets I Go

They showed me a lot of family photos, which unsurprisingly told me nothing. But of course, the ones they had were all from the time since I have known Paola. My childhood photos, if any, must be somewhere in Solara.

I spoke by phone with my sister in Sydney. When she learned I had not been well she wanted to come at once, but she had just undergone a rather delicate operation, and her doctors had prohibited her from making such a taxing journey.

Ada tried to remind me of something from the past, then gave up and started crying. I asked her to bring me a duck-billed platypus for the living room, next time she came—who knows why? Given these notions of mine, I might as well have asked her to bring me a kangaroo, but evidently I know they cannot be housebroken.

I spend only a few hours a day in the studio. Sibilla is getting the catalogue ready, and of course she knows her way around bibliographies. I give them a quick glance, say they look marvellous, then tell her I have a doctor's appointment. She watches me with apprehension as I leave. I feel sick, is that not normal? Or does she think I am avoiding her? What am I supposed to tell her? "I don't want to use you as a pretext for rebuilding fictitious memories, my poor dear love"?

I asked Paola what my political leanings were. "I don't want to find out I'm a Nazi or something."

"You're what they call a good liberal," Paola said, "but more from instinct than ideology. I always used to say politics bored you—and for the sake of argument you called me *La Pasionaria.* It was as if you sought refuge in your antique books out of fear, or contempt for the world. No, that's not fair, it wasn't contempt, because you were fervent about the great moral issues. You signed pacifist and non-violent petitions, you were outraged by racism. You even joined an antivivisection league."

"Animal vivisection, I imagine."

"Of course. Human vivisection is called war."

"And was I... always like that, even before meeting you?"

"You skated over your childhood and adolescence. And anyway I've never really been able to understand you about these things. You've always been a mix of compassion and cynicism. If there was a death sentence somewhere, you'd sign the petition, you'd send money to a drug rehab community. But if someone told you, say, that ten thousand babies had died in a tribal war in central Africa, you'd shrug, as if to say that the world was badly made and there's nothing to be done. You were always a jovial man, you liked good-looking women, good wine, and good music, but I always got the impression that all that was a shield, a way of hiding yourself. When you dropped it, you used to say that history is a blood-drenched enigma and the world an error."

"*Nothing can shake my belief that this world is the fruit of a dark god whose shadow I extend.*"

"Who said that?"

"I don't remember."

"It must be something that involved you. But you always bent over backwards if anyone needed anything—when they had the flood in Florence, you went as a volunteer to help pull books out of the mud at the Biblioteca Nazionale. That must be it, you were compassionate about the little things and cynical about the big things."

"That sounds fair. One does what one can. The rest is God's fault, as Gragnola used to say."

"Who is Gragnola?"

"I don't remember that either. I must have known once."

What did I know once?

One morning I woke up, went to make a coffee (decaf), and started humming *Roma non far la stupida stasera.* Why had that song come to mind? It's a good sign, Paola said, a beginning. Apparently every morning I would sing a song as I made coffee. No reason that one song came to mind as opposed to any other. None of Paola's enquiries (what did you dream last night? what did we talk about yesterday evening? what did you read before falling asleep?) produced a reliable explanation. Who can say—maybe the way I put my socks on, or the colour of my shirt, or a can I glimpsed out of the corner of an eye had triggered a sound memory.

"Except," Paola noted, "you only ever sang songs from the fifties or later. At most, you'd go back to the early San Remo festivals—songs like *Fly, Dove* or *Papaveri e papere.* You never went farther back than that, nothing from the forties or thirties or twenties." Paola mentioned *Sola me ne vò per la città,* the great post-war song, which had been on the radio so often that even she, though only a little girl at the time, still knew it. It certainly sounded familiar, but I did not react with interest; it was as if someone had sung *Casta Diva,* and indeed it seems I was never a great fan of opera. Not the way I am of *Eleanor Rigby,* say, or *Que será, será,* or *Sono una donna non sono una santa.* As for the older songs, Paola attributed my lack of interest to what she called a repression of childhood.

She had also noticed over the years that although I was something of a connoisseur of jazz and classical music and liked to go to concerts and listen to records, I never had any desire to turn on the radio. At best, I would listen to it in the background if someone else had turned it on. Evidently the radio was like the country house: it belonged to the past.

But the next morning, as I was waking up and making coffee, I found myself singing *Sola me ne vò per la città:*

All alone through city streets I go,
Walking through a crowd that doesn't know,
That doesn't see my pain.
I search for you, I dream of you, but all in vain...

All in vain I struggle to forget,
First love is impossible to forget,
Inside my heart a name is written, a single name.
I knew you well, and now I know that you are love,
The truest love, the greatest love...

The melody came of its own accord. And my eyes teared up.

"Why that song?" Paola asked.

"Who knows? Maybe because it's about searching for someone. No idea who."

"You've crossed the barrier into the forties," she reflected, curious.

"It's not that," I said. "It's that I felt something inside. Like a tremor. No, not like a tremor. As if... You know *Flatland,* you read it too. Well, those triangles and those squares live in two dimensions, they don't know what thickness is. Now imagine that one of us, who lives in three dimensions, were to touch them from above. They would feel something they'd never felt before, and they wouldn't be able to say what it was. As if someone were to come here from the fourth dimension and touch us from the inside—say on the pylorus—gently. What does it feel like when someone tickles your pylorus? I would say... a mysterious flame."

"What does that mean, a mysterious flame?"

"I don't know—that's what came to mind."

"Was it the same thing you felt when you looked at the picture of your parents?"

"Almost. Not really. Actually, why not? Almost the same."

"Now that's an interesting signal, Yambo, let's take note of that."

She is still hoping to redeem me. And me with my mysterious flame sparked, perhaps, by thoughts of Sibilla.

Sunday. "Go and take a stroll," Paola told me, "it will do you good. Stick to the streets you know. In Largo Cairoli, there's a flower stall that's usually open even on Sundays. Have him make you a nice spring bunch, or just some roses—this house feels like a morgue."

I went down to Largo Cairoli and the flower stall was closed. I meandered down Via Dante towards the Cordusio, then turned right towards the Borsa and saw the place where all the collectors in Milan gather on Sundays. Philatelic stalls along Via Cordusio, figurines and old postcards along all of Via Armorari, and the entire T of the Passaggio Centrale filled with vendors selling coins, toy soldiers, holy cards, wristwatches, even telephone cards. Collecting is anal—I should know. People collect all kinds of things, even Coca-Cola bottle caps, and after all, telephone cards are cheaper than my incunabula. In Piazza Edison, stalls to my left were selling books, newspapers, and advertising posters, while in front of me yet others were selling miscellaneous junk: art nouveau lamps, no doubt fake; flowered trays with black backgrounds; bisque ballerinas.

In one stall I found four cylindrical containers, sealed, filled with an aqueous solution (formalin?) in which were suspended various ivory-coloured forms—some round, some shaped like beans—linked together by snow-white filaments. Marine creatures—sea cucumbers, shreds of squid, faded coral—or perhaps the morbid figments of some artist's teratological imagination. Yves Tanguy?

The vendor explained to me that they were testicles: dog, cat, rooster, and some other beast, complete with kidneys and the rest. "Take a look, it's all from a scientific laboratory from the nineteenth century. Forty thousand apiece. The containers alone are worth twice that, this stuff is at least a hundred and fifty years old. Four times four is sixteen, I'll give you all four for a hundred and twenty. A bargain."

Those testicles fascinated me. For once, here was something I was not supposed to know about through my semantic memory, nor did it have anything to do with my personal history. Who has ever seen dog testicles in their pure state—I mean, without the dog attached? I rummaged around in my pockets. I had a total of forty thousand, and it's not as though a street vendor is going to take a cheque.

"I'll take the dog ones."

"A mistake to leave the others, you won't get that chance again."

You cannot have everything. I went back home with my dog balls and Paola blanched: "They're curious, they really do look like a work of art, but where will we keep them? In the living room, so that every time you offer guests some cashews or some Ascoli olives they can vomit on our carpet? In the bedroom? I think not. You can keep them in your studio, perhaps next to some lovely seventeenth-century book on the natural sciences."

"I thought it was a real find."

"Do you know you're the only man in the world, the only man on the face of the earth from Adam up to now, who when his wife sends him out to buy roses comes home with a pair of dog balls?"

"If nothing else, that's something for the *Guinness Book of Records*. And besides, you know, I'm a sick man."

"Excuses. You were crazy even before. It was no accident that you asked your sister for a platypus. Once you wanted to bring home a 1960s pinball machine that cost as much as a Matisse painting and made a hellish racket."

But Paola knew that street market already. Indeed, she said I should have known it too: once I found a first edition of Papini's *Gog* there, original covers, uncut, for ten thousand lire. And so the next Sunday she wanted to go with me: you never know, she said, you might come home with some dinosaur testicles and we'll have to call a mason to widen the doorway to get them inside.

Stamps and telephone cards did not arouse my interest, but the old newspapers did. Stuff from our childhood, Paola said. "Then forget it," I said. But at a certain point I saw a Mickey Mouse comic book. I picked it up instinctively. It could not have been really old—a 1970s reprint, judging from the back cover and the price. I opened it to the middle: "It's not an original, because those were printed in two colours, with shading from brick red to brown, and this one is printed in white and blue."

"How do you know that?"

"I don't know, I just do."

"But the cover is a reproduction of the original cover. Look at the date and the price: 1936; one and a half lire."

Clarabelle's Treasure: the title jumped out from a colourful background. "And they got the wrong tree," I said.

"What do you mean?"

I flipped quickly through the pages and immediately found the right panels. But it was as if I did not feel like reading what was written in the balloons—as if it were written in some other language or the letters had all been smeared together. Instead I told the story from memory.

"You see, Mickey Mouse and Horace Horsecollar, taking an old map, went in search of a treasure that had been buried by Clarabelle Cow's grandfather or great-uncle, and they're racing against the slimy Eli Squinch and the treacherous Peg-Leg Pete. They come to the place and consult the map. They're supposed to start from a big tree, make a line to a smaller tree, then triangulate. They dig and dig but find nothing. Until Mickey has a flash of inspiration: the map is from 1863, more than seventy years have passed, this little tree couldn't possibly have existed at that time, so the tree that now appears big must have been the little one then, and the big one must have fallen, but may have left traces. And indeed they look and look, find a piece of the old trunk, redo the triangulation, start digging again, and there it is, exactly in that spot, the treasure."

"But how do you know all that?"

"Doesn't everyone?"

"No, everyone does not," said Paola, excited. "That isn't semantic memory, that's autobiographical memory. You're remembering something that made an impression on you as a child! And this cover sparked it."

"No, not the image. If anything the name, Clarabelle."

"*Rosebud*."

Of course we bought the comic book. I spent the evening with that story but got nothing more from it. I knew it, and it was all there, but no mysterious flame.

"I'll never come out of this, Paola. I'll never enter the cavern."

"But you suddenly remembered that business about the two trees."

"Proust at least remembered three. Paper, paper, like all the books in this apartment, or those in my studio. My memory is made of paper."

"Use the paper, then, since madeleines don't tell you anything. So you're not Proust, fine. Zasetsky wasn't either."

"*What name, fair lady?*"

"I had almost forgotten about him; Gratarolo reminded me. In my line of work I couldn't have helped reading *The Man with a Shattered World*, a classic case. But I read it a long time ago, and for academic reasons. Today I reread it with a personal interest, it's a delicious little book you can skim in a couple of hours. In it, Luria, the great Russian psychologist, presents the case of this man Zasetsky, who during the last world war was hit with a piece of shrapnel that damaged the left occipitoparietal region of his brain. He wakes up, as you did, but in a terrible chaos. He isn't even able to discern the position of his body in space. He sometimes thinks certain of his body parts have changed—that his head has become inordinately large, that his torso is incredibly small, that his legs have moved onto his head."

"That doesn't seem much like my case. Legs on his head? And his penis in place of his nose?"

"Hang on. Never mind about the legs on the head, that happened only occasionally. The worst thing was his memory. Reduced to shreds, as if it had been pulverized—much worse than yours. Like you, he couldn't remember where he was born or the name of his mother—but he could no longer even read or write. Luria begins observing him. Zasetsky has an iron will and relearns how to read and write, and he writes and writes. For twenty-five years he records not only everything he disinters from the devastated caverns of his memory but also everything that happens to him day by day. It was as if his hand, with its automatisms, was able to put in order what his head couldn't. Which is like saying that what he wrote was more intelligent than he was. And thus, on paper, he gradually rediscovered himself. You're not him, but what struck me is that he reconstructed for himself a memory made of paper. And it took him twenty-five years. You already have plenty of paper here, but evidently it isn't the right paper. Your cavern is in the country house. I've given it a lot of thought in recent days, you know. All the papers of your childhood and your adolescence—you locked them away too abruptly. Maybe something there will hit home for you. So now, please do me the great favour of going to Solara. Alone, because for one thing I can't get away from work, and for another this is something, as I see it, that you have do by yourself. Just you and your distant past. Stay as long as you need to and see what happens. You'll lose a week at most, maybe two, and you'll get some good air, which won't hurt a bit. I've already phoned Amalia."

"And who's Amalia—Zasetsky's wife?"

"Yes, his grandmother. I didn't tell you quite everything about Solara. In your grandfather's time there were tenant farmers, Tommaso, who went by Masulu, and Maria, because in those days the house had quite a bit of land around it, mostly vineyards, and a fair amount of livestock. Maria watched you grow up and loved you with all her heart. As did Amalia, her daughter, who's about ten years older than you and who played the role of your big sister, nanny, everything. You were her idol. When your aunt and uncle sold the lands, including the farm on the hill, there was still a small vineyard left, and the fruit orchard, vegetable garden, pigsty, rabbit hutch, and henhouse. It no longer made sense to speak of tenant farming, so you just left it all to Masulu to use as he liked, with the proviso that his family would take care of the house. Eventually Masulu and Maria passed on, too, and because Amalia never married—she was never a great beauty—she's still there, selling her eggs and chickens in town, the pork butcher comes by when the time is right to kill the pig for her, some cousins help her apply the Bordeaux mixture to the vines and harvest her small crop of grapes; in short, she's content, except she feels a little lonely, so she's happy when the girls visit with the little ones. We pay her for any eggs, chickens, or salami we consume, for fruit and vegetables there's no charge—she says they belong to us. She's a gem, and you'll see what a cook she is. When she heard you might come, she was beside herself—Signorino Yambo this, Signorino Yambo that, how wonderful, you'll see, his illness will disappear when I fix him that salad he likes..."

"Signorino Yambo. How extravagant. By the way, why does everyone call me Yambo?"

"For Amalia, you'll always be *Signorino,* even when you're eighty. And as for Yambo, it was Maria who explained it to me. You chose it yourself when you were little. You used to say, My name is Yambo, the boy with the quiff. And you've been Yambo ever since."

"The quiff?"

"You must have had a cute little quiff. And you didn't like Giambattista, I can't say I blame you. But enough personal history. You're leaving. You can't really go by train, since you'd have to change four times, but Nicoletta will take you—she needs to pick up some things she left there at Christmas, then she'll turn right around and leave you with Amalia, who'll pamper you, who'll be around when you need her and disappear when you want to be alone. Five years ago we put a phone in, so we can be in touch at any time. Give it a try, please."

I asked for a few days to think about it. I was the one who had first brought up the idea of a trip, to escape those afternoons in my studio. But did I really want to escape those afternoons in my studio?

I was in a maze. No matter which way I turned, it was the wrong way. And besides, what did I want to get out of? Who was it who said *Open sesame, I want to get out*? I wanted to go in, like Ali Baba. Into the caverns of memory.

Sibilla was kind enough to solve my problem. One afternoon she emitted an irresistible hiccup, blushed slightly (*in your blood, which spreads its flames across your face, the cosmos makes its laughter*), tormented a stack of forms she had in front of her, and said: "Yambo, you should be the first to know...I'm getting married."

"What do you mean, married?" I replied, as if to say, "How could you?"

"I'm getting married. You know, when a man and woman exchange rings and everyone throws rice on them?"

"No, I mean...you're leaving me?"

"Why would I? He works for an architecture firm, but he doesn't make a whole lot yet—both of us will have to work. And besides, how could I ever leave you?"

The other planted the knife in his heart and turned it there twice.

The end of *The Trial,* and indeed, the end of the trial. "And is this something...that's been going on a long time?"

"Not long. We met a few weeks ago—you know how these things go. He's a great guy, you'll meet him."

How these things go. Perhaps there were other great guys before him, or perhaps she took advantage of my accident to wash her hands of an untenable situation. Maybe she threw herself on the first guy who came along, a shot in the dark. In which case I have hurt her twice. But who hurt her, you imbecile? Things are going as things go: she is young, meets someone her own age, falls in love for the first time...For the first time, okay? *And someone will pluck your flower, mouth of the wellspring, and not having sought you will be his grace and good fortune...*

"I'll have to get you a nice present."

"There's plenty of time. We decided last night, but I want to wait until you've recovered, so I can take a week of vacation without feeling guilty."

Without feeling guilty. How thoughtful.

What was the last quote I had seen about fog? *When we arrived at the Rome station, the evening of Good Friday, and she rode off in a coach into the fog, it seemed to me that I had lost her for ever, irrevocably.*

The story of our affair had ended on its own. Whatever had happened before, all erased. The blackboard shiny black. From now on, like a daughter only.

At that point I could leave. Indeed, I had to. I told Paola that I would be going to Solara. She was happy.

"You'll like it there, you'll see."

"*O flounder, flounder, in the sea, / it really isn't up to me, / it's just that tiresome wife I've got, / for she desires what I do not.*"

"You wicked man. To the countryside, to the countryside!"

That evening in bed, as Paola was giving me some last-minute advice before my trip, I caressed her breasts. She moaned softly, and I felt something that resembled desire, but mixed with gentleness, and perhaps recognition. We made love.

As with the toothbrushing, my body had apparently retained a memory of how it was done. It was a calm thing, a slow rhythm. She had her orgasm first (she always did, she later said), and I had mine soon after. After all, it was my first time. It really is as good as they say. I was not surprised by that fact; it was as if my brain already knew it, but my body was just then discovering it was true.

"That's not bad," I said, collapsing onto my back. "Now I know why people are so fond of it."

"Christ," Paola remarked, "on top of everything else, I've had to deflower my sixty-year-old husband."

"Better late than never."

But I couldn't help wondering, as I fell asleep with Paola's hand in mine, whether it would have been the same thing with Sibilla. Imbecile, I murmured to myself as I slowly lost consciousness, that is something you can never know.

I left. Nicoletta was driving, and I was looking at her, in profile. Judging by the photos of me at the time of my marriage, her nose was mine, and the shape of her mouth, too. She really was my daughter, I had not been saddled with the fruit of some indiscretion.

(Her blouse being slightly open, he suddenly espied a gold locket upon her breast, with a Y delicately engraved upon it. Great God, said he, who gave you that? I've always worn it, my lord, it was around my neck when I was found as an infant upon the steps of the Poor Clares convent at Saint-Auban, said she. The locket that belonged to your mother, the duchess, I exclaimed! Do you by chance have four moles in the shape of a cross upon your left shoulder? Yes, my lord, but how could you have known? Well then, then you are my daughter and I am your father! Father, oh Father! No, do not, my chaste innocent, lose your senses now. We'll run off the road!)

We were not talking, but I had already realized that Nicoletta was laconic by nature, and in that moment she was no doubt embarrassed, afraid to draw my attention to things I had forgotten, not wanting to upset me. I asked her only what direction we were heading: "Solara is right on the border between Langhe and Monferrato; it's a beautiful place, you'll see, Papà." I liked hearing myself called Papà.

At first, after we had left the highway, I saw signs that referred to well-known cities: Turin, Asti, Alessandria, Casale. Later we made our way onto secondary roads, where the signs began to refer to towns I had never heard of. After a few kilometres of plains, beyond a dip in the road, I glimpsed the pale blue outline of some hills in the distance. But the outline disappeared suddenly, because a wall of trees rose up in front of us and we drove into it, proceeding along a leafy corridor that brought to mind tropical forests. *Que me font maintenant tes ombrages et tes lacs?*

But once we had passed through the corridor, which felt like a continuation of the plains, we found ourselves in a hollow dominated by hills on each side and behind us. Evidently we had entered Monferrato after an imperceptible and continuous ascent, high ground had surrounded us without my noticing, and already I was entering into another world, into a festival of budding vineyards. In the distance, peaks of various heights, some barely rising above the low hills, some steeper, many dominated by structures—churches, large farmhouses, castles of a sort—that made their stands with disproportionate obtrusiveness and rather than gently completing their peaks, gave them a shove towards the sky.

At a certain point, after an hour or so of travelling through those hills, where a different landscape unfurled at every turn as if we were being suddenly transported from one region to another, I saw a sign that said Mongardello. I said: "Mongardello. Then Corseglio, Montevasco, Castelletto Vecchio, Lovezzolo, and we're there, right?"

"How do you know that?"

"Everyone knows that," I said. But apparently that was not true; do any encyclopaedias mention Lovezzolo? Was I beginning to penetrate the cavern?

Part Two

PAPER MEMORY

5. Clarabelle's Treasure

As I drew near the places of my childhood, I tried and failed to grasp why as an adult I had never willingly gone to Solara. It was not so much Solara itself—little more than a big village that one skirts before leaving it in its hollow amid the vineyards on the low hills—but what lay beyond and above it. At a certain point, after various hairpin curves, Nicoletta turned onto a narrow side road, and we drove for at least two kilometres along an embankment that was barely wide enough for two cars to pass and that sloped away on both sides, revealing two distinct landscapes. On the right, typical Monferrato country, gently rolling hills festooned with rows of vines, proliferating languidly, green against a clear early-summer sky, at that hour when (I knew) the midday demon rages. On the left, the first foothills of the Langhe region, with its harsher, less modulated contours, like a series of ranges one after the other, each given perspective by a different hue, until the farthest ones vanish in a pale blue haze.

I was discovering that landscape for the first time, yet I felt it was mine and had the impression that, had I launched into a mad run down towards the valleys, I would have known where I was going and how to get there. In a way it was like leaving the hospital and being able to drive that car I had never seen. I felt at home. I was gripped by a vague joy, an absent-minded happiness.

The embankment continued its ascent along the flank of a hill that suddenly loomed above it, and there, at the end of a drive lined with horse chestnuts, was the house. We came to a stop in front of a kind of courtyard splashed with beds of flowers, and behind the building you could glimpse a slightly higher hill, over which stretched what must have been Amalia's little vineyard. From the front it was difficult to discern the shape of that huge house with its tall second-storey windows: you could see the vast central wing, which featured a lovely oak door set in a rounded archway beneath a balcony that overlooked the drive, and two smaller wings on either side with humbler entryways, but it was hard to tell how far the house extended at the back, towards the hill. The courtyard looked out, behind me, onto the two landscapes I had just admired, and with a 180-degree panorama, for the driveway ascended gradually and the road that had led us here disappeared below us, without blocking the view.

It was a brief impression, because almost at once we heard shrieks of jubilation, and there emerged a woman who, from the descriptions I had been given, could have been no one but Amalia: short of leg, rather robust, of uncertain age (as Nicoletta had said earlier, between twenty and ninety), with a dried-chestnut face that was lit by an irrepressible joy. In short, the welcoming ceremony, hugs and kisses, demure gaffes quickly followed by little cries cut off by a hand clapped over a mouth (does Signorino Yambo remember this and that, surely you recognize, and so on, with Nicoletta, behind me, no doubt giving her looks).

A whirlwind, no room to think or ask questions, barely enough time to unload my suitcases and carry them to the left wing, the one where Paola had settled with the girls and where I too could stay, unless I preferred to stay in the central wing, the wing of my grandparents and my childhood, which had remained closed upstairs, like a sanctum ("Well, you know, I go in pretty regular to give things a good dusting, and every now and again I air it out some, but just every now and again, so as you don't get nasty smells, and without bothering the rooms, which for me is like being in church"). But on the ground floor those big empty rooms remained open, because that was where they set out the apples, the tomatoes, and many other good things, to ripen and to keep cool. And indeed, just a few steps into those entrance halls you could smell the pungent scent of spices and fruits and vegetables, and the first figs were already laid out on a long table, the very first, and I could not help tasting one and venturing to say that that tree always had been bountiful, but Amalia shouted, "What do you mean *that* tree: *those* trees, there's five as you well know, each prettier than the last!" Forgive me, Amalia, I was distracted. And no wonder, with all the important things you've got in that head of yours, Signorino Yambo. Thank you, Amalia, if only I really did have lots of things in my head—the trouble is they all flew away, *whoosh,* one morning in late April, and one fig or five, it's all the same to me.

"Are there already grapes on the vines?" I asked, if only to show I still had my wits about me.

"Well, the grapes are still just itty-bitty clusters like babies in a mamma's belly, though this year what with all the heat everything's ripening sooner than usual—sure hope we get some rain. They'll be ripe in time for you to see, I reckon you ought to stay till September. I know you've been a mite under the weather, and Signora Paola tells me I've got to give you a boost, something good and nourishing. For tonight I'm fixing what you liked when you was a boy, salad with a dressing of oil and tomato, with little pieces of celery and chopped green onion and all the herbs God could want, and I got them rolls you used to like for sopping up the dressing. Then one of my cockerels—none of that store-bought chicken fatted on garbage—or if you'd favour rabbit with rosemary.... Rabbit? Rabbit; I'll go right over and give the prettiest one a whack on the neck, poor little critter, but that's life. Lord, can it be true Nicoletta is leaving so quick? What a shame. That's all right, we'll stick around just the two of us and you can do whatever you like and I won't get in your hair. You'll see me in the morning, when I bring you your coffee, and at mealtimes, and the rest of the time you just come and go as you please."

"So, Papà," said Nicoletta as she was loading the stuff she had come to retrieve, "Solara may seem a long way from here, but behind the house there's a path that goes straight down into the town, cutting out all the switchbacks of the road. It's a fairly steep descent, but there's a kind of stairway, and before you know it you're down on the plain. Fifteen minutes to get down and twenty to get back up, but you always said it was good for the cholesterol. In town you'll find newspapers and cigarettes, but if you tell Amalia she'll go at eight in the morning. She goes in any case for all her errands and for mass. But be sure to write down for her the name of the paper you want, every day, otherwise she'll forget and bring you the same issue of *Gente* or some other celebrity rag seven days in a row. You really don't need anything else? I'd like to stay with you, but Mamma says it'll do you good to be alone among your old things."

Nicoletta left. Amalia showed me to the room that was mine and Paola's (lavender scent). I arranged my things, changed into some comfortable old rags that I rounded up, including some down-at-heel shoes that must have been twenty years old, real landowner's shoes, and then sat at the window for half an hour looking out at the hills on the Langhe side.

On the kitchen table was a newspaper from around Christmastime (we were last there for the holidays), and I began reading it, after pouring myself a glass of moscato, a bottle of which was waiting in a bucket of ice-cold well water. In late November the United Nations had authorized the use of force to free Kuwait from the Iraqis, the first shipments of American equipment had recently left for Saudi Arabia, and there was talk of one last attempt by the U.S. to negotiate in Geneva with Saddam's ministers and convince him to withdraw. The newspaper was helping me reconstruct certain events, and I read it as if it were the latest news.

I suddenly realized that in the confusion of departure I had not had a bowel movement that morning. I went into the bathroom, an excellent place to finish reading the paper, and from the window I saw the vineyard. A thought came to me, or rather an ancient urge: to do my business between the rows. I put the newspaper in my pocket and, either at random or by virtue of my internal radar, opened a little back door. I passed through a very well kept garden. The other wing of the house was the farming wing, and behind it I saw some wooden pens that, given all the clucking and rooting that could be heard, must have been the henhouse, the rabbit hutches, and the pigsties. At the end of the garden was a path leading up to the vineyard.

Amalia was right, the vine leaves were still small and the grapes looked like berries. But it felt like a vineyard to me, with clumps of earth beneath my dilapidated soles and tufts of weeds between one row and the next. I instinctively looked around for peach trees, but I saw none. Strange, I had read in some novel that between the rows—but you have to walk barefoot among them, your heels calloused since childhood—are yellow peaches that grow only in vineyards and split in half at the pressure of your thumb, the pit popping out almost by itself, as clean as if it had been chemically treated, except for an occasional fat little worm of white pulp left hanging by an atom. You can eat them almost without noticing the velvet of their skin, which makes you shiver from tongue to groin. For an instant, I felt that shiver in my groin.

I hunkered down in the great midday silence—broken only by the voices of a few birds and the stridulations of cicadas—and I defecated.

Silly season. He read on, seated calm above his own rising smell. Human beings love the perfume of their own excrement but not the odour of other people's. It is, after all, part of our bodies.

I was feeling an ancient satisfaction. The calm motion of the sphincter, among all that green, seemed to summon up my muddled past. Or was it an instinct of the species? I have so little that is individual and so much that is specific (I have the memory of humanity, not of a human being) that perhaps I was simply enjoying a pleasure that went back to Neanderthal man. His memory must have been worse than mine—he did not know the first thing about Napoleon.

When I finished, it occurred to me that I should clean myself with some leaves; that must have been an automatism. But I had the newspaper with me, and I ripped out the page with the TV schedule (it was six months old, after all, and in any case we have no TV in Solara).

I stood back up and looked down at my faeces. A lovely snail-shell architecture, still steaming. Borromini. My bowels must be in good shape, because everyone knows you have nothing to worry about unless your faeces are too soft or downright liquid.

I was seeing my own shit for the first time (in the city you sit on the bowl, then flush the toilet right away, without looking). I was now calling it shit, which I think is what people call it. Shit is the most personal and private thing we have. Anyone can get to know the rest—your facial expression, your gaze, your gestures. Even your naked body: at the beach, at the doctor's, making love. Even your thoughts, since usually you express them, or else others guess them from the way you look at them or appear embarrassed. Of course, there are such things as secret thoughts (Sibilla, for example, though I later betrayed myself in part to Gianni, and I wonder whether she herself intuited something—maybe that is precisely why she is getting married), but in general thoughts too are revealed.

Shit, however, is not. Except for an extremely brief period of your life, when your mother is still changing your nappies, it is all yours. And since my shit at that moment must not have been all that different from what I had produced over the course of my past life, I was in that instant reuniting with my old, forgotten self, undergoing the first experience capable of merging with countless previous experiences, even those from when I did my business in the vineyards as a boy.

Perhaps if I took a good look around, I would find the remains of those shits past, and then, triangulating properly, Clarabelle's treasure.

But I stopped there. Shit was not my linden-blossom tea—of course not, how could I have expected to conduct my *recherche* with my sphincter? In order to rediscover lost time, one should have not diarrhoea but asthma. Asthma is pneumatic, it is the breath (however laboured) of the spirit: it is for the rich, who can afford cork-lined rooms. The poor, in the fields, attend less to spiritual than to bodily functions.

And yet I felt not disinherited but content, and I mean truly content, in a way I had not felt since my reawakening. The ways of the Lord are infinite, I said to myself, they go even through the butthole.

That is how the day ended. I rambled around a bit in the rooms of the left wing, saw what must have been my grandchildren's bedroom (a large room with three beds, dolls, and abandoned tricycles in the corners), and found in my bedroom the books I had left on the night table—nothing particularly meaningful. I did not dare enter the old wing. There was time, and I needed to feel more comfortable with the place.

I ate in Amalia's kitchen, amid old kneading troughs, tables and chairs that had belonged to her parents, and the scent of garlic from heads that hung from the beams. The rabbit was exquisite, but the salad was worth the whole trip. I took pleasure in dipping the bread in that rosy dressing with its splotches of oil, but it was the pleasure of discovery, not memory. I could expect no help from my taste buds—I knew that already. I drank abundantly: the wine of those parts is worth all the wines of France put together.

I made the acquaintance of the household pets: a hairless dog named Pippo—according to Amalia it kept excellent watch, though it inspired little confidence, old as it was, blind in one eye, and apparently addled—and three cats. Two were peevish and wilful, the third, a sort of Angora, with thick, soft black fur, was graceful when asking for food, rubbing against my pant leg and emitting a seductive rumble. I love all animals, I think (did I not join an antivivisection league?), but one cannot control instinctive attraction. I liked the third cat best and gave it the choicest morsels. I asked Amalia what the cats' names were, and she replied that cats don't have names since they're not God-fearing creatures like dogs. I asked if I could call the black cat Matù, and she said I could, if kitty, kitty, kitty wasn't good enough for me, but I could tell she was thinking that city people, even Signorino Yambo, had crickets in their heads.

Crickets (real ones) were making a great racket outside, and I went into the courtyard to listen to them. I looked at the sky, hoping to discover familiar figures. Constellations, just constellations from an astronomy atlas. I recognized the Great Bear, but as one of those things I had always heard about. I had come this far to learn that the encyclopaedias were right. Return to the *interiorem hominem* and you will find Larousse.

I said to myself: Yambo, your memory is made of paper. Not of neurons, but of pages. Maybe some day someone will invent an electronic contraption allowing people to travel by computer among all the pages ever written, from the beginning of the world till today, and to pass from one to another with the touch of a finger, without knowing any longer where or who they are, and then everyone will be like you.

Still awaiting my misery's company, I went to bed.

I had just dozed off when I heard a voice calling me. It invited me to the window with a rasping, insistent *pssst pssst.* Who could be calling me from outside, hanging from the shutters? I flung them open and saw a whitish shadow flee into the night. It was, as Amalia explained to me the next morning, a barn owl: when houses are empty these creatures like to take up residence in attics or gutters, I'm not sure which, but as soon as they detect the presence of humans, they move elsewhere. Too bad. Because that barn owl fleeing into the night caused me to feel again what I had described to Paola as a mysterious flame. That barn owl, or one of its kind, must have belonged to me, must have woken me on other nights and on other nights fled into the dark, a clumsy, pea-witted ghost. *Pea-witted*? I could not have learned that word from the encyclopaedias either. It must have come from within, or from before.

My sleep was full of restless dreams, and at a certain point I woke up with a sharp pain in my chest. The first thing I thought was *heart attack*—they say they start like that—but then I got up without thinking and went to look in the medicine bag that Paola had given me, and took a Maalox. Maalox, so gastritis. You have an attack of gastritis when you eat something you should not. In reality I had simply eaten too much: Paola had told me to practise self-control, and when she was around had watched me like a hawk, but now it was time I learned to watch myself. Amalia would be of no help, since in the peasant tradition eating a lot is always healthy—what is unhealthy is when there is nothing to eat.

There was so much I still had to learn.

6. Il Nuovissimo Melzi

I went down into the village. The hike back was a strain, but it was a lovely walk, and invigorating. Good thing I brought a few cartons of Gitanes with me, because here they carry only Marlboro Lights. Country people.

I told Amalia about the barn owl. She was not amused when I said I had taken it for a ghost. She looked serious: "Barn owls, no, good critters that never hurt a body. But over yonder," and she gestured towards the slopes of the Langhe hills, "yonder they've still got hellcats. What's a hellcat? I'm almost afraid to say, and you should know, seems like my poor old pa was always telling you some story or other about them. Don't worry, they don't come up here, they stick to scaring ignorant farmers, not gentlemen who just might know the right word to send them running off. Hellcats are wicked women who traipse around at night. And if it's foggy or stormy, all the better, then they're happy as clams."

That was all she would say, but she had mentioned the fog, so I asked her if we got much of it here.

"Much of it? Jesus and Mary, too much. Some days I can't see the edge of the driveway from my door—but what am I saying, I can't even see the front of the house from here, and if someone's home at night you can just make out the light ever so faint coming from the window, but like it was just a candle. And even when the fog doesn't quite reach us, you should see the sight towards the hills. Maybe you can't see a thing for a ways, and then something pokes up—a peak, a little church—and then just white again after. Like somebody down there had knocked over the milk pail. If you're still around come September, you can bet you'll see it yourself, because in these parts, except for June to August, it's always foggy. Down in the village there's Salvatore, a fellow from Naples who fetched up here twenty years ago looking for work, you know how bad things are down south, and he's still not used to the fog, says that down there the weather's nice even for Epiphany. You wouldn't believe how many times he got lost in them fields and almost fell into the torrent and folks had to go and find him in the dark with flashlights. Well, his kind might be decent folk, I can't say, but they're not like us."

I recited silently to myself:

And I looked towards the valley: it was gone,
utterly vanished! A vast flat sea remained,
grey, without waves or beaches; all was one.
And here and there I noticed, when I strained,
the alien clamouring of small, wild voices:
birds that had lost their way in that vain land.
And high above, the skeletons of beeches
as if suspended in the sky, and dreams
of ruins and the hermit's hidden reaches.

But for now, the ruins and hermitages I was seeking, if they existed, were right there in broad daylight, yet no less invisible, for the fog was within me. Or perhaps I should be looking for them in the shadows? The moment had come. I had to enter the central wing.

When I told Amalia that I wanted to go alone, she shook her head and gave me the keys. There were a lot of rooms, it seemed, and Amalia kept them all locked, because you never knew when there might be a ne'er-do-well about. She gave me a bunch of keys, large and small, some of them rusty, telling me that she knew them all by heart, and if I really wanted to go on my own I would just have to try each key in each door. As if to say, "Serves you right, you're just as headstrong now as when you were little."

Amalia must have been up there in the early morning. The shutters, which had been closed the day before, were now partly open, just enough to let light into the corridors and rooms so you could see where you were going. Despite the fact that Amalia came from time to time to air the place out, there was a musty smell. It was not bad, it simply seemed to have been exuded by the antique furniture, the ceiling beams, the white fabric draped over the armchairs (shouldn't Lenin have been sitting there?).

Never mind the adventure, the trying and retrying of the keys, that made me feel like the head jailer at Alcatraz. The stairway led up into a room, a sort of well-furnished antechamber, with those Lenin chairs and some horrible landscapes, oils in the style of the nineteenth century, nicely framed on the walls. I had yet to get a sense of my grandfather's tastes, but Paola had described him as a curious collector: he could not have loved those daubs. They must have been in the family, then, maybe the painting exercises of some great-grandparent. That said, in the penumbra of that room they were barely noticeable—dark blotches on the walls—and maybe it was right that they were there.

That room led at one end onto the façade's only balcony and at the other into the midpoint of a long hallway, wide and shadowy, that ran along the back of the house, its walls almost completely covered in old colour prints. Turning right, one encountered pieces from the *Imagerie d'Épinal* that depicted historical events: "Bombardement d'Alexandrie", "Siège et bombardement de Paris par les Prussiens", "Les grandes journées de la Révolution Française", "Prise de Pékin par les Alliées". And others were Spanish: a series of little monstrous creatures called "Los Orrelis", a "Colección de monos filarmónicos", a "Mundo al revés", and two of those allegorical stairways, one for men and another for women, that depict the various stages of life—the cradle and babies with leading strings on the first step; then, step by step, the approach to adulthood, which is represented by beautiful, radiant figures atop an Olympic podium; from there, the slow descent of increasingly elderly figures, who by the bottom step are reduced, as the Sphinx described, to three-legged creatures, two wobbly sticks and a cane, with an image of Death awaiting them.

The first door on the right opened into a vast old-style kitchen, with a large stove and an immense fireplace with a copper cauldron still hanging in it. All the furnishings were from times past, maybe going back to the days of my grandfather's great-uncle. It was all antique by now. Through the transparent panes of the credenza I could see flowered plates, coffee pots, coffee cups. Instinctively I looked for a newspaper rack, so I must have known there was one. I found it hanging in a corner by the window, in pyrographed wood, with great flaming poppies etched against a yellow background. During the war, when there were shortages of firewood and coal, the kitchen must have been the only heated place, and who knows how many evenings I had spent in that room...

Next came the bathroom, also old-fashioned, with an enormous metal tub and curved taps that looked like drinking fountains. And the sink looked like a font for holy water. I tried to turn on the taps, and after a series of hiccups some yellow stuff came out of them that began to clear only after two minutes. The toilet bowl and flusher called to mind the Royal Baths of the late nineteenth century.

Past the bathroom, the last door opened into a bedroom that contained a few small items of furniture, in pale green wood decorated with butterflies, and a small single bed. Propped against the pillow sat a Lenci doll, mawkish as only a cloth doll from the thirties can be. This was no doubt my sister's room, as several little dresses in a drawer confirmed, but it seemed to have been stripped of every other furnishing and closed up for good. It smelled of damp.

Past Ada's room, at the end of the hall, stood an armoire, which I opened: it still gave off a strong odour of camphor, and inside were neatly folded embroidered sheets, some blankets, and a quilt.

I walked back down the hall towards the antechamber and then started down the left-hand side. On these walls were German prints, very finely worked, *Zur Geschichte der Kostüme:* splendid Bornean women, beautiful Javanese, Chinese mandarins, Slavs from Sibenik with pipes as long as their moustaches, Neapolitan fishermen and Roman brigands with blunderbusses, Spaniards in Segovia and Alicante... And also historical costumes: Byzantine emperors, popes and knights of the feudal era, Templars, fourteenth-century ladies, Jewish merchants, royal mousketeers, uhlans, Napoleonic grenadiers. The German engraver had captured each subject dressed for a great occasion, so that not only did the high and mighty pose weighed down by jewels, armed with pistols with decorated stocks, or decked out in parade armour or sumptuous dalmatics, but even the poorest African, the lowest commoner, appeared in colourful scarves that hung to their waists, mantles, feathered hats, rainbow turbans.

It may be that before reading many adventure books I explored the polychromatic multiplicity of the races and peoples of the earth in these prints, hung with their frames almost touching, many of them now faded from years and years of the sunlight that had rendered them, in my eyes, epiphanies of the exotic. "Races and peoples of the earth," I repeated aloud, and a hairy vulva came to mind. Why?

The first door belonged to a dining room, which also communicated with the antechamber. Two faux fifteenth-century sideboards, the doors of which were inset with circular and lozenge-shaped panes of coloured glass, a few Savonarola-style chairs like something out of *The Jester's Supper,* and a wrought-iron chandelier rising above the grand table. I whispered to myself, "capon and royal soup," but I did not know why. Later I asked Amalia why there should be capon and royal soup on the table, and what royal soup was. She explained to me that at Christmas time, each year our Good Lord granted us on this earth, Christmas dinner consisted of capon with sweet and spicy relishes, and before that the royal soup: a bowl of capon broth full of little yellow balls that melted in your mouth.

"Royal soup was so good, such a crime they don't make it any more, I reckon because they sent the king packing, poor man, and I'd like a word or two with Il Duce about that!"

"Amalia, Il Duce isn't around any more, even people who've lost their memories know that."

"I've never been much on politics, but I know they sent him off once and he came back. I'm telling you, that fellow is off biding his time somewhere, and one day, well, you never know.... But be that as it may, your good grandfather, may God rest his soul in glory, was partial to capon and royal soup, it wasn't Christmas without them."

Capon and royal soup. Had the shape of the table brought them to mind? Or the chandelier that must have illuminated them each December? I did not remember the taste of the soup, just the name. It was like that word game called Target: *table* gives rise to *chair* or *dining* or *wine*. For me, it called to mind *royal soup,* purely through word association.

I opened another door. I saw a double bed, and I hesitated a moment before entering the room, as though it were off limits. The silhouettes of furniture loomed large in the shadows, and the four-poster bed, its canopy intact, seemed like an altar. Could it have been my grandfather's bedroom, which I had not been allowed to enter? Had he died there, done in by grief? And had I been there to say my last goodbyes?

The next room was also a bedroom, with furnishings from an indeterminate epoch, pseudo-Baroque. No right angles, everything curved, including the doors of the great wardrobe, with its mirror and chest of drawers. I suddenly felt a knot in my pylorus, as I had in the hospital when I saw the photo of my parents on the day of their honeymoon. The mysterious flame. When I had tried to describe the feeling to Dr. Gratarolo, he had asked me if it was like an extrasystole. Perhaps, I said, but accompanied by a warmth that rises in my throat.... In that case, no, Gratarolo had said, extrasystoles are not like that.

It was in this room that I caught sight of a book, a small one, bound in brown leather, on the marble surface of the right-hand bedside table, and I went straight to it and opened it, saying to myself *riva la filotea.* In the Piedmontese dialect *riva* means "arrives"... but what was arriving? I sensed that this mystery had been with me for years, with its question in dialect (but did I speak dialect?): *La riva? Sa ca l'è c'la riva?* Something is arriving, but what is a *filotea*? A filobus, a trolley car, a tram of some kind?

I opened the book—which felt like a sacrilegious act—and it was *La Filotea,* by the Milanese priest Giuseppe Riva, an 1888 anthology of prayers and pious meditations, with a list of feast days and a calendar of the saints. The book was falling apart, and the pages cracked beneath my fingers when I touched them. I put it back together with religious care (part of my job, after all, is taking care of old books), and as I did I saw the spine, on which was printed, in faded gilt letters, RIVA LA FILOTEA. It must have been someone's prayer book, which I had never dared to open, but which, with the ambiguous wording on its spine that failed to distinguish between author and title, had seemed to herald the imminent arrival of some disquieting streetcar, which might have been named Desire.

Then I turned, and I saw that on the curved sides of the dresser were two smaller doors: with a quickening pulse, I hurried over and opened the one on the right, meanwhile looking around as though I were afraid of being observed. There were three shelves inside, curved too, but empty. I felt distressed, as if I had committed a theft. An ancient theft, perhaps: I must have snooped around in those drawers; perhaps they once contained something I was not supposed to touch, or see, and so I did it on the sly. By this time I was certain, reasoning almost like a detective: this had been my parents' bedroom, *La Filotea* was my mother's prayer book, and I used to go to those hiding places in the dresser in order to lay my hands on something intimate—old correspondence, perhaps, a wallet, packets of photographs that could not be put in the family album...

But if this was my parents' bedroom, and if I was born in Solara, as Paola said, then this room was where I had come into the world. Not to recall the room where one was born is normal. But if for years people have pointed to a place and told you, That is where you were born, on that big bed, a place where you sometimes insisted that you be allowed to spend the night between papà and mamma, where who knows how often, already weaned, you tried to smell again the scent of the breast that suckled you—all that should have left at least a trace in these damn lobes of mine. But no, even here my body retained only the memory of certain oft repeated gestures, that was all. In other words, if I wanted I could instinctively repeat the sucking motion of a mouth on a nipple, but nothing more; I could not tell you whose breast it was or what the taste of the milk was like.

Is it worth it to be born if you cannot remember it later? And, technically speaking, had I ever been born? Other people, of course, said that I was. As far as I know, I was born in late April, at sixty years of age, in a hospital room.

Signor Pipino, born an old man and died a bambino. What story was that? Signor Pipino is born in a cabbage at sixty years of age, with a nice white beard, and over the course of his adventures he grows a little younger each day, till he becomes a boy again, then a nursling, and then is extinguished as he unleashes his first (or last) scream. I must have read that story in one of my childhood books. No, impossible, I would have forgotten it like the rest, I must have seen it quoted when I was forty, say, in a history of children's literature—did I not know more about George Washington's cherry tree than my own fig trees?

In any case, I had to begin the recovery of my personal history there, in the shadows of those corridors, so that if I was going to die in swaddling bands at least I would be able to see my mother's face. My God, though, what if I expired with some blubbery, bewhiskered midwife looming over me?

At the end of the hallway, past a settle beneath the last window, were two doors, one on the end wall and one on the left. I opened the one on the left and entered a spacious study, aquarial and severe. A mahogany table dominated by a green lamp, like those in the Biblioteca Nazionale, was illuminated by two windows with panes of coloured glass that opened out on the side of the left wing, onto perhaps the quietest, most private area of the house, offering a superb view. Between the two windows, a portrait of an elderly man with a white moustache, posing as if for a rustic Nadar. The photo could not possibly have been there when my grandfather was still alive, a normal person does not keep his own portrait in front of his eyes. My parents could not have put it there, since he died after they did, indeed as a result of his grief over their passing. Perhaps my aunt or uncle, after selling the city house and the land around this house, had redone this room as a kind of cenotaph. And in fact nothing testified that it had been a place of work, an inhabited space. Its sobriety was deathly.

On the walls, another series from the *Imagerie d'Épinal,* with lots of little soldiers in blue and red uniforms: Infantry, Cuirassiers, Dragoons, Zouaves.

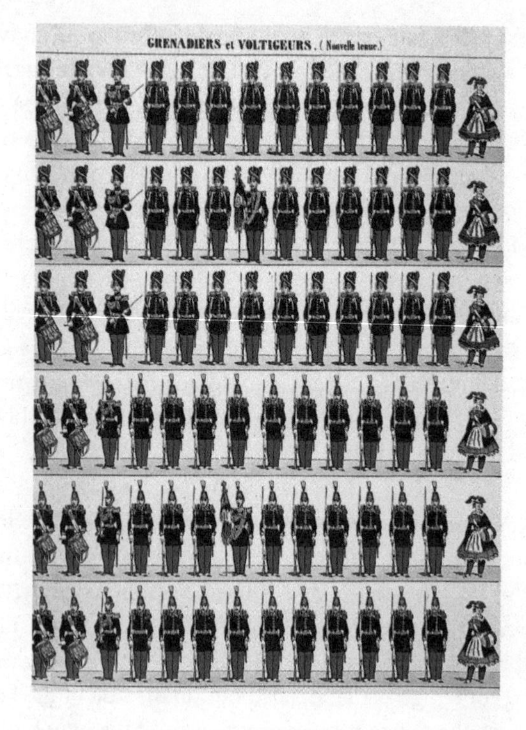

I was struck by the bookcases, which, like the table, were mahogany: they covered three walls but were practically empty. Two or three books had been placed on each shelf, for decoration—exactly what bad designers do to provide their clients with a bogus cultural pedigree while leaving space for Lalique vases, African fetishes, silver plates, and crystal decanters. But these shelves lacked all such expensive trinkets: just a few old atlases, a set of glossy French magazines, the 1905 edition of the *Nuovissimo Melzi* encyclopaedia, and French, English, German, and Spanish dictionaries. It was unthinkable that my grandfather, a seller and collector of books, had spent his life next to empty bookcases. And indeed, up on one shelf, in a silver-plated frame, I found a photograph, evidently taken from one corner of the room as sunlight from the windows shone on the desk: Grandfather was seated, looking surprised, in shirtsleeves (but with a waistcoat), barely fitting between two heaps of papers that cluttered the table. Behind him, the shelves were crowded with books, and among the books rose piles of newspapers, stacked sloppily. In the corner, on the floor, other heaps could be glimpsed, perhaps magazines, and boxes full of other papers that looked as though they had been tossed there to save them from being tossed out. Now that was what my grandfather's room must have been like when he was alive, the warehouse of one who hoarded all manner of printed matter that others would have thrown in the trash, the hold of a ghost ship transporting forgotten documents from one sea to another, a place in which to lose oneself, to plunge into those untidy tides of paper. Where had all those marvels gone? Well-meaning vandals had apparently whisked away everything that could be seen as messy, all of it. Sold perhaps at some wretched junk shop? Perhaps it was after such a spring cleaning that I decided not to visit these rooms any more, tried to forget Solara? And yet I must have spent hour after hour, year after year, in that room with my grandfather, discovering with him who knows what wonders. Had even this last handhold on my past been taken from me?

I went out of the studio and into the room at the end of the hall, which was much smaller and less austere: light-coloured furniture, made perhaps by a local carpenter, in a simple style, sufficient no doubt for a boy. A small bed in a corner, a number of shelves, virtually empty except for a row of nice red hardbacks. On a little student desk, neatly arranged with a black book bag in the centre and another green lamp, lay a worn copy of *Campanini Carboni,* the Latin dictionary. On one wall, attached with two tacks, an image that caused me to feel another very mysterious flame. It was the cover of a songbook, or an ad for a record, *It's in the Air,* but I knew it came from a film. I recognized George Formby with his horsy smile, I knew he sang while playing his ukulele, and now I was seeing him again, riding an out-of-control motorcycle into a haystack and coming out the other side amid a din of chickens, as the colonel in the sidecar catches an egg that falls into his hand, and then I saw Formby spiralling downwards in an old-style plane he had got into by mistake, but he righted himself, then rose and fell again in a nose-dive—oh, how funny, I was dying of laughter, "I saw it three times, I saw it three times," I was nearly yelling. "The funniest picture show I ever saw," I kept repeating, saying *picture show,* as we apparently did in those days, at least in the country.

That was certainly my room, my bed and desk, but except for those few items it was bare, as if it were the great poet's room in the house of his birth: a donation at the door and a mise-en-scène designed to exude the scent of an inevitable eternity. This is where he composed *August Song, Ode for Thermopylae, The Dying Boatman's Elegy*.... And where is he now, the Great One? No longer with us, consumption carried him away at the age of twenty-three, on this very bed, and notice the piano, still open just as He left it on his last day upon this earth, do you see? The middle A still shows traces of the spot of blood that fell from his pale lips as he was playing the *Water Drop Prelude*. This room is merely a reminder of his brief sojourn on this earth, hunched over sweat-drenched pages. And the pages? Those are locked away in the Biblioteca del Collegio

Romano and can be seen only with the grandfather's consent. And the grandfather? He is dead.

Furious, I went back into the hallway, leaned out of the window that looked out on the courtyard, and called Amalia. How can it be, I asked her, that there are no more books or anything else in these rooms? Why are my old toys not in my bedroom?

"Signorino Yambo, that was still your room when you was sixteen, seventeen years old. What would you have been wanting with toys then? And why worry your head about them fifty years later?"

"Never mind. But what about Grandfather's study? It must have been full of stuff. Where did that end up?"

"Up in the attic, it's all in the attic. Remember the attic? It's like a cemetery, breaks my heart just to go in, and I only go to set out the saucers of milk. Why? Well that's how I put the three cats in a mind to go up there, and once they get there they have fun hunting the mice. One of your grandfather's notions: Lots of papers up in the attic, got to keep the mice away, and you know in the country no matter how hard you try...As you got bigger, your old things would end up in the attic, like your sister's dolls. And later, when your aunt and uncle got their hands on the place, well, I don't mean to criticize, but they could at least have left out what was out. But no, it was like house-cleaning for the holidays. Everything up to the attic. So of course that floor you're on now turned into a morgue, and when you came back with Signora Paola nobody wanted to bother with it and that's why you all went to stay in the other wing, which it's not as nice but easier to keep clean, and Signora Paola got it fixed up real good..."

If I had been expecting the main wing to be the cave of Ali Baba, with its amphorae full of gold coins and walnut-sized diamonds, with its flying carpets cleared for take-off, we had completely miscalculated, Paola and I. The treasure rooms were empty. Did I need to go up into the attic and bring whatever I discovered back down, so I could return the rooms to their original state? Sure, but I would have to remember what their original state had been, and that state was precisely what I needed to spur my memory.

I went back to my grandfather's study and noticed a record player on a little table. Not an old gramophone, but a record player, with a built-in case. It must have been from the fifties, judging by the design, and only for 78s. So my grandfather listened to records. Had he collected them, as he collected everything else? If so, where were they now? In the attic, too?

I began to flip through the French magazines. They were de luxe magazines with a flowery, nouveau aesthetic and pages that looked illuminated, with illustrated margins and colourful Pre-Raphaelite images of pallid damsels in colloquy with knights of the Holy Grail. And there were stories and articles, these too in frames with lily scrolls, and fashion pages, already in the art deco style, featuring wispy ladies with bobs, chiffon or embroidered silk dresses with low waists, bare necks, and plunging backs, lips as blood-red as wounds, wide mouths from which to draw out lazy spirals of bluish smoke, little hats with veils. These minor artists knew how to draw the scent of powder puffs.

The magazines alternated between a nostalgic return to art nouveau, which had just gone out of fashion, and an exploration of what was currently in vogue, and perhaps that backward glance at charms that were ever so slightly outmoded lent a patina of nobility to their plans for the Future Eve. But it was over an Eve who was, apparently, slightly passé that I paused with a fluttering heart. It was not the mysterious flame, it was actual tachycardia this time, a flutter of nostalgia for the present.

It was the profile of a woman with long golden hair and something of the fallen angel about her. I recited silently:

Long-stemmed lilies, pale, devout,
were dying in your hands, candles gone cold.
Their perfume slipping through your fingers' hold
was the last gasp of great pain snuffing out.
And your bright clothes gave off the life breath of
both agony and love.

MODE- BALL
1 9 2 8
CANDEE
GALOCHES-SNOW BOOTS

VOGUE

My God, I must have seen that profile before, as a child, as a boy, as an adolescent, perhaps again on the threshold of adulthood, and it had been stamped on my heart. It was Sibilla's profile. I had known Sibilla, then, from time immemorial; a month ago in my studio I had simply recognized her. But this realization, rather than gratifying me and moving me to renewed tenderness, now withered my spirit. Because in that moment I realized that, seeing Sibilla, I had simply brought a childhood cameo back to life. Perhaps I had already done that, when we first met: I thought of her at once as a love object, because that image had been a love object. Later, when I met her again after my reawakening, I imagined an affair between us that was nothing more than something I had longed for in the days when I wore short pants. Was there nothing between myself and Sibilla but this profile?

And what if there were nothing but that face between me and all the women I have known? What if I have never done anything but follow a face I had seen in my grandfather's study? Suddenly the project I was undertaking in those rooms took on a new valence. It was no longer simply an attempt to remember what I had been before I left Solara, but also an investigation of why I had done what I had done after Solara. But was that really what happened? Don't exaggerate, I told myself, so you saw an image that reminds you of a woman you just met. Maybe for you this figure suggests Sibilla simply because she is slender and blonde, but for someone else she might call to mind, who knows, Greta Garbo, or the girl next door. You are simply still obsessed, and like the guy in the joke (Gianni had told it to me when I was telling him about the hospital tests), you always see the same thing in every inkblot the doctor shows you.

So, here you are looking for your grandfather, and your mind is on Sibilla?

Enough with the magazines, I would look at them later. I was suddenly drawn to the *Nuovissimo Melzi,* 1905 edition, 4,260 plates, seventy-eight tables of illustrated nomenclature, 1,050 portraits, twelve chromolithographs, Antonio Vallardi publisher, Milan. As soon as I opened it, at the sight of those yellowed pages in 8-point type and the little illustrations at the beginning of the most important entries, I immediately went to look for what I knew I would find. The tortures, the tortures. And indeed, there they were, the page with various types of tortures: boiling, crucifixion, the equuleus (with the victim hoisted and then dropped buttocks-first onto a cushion of whetted iron spikes), fire (where the soles of the feet are roasted), the gridiron, live burial, pyres, burnings at the stake, the wheel, flaying, the spit, the saw (hideous parody of a magic show, with the victim in a box and two executioners with a great toothed blade, except that the subject actually ended up in two pieces), quartering (much like the previous one, except that here a lever-like blade must have presumably divided the unfortunate one lengthwise as well), then dragging (with the guilty party tied to a horse's tail), foot screws, and, most impressive of all, impaling (and at that time I would have known nothing of the forests of burning impalees by the light of which Voivode Dracula dined), and on it went, thirty types of torture, each more gruesome than the last.

The tortures... Had I closed my eyes immediately after coming to that page, I could have named them one by one, and the bland horror, the mute exaltation I was feeling, were my own, in that moment, not those of someone else I no longer knew.

How long I must have lingered over that page. And how long, too, over other pages, some in colour, to which I turned without relying on alphabetical order, as if I were following the memory of my fingertips: mushrooms, fleshy ones, the most beautiful among them poisonous—the fly agaric with its red cap flecked with white, the noxious yellow bleeding milk cap, the smooth parasol, Satan's bolete, the sickener like a fleshy mouth opened in a grimace; then fossils, with the megathere, the mastodon, and the moa; ancient instruments (the ramsinga, the oliphant, the Roman bugle, the lute, the rebec, the aeolian harp, Solomon's harp); the flags of the world (with countries named Cochin China, Anam, Baluchistan, Malabar,

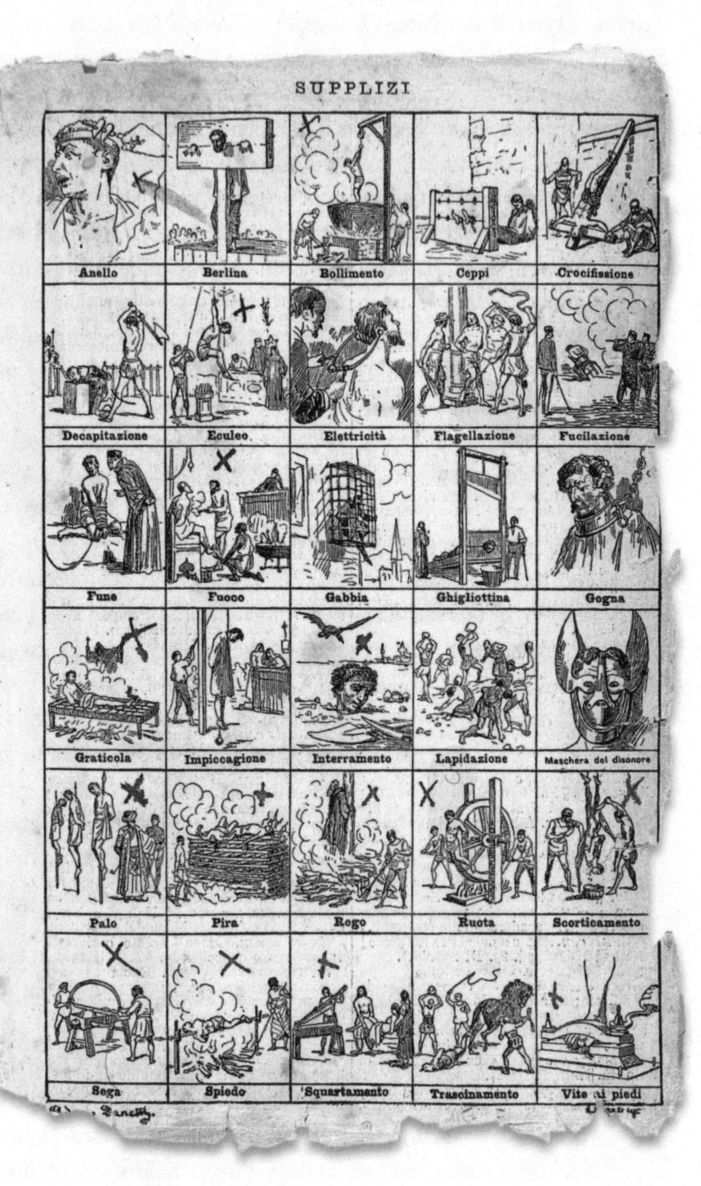
SUPPLIZI
Anello
Berlina
Bollimento
Ceppi
Crocifissione
Decapitazione
Eculeo
Elettricità
Flagellazione
Fucilazione
Fune
Fuoco
Gabbia
Ghigliottina
Gogna
Graticola
Impiccagione
Interramento
Lapidazione
Maschera del disonore
Palo
Pira
Rogo
Ruota
Scorticamento
Sega
Spiedo
Squartamento
Trascinamento
Vite ai piedi

Tripoli, Congo Free State, Orange Free State, New Granada, the Sandwich Islands, Bessarabia, Wallachia, Moldavia); vehicles, such as the omnibus, the phaeton, the hackney, the landau, the coupé, the cabriolet, the sulky, the stagecoach, the Etruscan chariot, the Roman biga, the elephant tower, the carroche, the berlin, the palanquin, the litter, the sleigh, the curricle, and the oxcart; sailing ships (and I had thought some sea-adventure tale had taught me such terms as brigantine, mizzen sail, mizzen topsail, mizzen-topgallant sail, crow's nest, mainmast, foremast, foretopmast, fore-topgallant sail, jib and flying jib, boom, gaff, bowsprit, top, broadside, luff the mainsail you scurvy boatswain, hell's bells and buckets of blood, shiver my timbers, take in the topgallants, man the port broadside, Brethren of the Coast!); on to ancient weaponry—the hinged mace, the scourge, the executioner's broadsword, the scimitar, the three-bladed dagger, the dirk, the halberd, the wheel-lock harquebus, the bombard, the battering ram, the catapult; and the grammar of heraldry: field, fess, pale, bend, bar, per pale, per fess, per bend, quarterly, gyronny... This had been the first encyclopaedia in my life, and I must have pored over it at great length. The margins of the pages were badly worn, many entries were underlined, and sometimes there appeared beside them quick annotations in a childish hand, usually transcriptions of difficult terms. This volume had been used nearly to death, read and reread and creased, and many pages were now coming loose.

Was this where my early knowledge had been shaped? I hope not; I sneered at the sight of certain entries, particularly those most underlined:

Plato. *Emin. Gr. phil., greatest of ancient phils. Disciple of Socrates, whose doctrine he espoused in the* Dialogues. *Assembled fine collection of antiques. 429–347* B.C.

Baudelaire. *Parisian poet, peculiar and artificial in his art.*

Apparently one can overcome even a bad education. Later I grew older and wiser, and at college I read nearly all of Plato. Nowhere did I ever find evidence that he had put together a fine collection of antiques. But what if it were true? And what if it had been, for him, the most important thing, and the rest was a way to make a living and allow himself that luxury? As for the tortures, they no doubt existed, though I do not believe that the history books used in schools have much to say about them, which is too bad—we really should know what stuff we are made of, we children of Cain. Did I, then, grow up believing that man was irremediably evil and life a tale full of sound and fury? Was that why I would, according to Paola, shrug my shoulders when a million babies died in Africa? Was it the *Nuovissimo Melzi* that gave rise to my doubts about human nature? I continued to leaf through its pages:

Schumann (Rob.). *Celeb. Ger. comp. Wrote* Paradise and the Peri, *many* Symphonies, Cantatas, *etc. 1810–1856.* —(Clara). *Distinguished pianist, widow of preced. 1819–1896.*

Why "widow"? In 1905 they had both been dead for some time. Would we describe Calpurnia as Julius Caesar's widow? No, she was his wife, even if she survived him. Why then was Clara a widow? My goodness, the *Nuovissimo Melzi* was also susceptible to gossip: after the death of her husband, and perhaps even before, Clara had had a relationship with Brahms. The dates are there (the *Melzi,* like the oracle of Delphi, neither reveals nor conceals; it indicates), Robert died when she was only thirty-seven, with forty more years ahead of her. What should a beautiful, distinguished pianist have done at that age? Clara belongs to history as a widow, and the *Melzi* was recording that. But how had I come to learn Clara's story? Perhaps the *Melzi* had piqued my curiosity about that "widow". How many words do I know because I learned them there? Why do I know even now, with adamantine certainty, and in spite of the tempest in my brain, that the capital of Madagascar is Antananarivo? It was in that book that I had encountered terms that tasted like magic words: avolate, baccivorous, benzoin, cacodoxy, cerastes, cribble, dogmatics, glaver, grangerism, inadequation, lordkin, mulct, pasigraphy, postern, pulicious, sparble, speight, vespillo, Adrastus, Allobroges, Assur-Bani-Pal, Dongola, Kafiristan, Philopator, Richerus...

I leafed through the atlases: some were quite old, from before the First World War, when Germany still had African colonies, marked in bluish grey. I must have looked through a lot of atlases in my life—had I not just sold an Ortelius? But some of these exotic names had a familiar ring, as if I needed to start from these maps in order to recover others. What was it that linked my childhood to German West Africa, to the Dutch West Indies, and above all to Zanzibar? In any case, it was undeniable that there in Solara every word gave rise to another. Would I be able to climb back up that chain to the final word? What would it be? "I"?

I had gone back to my room. I felt absolutely sure about one thing. The *Campanini Carboni* did not include the word "shit". How do you say that in Latin? What did Nero shout when, hanging a painting, he smashed his thumb with the hammer? *Qualis artifex pereo*? When I was a boy, those must have been serious questions, and official culture offered no answers. In such cases one turned to non-scholastic dictionaries, I imagined. And indeed the *Melzi* records *shit, shite, shitten, shitty*... Then like a flash I heard a voice: "The dictionary at my house says that a *pitana* is a woman who sells by herself." Someone, a schoolmate, had flushed out from some other dictionary something not found even in the *Melzi;* he pronounced the forbidden word in a kind of semidialect (the dialect form was *pütan'na*), and I must have long been fascinated by that phrase "sells by herself". What could be so forbidden about selling, as it were, without a clerk or bookkeeper? Of course, the word in his prim dictionary must have been *puttana,* whore, a woman who *sells herself,* but my informer had mentally translated that into the only thing he thought might have some malicious implication, the sort of thing he might hear around the house: "Oh, she's a wily one, she does all her selling by herself..."

Did I see anything again—the place, the boy? No, it was as though phrases were resurfacing, sequences of words, written about a story I once had read. *Flatus vocis.*

The hardbacks could not have been mine. I must have taken them from my grandfather, or maybe my aunt and uncle had moved them here from my grandfather's study, for decorative reasons. Most of them were *cartonnés* from the Collection Hetzel, the complete works of Verne, red bindings with gilt ornaments, multicoloured covers with gold decorations... Perhaps I had learned my French through these books, and once again I turned confidently to the most memorable images: Captain Nemo looking through the porthole of the *Nautilus* at the gigantic octopus, the airship of Robur the Conqueror abristle with its high-tech yards, the hot-air balloon crash-landing on the Mysterious Island ("Are we rising again?" "No! On the contrary! We're descending!" "Worse than that, Mr. Cyrus! We're falling!"), the enormous projectile aimed at the moon, the caverns at the centre of the earth, the stubborn Kéraban, and Michel Strogoff... Who knows how much those figures had unsettled me, always emerging from dark backgrounds, outlined by thin black strokes alternating with whitish gashes, a universe void of solid chromatic zones, a vision made of scratches, of streaks, of reflections dazzling for their lack of marks, a world viewed by an animal with a retina all its own—maybe the world does look like that to oxen or dogs, to lizards. A ruthless nightworld seen through ultra-thin Venetian blinds. Through these engravings, I entered the chiaroscuro world of make-believe: I lifted my eyes from the book, emerged from it, was wounded by the full sun, then went back down again, like a submarine sinking to depths at which no colour can be distinguished. Had they made any Verne books into colour movies? What does Verne become without those engravings, those abrasions that generate light only there where the graver's tool has hollowed out the surface or left it in relief?

My grandfather had had other volumes bound, though he kept the old illustrated covers: *The Adventures of a Parisian Lad, The Count of Monte Cristo, The Three Musketeers,* and other masterpieces of popular romanticism.

There were two versions of Jacolliot's *Les ravageurs de la mer,* the French original and Sonzogno's Italian edition, retitled *Captain Satan.* The engravings were the same, who knows which I had read. I knew there were two terrifying scenes: first the evil Nadod cleaves the good Harald's head with a single hatchet blow and kills his son

Olaus; then at the end Guttor the executioner grasps Nadod's head and begins squeezing it by degrees between his powerful hands, until the wretch's brains spurt straight up to the ceiling. In the illustration of that scene, the eyes of both victim and executioner are bulging nearly out of their sockets.

Most of the action takes place on icy seas covered by hyperborean mist. In the engravings, foggy, mother-of-pearl skies contrast with the whiteness of the ice. A wall of grey vapour, a milky hue more evident than ever... A fine white powder, resembling ashes, falling over the canoe... From the depths of the ocean a luminous glare arose, an unreal light... A downpour of white ashy powder, with momentary rents within which one glimpsed a chaos of indistinct forms...And a human figure, infinitely larger in its proportions than any dweller among men, wrapped in a shroud, its face the immaculate whiteness of snow...No, what am I saying, these are memories of another story. Congratulations, Yambo, you have a fine short-term memory: were these not the first images, or the first words, that you remembered as you were waking in the hospital? It must be Poe. But if these lines by Poe are so deeply etched in your public memory, might that not be because when you were small you had these private visions of the pallid seas of Captain Satan?

I stayed there reading (rereading?) that book until evening. I know that I was standing when I began, but I ended up sitting with my back against the wall, the book on my knees, forgetful of time, until Amalia came to wake me from my trance, shouting, "You'll ruin your eyes like that, your poor mother tried to teach you! My goodness gracious, you didn't set foot outside today, and it was the prettiest afternoon a body could ask for. You didn't even come and see me for lunch. Come on, let's go, time for supper!"

So I had repeated an old ritual. I was worn out. I ate like a boy at the height of a growth spurt, then was overcome by drowsiness. Usually, according to Paola, I read for a long time before falling asleep, but that night, no books, as if on Mother's orders.

I dozed off at once, and I dreamed of the lands of the South Seas, made of streaks of cream arranged in long strands across a plate of mulberry jam.

7. Eight Days in an Attic

What did I do for the past eight days? I read, mostly in the attic, but the memory of one day blurs into the next. I know only that I was reading in a wild, disorderly fashion.

I did not read everything word for word. Some books and magazines I skimmed as though I were flying over a landscape, and as I did I was aware of already knowing what was written in them. As though a single word could summon back a thousand others, or could blossom into a full-bodied summary, like those Japanese flowers that open in water. As though something were striking out on its own to settle in my memory, to keep Oedipus and Don Quixote company. At times the short circuit was caused by a drawing, three thousand words for one picture. At times I would read slowly, savouring a phrase, a passage, a chapter, experiencing perhaps the same emotions sparked by my first, forgotten reading.

It is pointless to speak of the gamut of mysterious flames, mild tachycardias, and sudden flushes that many of those readings gave rise to for a brief instant, which dissolved as quickly as they had come, making way for new waves of heat.

For eight days, I rose early to take advantage of the light, went upstairs, and remained there until sundown. Around noon, Amalia, who was alarmed the first time she could not find me, would bring me a plate with bread, salami or cheese, two apples, and a bottle of wine. ("Lordy, Lordy, he'll get himself sick again and then what will I tell Signora Paola, at least do it for me, stop or you'll go blind!") Then she would leave in tears, and I would drink down nearly all the wine and keep turning pages in an inebriated state, and of course I can no longer reconstruct the befores and afters. Sometimes I would go downstairs with an armful of books to hole up elsewhere, so as not to be a prisoner of the attic.

Before my first ascent I called home, to give Paola an update. She wanted to know about my reactions, and I was circumspect: "I'm getting settled in, the weather is splendid, I take walks outside, Amalia is a sweetheart." She asked me if I had been to the local pharmacist yet to have my blood pressure checked. I was supposed to do it every two or three days. After what had happened to me, I should not mess around. And above all, my pills, each morning and evening.

Right after that, with some guilt, but with a sound professional alibi, I called the office. Sibilla was still working on the catalogue. I could expect the proofs in two or three weeks. After many encouraging, paternal words, I hung up.

I asked myself whether I still felt anything for Sibilla. Strangely, the first few days in Solara had cast everything in a different light. Sibilla was now beginning to seem like a distant childhood memory, while everything I was gradually excavating from the fog of my past was becoming my present.

Amalia had told me that one entered the attic from the left wing. I had imagined a spiral wooden staircase, but instead there were stone steps, quite comfortable and practical—otherwise, I later realized, how would they have been able to carry up all that stuff they stashed away?

As far as I knew, I had never seen the inside of an attic. Nor of a cellar, for that matter, but everyone knows what cellars are like: subterranean, dark, damp, always cool, and you have to bring a candle, or a torch. The Gothic romance is rich in the subterranean, the monk Ambrosio wandering gloomily among crypts. Natural underground passageways, like Tom Sawyer's caverns. The mystery of darkness. All houses have cellars, but not all have attics, especially in cities, where they have penthouses. But is there really no literature of attics? And in that case what is *Eight Days in an Attic*? The title came to mind, but nothing else.

Even if you do not go through them all at once, you can tell that the attics of the Solara house extend over all three wings: you enter an area that stretches from the façade to the rear of the building, but then narrower passages open and bulkheads appear, wooden partitions that divide the spaces, routes defined by metal shelving units or old chests of drawers, the interchanges of an endless labyrinth. Having ventured down one of the corridors on the left, I turned once or twice more and found myself back in front of the entrance.

Immediate sensations: heat, above all, which is natural just beneath a roof. Then light: it comes in part from a series of dormer windows, which can be seen when you look at the front of the house, but which on the inside are largely obstructed by piles of junk, so that in some cases the sunlight barely filters through, reduced to yellow blades astir with an infinity of particles, revealing that the penumbra must also be crazed with a multitude of motes, spores, primordial atoms caught up in their Brownian skirmishes, primal bodies swarming in the void—who spoke of those, Lucretius? Sometimes those slants of light ricocheted off the glass panes of a dismantled buffet or a full-length mirror that from another angle had looked like merely another dull surface propped against the wall. And then the occasional skylight, darkened by decades of encrusted pluvial detritus but still able to make a pale zone of illumination on the floor.

Finally, the colour: the attic's dominant colour, imparted by the roof beams, by the crates piled here and there, by the remains of wobbly chests of drawers, is the colour of carpentry, composed of many shades of brown, from the yellowish-brown of unfinished wood to the warmth of maple to the darker tones of old dressers, their finishes flaking off, to the ivory of old papers overflowing their boxes.

If a cellar prefigures the underworld, an attic promises a rather threadbare paradise, where the dead bodies appear in a pulverulent glow, a vegetal elixir that, in the absence of green, makes you feel you are in a parched tropical forest, an artificial canebreak where you are immersed in a tepid sauna.

I had thought cellars symbolized the welcome of the mother's womb, with their amniotic dampness, but this aerial womb made up for that with an almost medicinal heat. And in that luminous maze, where if you pushed aside a couple of roof tiles you would see the open sky, a complicit mustiness hung in the air, the odour of silence and calm.

After a while, however, I no longer noticed the heat, gripped as I was by the frenzy of discovery. Because my Clarabelle's treasure was certainly there, though it would take a lot of digging and I had no idea where to begin.

I had to tear a lot of spiderwebs: the cats had taken care of the mice, as Amalia had said, but Amalia never worried about the spiders. If they had not overrun everything, it was thanks to natural selection; one generation died and their webs crumbled away, and so on, from season to season.

I began rummaging through several shelves, at the risk of toppling the stacks of containers that had accumulated there. My grandfather, apparently, had also collected containers, especially colourful metal ones: illustrated tins of Wamar biscotti showing cherubic children on swings, an Arnaldi cachet box, the Coldinava pomade tin with the gold borders and the plant motifs, a box of assorted Perry nibs, a sumptuous, shiny coffer of Presbitero pencils, all still perfectly aligned and untouched, like a scholar's ammo belt, and finally a can of Talmone cocoa featuring an old woman tenderly offering that easily digested beverage to a smiling old man, *ancien régime,* still wearing breeches. I could not help identifying the elderly couple with my grandfather and the grandmother I must have barely known.

Next I came across a tin, late-nineteenth-century in style, of Effervescente Brioschi. A couple of cheerful gentlemen are tasting flutes of table water proffered by a charming waitress. My hands remembered first: you take an envelope containing a soft white powder, you pour it slowly into the neck of the bottle after it has been filled with tap water, and you swirl it around a little to make sure no powder sticks to the neck; then you take another envelope, which contains a grainy powder made of tiny crystals, and you pour that in too, and quickly, because the water begins to seethe immediately and you have to hurry to get the cap on and then wait for the chemical miracle to take place in that primordial soup, as the liquid gurgles and tries to bubble out around the rubber gasket. Finally the tempest subsides, and the sparkling water is ready to drink: table water, children's wine, home-made mineral water. I said to myself: *vichy water.*

But besides my hands, something else had been set in motion, almost as it had been that day in front of *Clarabelle's Treasure.* I looked for another container, this one not a tin but a small carton, definitely from a later period, one which I had opened on countless occasions before we sat down to our meals. Its illustration would have been slightly different: still the same gentlemen, who still were drinking the amazing water from champagne glasses, except that clearly visible on the table before them was a carton identical to the actual carton, and on that second one were depicted the same

gentlemen, drinking in front of a table on which appeared yet another carton of powder, that one also with gentlemen who . . . and so on for ever. You knew that all you needed was a magnifying glass or a high-powered microscope to see other cartons within cartons, *en abîme,* like Chinese boxes or Matrioshka dolls. Infinity, as seen through the eyes of a boy who has yet to study Zeno's paradox. The race towards an unreachable goal; neither the tortoise nor Achilles would ever have reached the last carton, the last gentlemen, the last waitress. We learn as children the metaphysics of the infinite and infinitesimal calculus, though we are unaware of what we are learning, and it might be the image of an Endless Regress or its opposite, the dreadful promise of the Eternal Return and of the turning of the ages that bite their own tails, because upon reaching the final carton, were there such a thing, we might have discovered, at the bottom of that vortex, ourselves, holding the first carton in our hands. Why had I decided to become an antiquarian book dealer if not in order to have a fixed point, the day that Gutenberg printed the first Bible in Mainz, to go back to? At least you know that nothing existed before that, or rather, other things had existed, but you know that *you* can stop there; otherwise you would be not a book dealer but a decipherer of manuscripts. One chooses a profession that involves only five and a half centuries because as a child one daydreamed about the infinitude of vichy water tins.

The attic's entire accumulation would not have fitted in my

grandfather's study or anywhere else in the house, so even in the days when the study was crowded with stacks of papers, a lot of stuff must already have been up there. No doubt that was where many of my childish explorations had been undertaken, my Pompeii, the place I used to go to disinter remote artefacts dating back to a time before my birth. To get a whiff of the past, as I was doing now. Thus I was again enacting a Repetition.

Beside the tin were two cardboard boxes full of packs and cases of cigarettes. So he collected those too, my grandfather, and it must have cost him no little trouble to go out and filch them from travellers, who knows where or from where, because in those days collecting ephemera was not as organized as it is now. They were brands I had never heard of—Mjin Cigarettes, Makedonia, Turkish Atika, Tiedemann's Birds Eye, Calypso, Cirene, Kef Orientalske Cigaretter, Aladdin, Armiro Jakobstad, Golden West from Virginia, El Kalif from Alexandria, Stambul, Sasja Mild Russian Blend—in sumptuous cases, with images of pashas and khedives and (as on the Cigarrillos Excélsior de la Abundancia) Oriental odalisques, or else spiffy English sailors sporting white and blue outfits and King George (V?) beards. And there were also packs I seemed to recognize, as though I had seen them in some gentleman's hand, such as the ivory-white Eva or the Serraglio; and finally the flimsy paper packets, crushed and wrinkled, of working-class cigarettes, such as Africa or Milit, that no one would have ever thought to save, that by pure luck had been snatched from the garbage for future memory.

I lingered for at least ten minutes over a flattened, tattered toad of a packet, No. 10 Macedonia Cigarettes, 3 lire, murmuring, "Duilio, the Macedonias are turning your fingertips yellow..." I had still learned nothing about my father, but now I was sure that he had smoked Macedonias, perhaps even *those* Macedonias, from that very packet, and that my mother had complained about his nicotine-yellow fingertips: "yellow as quinine tablets." A guess at my father's image based on pale shades of tannin was not much, but it was enough to justify the trip to Solara.

"GOLD FLAKE"
CIGARETTES
W.D.&H.O.WILLS
GOLD FLAKE
HONEY DEW
W.D.&H.O.WILLS,
BRISTOL & LONDON.
FEZ
CORK TIP
FAROS
PAPEL ARROZ
Cia INDUSTRIAL DEL CENTRO
S.A.
IRAPUATO, GTO.
MURAD
THE TURKISH CIGARETTE
S. ANARGYROS.
P. LORILLARD CO., SUCCESSOR.
BELLE OF TURKEY
CIGARETTES
PLAIN END
PLAYER'S
CLIPPER
CIGARETTES
SUBLIMES
EL BUEN TONO S.A
FABRICA Y DEPOSITO
PLAZA SAN JUAN
MEXICO
LA
MARQUISE
CIGARETTE
DE
QUALITÉ SURFINE
No 10
SIGARETTE
MACEDONIA
Lire 3.00

I recognized, too, the marvels of the next box, to which I was drawn by the reek of their cheap perfumes. You can still find them, though they are quite expensive now (I had seen some a few weeks earlier among the stalls at the Cordusio market): the wallet-sized calendarettes that barbers used to give out at year's end, so unbearably perfumed that after more than fifty years they still retained a certain fragrance, a symphony of cocottes, of ladies clad in crinolines and little more, of beauties on swings and lost lovers, of exotic dancers and Egyptian queens... Women's Hairstyles Through the Ages; Good Luck Ladies; The Italian Firmament, with Maria Denis and Vittorio de Sica; Her Majesty, Woman; Salomé; the Empire-Style Perfumed Almanac with Madame Sans-Gêne; Tout Paris; the Grand Savon Quinquine, an all-purpose soap that cleanses and disinfects, invaluable in hot climates, effective against scurvy, malarial fevers, dry ezema (*sic*)—it bears Napoleon's monogram, God knows why, and the first image shows the Emperor receiving news of the great soap's invention from a Turk, and approving it. There was even a calendarette devoted to The Poet-Prophet Gabriele d'Annunzio—barbers had no shame.

I was nosing around hesitantly, as if I were an intruder in a forbidden kingdom. The barbers' calendarettes might have seriously

Tentazioni!
DANZE MODERNE
VITA PRIMITIVA
ALMANACCO PROFUMATO
1904
VALSECCHI & MOROSETTI
MILANO
Ricordati di me, che son la Pia,
Siena mi fe, disfecemi Maremma;
Salsi colui che innanellata pria,
Disposando, m'avea con la sua
gemma.
PIA DE TOLOMEI

inflamed a boy's imagination; perhaps they had been off limits to me. Perhaps I could learn something in that attic about the formation of my sexual consciousness.

By now the sun was beating straight down on the skylights, yet I was not content. I had seen many things, but no object that had been truly and wholly mine. I wandered at random and was drawn towards a closed chest. I opened it, and it was full of toys.

Over the course of the preceding weeks I had seen my grandkids' toys: all of them colourful plastic, most electronic. When I gave Sandro a new motorboat, the first thing he said was not to throw the box away, since the battery must still be inside. The toys of my childhood were made of wood and metal. Sabres, cap guns, a little colonial helmet from the period of the Ethiopia conquest, an entire army of lead toy soldiers, and other, larger soldiers made of a sort of friable clay, some now with no heads, some with no arms, or rather with nothing but the jutting wire that once supported the painted clay arms. I must have spent day after day with those guns and those mutilated heroes, in the grip of warlike passions. It was a necessity of the times that boys be schooled in the cult of war.

Beneath all that were some of my sister's dolls, which she must have been given by my mother, who had no doubt received them from my grandmother (toys in those days were passed down). Porcelain complexions, dainty pink mouths and fiery cheeks, little organdy dresses, eyes that still moved languidly. One, when I shook it, still said "mamma".

Foraging between one toy rifle and another I uncovered some curious soldiers: flat wooden cut-outs with red kepis, blue tunics, and long red trousers with yellow stripes, mounted on little wheels. Their faces were not martial, but rather grotesque, with potato-shaped noses. It occurred to me that one of them was Captain Potato of the Soldiers-of-Cockaigne Regiment. I was certain that was what they were called.

Finally I pulled out a tin frog, which, when I pressed its belly, still emitted the faintest *croak croak*. If she doesn't want Dr. Osimo's milk candies, I thought, she'll want to see the frog. What did Dr. Osimo have to do with the frog? And whom did I want to see it? Pitch darkness. I would have to give it some thought.

After looking at the frog and touching it, I spontaneously said that Angelo Bear must die. Who was Angelo Bear? What was his relationship to the tin frog? I felt something thrumming; I was sure that both the frog and Angelo Bear connected me to someone, but in the aridity of my purely verbal memory, I had nothing else to go on. Except I murmured a rhyme: "The procession is set to begin, Captain Potato says when." Nothing more: I was back in the present, in the hazel silence of the attic.

On the second day, Matù paid me a visit. He immediately climbed onto my lap as I was eating, earning himself the rinds of my cheese. After the now standard-issue bottle of wine, I went about haphazardly until I saw, in front of a dormer window, two large, wobbly armoires that stood more or less upright, thanks to a few rudimentary wooden chocks slipped beneath them. I had some trouble opening the first, which continually threatened to collapse, and when it did open a shower of books fell at my feet. I was unable to stave off the landslide; it seemed that those owls, those bats that had been imprisoned for centuries, those bottled genies, had been awaiting nothing other than some imprudent man who would grant them their vengeful freedom.

Between the books that were piling up around my feet and those I was trying to grab to keep them from tumbling down, too, I had discovered an entire library—or, more likely, the inventory of the old shop that my grandfather had owned in the city and that my aunt and uncle had liquidated.

I could never have managed to see it all, but I was already dazed by recognitions that flared and were snuffed in an instant. Books in various languages, from various eras, some with titles that sparked no flames, because they belonged to the repertoire of the already known, like the many old editions of Russian novels, though even glancing at their pages I was struck by the muddled Italian, the work (according to the title page) of a lady with a double surname who had evidently translated the Russians from French, for the characters' names all ended in *ine,* like Myskine and Rogozyne.

The pages of many of these volumes crumbled in my hands when I touched them, as if the paper, after decades of sepulchral darkness, could not bear the light of the sun. It certainly could not bear the touch of a finger and had been lying there for years waiting to be reduced to tiny shreds, shattering at the margins and corners into thin shavings.

Jack London's *Martin Eden* caught my eye, and I turned mechanically to the last sentence, as if my fingers knew what they would find there. Martin Eden, at the height of his fame, kills himself by slipping out through the porthole of his steamer cabin into the Pacific, and as he feels the water slowly filling his lungs, he gains, in a final glimmer of lucidity, some understanding, maybe of the meaning of life, but "at the instant he knew, he ceased to know."

Should one really demand a final revelation, if as soon as one has it one sinks into darkness? That rediscovery cast something of a pall over what I was doing. Perhaps I should have stopped there, seeing that fate had already granted me oblivion. But I had begun and could not help but keep going.

I spent the day skimming this and that, at times discovering that some great masterpiece that I thought had been absorbed by my public, adult memory, had probably come to my attention for the first time in the abridged Golden Stairway children's editions. The lyrical verses of *The Basket,* poems for children by Angiolo Silvio Novaro, sounded familiar to me: *What does the March rain say / when it sprinkles its silvery way / down from the eaves / to clatter against the parched leaves / of the holly?* Or: *When the springtime comes a-dancing, / comes a-dancing to your door, / what do you think it has in store? / Little wreaths of butterflies, / little bells of morning glory...* Did I know back then what morning glory was, or holly? Right after that my eyes lit upon the covers of the Fantômas stories—*The Hanged Man of London, The Red Wasp, The Hempen Necktie*—with their dark episodes involving chases through Parisian sewers, girls emerging from crypts, dismembered

NICK CARTER
IL GRAN POLIZIOTTO AMERICANO
Carrothers il Re dei Delinquenti.
Fascicolo I°
Prezzo: 25 Centesimi.
THE MASTER CRIMINAL
WITH THE DEVIL IN HIS EYE
EDMONDO DE AMICIS
CUORE
Libro per i ragazzi
MILANO
CURTI BÒ
E LA
PICCOLA TIGRE BIONDA
Romanzo di AUGUSTO DE ANGELIS
I PROMESSI SPOSI
ALESSANDRO MANZONI
40 QUADRI di TANCREDI SCARPELLI
CASA EDITRICE G. NERBINI - FIRENZE
Un problema difficile
NEW NICK CARTER WEEKLY
A MENTAL MYSTERY
MAURICE LEBLANC
LES AVENTURES EXTRAORDINAIRES
d'Arsène Lupin
L'AIGUILLE CREUSE
Carolina Invernizio
Il Treno della Morte.
GIALLI ECONOMICI MONDADORI
IL CONSIGLIO DEI QUATTRO
di
EDGAR WALLACE
VIDOCQ
L'UOMO DALLE CENTO FACCE
di MARC MARIO et LOUIS LAUNAY
Società Editrice "LA MILANO"
MILANO - Via S. Pietro all'Orto N. 12 - MILANO

LA SCALA D'ORO
I Miserabili
SERIE VII
N. 8
EMILIO SALGARI
I CORSARI DELLE BERMUDE
ILLUSTRAZIONI DI
G. AMATO
CASA EDITRICE SONZOGNO - MILANO
SATURNINO FARANDOLA
NELLE 5 O 6 PARTI DEL MONDO
PER
G. ROBIDA
CASA EDITRICE SONZOGNO MILANO
GIULIO VERNE
I FIGLI DEL CAPITANO GRANT
ROMANZO
E. SUE
I Misteri del Popolo
STORIA
LA STRANA MORTE DEL
Ogni pagina un'emozione!
A·M
SIGNOR BENSON
S.S. VAN DINE
Il più bel libro per la gioventù!
SENZA FAMIGLIA
ROMANZO DI ETTORE MALOT
IL ROMANZO MENSILE
LIRE 2
IL BARONE ALLE STRETTE
A. MORTON
IL DELITTO DI ROULETABILLE
G. LEROUX
L 6

FANTOMAS

bodies, severed heads, and the prince of crime in his tailcoat, always ready with his derisive laugh to conjure and control a nocturnal, subterranean Paris.

And together there with Fantômas were the tales of Rocambole, another crime lord. *The Woes of London* fell open to a page on which I read this description:

At the south-west corner of Wellclose Square is an alley about ten feet wide; halfway down there stands a theatre where the best seats in the house go for a shilling, and for a penny you may sit in the stalls. The leading actor is a Negro. There one may smoke and drink during the performance. The prostitutes who frequent the boxes are barefoot; the stalls are full of thieves.

Unable to resist the allure of evil, I spent the rest of the day with Fantômas and Rocambole, among their errant, dazzling pages, interspersing their stories with those of two other criminals: the gentleman burglar Arsène Lupin and an even greater gentleman, the supremely elegant Baron, an aristocratic jewel thief of many disguises, and of an exaggeratedly Anglo-Saxon appearance—thanks, I imagine, to some Anglophilic Italian artist.

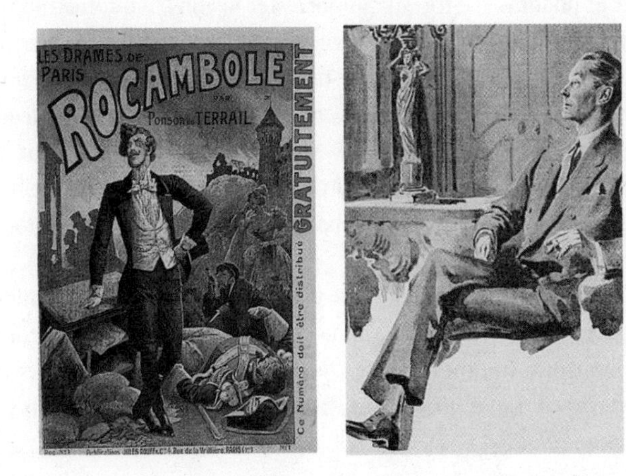

I trembled before a lovely edition of *Pinocchio,* illustrated by Mussino in 1911, its pages torn and coffee-stained. Everyone knows the story of Pinocchio; I had retained a cheerful, fairy-tale image of him, and who knows how often I told my grandkids his story to entertain them, and yet now I shuddered before those terrifying illustrations, most of them done in only two colours, either yellow and black or green and black, whose art nouveau whorls assaulted me in Fire-Eater's riverlike beard, in the fairy's unsettling blue hair, in the nocturnal visions of the Assassins, and in the Green Fisherman's rictus. Did I cringe beneath the covers on stormy nights after having looked at that *Pinocchio*? Weeks ago, I asked Paola whether all those movies on television, full of violence and the living dead, were bad for children, and she told me that one psychologist had revealed to her that in his entire clinical career he had never seen children seriously traumatized by a movie except in one case, and that child was irrevocably wounded to the core: devastated by Walt Disney's *Snow White.*

And elsewhere I learned that equally terrifying visions lay behind my very name. I found *The Adventures of Ciuffettino,* by a certain Yambo, along with other adventure books by the same author, with more art nouveau drawings and dark scenery: castles standing out above steep hills, black against the dark night; flame-eyed wolves in phantasmal forests; underwater visions like something out of a home-grown, latter-day Verne; and Ciuffettino, the charming little boy with the quiff of a fairy-tale bravo: "An immense quiff that gave him a curious appearance, causing him to resemble a feather duster. And do you know, he was fond of his quiff!" That was where the Yambo I am now, and the one I wanted to be, was born. In the end I suppose it is better than identifying with Pinocchio.

Was this my childhood? Or worse? Still rummaging around, I brought to light (wrapped in blue sugar paper and held by rubber bands) various volumes of the *Illustrated Journal of Voyages and Adventures on Land and at Sea.* It had come in weekly instalments,

.... il serpente si rizzò all'improvviso come una molla....

YAMBO
LE AVVENTURE
DI CIUFFETTINO
Libro per
i ragazzi

and my grandfather's collection included issues from the first decades of the century, as well as a few copies of the original French edition, *Journal des Voyages*.

Many of the cover images depicted ferocious Prussians shooting valiant Zouaves, but for the most part they had to do with exploits of ruthless cruelty in foreign lands: impaled Chinese coolies, scantily clad virgins kneeling before a gloomy Council of Ten, rows of decapitated heads atop sharpened poles in front of the buttresses of some mosque, children slaughtered by scimitar-wielding Tuareg raiders, the bodies of slaves torn apart by huge tigers—as if the *Nuovissimo Melzi*'s table of tortures had inspired these perverse illustrators, arousing an unnatural imitative frenzy. It was an overview of Evil in all its guises.

Faced with such abundance and stiff from sitting in the attic, and because the heat had become unbearable, I brought the stack of issues downstairs into the big room with the apples, and my first thought was that the apples lined up on the big table must all be mouldy. Then I realized that the smell of mould came from the pages in my hands. But how could they smell musty after fifty years in the dry atmosphere of the attic? Perhaps in the cold, rainy months moisture came in through the roof and the attic was not quite so dry, or perhaps those issues, prior to being stored there, had spent decades in some cellar, where water trickled down the walls, before my grandfather discovered them (he too must have courted widows) in a state so rotten that they had never lost their odour, even in this heat that had shrivelled them. But as I was reading about atrocious events and ruthless vendettas, the scent of mould conjured up not cruel feelings but rather thoughts of the Wise Men and Baby Jesus. Why? When did I ever have anything to do with the Wise Men, and what had they to do with massacres in the Sargasso Sea?

My concern at the moment was something quite different, however. If I had read all those stories, if I had really seen all those cover images, how could I have accepted that springtime comes

Anno XXXVI. — N. 20.
Milano, 16 Maggio 1920.
Giornale Illustrato dei Viaggi
e delle Avventure di Terra e di Mare
SI PUBBLICA LA DOMENICA
IL PROFETA TI GUIDI!
Giornale Illustrato dei Viaggi
e delle Avventure di Terra e di Mare
SI PUBBLICA LA DOMENICA
LA VERGINE DELLA LAGUNA.
Anno XXXV. — N. 8.
Milano, 23 Febbraio 1919.
Giornale Illustrato dei Viaggi
e delle Avventure di Terra e di Mare
SI PUBBLICA LA DOMENICA
IL SEGRETO DEL LAGO.
Anno XXXVI. — N. 15.
Milano, 11 Aprile 1920.
Giornale Illustrato dei Viaggi
e delle Avventure di Terra e di Mare
SI PUBBLICA LA DOMENICA
L'AMULETO INSANGUINATO.

a-dancing? Did I have some instinctive ability to keep the realm of good, domestic feelings separate from those adventure stories that spoke to me of a cruel world modelled on the Grand Guignol, that realm of the torn asunder, the flayed, the burned at the stake, the hung?

The first armoire had been completely emptied, though I had not been able to look at everything. On the third day I started in on the second one, which was less congested. These books did not appear to have been tossed aside by my aunt and uncle in their rabid haste to divest themselves of unwanted junk, but instead had been arranged in nice rows, as if by my grandfather in earlier times. Or by me. They were all books that were more suited to childhood, and perhaps they had belonged to my personal mini-library.

I took out the entire collection of My Children's Library, the series published by Salani, whose covers I recognized and whose titles I began reciting, even before pulling out the individual volumes, as surely as I identified the most famous books—Münster's *Cosmographia* or Campanella's *De Sensu Rerum et Magia*—in a competitor's catalogue or a widow's library. *The Boy Who Came from the Sea, The Gypsy's Legacy, The Adventures of Sun-Blossom, The Tribe of Wild Rabbits, The Mischievous Ghosts, The Pretty Prisoners of Casabella, The Painted Chariot, The North Tower, The Indian Bracelet, The Iron Man's Secret, The Barletta Circus*...

Too many—had I stayed in the attic, I would have cramped into the hunchback of Notre Dame. I took an armful and went downstairs. I could have gone to the study, I could have sat in the garden, but instead, for some obscure reason, I wanted something else.

I went behind the house, to the right, towards the place where, on the first day, I had heard pigs rooting and hens twittering. There, behind Amalia's wing of the house, was a threshing floor, just as in the old days, with chickens scratching around on it, and beside it were the rabbit hutches and pigsties.

LA TELEFERICA
MISTERIOSA
A.F. PESSINA
BIBLIOTECA DEI MIEI RAGAZZI
ANTASMI
ALIZIOSI
M. GOUDAREAU
BIBLIOTECA DEI MIEI RAGAZZI
OTTO GIORNI
IN UNA SOFFITTA
H. GIRAUD
BIBLIOTECA DEI MIEI RAGAZZI
La Torre
del Nord
M. GOUDAREAU
Biblioteca dei miei ragazzi
IL CIRCO
BARLETTA
M. CATALANY
BIBLIOTECA DEI MIEI RAGAZZI
L'erede
di Ferralba
M. BOURCET

GUARDIANI
DEL FARO
BIBLIOTECA DEI MIEI RAGAZZI

LA TRIBÙ DEI
CONIGLI SELVATICI
A. BRUYÈRE
BIBLIOTECA DEI MIEI RAGAZZI

LA PICCOLA
PANTOFOLA D'ARGENTO
M. DE CARNAC
BIBLIOTECA DEI MIEI RAGAZZI

On the ground level was a huge room full of farming tools—rakes, pitchforks, shovels, lime buckets, old tuns.

On the other side of the threshing floor, a path led into a fruit orchard, wonderfully lush and cool, and my first impulse was to climb a tree, straddle a branch, and do my reading there. Maybe that was what I had done as a boy, but at sixty you can never be too careful, and besides, my feet were already leading me elsewhere. In the midst of that greenery I came upon a small stone stairway, at the bottom of which was a circular area enclosed by low, ivy-covered walls. Directly across from the steps, against the wall, a trickling fountain gurgled. A gentle breeze was blowing, the silence was total, and I squatted on a jutting rock between the fountain and the wall, ready to read. Something had carried me to that place, perhaps I used to go there with those same books. Accepting the choice of my animal spirits, I plunged into those slim volumes. Often a single illustration brought the entire plot to mind.

Several, judging from the forties-style drawings and the authors' names, were clearly Italian in origin (*The Mysterious Cableway* and *The Pure-Blooded Milanese Boy*), and many were inspired by patriotic, nationalistic sentiments. But most were translated from the French and written by people with names like B. Bernage, M. Goudareau, E. de Cys, J. Rosmer, Valdor, P. Besbre, C. Péronnet, A. Bruyère, M. Catalany—an eminent roster of unknowns; even the Italian publisher may not have known their first names. My grandfather had also collected some of the French originals, which had appeared in the Bibliothèque de Suzette series. The Italian editions came out a decade or more later, but their illustrations harked back at least to the twenties. As a young reader, I must have detected a pleasantly old-fashioned air about them, and so much the better: all the stories were set in a bygone world, and seemed to be told by gentle ladies writing for young girls from good families.

In the end, it seemed to me, all those books told the same story: typically three or four kids of noble lineage (whose parents for some reason were always off travelling) come to stay with an uncle in an old castle, or a strange country house, and they get caught up in thrilling, mysterious adventures involving crypts and towers, finally unearthing some treasure, or the plot of a treacherous local official, or a document that restores to an impoverished family the estate some wicked cousin has usurped. Happy ending, celebration of the children's bravery, and good-natured remarks from the uncles or grandparents about the dangers of such reckless behaviour, no matter how well motivated.

You could tell from the peasants' work shirts and clogs that the stories were set in France, but the translators had performed miraculous balancing acts, shifting the names into Italian and making it appear that the events were taking place somewhere in our country, despite landscapes and architecture that suggested now Brittany, now Auvergne.

I found two Italian editions of what was clearly the same book (by M. Bourcet), but the 1932 edition was called *The Ferlac Heiress,* and the names and characters were French, whereas the 1941 edition was called *The Ferralba Heiress* and featured Italian characters. Clearly in the intervening years an order from on high, or spontaneous self-censorship, had brought about the story's Italianization.

And I finally came across the explanation for that phrase that had come into my head while I was in the attic: one of the books in the series was *Eight Days in an Attic* (I had the original too, *Huit jours dans un grenier*), a delightful story about some children who hide a girl named Nicoletta, who has run away from home, in the attic of their villa for a week. Who knows whether my love for attics derived from that book, or whether I had discovered the book while exploring the attic. And why had I named my daughter Nicoletta?

Nicoletta shared the attic with a cat named Matù, an Angora type, jet-black and majestic—so that was where I had got the idea to have a Matù of my own. The illustrations depicted little boys and girls who were well dressed, sometimes in lace, with blond hair, del-

icate features, and mothers who were no less elegant: neat bobbed hair, low waists, triple-flounced skirts to their knees, and barely pronounced, aristocratic breasts.

In my two days beside the fountain, when the light waned and I could make out only pictures I would think about the fact that I had no doubt cultivated my taste for the fantastic in the pages of My Children's Library, while living in a country where even if the author's name was Catalany the protagonists had to be named Liliana or Maurizio.

Was this nationalistic education? Had I understood that these children, who were presented to me as brave little compatriots of my own time, had lived in a foreign land decades before I was born?

Back in the attic, having returned from my vacation by the fountain, I found a package tied with string that contained thirty or so instalments (sixty centesimi each) of the adventures of Buffalo Bill. They were not stacked in sequential order, and the first cover I saw sparked a burst of mysterious flames. *The Diamond Medallion:* Buffalo Bill, his fists tensed behind him, his gaze grim, is about to hurl himself upon a red-shirted outlaw who is threatening him with a pistol.

And as I looked at that issue, No. 11 in the series, I could anticipate other titles: *The Little Messenger, Big Adventures in the*

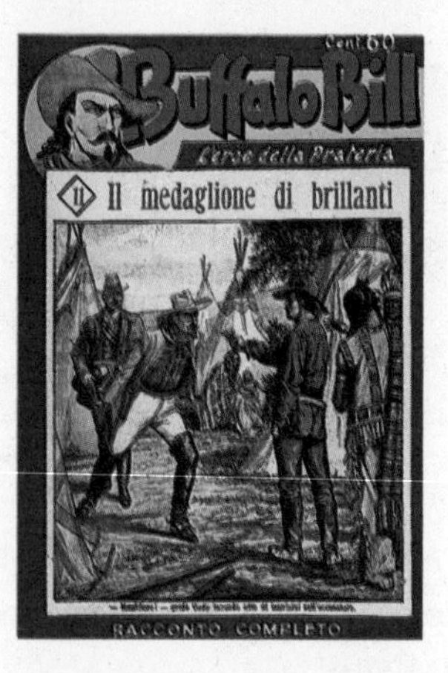

Forest, Wild Bob, Don Ramiro the Slave Trader, The Accursed Estancia... I noticed that the covers referred to *Buffalo Bill, the Hero of the Plains,* whereas the inside heading said *Buffalo Bill, the Italian Hero of the Plains.* To an antiquarian book dealer, at least, it was clear what had happened, you had only to look at the first issue of a new series, dated 1942: it featured a large boldfaced notice explaining that William Cody's real name was Domenico Tombini and that he was from Romagna (just as Mussolini was, though the note passed over that amazing coincidence in modest silence). By 1942 we had, I felt sure, already entered the war with the United States, and that explained everything. The publisher (Nerbini of Florence) had printed the covers at a time when Buffalo Bill could simply be American; later, it was decided that heroes must always and only be Italians. The only thing to do, for economic reasons, was to keep the old colour cover and reset only the first page.

Curious, I said to myself, falling asleep over Buffalo Bill's latest adventure: I was raised on adventure stories that had come from France and America but had then been naturalized. If this was the nationalistic education that a boy received under the dictatorship, it was a fairly mild one.

No, it had not been mild. The first book I picked up the next day was *Italy's Boys in the World,* by Pina Ballario, with sinewy modern illustrations dominated by black and red.

A few days earlier, on finding the Verne and Dumas books in my bedroom, I had the feeling that I had read them curled up on some balcony. I paid little attention to this at the time, it was just a flash, a simple sense of déjà vu. But now it occurred to me that there was indeed a balcony in the centre of the main wing, and that was where I must have devoured those adventures.

To recreate the balcony experience, I decided to read *Italy's Boys in the World* out there, and so I did, even attempting to sit with my legs dangling down, sticking through the narrow gaps in the railing. My legs, however, no longer fitted. I roasted for hours beneath the sun, until it had travelled around to the other side of the house and things had cooled off. In that way I was able to experience the Andalusian sun, at least as I must have imagined it back then, even though the story I was reading was set in Barcelona. A group of young Italians, having emigrated with their family to Spain, were caught up in Generalísimo Franco's anti-Republican rebellion, except in this book the usurpers seemed to be the Red Militia, drunk and out for blood. The young Italians regained their Fascist pride, ran intrepidly in their black shirts through the streets of a Barcelona in the throes of upheaval, and saved the pennant of the Fascist headquarters after the building had been closed down by the Republicans; the brave protagonist even managed to convert his father—a socialist and a drunkard—to the Word of Il Duce. A story that must have made me glow with Fascist pride. Did I identify back then with those Italian boys, or with the little Parisian kids Bernage described, or with a man who at the end of the day was still named Cody and not Tombini? Who had inhabited my childhood dreams? Italy's boys in the world, or the little girl in the attic?

A return to the attic offered two new thrills. The first was *Treasure Island.* Of course I recognized the title, a classic, but I had forgotten the story, a sign that it had become part of my life. I spent two hours reading through it in a single sitting, each chapter bringing to mind what would happen in the next. I had gone back to the fruit orchard, where I had glimpsed, at one end, some wild hazelnut bushes, and there I sat, on the ground, alternately reading and stuffing myself with hazelnuts. I would crack three or four at a time with a stone, blow away the shell fragments, and toss the plunder into my mouth. I lacked the apple barrel into which Jim climbs to eavesdrop on Long John Silver's councils, but I really must have read that book that way, munching dry foods, as they do on ships.

It was my story. Relying on a slender manuscript, the characters go off to discover Captain Flint's treasure. Towards the end of it, I went to get myself a bottle of grappa I had noticed on Amalia's sideboard, and I alternated my reading of that pirate tale with long sips. Fifteen men on the dead man's chest—Yo-ho-ho, and a bottle of rum.

After *Treasure Island,* I came across *The Tale of Pipino, Born an Old Man and Died a Bambino,* by Giulio Gianelli—the story that had come to mind a few days earlier, except this book was about a pipe that had been left, still hot, on a table beside a clay statue of a little old man, and the pipe decided to breathe warmth into that dead thing to bring it to life, and thus an elderly man was born. *Puer senex,* an ancient commonplace. In the end, Pipino dies as an infant in his cradle and is carried up to heaven by fairies. It was better the way I had remembered it: Pipino was born as an old man in one cabbage and died as a nursling in another. In either case, Pipino's journey towards infancy was my own. Perhaps when I reached back to the moment of my birth, I would dissolve into nothing (or All), as he had.

That evening Paola called, worried because I had not been in touch. I'm working, I'm working, I said. Don't worry about my blood pressure, everything's fine.

But the next day I was once again rummaging around in the armoire, where I found all the Salgari novels, with their art nouveau covers that featured, among gentle swirls, the brooding, ruthless Black Corsair, with his raven hair and his pretty red mouth, finely drawn upon his melancholy face; the Sandokan of *Two Tigers,* with his fierce Malay-prince head grafted on to a catlike body; the voluptuous Surama and the prahus from *The Pirates of Malay.*

E. SALGARI
SANDOKAN
ALLA RISCOSSA
I MISTERI DELLA
JUNGLA NERA
LE TIGRI DI
MOMPRACEM
E. SALGARI
SALGARI
IL
CORSARO
NERO

It was hard to say whether I was rediscovering anything or simply triggering my paper memory, because people today still talk about Salgari all the time, and sophisticated critics devote nostalgia-drenched screeds to him. Even my grandkids, a few weeks ago, were singing "Sandokan, Sandokan"—apparently they had seen him on television. I could have written an entry on Salgari for a children's encyclopaedia even without coming to Solara.

Certainly I had devoured those books as a child, but if I had any individual memory to reactivate, it was blurring with my general memory. It might be that the books that had marked my childhood most indelibly were those that sent me smoothly back to my adult, impersonal knowledge.

Still guided by instinct, I read most of Salgari in the vineyard (and later brought several volumes to bed and spent the following nights with them). Even among the vines it was quite hot, but the sunny blaze acclimatized me to deserts, prairies, and flaming forests, to tropical seas plied by trepang fishermen, and every so often, lifting my eyes to wipe sweat from my face, I glimpsed, among the scant vines and the trees that rose at the hill's edge, a baobab, pombos as huge as those that surrounded Giro-Batol's hut, mangrove swamps, palm cabbages with their mealy flesh that tastes of almonds, the sacred banyan of the black jungle. I could almost hear the sound of the ramsinga, and I kept expecting to see a nice babirusa pop out from between the rows of vines, perfect for roasting over a spit between two forked branches planted in the earth. For dinner, I would have liked Amalia to prepare some *blachan,* highly prized by Malayans: that potpourri of shrimp and fish ground together, left to rot in the sun, and then salted, with a smell that even Salgari thought vile.

Delicious. Perhaps that is why, according to Paola, I love Chinese food, and in particular shark fins, birds' nests (harvested amid their guano), and abalone, the more putrid the better.

But, *blachan* aside, what happened when an "Italian boy in the world" read Salgari, where often the heroes were dark-skinned and the whites evil? It was not only the English who were odious, but also the Spanish (how I must have loathed the Marquis of Montelimar). The Black, Red, and Green Corsairs may have been Italians, and counts of Ventimiglia to boot, but other heroes were named Carmaux, Wan Stiller, or Yanez de Gomera. The Portuguese had to seem good because they were a bit Fascist, but were not the Spanish also Fascists? Perhaps my heart raced for the valiant Sambigliong as he fired off cannonades of nailshot, without my wondering which of the Sunda Islands he had come from. Kammamuri could be good and Suyodhana bad, though both were Indian. Salgari must have made my first forays into cultural anthropology rather confusing.

Then, from the bottom of the armoire, I pulled out magazines and books in English. Many issues of *The Strand*, with all of Sherlock Holmes's adventures. I certainly did not know English in those days (Paola told me I had learned it only as an adult), but luckily there were also many translations. The majority of the Italian editions, however, were not illustrated, so perhaps I had read the Italian and then looked up the corresponding illustrations in *The Strand*.

I dragged all the Holmes into my grandfather's study, which had a more civil atmosphere, better suited to reviving that universe where well-mannered gentlemen sat beside the hearth in the lodgings on Baker Street, intent on their calm conversations—so different from the damp cellars and the macabre sewers haunted by the characters in the French *feuilletons*. The few times that Sherlock Holmes was shown pointing a pistol at a criminal, he always had his right leg and arm stretched forward in an almost statuesque pose, maintaining his aplomb, as befits a gentleman.

I was struck by the almost obsessive recurrence of images of Holmes seated, with Watson or others, in a train compartment, in a brougham, before the fire, in an armchair covered with white fabric, in a rocking chair, beside a small table, in the perhaps greenish lamplight, in front of a just-opened chest, or standing, while reading a letter or deciphering a coded message. Those images said to me: *de te fabula narratur.* At that very moment Sherlock Holmes was me, intent on retracing and reconstructing remote events of which he had no prior knowledge, while remaining at home, shut away, perhaps even in an attic. He too, like me, motionless and isolated from the world, deciphering pure signs. He always succeeded in making the repressed resurface. Would I be able to? At least I had a model.

And like him, I had to combat the fog. It was enough to open *A Study in Scarlet* or *The Sign of Four* at random:

It was a September evening, and not yet seven o'clock, but the day had been a dreary one, and a dense drizzly fog lay low upon the great city. Mud-coloured clouds drooped sadly over the muddy streets. Down the Strand the lamps were but misty splotches of diffused light which threw a feeble circular glimmer upon the slimy pavement. The yellow glare from the shop-windows streamed out into the steamy, vapourous air, and threw a murky, shifting radiance across the crowded thoroughfare. There was, to my mind, something eerie and ghostlike in the endless procession of faces which flit-

ted across these narrow bars of light—sad faces and glad, haggard and merry.

It was a foggy, cloudy morning, and a dun-coloured veil hung over the housetops, looking like the reflection of the mud-coloured streets beneath. My companion was in the best of spirits, and prattled away about Cremona fiddles and the difference between a Stradivarius and an Amati. As for myself, I was silent, for the dull weather and the melancholy business upon which we were engaged, depressed my spirits.

By contrast, that evening in bed, I opened Salgari's *The Tigers of Mompracem:*

On the night of December 20, 1849, a ferocious hurricane raged over Mompracem, an untamed island of sinister repute, the lair of fearsome pirates, located in the Malay Sea a few hundred miles off the western shores of Borneo. Black masses of vapour, driven by an irresistible wind, raced through the sky like unbridled steeds, roiling tumultuously, unleashing at intervals furious downpours onto the island's gloomy forests.... Who would be awake at that hour, amid such a storm, on an island of bloodthirsty pirates?... One room in that dwelling is illumined, its walls covered with heavy red fabrics, velvets and brocades of great price, though creased in places, or torn, or stained; its floor disappearing beneath a thick layer of Persian carpets, blazing with gold.... In the room's centre stands an ebony table, inlaid with mother-of-pearl and trimmed in silver, laden with bottles and glasses of the purest crystal; in the corners rise great dilapidated shelves, filled with jugs overflowing with gold bracelets, earrings, rings, medallions, precious sacred objects now twisted or flattened, pearls that had doubtless come from the pearl fishers of Ceylon, emeralds, rubies, and diamonds that glinted like stars beneath the light of a gilded lamp that hung from the ceiling.... In that strangely furnished room, in a decrepit armchair, sits a man: tall and slim of stature, powerfully built, with vigorous, masculine, proud features, and a strange beauty.

Who had been my hero? Holmes, reading a letter by the fire, rendered politely amazed by his seven-per cent solution, or Sandokan, tearing his chest madly as he utters the name of his beloved Marianna?

I then gathered up a number of paperback editions; they had been printed on cheap paper, but I must have finished them off, slowly wearing them out through repeated readings, writing my name in the margins of many pages. Some, their bindings completely destroyed, held together only by a miracle; others had been patched up, probably by me, with new spines of sugar-paper and carpenter's glue.

But I could no longer read even the titles; I had been in that attic for eight days. I knew I should have reread everything, word for word, but how long would that have taken? Assuming that I learned to read at the end of my fifth year, and that I had lived among those artefacts at least until high school, it would have taken at least ten years, on top of those eight days. And that is without counting all the other books, especially the ones with pictures, that were read to me by my parents or my grandfather before I was literate.

Had I tried to remake myself completely among those pages, I would have become Funes the Memorious, I would have relived moment by moment all the years of my childhood, every leaf I heard rustling in the night, every whiff of coffee in the morning. Too much. And what if they remained merely and for ever and nevertheless words, confusing my ailing neurons even more without throwing the hidden switch that would open the way to my truest, most hidden memories? *What is to be done?* Lenin in his white armchair in the anteroom. Maybe I have been all wrong about this, and Paola too: had I not come back to Solara, I would have remained merely feeble-minded; having come back might drive me truly mad.

I put all the books back into the two armoires, then decided to give up on the attic. But as I was leaving, I spotted a series of cardboard boxes with labels written in a lovely, almost Gothic hand: "FASCISM", "THE '40S", "WAR"... Those had to have been put together by my grandfather himself. The other boxes looked more recent; my aunt and uncle seemed to have made indiscriminate use of the empty containers they had found up there: Bersano Brothers Winery, Borsalino, Cordial Campari, Telefunken (was there a radio in the house?).

I could not bring myself to open them. I had to get out of there and go for a walk in the hills, I would come back later. I had reached my limit. Perhaps I was running a fever.

The sunset hour was fast approaching, and Amalia was already calling up in a loud voice to announce that her mouthwatering *finanziera*—that rustic Piedmontese concoction of calf brains and sweetbreads, giblets and wattles and cockscombs—was almost ready. The first vague shadows, gathering in the hidden corners of the attic, seemed to portend some lurking Fantômas, awaiting my collapse so he could pounce on me, bind me with a hempen rope, and dangle me in the abyss of a bottomless well. Mainly in order to prove to myself that I was no longer the child that I would have liked to become again, I fearlessly lingered to peer into those unlit areas. Then I was assailed once more by an ancient mustiness.

Near one of the dormer windows that was letting in the last rays of late afternoon, I dragged out a large crate, its lid carefully protected with brown wrapping paper. In removing that dusty covering, I disturbed two layers of moss, real moss, though now desiccated—enough penicillin to send everyone in *The Magic Mountain*'s sanatorium home in a week, and goodbye to those wonderful conversations between Naphta and Settembrini. Each tuft was like a clump of sod, and putting them all together you could have made a field as large as my grandfather's desk. Who knows by what miracle—maybe the layer of paper had created a humid zone beneath it, thanks to all those winters, those days when the attic roof was pounded with rain, snow, or hail—but the moss had retained something of its pungent stench.

Beneath the moss, packed in curly wood shavings, which I plucked out carefully so as not to damage the contents, were a hut made of wood or cardboard covered with coloured plaster, with a roof of compressed straw, a windmill of straw and wood with a wheel that still turned, though barely, and a number of little painted-cardboard houses and castles, which placed on some hill must have served as background scenery for the hut, lending perspective. And finally, deep in the shavings, I found the statuettes: the shepherds with the baby lamb in tow, the knife grinder, the miller with his two little donkeys, the peasant woman with a fruit basket on her head, a pair of pipers, an Arab with two camels, and—here they are—the Wise Men, they too smelling more like mould than incense or myrrh. Then at last the donkey, the ox, Joseph, Mary, the cradle, the Baby Jesus, two angels, arms flung wide, stiffened with a glory that had lasted at least a century, the golden comet, a rolled-up blue cloth that was stitched with stars, a metal basin filled with cement so as to form the bed of a creek, with two holes through which the water came and went, and something that made me put off dinner for half an hour while I studied it: a strange contraption consisting of a glass cylinder out of which came long rubber tubes.

A complete Nativity scene. I had no idea whether my grandfather or my parents had been believers (my mother must have been, given the *Filotea* on her nightstand), but clearly someone used to exhume this crate as Christmas approached in order to set up the crèche in one of the downstairs rooms. And yet those little statues were calling to mind not more words, but an image, something I had not seen in the attic but that must have been around somewhere, so vivid did it seem to me in that moment.

What had the Nativity scene meant to me? Between Jesus and Fantômas, between Rocambole and *The Basket,* between the mould on the Wise Men and that on the impaled corpses in the pages of the *Illustrated Journal of Voyages and Adventure,* where did I stand?

3 e, con passo lieve lieve
sul tappeto della neve,
s'incolonnan dietro a quello
misterioso pastorello

I realized that those days in the attic had been badly spent: I had reread pages I had first encountered at the age of six or twelve or fifteen, falling under the spells of different books at different times. That is no way to reconstruct a memory. Memory amalgamates, revises, and reshapes, no doubt, but it rarely confuses chronological distances. A person should know perfectly well whether something happened to him at seven years of age or at ten. Even I could now distinguish the day I woke up in the hospital from the day I departed for Solara, and I knew perfectly well that between one and the other some maturation had taken place, a change in my thinking, a weighing of experiences. And yet in the past three weeks I had taken everything in as if as a boy I had swallowed it down all at once, in one gulp—no surprise that I felt dazed as if by some intoxicating brew.

So I had to give up that *grande bouffe* of old papers, put things back in their places, and savour them over the course of time. Who could tell me what I had read or seen when I was eight as opposed to thirteen? I thought awhile and understood: my old schoolbooks and notebooks simply had to be somewhere among all those containers. Those were the documents to track down: I had only to listen to their lesson, letting them lead me by the hand.

At dinner, I asked Amalia about the Nativity scene. Indeed it had been my grandfather's, and had meant a lot to him. He was not a churchgoer, but the Nativity scene was like royal soup: it was not

Christmas without it, and even if he had had no grandchildren he might have set it up just for himself. He began working on it in early December, and if I looked around the attic I would find all the framework, which had supported the sky backdrop and contained lots of little bulbs in the front part that made the stars twinkle. "A thing of beauty it was, your dear grandfather's Nativity scene, made me cry every year. And water truly flowed in the river, why in fact one year it overflowed and got the moss wet that had come in fresh that very year, and then the moss all bloomed with itty-bitty blue flowers, which it was truly a miracle of the Christ child, and even the parish priest came who couldn't believe his eyes."

"But how did he make the water flow?"

Amalia blushed and mumbled something, then made up her mind: "In that Nativity scene crate, which every year I helped to put it all away after Epiphany, there ought to be something, like a big bottle with no neck. You saw it? Well, I don't know if folks still use them things or not, but it was a contraption, pardon my French, for giving enemas. Do you know what enemas are? Good, then I don't have to explain, which would embarrass me. And so your dear grandfather got the bright idea that if he put that enema contraption underneath the Nativity scene, and hooked up the tubes in the right places, the water would come up and then go back down again. That was something, I can tell you, forget the picture shows."

8. When the Radio

After my eight days in the attic, I decided to go into town to get my blood pressure checked by the pharmacist. Too high: 170. Gratarolo had released me from the hospital with orders to keep it in the 130s, and 130 it was when I left for Solara. The pharmacist said that if I measured it after walking all the way down the hill to town, of course it would be high. If I checked it in the morning when I woke up, it would be lower. Nonsense. I knew what it had been, and for days I had lived like a man possessed.

I called Gratarolo, and he asked if I had done anything I should not have, and I had to admit that I had been moving crates, drinking at least a bottle of wine per meal, smoking a pack of Gitanes a day, and causing myself frequent bouts of mild tachycardia. He reproached me: I was convalescing, if my pressure went through the roof I could have another incident, and I might not be as lucky as I was the first time. I promised him I would take care of myself, and he raised the dosage of my pills and added others to help me get rid of salt through my urine.

I asked Amalia to use less salt in my food, and she said that during the war they had to go to the ends of the earth and give away two or three rabbits to get a kilo of salt, so salt is a gift from God and when you don't have it nothing tastes like anything. I told her that the doctor had prohibited it, and she replied that doctors do all that studying and then they're dumber than anybody and you shouldn't pay them any mind—just look at her, never seen a doctor in her life and here she was well past seventy breaking her back every blessed day doing a thousand things, and she didn't even have sciatica like everybody else. Never mind, I can pass her salt out in my urine.

It was more important to quit spending all my time in the attic, to move around a little, distract myself. I called Gianni: I wanted to see if all the things I had been reading in recent days meant anything to him. We seem to have had different experiences—his grandfather had not collected old-fashioned objects—but we had read many of the same things, in part because we used to borrow each other's books. We spent half an hour quizzing each other on Salgari trivia, as if we were on a game show. What was the name of the Greek, the Rajah of Assam's lackey? Teotokris. What was the last name of the lovely Honorata whom the Black Corsair could not love because she was his enemy's daughter? Wan Guld. And who married Darma, Tremal-Naik's daughter? Sir Moreland, son of Suyodhana.

I asked about Ciuffettino, too, but that meant nothing to Gianni. He had preferred comic books, and here he turned the tables, bombarding me with a barrage of titles. I must surely have read some of them, too, and a few of the names Gianni mentioned sounded familiar: *The Phantom, Fulmine vs. Flattavion, Mickey Mouse and the Phantom Blot,* and above all, *Tim Tyler's Luck*...But I had found no trace of them in the attic. Maybe my grandfather, who had loved Fantômas and Rocambole, considered comic books inferior rags that were bad for children. And Rocambole was not?

Did I grow up without comic books? It was pointless to impose on myself long breaks and forced rest. I was being gripped once more by research fever.

Paola saved me. That very morning, towards noon, she showed up unexpectedly with Carla, Nicoletta, and the three little ones. My few phone calls had not convinced her. A quick trip, just to give you a hug, she said, we'll leave again before dinner. But she was watching me closely, weighing me.

"You're getting fat," she said. Luckily, I was not pale, what with all the sun I had got on the balcony and in the vineyard, but no doubt I had put on a little weight. I said it was Amalia's little suppers, and Paola promised to set her straight. I failed to mention that I had spent days on end curled up in some corner, not moving for hours and hours.

A nice walk is what you need, she said, and our whole family headed off towards the Conventino, which was not a convent at all, but rather a small chapel sitting atop a hill a few kilometres away. The rise was continuous, and therefore nearly imperceptible, except for the last few dozen metres. While I was catching my breath I encouraged the little ones to gather *a spray of roses and of violets.* Paola grumbled that I should smell the flowers and not quote the Poet—especially since Leopardi, like all poets, was lying: the first roses do not bloom until after violets are gone for the season, and in any case roses and violets cannot be put together in the same bouquet, try it and see.

To prove that I did not remember only passages from encyclopaedias, I showed off a few of the stories I had learned in recent days, and the children sidled up with wide eyes; they had never heard those tales before.

Sandro was the biggest little one, and I recounted *Treasure Island* for him. I told him how, departing from the Admiral Benbow Inn, I had sailed off on the schooner *Hispaniola,* along with Lord Trelawney, Dr. Livesey, and Captain Smollett, but by the end his two favourite characters seemed to be Long John Silver, because of his wooden leg, and that poor wretch Ben Gunn. His eyes grew big with excitement, he began seeing pirates lying in wait in the shrubs, kept saying, "More, more," and then, "That's enough," because once we had gained Captain Flint's treasure the story was over. As compensation we sang *Fifteen men on the dead man's chest—Yo-ho-ho, and a bottle of rum* over and over.

———

For Giangio and Luca, I did my best to conjure up the naughtiness of Giannino Stoppani from *The Diary of the Hurricane Boy.* When I inserted the stick up through the drainage hole in the bottom of Aunt Bettina's pot of dittany, or when I yanked Signor Venanzio's last tooth out with a fishhook, they laughed endlessly, though who knows how much sense those stories made to three-year-olds. The tales' best audience may have been Carla and Nicoletta, who had never been told a thing (a sad sign of the times) about Gian the Hurricane Boy.

But for them, I was more interested in explaining how, in the guise of Rocambole, I had eliminated my mentor in the art of crime, Sir William, now blind but nonetheless an embarrassing witness to my past, by throwing him to the ground and driving a long, sharp hat pin into the nape of his neck, and I had only to remove the small spot of blood that had formed in his hair for everyone to think he had had an apoplectic stroke.

Paola yelled that I should not be telling such stories in front of the children, and thank God nobody kept hat pins lying around the house these days, otherwise they would probably try one out on the cat. But more than anything she was intrigued by the fact that I had told all those things as if they had happened to me.

"If you're doing that to entertain the kids," she said, "that's one thing, but if not, then you're identifying too much with what you're reading, which is to say you're borrowing other people's memory. Are you clear about the distance between you and these stories?"

"Come on," I said, "I may be an amnesiac, but I'm not crazy. I do it for the kids!"

"Let's hope so," she said. "But you came to Solara to rediscover yourself, because you felt oppressed by an encyclopaedia full of Homer, Manzoni, and Flaubert, and now you've entered the encyclopaedia of pulp literature. It's not a step forward."

"Yes it is," I replied, "first of all because Stevenson isn't pulp literature, and second because it's not my fault if the guy I'm trying to rediscover devoured pulp literature, and, finally, you're the very one, with that business about Clarabelle's treasure, who sent me here."

"That's true, I'm sorry. If you feel it's useful for you, go ahead. But be careful, don't get drunk on what you're reading." Changing the subject, she asked me about my blood pressure. I lied: I said I had just had it checked and it was 130. That made her happy, poor thing.

When we returned from our outing, Amalia had prepared a lovely snack, with water and fresh lemon for everyone. Then they left.

That evening I was a good boy and went early to bed.

The next morning, I revisited the rooms of the old wing, which I had only breezed through the first time. I went back to my grandfather's bedroom, at which I had barely glanced, daunted by some reverential awe. There, too, as in all the old bedrooms, was a chest of drawers and a large wardrobe with a mirror.

Inside the wardrobe I found a tremendous surprise. In the back, almost hidden behind several hanging suits to which the scent of old mothballs still clung, were two objects: a horn gramophone, the kind you crank by hand, and a radio. Both were covered with pages from a magazine, which I reassembled: it was the *Radiocorriere*, a publication devoted to radio programmes, an issue from the forties.

An old 78, covered with a layer of dirt, was still in place on the gramophone. I spent half an hour cleaning it, spitting on my handkerchief. The song was "Amapola". I set the gramophone on the chest of drawers, cranked it, and a few muddled sounds came through the horn. You could barely make out the melody. The old gadget had by now attained a state of senile dementia, nothing to be done. After all, it must already have been a museum piece when I was a boy. If I wanted to listen to music of that era, I would have to use the record player I had seen in my grandfather's study. But the records—where were they? I would have to ask Amalia.

The radio, though it had been protected, was nonetheless coated with fifty years of dust, enough that you could write on it with your finger, and I had to clean it with care. It was a nice mahogany-coloured Telefunken (that explained the box I had seen in the attic), with a speaker that was covered in a coarse grille cloth, which may have helped the sound resonate better.

Beside the speaker was the station panel, dark and illegible, and below that three knobs. Evidently it was a valve radio, and when I shook it I could hear something rattle inside. It still had its cord and plug.

I took it into the study, set it gently on the table, and plugged it into an outlet. A near miracle, and a sign that back then they built things to last: the station-panel bulb, though weak, still worked. The rest did not; the valves must have been shot. I knew that somewhere, perhaps in Milan, I could find one of those enthusiasts who are able to refurbish these receivers, because they have warehouses of old parts, like the mechanics who put cars of that period back together using the good bits of junked cars. Then I imagined what an old electrician full of good common sense might tell me: "I don't want to steal your money. Look, if I get it working again for you, you won't hear what they broadcast back in those days, you'll hear what they broadcast today, and so you're better off buying a new radio, and it'll cost you less than fixing this one." A clever man. I was playing a losing game. A radio is not an antique book, which you can open and discover what people thought, said, and printed five hundred years ago. That radio would have subjected me, with all its crackling, to horrendous rock music or whatever they call it these days. Like pretending to feel again the fizzy touch of vichy water on your taste buds as you drink a bottle of San Pellegrino just purchased from the supermarket. That broken box in the attic promised me sounds that have been for ever lost. If only I could bring them back, like the frozen words of Pantagruel... But although my brain's memory could conceivably return some day, the memory that consisted of Hertzian waves was now irrecoverable. Solara was of no help when it came to sounds other than the deafening noise of its silences.

But I still had the illuminated panel with the names of the stations—in yellow for medium-wave, red for shortwave, green for long-wave—names that must have mesmerized me as I moved the station indicator in search of unfamiliar sounds from magical cities like Stuttgart, Hilversum, Riga, Tallinn. Names I had never heard before, which I may have associated with Makedonia, Turkish Atika, Virginia, El Kalif, and Stambul. Had I daydreamed more over atlases, or more over that list of stations and their whispers? But there were also domestic names like Milan and Bolzano. I began humming:

When her radio broadcasts from Turin,
it means: I'll wait for you down by the Po,
but if she suddenly changes the station,
it means: Be careful, my mother is home.
Radio Bologna means: I am dreaming about you,
Radio Milan means: You feel so far away,
Radio Igea, I feel like I'm dying without you,
Radio San Remo, I'll see you later today...

The names of the cities were once again words that called to mind other words.

By the look of it, the radio dated from the thirties. Radios must have been quite expensive at that time, and no doubt it entered the family only at a certain point, as a status symbol.

I wanted to figure out what people did with radios during the thirties and forties. I called Gianni again.

The first thing he said was that I should pay him by the job, since I was using him like a diver to bring submerged amphorae up to the surface. But then he added, with some emotion in his voice, "Ah, the radio... We didn't get one until around 1938. They were expensive; my father was an office worker, but unlike yours he worked for a small company and didn't make much. Your family went on vacation in the summer, and we stayed in the city, visited the public gardens in the evenings to enjoy the cool air, and had gelato once a week. My father was not a talkative man. That day he came home, sat down at the table, ate dinner in silence, and afterwards took out a bag of pastries. Why, it isn't Sunday? my mother asked. And he: Just because, I felt like it. We ate the pastries and then, scratching his head, he said: Mara, apparently things have been going well the past few months, and today the boss gave me a thousand lire. My mother nearly had a stroke, she brought her hands up to her mouth and screamed: Oh Francesco, now we can buy a radio! Just like that. A popular song of the time was called "If I Could Make a Thousand Lire a Month". It was the song of a humble office worker who dreamed of making a thousand lire a month, so he could buy lots of things for his pretty young wife. A thousand lire must have been the equivalent of a good month's salary, maybe it was more than my father made, and in any case it was like a Christmas bonus no one was expecting. That's how the radio came into our house. Let me think—it was a Phonola. Once a week there was the Martini and Rossi opera concert, on some other day there was a play. Ah, Tallinn and Riga, I wish they were still on the radio I've got now—it just has numbers... And then during the war the only heated room was the kitchen, so we moved the radio there, and in the evenings, with the volume turned way down, otherwise they'd have thrown us in jail, we'd listen to Radio London. Shut up in our house with the windows covered with light blue paper, the kind sugar came in, for the blackout. And the songs! When you come back, I'll sing them all to you if you want, even the Fascist anthems. You know, I'm not a nostalgic man, but now and then I get the urge to hear those Fascist anthems; they remind me how it felt to be sitting by the radio in the evening... What did the ad say? *Radio, the voice that enchants.*"

I asked him to stop. True, I was the one who had prompted him, but now he was polluting my tabula rasa with *his* memories. I needed to relive those evenings by myself. Things would have been different for me: he had a Phonola, and I had a Telefunken, and besides, maybe he tuned in to Riga and I to Tallinn. But could we really pick up Tallinn, and did we then listen to people speaking Estonian?

I went downstairs to eat and, in spite of Gratarolo, to drink, but only to forget. I of all people. But I had to forget the upheavals of the past week, had to bring on the desire to sleep in the afternoon shadows, stretched out in bed with *The Tigers of Mompracem,* which may once have kept me awake into the small hours, but which the past two evenings had proved blessedly soporific.

But between a forkful for myself and a scrap for Matù, I had a simple but enlightening thought: the radio transmits whatever is on the airwaves now, but the gramophone allows you to hear what was on the records of the past. They are the frozen words of Pantagruel. To feel what it was like to listen to the radio fifty years ago, I needed records.

"Records?" Amalia muttered. "Keep your mind on your food, why don't you, instead of records, or this good stuff will go down wrong and turn toxic and then you'll need a doctor! Records, records, records... Jumping Jehoshaphat, they're not in the attic at all! When your aunt and uncle put everything away, I helped, and... hang on here... I thought to myself that them records in the study, if I was to carry them all up to the attic I'd drop them and they'd go to pieces on the stairs. And so I put them... I put them... I'm sorry, you know it's not that my memory doesn't work any more, which at my age I could be forgiven that, but it's been more than fifty years, and it's not like I've been sitting here all that time thinking about them records. But that's it, what a noggin! I bet I stuck them in the settle outside your dear grandfather's study!"

I skipped the fruit and went upstairs to find the settle. I had paid little attention to it in the course of my first visit, but I opened it and there they were, one on top of the other, all of them good old 78s in their protective sleeves. Amalia had set them down in no particular order, and there were all kinds of things. I spent half an hour transporting them onto the desk in the study, then began to put them in some kind of order on the shelves. My grandfather must have been a lover of good music: Mozart was there, and Beethoven, opera arias (even a Caruso), and a lot of Chopin, but also a fair share of popular songs.

I looked at the old *Radiocorriere:* Gianni was right, the listings included a weekly opera programme, plays, the occasional symphonic concert, the Radio News, and the rest was light music, or melodic music, as they called it then.

I had to listen to the songs again, then; they must have been the sonic furnishings of my childhood. Perhaps my grandfather had sat in his study listening to Wagner while the rest of the family listened to those pop songs on the radio.

I immediately picked out "If I Could Make a Thousand Lire a Month", by Innocenzi and Soprani. My grandfather had written dates on many of the jackets: whether these represented the year each song had come out or the year he had acquired it I was not sure, but the dates gave me a rough sense of when the songs were being played on the radio. In this case, the year was 1938. Gianni had remembered well; the song had come out around the time his family purchased their Phonola.

I turned the record player on. It still worked: the speaker was no prodigy, but perhaps it was proper that everything crackled as it once had. And so it was that, with the radio panel illuminated, as if broadcasting, and the record player spinning, I listened to a transmission from the summer of 1938:

If I could make a thousand lire a month,
it wouldn't be a lie to say that it would buy
all the joy a man could want.
I'm just an office man, I don't aim too grand,
and if I keep on trying, maybe I can find
all the peace a man could want.
A nice little house on the edge of the city,
and a little wife too, so young and so pretty
and so very much like you.
If I could make a thousand lire a month,
I'd buy so many things, such beautiful things,
oh anything you want.

Over the previous few days, I had been trying to imagine the divided self of a boy exposed to messages of national glory while at the same time daydreaming about the fogs of London, where he would encounter Fantômas battling Sandokan amid a hail of nailshot that ripped holes in the chests and tore off the arms and legs of Sherlock Holmes's politely perplexed compatriots—and now here I was learning that in those same years the radio had been proposing as an ideal the life of a humble accountant who longed for nothing more than suburban tranquillity. But perhaps that song was an exception.

I had to reorganize the records, by date when possible. I had to retrace year by year the formation of my consciousness through the songs I used to hear.

During my rather frantic reorganization—among a succession of my love my love bring me all your roses, you're not my baby any more, oh baby how I love you, there is a chapel love hidden in an apple grove, come back my darling, play just for me o gypsy violin, you divine music, just a single hour with you, little flower in the field, and ciribiribin, and among the orchestral stylings of Cinico Angelini, Pippo Barzizza, Alberto Semprini, and Gorni Kramer, on records labelled Fonit, Carisch, and His Master's Voice, with the little dog listening with pointed snout to the sounds emanating from the horn of a gramophone—I stumbled across some Fascist anthems, which my grandfather had tied together with string, as if to protect them, or segregate them. Had my grandfather been Fascist, or anti-Fascist, or neither?

I spent the night listening to things that sounded familiar to me, though with some songs only the words came to mind and with others only the melodies. I could not help but know a classic like "Youth of Italy", which must have been the official anthem of every rally, but neither could I overlook the fact that it had probably emanated from my radio in close proximity to "Penguin in Love", sung, as the record jacket noted, by the great Trio Lescano.

I felt as if I had known those female voices for ages. The three of them managed to sing in intervals of thirds and sixths, creating an apparent cacophony that was sheer delight to the ear. And while Italy's boys in the world were teaching me that the greatest privilege was to be Italian, the Lescano sisters sang to me of Dutch tulips.

I decided to go back and forth between anthems and songs, the way they had likely come to me through the radio. I went from the tulips to Balilla's anthem, and as soon as I put the record on I began singing along, as if reciting from memory. It exalted that courageous youth (a proto-Fascist, since—as every encyclopaedia knows—Giovan Battista Perasso, known as Balilla, lived in the eighteenth century) who hurled his stone against the Austrian troops, sparking the revolt of Genoa.

The Fascists must not have disapproved of acts of terrorism, and my version of "Youth of Italy" even included the lines "Now I have Orsini's bomb / I will sharpen terror's blade"—I think Orsini was the man who tried to kill Napoleon III.

But as I was listening, night fell, and from the orchard or the hill or the garden came a strong scent of lavender, and other herbs I did not recognize (thyme? basil? I think I was never very good at botany, and after all I was still the guy who, when sent out to buy roses, came home with dog testicles—maybe they were Dutch tulips). I could smell some other flower that Amalia had taught me to recognize: dahlias or zinnias?

Matù appeared and began rubbing up against my pant leg, purring. I had seen a record with a cat on the cover—"Maramao, Why Did You Die?"—and so I put it on in place of Balilla's anthem and succumbed to its feline threnody.

But did Balilla Boys really sing "Maramao"? Perhaps I should return to the Fascist anthems. It would matter little to Matù if I changed songs. I got comfortable, put him on my lap and began scratching his right ear, lit a cigarette, and prepared for full immersion in Balilla's world.

After I had listened for an hour, my brain was a hotchpotch of heroic phrases, incitements to attack and kill, and oaths of obedience to Il Duce even to the point of ultimate sacrifice. Like Vesta's fire erupting from her temple our youth goes forth on wings of flame a manly corps of youth with Roman will and might will stand and fight we don't care a whit about the jails we don't care a whit about

From the trenches comes the call
when the battle hour is near,
the black flame ahead of all
raging onward, sowing fear.
With a grenade in his hand,
with allegiance in his heart,
he advances o'er the land
as he bravely does his part.

Youth of Italy, youth of Italy,
you are the lovely spring
in this life of suffering,
your song will ring out, and then will
fade.

Now I have Orsini's bomb,
I will sharpen terror's blade,
Let the roar of the howitzer come,
I am strong and unafraid.
I with honour have defended
our splendid banner from the start,
the black flame has never ended,
it brightly burns in every heart.

Youth of Italy, youth of Italy,
you are as the lovely spring
in this life of suffering,
your song will ring out, and then will
fade.

For Benito Mussolini
Eia Eia Alalà.

Round above the trees
like a wheel of Dutch cheese in the sky,
The May moon makes its way,
sending us rays from on high...
Love is before us,
say the tuli tuli tuli tulips,
They murmur in chorus,
all the tuli tuli tuli tulips...
You hear their wonderful tune,
beneath the spell of the moon,
Love's in the air,
say the tuli tuli tuli tulips,
Two hearts make a pair,
say the tuli tuli tuli tulips...
And they will speak of me to you,
Those marvellous flowers,
the tuli tuli tuli tuli tuli tulips!

The whistling stone, the blaring name,
of the daring Portorian...
The little boy they call Balilla
history calls a giant man.
There was a cannon made of bronze
sinking in the muddy street.
But the boy was made of steel
and he set his Mother free.

His eye is proud, his feet are swift,
valour's cry rings loud and clear.
Against his foes he hurls a stone,
as for his friends, he holds them dear.

We're the seed of the coming harvest,
we're the flame of bravery.
The crystal spring is singing for us,
May for us shines happily.
But if some day the battlefield
claims our heroes, we shall be
the ammunition and the gun
defending Sacred Liberty.

When all is quiet and the moon
appears up in the sky,
I use my friendliest miaow
to call back Maramao.
I watch the cats up on the roof
as they walk slowly by,
for they have also come to be,
without you, as sad as me.

Maramao, why did you die?
You had bread and wine and more,
you had salad out in the yard,
a roof above you, below a floor.
The pretty kitties, they all love you,
they are purring for you still.
But your door is always closed,
you don't answer, and never will.

Maramao, Maramao,
say the kitties in chorus...
Maramao, Maramao,
mao, mao, mao, mao, mao...

sad fate the mighty people of the mighty State don't care a whit when it's time to die the world knows the Black Shirt never fails we wear it when we fight and when we die for Il Duce and for the Empire eia eia alalà hail O Emperor King Il Duce gave new law to Earth and to Rome new Empire this is goodbye I'm off to Abyssinia my dear Virginia I'll see you later I'll send from Africa a lovely flower that blooms in the sun of the equator Savoy and Nice and deadly Corsica Malta that bulwark of Rome Tunisian shores mountains and sea resound with liberty at home.

Did I want Nice to belong to Italy, or did I want a thousand lire a month, the value of which I did not know? A boy who plays with guns and toy soldiers would rather liberate deadly Corsica than terrorize tulips and love-struck penguins. Still, Balilla aside, had I listened to "Penguin in Love" while reading *Captain Satan,* and if so, had I imagined penguins in the icy North Seas? And as I followed *Around the World in Eighty Days,* had I seen Phileas Fogg traversing fields of tulips? And how had I reconciled Rocambole and his hat pin with Giovan Battista Perasso and his stone? "Tulips" was from 1940, the beginning of the war: no doubt I was singing "Youth of Italy" at the same time. Or perhaps I did not read about Captain Satan and Rocambole until 1945, after the war was over and every trace of those Fascist songs had vanished?

It was vital now that I find my old schoolbooks. In them, my true first readings would appear before my eyes, the songs with their dates would let me know what sounds had accompanied what readings, and perhaps I could then clarify the relationship between "We don't care a whit about sad fate" and the massacres that drew me to *The Illustrated Journal of Voyages and Adventures.*

Futile to try to impose a few days of truce. The next morning, I had to go back up into the attic. If my grandfather had been methodical, my schoolbooks would be near the crates of children's books. Unless my aunt and uncle had misplaced everything.

For the time being, I was tired of calls to glory. I looked out of the window. The outline of the hills stood dark against the sky, and the moonless night was *stitched with stars.* Why had that tattered old expression come to mind? It must have come from a song. I was seeing the sky as I had once heard it described by some singer.

I began rummaging among the records and picked out all the ones whose titles evoked the night and some sidereal space. My grandfather's record player was the kind that allowed you to stack several records, one on top of the other, so that as soon as one finished another would fall onto the turntable. Just as if the radio were singing to me all by itself, without my having to turn any knobs. I started the first record and stood swaying by the window, with the starry sky above me, to the sounds of so much good bad music that something should have woken up inside me.

Tonight the stars are shining by the thousand... One night, with the stars and you... Speak, oh speak in the starlight so clear, whisper sweet words in my ear, under the spell of love... Beneath the Antilles night, with the stars burning bright, there flowed the streaming light of love... Mailù, under the Singapore sky, its golden stars dreamily high, we fell in love, you and I... Beneath the maze of stars that gazes down on all of this, beneath the craze of stars I want to give your lips a kiss... With you, without, we sing to the stars and the moon, you can't rule it out, good fortune may come to me soon... Harbour moon, love is sweet if you never learn, Venice the moon and you, you and me all alone in the night, you and me humming a tune... Hungarian sky, melancholy sigh, I'm thinking of you with infinite love... I wander where the sky is always blue, listening to thrushes as they flutter in the bushes, their twittering coming through...

The next record had been put in the stack by mistake, it had nothing to do with the sky, just a sensual voice, like a saxophone in heat, that sang:

Up there at Capocabana, at Capocabana the woman is queen, and she reigns supreme...

tango del ritorno
di mendes-rusconi
Edizioni JOLY - Milano
Finestra chiusa
TANGO SERENATA
MUSICA DI G. D'ANZI
PAROLE DI A. BRACCHI
£ 2-
EDIZIONI CURCI MILANO
LA S.A.E.A. FILM PRESENTA IL CELEBRE TENORE GIUSEPPE LUGO IN
la mia canzone al vento
FOX-TROT dal film omonimo
PAROLE DI B. Cherubini
MUSICA DI C.A. Bixio
£.2
Edizioni S.a.m. Bixio - Milano
Musica di E. Lecuona
Parole di Nisa
tango
Maria la o
EDIZIONI LEONARDI
MILANO

I was disturbed by the noise of a distant engine, maybe a car going through the valley. I felt a hint of tachycardia and said to myself: "It's Pipetto!" As if someone had shown up precisely at the expected moment, someone whose arrival had disturbed me nonetheless. Who was Pipetto? *It's Pipetto,* I kept saying, but once again it was just my lips that remembered. Just *flatus vocis*. I did not know who Pipetto was. Or rather, something in me knew, but that something was simmering slyly in the injured region of my brain.

An excellent topic for My Children's Library: *The Secret of Pipetto*. Perhaps it was the Italian adaptation of *The Secret of Lantenac*?

I racked my brain for the secret of Pipetto, and maybe there was no secret, except the one whispered to the world from a radio late at night.

9. But Pippo Doesn't Know

Other days (five, seven, ten?) have blurred together in my memory, which is just as well, since what that left me with was, so to speak, the quintessence of a montage. I put disparate pieces of evidence together, cutting and joining, sometimes according to a natural progression of ideas and emotions, sometimes to create contrast. What resulted was no longer what I had seen and heard in the course of those days, nor what I might have seen and heard as a child: it was a figment, a hypothesis formed at the age of sixty about what I could have thought at ten. Not enough to say, "I know it happened like this," but enough to bring to light, on papyrus pages, what I presumably might have felt back then.

I had returned to the attic, and I was beginning to worry that none of my school things remained when my eyes lit upon a cardboard box, sealed with adhesive tape, on which appeared the words ELEMENTARY AND MIDDLE YAMBO. There was another, labelled ELEMENTARY AND MIDDLE ADA, but I did not need to reactivate my sister's memory. I had enough to do with my own.

I wanted to avoid another week of high blood pressure. I called Amalia and had her help me carry the box down to my grandfather's study. Then it occurred to me that I must have been in elementary and middle school between 1937 and 1945, and so I also brought down the boxes labelled WAR, 1940s, and FASCISM.

In the study, I took everything out and arranged it on various shelves. Books from elementary school, history and geography texts from middle school, and lots of notebooks, with my name, year, and class. There were lots of newspapers. Apparently my grandfather, from the war in Ethiopia on, had kept the important issues: the one with the historic speech by Mussolini proclaiming the birth of the Italian Empire, the one from June 10, 1940, with the declaration of war, and so on until the dropping of the atom bomb on Hiroshima and the end of the war. There were also postcards, posters, leaflets, and a few magazines.

I decided to proceed using the historian's method, subjecting evidence to cross-comparison. That is to say, when I was reading my books and notebooks from fourth grade, 1940–41, I would also browse through the newspapers from the same years and, whenever I could, put songs from those years on the record player.

Because the books of the period were pro-Fascist, I had assumed that the newspapers would be, too. Everyone knows, for example, that *Pravda* in Stalin's day didn't provide the good citizens of the Soviet Union with accurate news. But I was forced to reconsider. As breathlessly propagandistic as the Italian papers could be, still they allowed readers, even in wartime, to figure out what was going on. Across a distance of many years, my grandfather was giving me a great lesson, civic and historiographic at once: You have to know how to read between the lines. And read between the lines he had, underscoring not so much the banner headlines as the in-briefs, the also-noteds, the news one might miss on a first reading. One issue of *Corriere della Sera,* from January 6–7, 1941, offered this headline: BATTLE ON THE BARDIA FRONT WAGED WITH GREAT FEROCITY. In the middle of the column, the war bulletin (there was one each day, a bureaucratic listing of such things as the number of enemy aircraft shot down) stated coolly that "other strongholds fell after courageous resistance from our troops, who inflicted substantial losses on the adversary." Other strongholds? From the context it was clear that Bardia, in North Africa, had fallen into British hands. In any case, my grandfather had made a note in red ink in the margin, as he had in many issues: "RL, lost B. 40,000 pris." RL apparently meant Radio London, and my grandfather was comparing the Radio London news with the official news. Not only had Bardia been lost, but forty thousand soldiers had been handed over to the enemy. As one can see, the *Corriere* had not lied, it had merely taken for granted the facts about which it had remained reticent. The same paper, on February 6, ran the headline OUR TROOPS COUNTERATTACK ON NORTHERN FRONT OF EAST AFRICA. What was the northern front of East Africa? Whereas many issues from the previous year, when giving news of our first inroads into Kenya and British Somalia, had provided detailed maps to show where we were victoriously trespassing, that article about the northern front gave no map, yet all you had to do was go and look in an atlas to understand that the British had entered Eritrea.

The *Corriere* of June 7, 1944 ran this triumphant headline over nine columns: GERMAN DEFENSIVE FIREPOWER POUNDS ALLIED FORCES ALONG NORMANDY COAST. Why were the Germans and the Allies fighting on the coast of Normandy? Because June 6 had been the famous D-day, the beginning of the invasion, and the newspaper, which obviously had not had any news of that event on the previous day, was treating it as though it were already understood, except for pointing out that Field Marshal von Rundstedt had certainly not allowed himself to be surprised and that the beach was littered with enemy corpses. No one could say that was not true.

Proceeding methodically, I could have reconstructed the sequence of actual events simply by reading the Fascist press in the right light, as everyone probably had then. I turned on the radio panel, started the record player, and went back. Of course, it was like reliving someone else's life.

First school notebook. In those days, we were taught before anything else to make strokes, and we moved on to the letters of the alphabet only when we could fill a page with neat rows of straight lines. Training of the hand, the wrist: handwriting counted for something in the days when typewriters were found only in offices. I moved on to *The First Grade Reader,* "compiled by Miss Maria Zanetti, illustrations by Enrico Pinochi," Library of the State, Year XVI.

On the page of basic diphthongs, after *io, ia, aia,* and so on, there was *Eia! Eia!* next to the Fascist emblem. We learned the

Ba- ba- baby come and kiss me,
you're buh- buh- beauty makes me dizzy,
come and gi- gi- give your kisses all to me!
Tadatadatadatadatadee…

Be- be- be my naughty girl,
you're a bo- bo- bold audacious girl,
what a tem- tem- ptation you can be to me!
Tadatadatadatadatadee…

B and A make BA, B and E make BE.
These are syllables, you see.
B and O make BO, B and U make BU.
Lovely syllables for you!

alphabet to the sound of "Eia eia alalà!"—as far as I know one of D'Annunzio's cries. For the letter B there were words like *Benito*, and a page devoted to Balilla. At that very moment, *my* radio began belting out a different syllabication: *ba- ba- baby come and kiss me*. I wonder how I learned the B, seeing that my little Giangio still confuses it with the V, saying things like *bery* instead of *very*?

The Balilla Boys and the Sons of the She-Wolf. A page with a boy in uniform: a black shirt and a sort of white bandolier crossed over his chest with an *M* at the centre. "Mario is a man," the text said.

Son of the She-Wolf. It is May 24. Guglielmo is putting on his brand-new uniform, the uniform of the Sons of the She-Wolf. "Daddy, I'm one of Il Duce's little soldiers, too, aren't I? Soon I'll become a Balilla Boy, I'll carry the standard, I'll have a musket, and later I'll become a Vanguard Youth. I want to do the drills, too, just like the real soldiers, I want to be the best of all, I want to earn lots of medals..."

Right after that, a page that resembled the *images d'Épinal*, except that these uniforms did not belong to Zouaves or French cuirassiers, but rather to the various ranks of Fascist youth.

In order to teach the *l*-sound, the book offered examples such as *bullet, flag,* and *battle*. For six-year-old children. The ones for whom springtime comes a-dancing. Towards the middle of the syllabary, however, I was taught something about the Guardian Angel:

A boy walks along, down the long road,
alone, all alone, where will he go?
Small is the boy and the country is wide,
but an Angel sees him and walks by his side.

Where was the Angel supposed to lead me? To the place where bullets danced? From what I knew, the Conciliation between

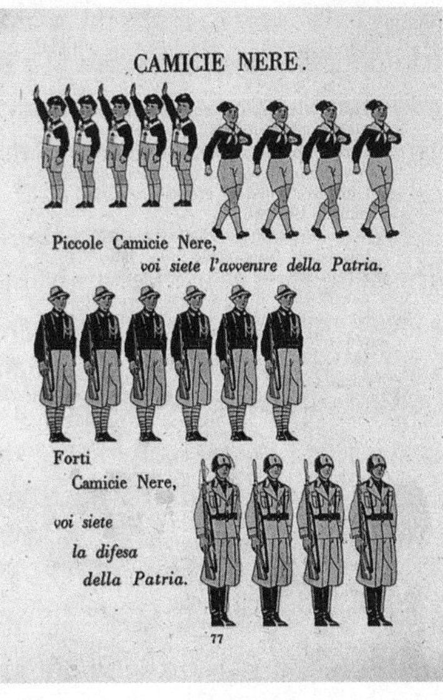

the Church and Fascism had been signed some years earlier, and so by this time they were supposed to educate us to become Balilla Boys without forgetting the Angels.

Did I, too, march in uniform through the streets of the city? Did I want to go to Rome and become a hero? The radio at that moment was singing a heroic anthem that evoked the image of a procession of young Blackshirts, but with the next song the view suddenly changed: walking down the road now was a certain Pippo, who had been poorly served by both Mother Nature and his personal tailor, given that he was wearing his shirt over his waistcoat. With Amalia's dog in mind, I envisioned this wanderer with a downcast expression, lids drooping over two watery eyes, a dim-witted, toothless smile, two disjointed legs and flat feet. And what connection was there between Pippo and Pipetto?

The Pippo in the song wore his shirt over his waistcoat. But the voices on the radio did not say "shirt", but rather "shir-irt" (*he wears his overcoat under his jacket / and he wears his shir-irt over his waistcoat*). It must have been to make the words fit the music. I had the feeling I had done the same thing but in a different context. I sang *Youth of Italy* aloud again, as I had the night before, but this time I sang *For Benito and Mussolini, Eia Eia Alalà*. We never sang *For Benito Mussolini*, but rather *For Benito* and *Mussolini*. That *and* was clearly euphonic, serving to give extra oomph to *Mussolini*. For Benito and Mussolini, his shir-irt over his waistcoat.

But who was walking through the streets of the city, the Balilla Boys or Pippo? And at whom were people laughing? Might the regime have recognized in the figure of Pippo a subtle allusion? Might our popular wisdom have been offering us that almost infantile drivel as consolation for continually having to endure that heroic rhetoric?

My thoughts wandering, I came to a page about the fog. An image: Alberto and his father, two shadows outlined against other shadows, all of them black, the whole crowd silhouetted against a grey sky, from which emerge the profiles, in a slightly darker grey, of city houses. The text informed me that in the fog people look like shadows. Was that what fog was like?

Should not the grey of the sky have enveloped, like milk, or like water and anisette, even the human shadows? According to my collection of quotations, shadows are not outlined against the fog, but are born from it, confused with it—the fog makes shadows appear even where nothing is, and nothing precisely where shadows will emerge... My first-grade reader, then, was lying to me even about the fog? In fact, it concluded with an invocation to the beautiful sun to clear away the fog. Its message was that fog was inevitable, but undesirable. Why did they teach me fog was bad, if later I was to harbour an obscure nostalgia for it?

Grey, black, *blackout*. Words that call to mind other words. During the war, Gianni had said, the city was plunged into darkness so as not to be visible to enemy bombers, and none of us could

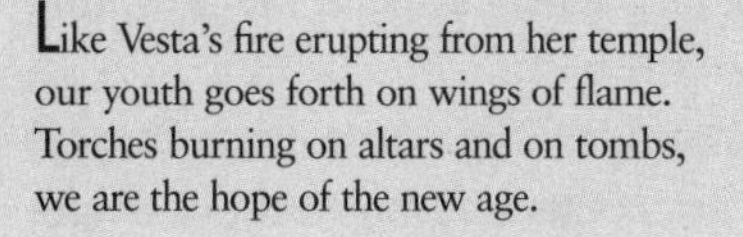

Like Vesta's fire erupting from her temple,
our youth goes forth on wings of flame.
Torches burning on altars and on tombs,
we are the hope of the new age.

Duce, Duce, who shall renounce his oath?
And who shall not know how to die?
Our swords are ready! And at your
command,
like standards in the wind, we'll come.
Let the arms and flags of ancient heroes
flash, O Duce, for Italy in the sun.

Life goes on, and on it goes,
carrying us along and promising the
future.

A manly corps of youth
with Roman will and might shall stand
and fight.

That day, that day will come,
when the Mother of all heroes calls on us,
for Duce, Fatherland, and King—on us!
And we'll go forth and bring an empire
home!

But Pippo, Pippo doesn't know
that everyone is laughing as they watch
him go,
and from their shops the sewing girls
wink at him and toss their curls.

But he, all serious, says, "Good day",
and makes a little bow and continues
on his way,
thinking himself a god among men,
strutting like a barnyard hen.

He wears his overcoat under his jacket
and he wears his shirt over his
waistcoat.
Over each shoe, a sock, maybe two,
and though belts might be best
for holding up pants, a pair of laces
will do.

But Pippo, Pippo doesn't know,
and so, all serious, through city streets
he'll go,
thinking himself a god among men,
strutting like a barnyard hen.

allow even a sliver of light to show through our windows. If that was true, we must have blessed the fog then, as it spread its protective mantle over us. Fog was good.

Of course my first-grade reader could not have had anything to tell me about blackouts, as it had been published in 1937. It spoke only of dreary fog, the kind that climbed the bristling hills. I paged through the books from subsequent years, but found no signs of the war even in the one for fifth grade, though it had been published in 1941 and the war was then a year old. It was still an edition from earlier years, and it mentioned only heroes from the Spanish Civil War and the conquest of Ethiopia. The hardships of war were not a seemly subject for schoolbooks, which avoided the present in favour of celebrating the glories of the past.

My reader from the fourth grade, 1940–1941 (that autumn we were in the first year of the war), contained only histories of glorious actions from World War One, with pictures that showed our infantrymen standing on the Carso, naked and muscled, like Roman gladiators.

But on other pages there appeared, perhaps to reconcile Balilla Boys with Angels, stories about Christmas Eve that were full of sweetness and light. Since we were to lose all of Italian East Africa only at the end of 1941, by which time that book was already making the rounds in schools, our proud colonial troops were still featured, and I was struck by a Somali Dubat in his handsome, characteristic uniform, which had been adapted from the style of dress of those natives we were civilizing: he was bare-chested except for a white sash knotted to his ammo belt. The caption was pure poetry: *The legionary Eagle spreads its wings—over the world: only the Lord shall stop it.* But Somaliland had already fallen into English hands by February, perhaps even as I was first reading that page. Did I know it at the time?

In any case, in that same syllabary I was also reading *The Basket* recycled: *Goodbye to the thunder blast! / Goodbye to the stormy day! / The clouds have run away / and the sky is clean at last... / The world, consoled, grows calm, / and on each afflicted thing, / quiet and comforting, / peace settles like a balm.*

And what about the war in progress? My fifth-grade reader included a meditation on racial differences, with a section on the Jews and the attention that should be paid to this untrustworthy breed, who "having shrewdly infiltrated Aryan regions... introduced among the Nordic peoples a new spirit made up of mercantilism and profit hunger." I also found in those boxes various issues of *Defence of the Race*, a magazine founded in 1938. (I do not know whether my grandfather ever allowed it to fall into my hands, but I suspect I poked my nose into everything sooner or later.) They contained photos that compared aborigines to an ape and others that revealed the monstrous consequences of crossing a Chinese with a European (such degenerate phenomena, however, apparently occurred only in France). They spoke highly of the Japanese race and pointed out the unmistakable stigmata of the English race—women with double chins, ruddy gentlemen with alcoholic noses—and one cartoon showed a woman wearing a British helmet, immodestly covered with nothing but a few pages of the *Times* arranged like a tutu: she was looking in the mirror, and TIMES, backwards, appeared as SEMIT. As for actual Jews, there was little to choose from: a survey of hooked noses and unkempt beards, of piggy, sensual mouths with buck-teeth, of brachycephalic skulls and scarred cheekbones and wretched Judas eyes, of the unchecked guts of well-dressed profiteers, their gold fobs dangling from their watch pockets and their greedy hands poised above the riches of the proletarian masses.

My grandfather, presumably, had inserted among those pages a propaganda postcard showing a repugnant Jew, with the Statue of Liberty in the background, thrusting his fists towards the viewer. And there was something for everyone: another postcard showed a grotesque, drunken Negro in a cowboy hat clutching a big, claw-like hand around the white midriff of the Venus de Milo. The artist had apparently forgotten that we had also declared war on Greece, so why should we have cared if that brute was groping a mutilated Greek woman, whose husband went around in a kilt with pompoms on his shoes?

For contrast, the magazine showed the pure, virile profiles of the Italic race, and when it came to Dante and a few of our leaders whose noses were not exactly small or straight, they spoke in terms of the "aquiline race". In case the appeal to uphold the Aryan purity of my countrymen had not completely convinced me, my schoolbook contained a fine poem about Il Duce (*Square is his chin, his chest is squarer yet, / His footstep that of a pillar walking, / His voice as biting as a fountain's jet*) and a comparison of the masculine features of Julius Caesar with those of Mussolini (I would learn only later, from encyclopaedias, that Caesar used to go to bed with his legionnaires).

Italians were all beautiful. Beautiful Mussolini himself, who appeared on the cover of *Tempo,* an illustrated weekly, on horseback, sword raised high (an actual photo, not some artist's allegorical invention—does that mean he went around carrying a sword?) to celebrate our entry into the war; beautiful the blackshirt proclaiming things like HATE THE ENEMY and WE WILL WIN!; beautiful the Roman swords stretching towards the outline of Great Britain;

With your delicate half-powdered face,
and that cheerful light-hearted grace,
you walk through crowds at a bustling
  pace,
with a box of something new.
Oh, lovely piccinina
you pass by every day,
skipping lightly through the crowd,
always humming along the way.
Oh, lovely piccinina,
why are you so coy?
You turn a dozen shades of red
if by chance some passing boy
makes eyes at you as he comes near
or whispers something in your ear,
Then says Good day and walks away…

Where are you going, beauty on a bike,
pedalling away in such a hasty fashion,
with legs so slim, so shapely and trim,
why, already they have filled my heart
  with passion.
Where are you going, hair blowing in
  the wind,
and your heart contented and your
  smile enthralling?
It's up to you, dreams can come true,
and this could be true love into which
  we're falling.

When we see a girl go walking by,
what do we do? We pursue,
and try to guess with our cunning
  eye
what doesn't show from head to toe.
Dark eyes might be pretty,
blue eyes might be swell,
but as for me, oh as for me,
it's their legs that I like well.
Blue eyes might be pretty,
and an impish nose is nice,
but as for me, oh as for me,
it's their legs I look at twice.

At dawn when the sun comes up
o'er the Abruzzo countryside,
the buxom girls of the country
go down into the valleys wide.
Oh beautiful country girl,
you are the queen of this world.
Your eyes have the sun's power,
and the tint of the prettiest flower
in all the blossoming valley!
And when you sing, your voice
is a harmony of peace
that spreads and seems to say:
"If you want to be happy and gay
then you must come live here!"

beautiful the rustic hand turning up its thumb as London burned; beautiful the proud legionnaire outlined against the backdrop of the ruins of Amba Alagi, promising WE WILL RETURN!

Optimism. My radio continued to sing Oh he was big but he wasn't tall, they called him Bombolo, he danced a jig then started to fall and tumbled head over toe, he tumbled here, he tumbled there, he bounced like a rubber ball, his luck was gone, he fell in a pond, but he floated after all.

But beautiful above all else were the images, in magazines and publicity posters, of pure-blooded Italian girls, with their large breasts and soft curves, splendid baby-making machines in contrast to those bony, anorexic English misses and to the "crisis woman" of our own plutocratic past. Beautiful the young ladies who seemed to be actively competing in the "Five Thousand Lire for a Smile" contest, and beautiful also that provocative woman, her rear well defined by a seductive skirt, who strode across a publicity poster as the radio assured me that dark eyes might be pretty, blue eyes might be swell, but as for me, oh as for me, it's their legs that I like well.

Utterly beautiful the girls in all the songs, whether they were rural, Italic beauties ("the buxom country girls") or urban beauties like the "lovely piccinina," that milliner's assistant from Milan with her delicate half-powdered face, walking through crowds at a bustling pace... Or beauties on bikes, symbols of a brash, dishevelled femininity, with legs so slim, so shapely and trim.

Ugly, of course, were our enemies, and several copies of *Balilla,* the weekly for the Italian Fascist Youth, contained illustrations by De Seta alongside stories that made fun of the enemy, always through brutish caricatures: *The war had him worried / so King Georgie scurried / for defence from things sinister / to Big Winston, his Minister*—and then there were the other two villains, Big Bad Roosevelt and the terrible Stalin, the red ogre of the Kremlin.

The English were bad because they used the equivalent of *Lei,* whereas good Italians were supposed to use, even when addressing people they knew, nothing but the oh-so-Italian *Voi.* A basic knowledge of foreign languages suggests that it is the English and French who use *Voi* (*you, vous*), whereas *Lei* is very Italian, though perhaps influenced by Spanish, and at the time we were thick as thieves with Franco's Spain. As for the German *Sie,* it is a *Lei* or a *Loro,* but not a *Voi.* In any case, perhaps as a result of poor knowledge of things foreign, *Lei* as the polite form of *you* had been rejected by the higher powers in favour of *Voi*—my grandfather had kept clippings that were quite explicit and rather inflexible on the matter. He had also had the presence of mind to save the last issue of a women's magazine called *Lei,* in which it was announced that beginning with the next issue it would be called *Annabella.* Obviously, the *Lei* in this context was not an address to "you", the magazine's ideal reader, but rather an instance of the pronoun "she", indicating that the magazine was aimed at women, not men. But regardless, the word *Lei,* even when serving a different grammatical function, had become taboo. I wondered if the whole episode had made the women who read the magazine laugh at the time, and yet it had happened and everyone had put up with it.

And then there were the colonial beauties, because even though Negroid types resembled apes and Abyssinians were plagued by a whole host of maladies, an exception had been made for the beautiful Abyssinian woman. The radio sang: *Little black face / sweet Abyssinian / just wait and pray / we're nearing our dominion / Then we'll be with you / and gifts we'll bring / yes we will give you / a new law and a new King.*

Just what should be done with the beautiful Abyssinian woman was made clear in De Seta's colour cartoons, which featured Italian legionnaires buying half-naked, dark-skinned females in slave markets and sending them to their pals back home, as parcels.

But the feminine charms of Ethiopia had been evoked from the very beginning of the colonial campaign in a nostalgic caravan-style song: *They're off / the caravans of Tigrai / towards a star that by and by / will shine and glimmer with love.*

And I, caught in this vortex of optimism, what had I thought? My elementary-school notebooks held the answer. It was enough to look at their covers, which immediately invited thoughts of daring and triumph. Except for a few that contained thick, white paper (they must have been more expensive) and bore on their covers the portraits of Great Men (I must have done some woolgathering around the name and the enigmatic, smiling face of a gentleman called Shakespeare—which I no doubt pronounced as it was spelled, with four syllables—seeing that I had gone over all the letters in pen, as if to interrogate or memorize them), the notebooks boasted images of Il Duce on horseback, of heroic combatants in black shirts lobbing hand grenades at the enemy, of slender PT boats sinking enormous battleships, of couriers with a sublime sense of sacrifice, who though their hands have been mangled by a grenade run on beneath the crackle of enemy machine-guns, carrying their messages between their teeth.

Our headmaster (why headmaster and not headmistress? I do not know, but I could hear myself saying "Mr. Headmaster") had dictated to us the key passages from Mussolini's historic address on the day he declared war, June 10, 1940, inserting, following the newspaper accounts, the reactions of the oceanic audience listening to him in Piazza Venezia:

Combatants on land, at sea, and in the air! Blackshirts of the revolution and of the legions! Men and women of Italy, of the Empire and of the kingdom of Albania! Listen! An hour signalled by destiny is striking in the skies of our fatherland. The hour of irrevocable decisions. The declaration of war has already been delivered (cheering, deafening cries of "War! War!") *to the ambassadors of Great Britain and of France. We are going to battle against the plutocratic and reactionary democracies of the West, who at every turn have hindered the advance and often threatened the very existence of the Italian people...*

According to the laws of Fascist morality, when one has a friend one marches with him wholeheartedly. (Shouts of "Duce! Duce! Duce!") *This is what we have done and will do with Germany, with her people, with her marvellous armed forces. On the eve of this event of historic import, we turn our thoughts to his Majesty the Emperor King* (the multitudes erupt in great cheers at the mention of the House of Savoy), *who, as always, has understood the spirit of the fatherland. And we salute the Führer, the head of allied Greater Germany.* (The crowd cheers at length at the mention of Hitler.) *Italy, proletarian and Fascist, is on her feet for the third time, strong, proud, and united as never before.* (The multitude cries out in a single voice: "Yes!") *The watchword is one word only, categorical and binding for all. It has already taken wing, stirring hearts from the Alps to the Indian Ocean: Victory! And we will win!* (The crowd erupts in deafening cheers.)

It was in those months that the radio must have begun playing "Victory", echoing the word of the Chief:

Steeled by a thousand passions,
the voice of our nation rang clear!
"Centuries, Cohorts, and Legions,
attention, the hour is here!"
March onward, young men!

Who holds us back
or blocks our track,
we'll knock them aside!
Slaves never again!
Our hands won't be tied
like prisoners by our own sea!
Victory, victory, victory!
We will triumph in the air, on land, at sea!
The highest powers say
it's the watchword of the day:
Victory, victory, victory!
At any cost: nothing will stand in our way!
Our hearts are eager to obey
even to our last breath.
And our voices swear today:
Victory or death!

How might I have experienced the beginning of a war? As a great adventure, undertaken at the side of my German comrade. His name was Richard, as the radio informed me in 1941: *Comrade Richard, welcome*... I learned how I, in those glorious years, might have imagined my comrade Richard (the song's rhythm obliged us to pronounce that name like the French *Richárd,* rather than the German *Ríchard*) from a postcard, on which he appeared alongside an Italian comrade, both in profile, both masculine and decisive, their gaze fixed on the finish line of victory.

But *my* radio, after "Comrade Richard", was already playing (by this point I was convinced it was a live broadcast) a different song. This one was in German, a sad dirge, almost a funeral march that seemed to me to keep time with some imperceptible rhythm in my gut, sung by a woman whose voice was deep and hoarse, mournful and sinful: *Vor der Kaserne / Vor dem großen Tor / Stand eine Laterne / Und steht sie noch davor*...

My grandfather had owned the record, but in those days I would not have understood the German.

And indeed I listened next to the Italian version, which was more a paraphrase or an adaptation than a translation:

Every evening
beneath the streetlamp's glow
not far from the garrison
I waited for you to show.
I'll be there this evening too,
forgetting all the world with you,
with you, Lili Marleen,
with you, Lili Marleen.

When I must walk
through the muck and mire
beneath my heavy pack
I feel unsure and tired.

Where will I go? What will I do?
Then I smile and think of you,
of you, Lili Marleen,
of you, Lili Marleen.

Though the Italian lyrics fail to say so, in the German the streetlamp emerges from the fog: *Wenn sich die späten Nebel drehn,* when the late fog swirls. But in any case, in those days I would not have understood that the sad voice in the fog beneath that streetlamp (my concern then was probably how a streetlamp could have been lit during a blackout) belonged to the mysterious *pitana,* "the woman who sells by herself." That song must be why, years later, I took note of this passage from Corazzini's poem "The Streetlamp": *Murky and scant in the lonely thoroughfare, / in front of the bordello doors, it dims, / and the good smoke that from the censer swims / might be this fog that whitens out the air.*

"Lili Marleen" came out not too long after the giddy "Comrade Richard". Either we were generally more optimistic than the Germans, or in the interim something had happened, our poor comrade had grown sad and, tired of walking through muck, longed to go back to his streetlamp. But I was coming to realize that the same series of propagandistic songs could explain how we had gone from a dream of victory to one of the welcoming bosom of a whore as hopeless as her clients.

After our initial enthusiasm, we grew accustomed not only to blackouts and, I imagine, to bombings, but also to hunger. Why else would it have been necessary to encourage the little Balilla Boy, in 1941, to cultivate a war garden on his apartment balcony, if not so that he could squeeze a few vegetables from the most paltry of spaces? And why has the boy received no news from his father at the front?

Dear Papà, my hand is shaking some,
but you will understand what I am saying.
It's been so many days since you left home

and yet you haven't told me where you're staying.
As for the tears that trickle down my cheek,
you can be sure they're only tears of pride.
I still can see you smile and hear you speak,
and your Balilla waits for you, arms wide.
I'm helping in the war, I'm fighting, too,
with discipline, with honour, and with faith.
I want this land of mine to bear good fruit,
so I tend my little garden every day
(my own war garden!) and ask God each night
to watch you, to make sure my dad's all right.

Carrots for victory. By contrast, in one of my notebooks I found a place where the headmaster had made us take note of the fact that our English enemies were a five-meal people. I must have thought to myself that I had five meals, too: coffee with bread and marmalade, a snack at ten at school, lunch, an afternoon snack, then dinner. But perhaps other children were not as fortunate, and a people who ate five meals a day could not but stir resentment among those who had to grow tomatoes on their balcony.

But then why were the English so skinny? And why did one of my grandfather's postcards feature (above the word *Hush!*) a crafty Englishman trying to overhear military secrets that some loose-lipped Italian comrade might let slip in some bar? How was such a thing possible if the entire population had rushed as one to take up arms? Were there Italians who spied? Had the subversives not been defeated, as the stories in my reader explained, by Il Duce with his march on Rome?

Various pages of my notebooks mentioned the now imminent victory. But as I was reading, a beautiful song dropped onto the turntable. It told the story of the last stand of Giarabub, one of our desert strongholds, where the exploits of our besieged soldiers, who finally succumbed to hunger and lack of munitions, attained epic dimensions. In Milan some weeks earlier, I had seen on television a

The snow melts away,
the fog and mist too,
those dastardly English
have nothing to do
but gulp down their swill
and suck on their pills,
while asking the rats
when will the weather change.
April won't bring
the sweet-tempered dove,
bombs on their targets
will rain from above,
torpedoes will fly
and drop from the sky—
it's April in Italy,
and glory is in range...
You vile Englishmen
have no chance to win,
our triumph instead
will sit proud on your head.

Blue skies are on the way,
blue skies are on the way...
We will send you back up north
to your little fishing port.
Blue skies are on the way,
blue skies are on the way...
Men of England, men of England,
your fate is in our hands.

Fixed above palms, the moon
casts its pale unblinking eye;
an ancient minaret nearby
rises high above its dune.
Clamour, banners, and machines,
explosions, blood—camel driver,
won't you tell me what it means?
It's the feast of Giarabub!

"Colonel, sir, I don't want bread,
put some bullets in my hand,
that and these bags of sand
will be enough for me today.
Colonel, sir, I don't want water,
give me fire's destructive flood,
that and my heart's own blood
will satisfy my thirst today.
Colonel, sir, I don't want rest,
no one here will turn or flinch,
we won't give even an inch,
if we do not meet death today."

"Colonel, sir, I don't want praise,
I died for my beloved land.
Just say old England's final stand
started here in Giarabub!"

colour movie about the last stand of Davy Crockett and Jim Bowie at the Alamo. Nothing is more exhilarating than the topos of the besieged fort. I imagine I once sang that sad elegy with the emotion of a boy watching a Western today.

I sang that England's final stand had begun at Giarabub, but the song must have reminded me of *Maramao, Why Did You Die,* because it was the celebration of a defeat—my grandfather's newspapers told me more: the Giarabub oasis in Cyrenaica had fallen, despite heroic resistance, in March of 1941. Using a defeat to electrify a population seemed to me a rather desperate measure.

And this other song, from the same year, that promised victory? "Blue Skies Are on the Way!" promised blue skies by April—by which time we were to lose Addis Ababa. In any case, people say "blue skies are on the way" when the weather is bad and they hope it will change. Why were blue skies supposed to be coming (in April)? A sign that during the winter, when the song was first sung, people had been looking forward to a reversal of fortune.

All the heroic propaganda we were raised on alluded to some frustration. What did the refrain "We will return" mean, if not that we looked forward to, hoped for, counted on a return to the place where we had been defeated?

And when did "The M Battalions" anthem come out?

Battalions of Il Duce, battalions
of death created in life's name,
in the springtime begins the game,
the continents will flame and flower!
We'll win with Mussolini's Lions,
made strong by his courageous power.

These battalions of death
they are life battalions, too,
there is no love without hate,
so the game begins anew.

The M we wear is red like fate,
our tassels black, and as for death
we've faced it with grenades in hand
and a flower between our teeth.

According to my grandfather's dates, it must have come out in '43, and once again, two years after Giarabub, springtime was invoked (we signed the armistice in September of '43). Leaving aside the image, which must have fascinated me, of greeting death with grenades in hand and a flower between our teeth, why did the game have to begin again in springtime, why did it have to start over? Had it been stopped? And yet they had us singing it, in a spirit of incorruptible faith in final victory.

The only optimistic anthem that the radio offered me was the "Song of the Submariners": *to creep through the ocean deep, laughing in the face of Lady Death and Fate*... But those words reminded me of others, and I went looking for a song called "Young Ladies, Keep Your Eyes Off Sailor Boys".

They would not have had me sing this at school. Apparently it was played on the radio. The radio, then, played both the submariner's song and the warning to young ladies. Two worlds.

The other songs, too, made it seem as if life were running on two different tracks: on one, the war bulletins; on the other, the endless lessons in optimism and gaiety that our orchestras offered in such abundance. Was war breaking out in Spain, with Italians dying on both sides, while our Chief passionately exhorted us to prepare for a larger, bloodier conflict? Luciana Dolliver sang (such an exquisite flame) don't forget my words, my darling one, you don't know what love is, the Barzizza Orchestra played oh baby how I love you, I've been dreaming of you, you slept, I stood above you, you smiled then in your sleep, and everyone was repeating Fiorin, Fiorello, l'amore è bello when you're by my side. Was the regime celebrating beautiful country girls and productive mothers by im-

LA DOMENICA DEL CORRIERE

They glide through murky waters
in the pitch dark of the deep,
and from proud conning towers
a sharp-eyed watch they keep.
Silent and unseen
departs the submarine!
The heart and the machine
of the brave marine
against Immensity!

To creep
through the ocean deep,
laughing in the face of Lady Death and
 Fate!
To leave
in a watery grave
every enemy you meet along the way!
That's how a sailor spends his day,
in the heart of the deep
and echoing sea!
No matter what the adversity
or who the enemy, he knows that he
will have victory!

Who knows why the young girls
 nowadays
all go so crazy for sailor boys...
They don't know it's dangerous to
 trust:
there's what they say and what they
 do,
and oceans lie between the two...

Young ladies, keep your eyes off sailor
 boys...
oh why, oh why?
because they stir up trouble that
 destroys...
oh why, oh why?

They teach the verb "to love"
by showing you how to swim,
then leaving you to drown.

Young ladies, keep your eyes off sailor
 boys...
oh why, oh why?

posing a bachelor tax? The radio gave notice that jealousy had gone out of fashion, that it had become uncouth.

Was war breaking out, and did we have to darken our windows and stay glued to the radio? Alberto Rabagliati whispered that we should turn the volume way down low to hear his heart beat through the radio. Had our campaign to "break the back of Greece" got off to a bad start, and had our troops begun dying in the mud? No worries, one does not make love when rain is falling.

Did Pippo really not know? How many souls did the regime have? The battle of El Alamein was raging beneath the African sun, and the radio was intoning that's how I want to live, sun on my face, singing happily, full of bliss. We were going to war against the United States and our papers were celebrating the Japanese bombing of Pearl Harbor, and the airwaves were bringing us beneath Hawaiian skies you'll watch the full moon rise and dream of paradise. (But perhaps the listening audience was not aware that Pearl Harbor was in Hawaii or that Hawaii was a U.S. territory.) Field Marshal Paulus was surrendering in Stalingrad amid stacks of bodies from both sides, and we were hearing I have a pebble in my shoe, and oh it's really killing me.

Allied troops were landing in Sicily, and the radio (in the voice of Alida Valli!) was reminding us that love is not that way, love won't turn to grey the way the gold fades in a woman's hair. Rome was experiencing its first air raids, and Jone Caciagli was twittering night and day, hand in hand, you and I away from everyone, till the rising of tomorrow's sun.

The Allies were landing at Anzio and the radio could not get enough of "Bésame, Bésame Mucho"; the Fosse Ardeatine massacre took place, and the radio kept our spirits high with "Baldy" and "Where Is Zazà Now"; Milan was being tortured with bombardments, and Radio Milan was broadcasting "The Dandy-Girl of the Biffi Scala"...

Don't forget my words, my darling one,
You don't know what love is, oh my sweet,
Love's as splendid as the summer sun,
Of the two love gives more heat.

It slowly seeps into the lover's veins,
It slowly fills the chambers of the heart.
And so the lover suffers the first pains
just when the first sweet dreams start.

But love is not that way...
My love won't blow away
in the wind with the petals of the rose.
My love is strong, my love is here to stay,
it won't fade away.
I will mend my love,
I'll defend my love
against the dangers that the world will pose,
against the snares that tear love from the heart,
tearing love apart.

Oh darling how I love you,
I've been dreaming of you,
You slept, I stood above you,
you smiled then in your sleep.
Oh darling how I miss you,
I leaned down to kiss you,
You rose from sleep's abyss, you
Must this memory keep.

Fiorin Fiorello,
l'amore è bello
with you by my side!
When dreaming of you
I tremble, I do,
oh who knows why.
The rose, the peony,
what good would life be
if we lacked the love
hearts need so much of
to make them beat?
The daisy, the carnation,
if love upon occasion
brings us grief or pain,
it blows in like the wind
stays a moment, then
it's gone again!
But when you're with me
I'm happy happily...
Fiorin Fiorello,
l'amore è bello
with you by my side.

Jealousy has now gone out of fashion,
nowadays it has become uncouth:
You must always wear a smile
in the modern style
in order to enjoy your youth.
If you're sad just have a whisky and soda,
then you won't give love a thought, you'll see.
You'll find the world a cheerful place,
a smile upon your face,
you'll be happy as happy can be.

And what about me, how did I experience this schizophrenic Italy? Did I believe in victory, did I love Il Duce, did I want to die for him? Did I believe in the Chief's historic phrases, which the headmaster dictated to us: It's the plough that makes the furrow but it's the sword that defends it; We will not back down; If I advance, follow, if I retreat, kill me?

In a notebook from fifth grade, 1942, Year XX of the Fascist Era, I found one of my in-class compositions:

TOPIC: *"O children, you must remain for the rest of your lives the guardians of the new heroic civilization that Italy is creating." (Mussolini)*

TREATMENT: *Here along the dusty road a column of young boys advances.*

They are the Balilla Boys, proud and robust beneath the mild sun of early spring, marching with discipline, obeying the terse commands imparted by their officers; it is those boys who at twenty years of age will set aside their pens in order to take up muskets to defend Italy against its insidious enemies. Those Balilla Boys who can be seen marching through the streets on Saturdays and hunching over their school desks studying on other days, will at the proper age become faithful and incorruptible guardians of Italy and its civilization.

Who would have imagined, watching the legions parading by during the "Youth March", that those beardless boys, many still Vanguard Youths at that time, would already have reddened the burning sands of Marmarica with their blood? Who imagines, seeing these boys now, cheerful and always in a joking mood, that within a few years they, too, may die on the battlefield with the name of Italy on their lips?

My insistent thought has always been this: when I grow up, I will be a soldier. And now that I hear on the radio about the countless deeds of courage, heroism, and self-denial performed by our brave soldiers, my desire has become even more deeply anchored in my heart, and no human force could uproot it.

Yes! I will be a soldier, I will fight and, if it is Italy's will, die for the new, heroic, holy civilization, which will bring well-being to the world and which God desired should be built by Italy.

Yes! The happy, playful Balilla Boys will become lions when they grow up should any enemy dare to profane our holy civilization. They would fight like wild beasts, fall and get back up to fight again, and they would triumph, bringing another victory to Italy, immortal Italy.

And with the guiding memory of past glories, with the results of present glories, and with the hope for future glories to be brought home by the Balilla Boys, youths today but soldiers tomorrow, Italy will continue its glorious path towards wingèd victory.

Did I really believe all that, or was I repeating stock phrases? What did my parents think when I brought home (with high marks) such compositions? Perhaps they believed it themselves, having absorbed phrases of the kind even prior to Fascism. Had they not, as is commonly known, been born and grown up in a nationalistic climate in which the First World War was celebrated as a purifying bath? Had the futurists not said that war was the world's only hygiene? Among the books in the attic, I had come across an old copy of *Heart,* the famous late nineteenth-century children's book by De Amicis, in whose pages, among the heroic deeds of the Little Paduan Patriot and the magnanimous acts of Garrone, I found this passage, in which Enrico's father writes to his son in praise of the Royal Army:

All these young people full of strength and hope may from one day to the next be called upon to defend our Nation and within a few hours be smashed by bullets and grapeshot. Every time you hear someone at a festival shout, "Long live the Army, long live Italy," I want you to picture, beyond the passing regiments, a field covered with corpses and flooded with their blood, and then your hurrahs for the army will spring from deeper in your heart, and your image of Italy will be more severe and grand.

So it was not only myself, but my elders, too, who had been raised to conceive of love for our country as a blood tribute, and to feel not horror but excitement when faced with a landscape flooded with blood. For that matter, had not the great Leopardi himself, gentlest of poets, written a hundred years earlier: *O providential, dear, and hallowed were / the days of old when for their fatherland / the people ran in squads to die*?

I understood that even the massacres in *The Illustrated Journal of Voyages and Adventures* must not have seemed exotic to me at all, since I had been raised in a cult of horror. And it was not simply an Italian cult, for in that same *Illustrated Journal* I had read other encomiums to war and to redemption through bloodbaths uttered by heroic French poilus, who had turned the Sedan debacle into their own rabid, vengeful myth, as we were to do with Giarabub. Nothing is more likely to incite a holocaust than the rancour of a defeat. That was how we, fathers and sons, were taught to live, through stories of how beautiful it was to die.

But how much did I really want to die and what did I know of death? In my fifth-grade reader, I found a story called "Loma Valente". Its pages were more tattered than the rest, the title had been marked in pencil with a cross, many passages were underlined. The story describes a heroic episode from the Spanish Civil War, involving a battalion of Black Arrows emplaced below a harsh, rugged hilltop (*loma* in Spanish) that offers little opening for an attack. But one platoon is commanded by a dark-haired athlete, twenty-four years of age, named Valente, who back home in Italy studied literature and wrote poetry, though he also won the boxing prize at the Fascist Games. Valente, who has volunteered in Spain, where "pugilists and poets both had something to fight for", orders the attack fully aware of the risks, and the story treats the various phases of the gallant undertaking: the Reds ("Damn them, where are they? Why won't they show themselves?") fire every weapon they have, a torrent, "as if throwing water on a wildfire that was spreading and coming closer." Valente has only a few steps left to conquer the hill, when a sudden, sharp blow to his head fills his ears with a terrible din:

Then, darkness. Valente's face lies in the grass. The darkness now grows less black; it is red. The eye of our hero that lies closest to the ground sees two or three blades of grass as thick as stakes.

A soldier comes up to him and whispers that the hill has been taken. The author now speaks for Valente: "What does it mean to die? It is the word, usually, that is frightening. Now that he is dying, and knows it, he feels neither heat, nor cold, nor pain." He knows only that he has done his duty and that the *loma* he has conquered will bear his name.

I understood from the tremor that accompanied my adult rereading of those few pages that they had offered me my first vision of actual death. That image of blades of grass as thick as stakes seemed to have inhabited my mind from time immemorial, I could almost see them as I was reading. Indeed I had the feeling that as a child I had often repeated, as a sacred rite, a descent into the garden, where I would lie prone, my face flattened against some patch of redolent grass, in order to really see those stakes. That reading had been the fall on the road to Damascus that had marked me, perhaps, for ever. It was during those same months that I had written the composition that now so disturbed me. Was such duplicity possible? Or had I read the story after writing the composition, and had everything changed from that moment?

I had come to the end of my elementary school years, which concluded with the death of Valente. The middle-school books were less interesting—Fascist or not, if your subject is the seven kings of

Rome or polynomials, you have to say more or less the same things. But among my middle-school materials were notebooks called "Chronicles". Some kind of curriculum reform had taken place, and we were no longer assigned compositions on fixed topics, but were apparently encouraged to recount episodes from our lives. And we had a different teacher, who read all the chronicles and marked them in red pencil, not with a grade but with a critical comment regarding their style or inventiveness. It was clear from the feminine endings of certain words in those comments that the teacher was a woman. Clearly an intelligent woman (perhaps we adored her, because reading those red messages I sensed that she must have been young and pretty and, God knows why, very fond of lilies of the valley), who had tried to push us to be sincere and original.

One of my most highly praised chronicles was the following, dated December 1942. I was eleven by then, but only nine months had passed since the earlier composition.

CHRONICLE: *The Unbreakable Glass*

Mother had purchased an unbreakable glass. But it was actual glass, real glass, and I was dumbfounded, because when this event took place, the undersigned was only a few years old, and his mental faculties were not yet so well developed that he could imagine that a glass, a glass similar to the ones that went crash! *when they fell (leading to a good cuffing) could be unbreakable.*

Unbreakable! It seemed like a magic word. The boy tries it once, twice, three times, and each time the glass falls, bounces with a terrible racket, and remains intact.

One evening some family friends come by and chocolates are passed around (note that back then those delicacies still existed, and in great number). With my mouth full (I no longer recall the brand, Gianduia or Strelio or Caffarel-Prochet), I proceed to the kitchen and return with the famous glass.

"Ladies and gentlemen," I exclaim, with the voice of a ring-master calling out to passers-by to attend the show, "I present to you a unique, magic, unbreakable glass. I will now throw it to the ground and you will see that it will not break," and in a grave and solemn manner I add, "IT WILL REMAIN INTACT."

I throw it, and... needless to say, the glass shatters into a thousand pieces.

I feel myself turn red, I stare in shock at those shards that, struck by the light of the chandelier, are gleaming like pearls... and I burst into tears.

End of my story. Now I was trying to analyse it as though it were a classic text. I was writing about a pre-technological society, in which an unbreakable glass was a rarity, and people would purchase a single glass to try it out. Breaking it was not only a humiliation, but also a blow to the family finances. It was thus a story of defeat on all fronts.

My story, from 1942, evoked the pre-war period as a happier era, when chocolates were still available, and foreign brands at that, when people received guests in their living rooms or in their dining rooms beneath a bright chandelier. The appeal I had made to my audience had not resembled Il Duce's appeals from the balcony of Palazzo Venezia, but had rather the ridiculous air of the barkers I may have heard at the market. I was evoking a gamble, an attempted triumph, an incorruptible certainty, and then, with a nice anticlimax, I reversed the situation and recognized that I had lost.

It was one of the first stories that was truly mine, not the repetition of schoolboy clichés nor the rehashing of some adventure novel. The drama of a promissory note not made good. In those shards that, lit by the chandelier, gleamed (falsely) like pearls, I was celebrating at the age of eleven my own *vanitas vanitatum* and professing a cosmic pessimism.

I had become the narrator of a failure, whose breakable objective correlative I represented. I had become existentially, if ironically, bitter, radically sceptical, impervious to all illusion.

How can a person change so much in the course of nine months? Natural growth, no doubt, one gets cleverer with age, but there was more: the disillusionment caused by broken promises of glory (perhaps I, too, still in the city then, was reading the newspapers my grandfather had underlined), and my encounter with the death of Valente, whose heroic act had resolved into that terrible image of rot-green stakes, the final fence separating me from the underworld and the fulfilment of every mortal's natural fate.

In nine months I had become wise, with a sarcastic, disenchanted wisdom.

And what of everything else: the songs, Il Duce's speeches, the oh-babys, and the idea of facing death with grenades in hand and a flower between our teeth? Judging by the headings in my notebooks, I spent the first year of middle school, during which I had written that chronicle, still in the city, then the next two years in Solara. Meaning that my family had decided to evacuate definitively to the country, because the first bombardments had finally reached our city. I had become a citizen of Solara in the wake of my remembrance of that broken glass, and my remaining chronicles, from the second and third years of middle school, were all remembrances of better, bygone times, when if you heard a siren you knew it came from the factory and you said to yourself, "It's noon, father will be home soon," stories about how great it would be to return to a peaceful city, reveries about the Christmases of yesteryear. I had taken off my Balilla Boy uniform and had become a little decadent, devoted already to the search for lost times.

And how had I spent the years from 1943 to the end of the war, the darkest years, with the Partisan struggle and the Germans no longer our comrades? Nothing in the notebooks, as if speaking of the horrid present had been taboo and our teachers had encouraged us not to do it.

I was still missing some link, perhaps many links. At some point I had changed, but I did not know why.

10. The Alchemist's Tower

I felt more confused than I had when I arrived. At least before I remembered nothing, absolute zero. Now, I still could not remember, but I had learned too much. Who had I been? The Yambo shaped by school and by the kind of "public education" carried out through Fascist architecture, propaganda postcards, street posters, and songs, the Yambo of Salgari and Verne, of Captain Satan, of the savagery of *The Illustrated Journal of Voyages and Adventures,* of the crimes of Rocambole, of the Paris Mysterieux of Fantômas, and of the fog of Sherlock Holmes; or the Yambo of Ciuffettino, and of the unbreakable glass? Or all of them?

I phoned Paola, bewildered, and explained my anxieties, and she laughed.

"Yambo, for me those are just blurred memories. I have an image of a few nights in an air-raid shelter, someone waking me up suddenly and taking me downstairs, I must have been four. But excuse me, let me play the psychologist: a child can live in different worlds, just as our little ones do; they figure out how to turn on the TV and they watch the news, then they listen to fairy tales and page through picture books of green monsters with kind eyes and talking wolves. Sandro is always going on about dinosaurs, which he saw in some cartoon, but he doesn't expect to meet one on the street corner. I read him *Cinderella* at bedtime, and then he gets out of bed at ten o'clock, and without his parents noticing peeks at the television from the doorway and sees a marine kill ten gooks with a single machine-gun burst. Children are much more balanced than we are, they can tell the difference between fairy tale and reality just fine; they keep one foot here and one there but never get them confused, with the exception of a few sick children who see Superman fly, then attach a towel to their shoulders and throw themselves out of the window. But those are clinical cases, and it's nearly always the parents' fault. You weren't a clinical case, and you managed perfectly well between Sandokan and your schoolbooks."

"Sure, but which one did I think was imaginary? The world of Sandokan or that of Il Duce sweet-talking the Sons of the She-Wolf? I told you about that composition, right? At ten, did I really want to fight like a wild beast and die for immortal Italy? I'm talking ten years old, and I don't doubt that there was censorship at the time, but the bombs were already raining down on us, and in 1942 our soldiers in Russia were dropping like flies."

"But Yambo, when Carla and Nicoletta were little, and even recently with the grandkids, you used to say that children are manipulative bastards. You should remember this, it happened just a few weeks ago: Gianni came over to our place when the little ones were there too, and Sandro said to him: 'I'm so happy when you come see us, Uncle Gianni.' 'You see how much they love me,' Gianni said. And you: 'Gianni, children are manipulative bastards. This one knows that you always bring him chewing gum. That's all.' Children are manipulative bastards. And you used to be. All you wanted was to get a good grade, and you wrote what the teacher liked."

"You're oversimplifying. It's one thing to be a manipulative bastard when it comes to Uncle Gianni, it's another when it comes to Immortal Italy. And besides, why in that case was I a master of scepticism less than a year later, writing that story of the unbreakable glass as an allegory of a pointless world—because that's what I wanted to say, I can feel it."

"Simply because you had changed teachers. A new teacher can liberate the critical spirit that another might not have allowed you to develop. And besides, at that age, nine months is a century."

Something must have happened in those nine months. I understood that when I went back to my grandfather's study. Browsing at random as I drank a coffee, I pulled from the magazine pile a humorous weekly from the late thirties, *Il Bertoldo*. It was a 1937 issue, but I must have read it later than that, because at that time I would not have been able to appreciate those filiform drawings and that twisted sense of humour. But now I was reading a dialogue (one appeared each week in the little opening column on the left of the front page) that may well have caught my attention during those nine months of profound transformation:

Bertoldo walked past all those gentlemen of the retinue and went at once to sit beside the Grand Duke Windbag, who, gentle in nature and fond of wit, began in that spirit to question him pleasantly.

GRAND DUKE: *Good day, Bertoldo. How was the crusade?*
BERTOLDO: *Noble.*
GRAND DUKE: *And the task?*
BERTOLDO: *Lofty.*
GRAND DUKE: *And the impulse?*
BERTOLDO: *Generous.*
GRAND DUKE: *And the surge of human solidarity?*
BERTOLDO: *Moving.*
GRAND DUKE: *And the example?*
BERTOLDO: *Enlightening.*
GRAND DUKE: *And the initiative?*
BERTOLDO: *Courageous.*
GRAND DUKE: *And the offer?*
BERTOLDO: *Spontaneous.*

GRAND DUKE: *And the gesture?*

BERTOLDO: *Exquisite.*

The Grand Duke laughed, and calling for all the Gentlemen of the Court to gather around him, ordered the Revolt of the Wool Carders (1378), upon completion of which the courtiers all returned to their places, leaving the Grand Duke and the peasant to resume their conversation.

GRAND DUKE: *How are the workers?*

BERTOLDO: *Unrefined.*

GRAND DUKE: *And their fare?*

BERTOLDO: *Plain, but hearty.*

GRAND DUKE: *And the province?*

BERTOLDO: *Fertile and sunny.*

GRAND DUKE: *And the populace?*

BERTOLDO: *Welcoming.*

GRAND DUKE: *And the view?*

BERTOLDO: *Superb.*

GRAND DUKE: *And the outskirts?*

BERTOLDO: *Enchanting.*

GRAND DUKE: *And the villa?*

BERTOLDO: *Stately.*

The Grand Duke laughed, and calling for all his courtiers to gather around him, ordered the Storming of the Bastille (1789) and the Battle of Montaperti (1260), upon completion of which the courtiers all returned to their places, leaving the Grand Duke and the peasant to resume their conversation...

At one and the same time that dialogue mocked the language of poets, of newspapers, and of official rhetoric. If I was a clever lad, I would no longer have been able, after those dialogues, to write compositions such as the one of March 1942. I was ready for the unbreakable glass.

These were only hypotheses. Who knows how many other things happened to me between the heroic composition and the disillusioned chronicle. Again I decided to suspend my research and reading. I went into town: I had finished my Gitanes by then and had to make do with Marlboro Lights—better that way: I would smoke less, since I do not like them. I went back to the pharmacist to get my blood pressure checked. The conversation with Paola must have relaxed me—it was around 140. Getting better.

Back at the house, I had a craving for an apple, and I entered the lower rooms of the central wing. Strolling among the fruits and vegetables, I noticed that some of the large rooms on the ground floor were being used for storage and that in the back of one room were stacks of deckchairs. I carried one into the yard. I sat down facing the panorama, skimmed the newspapers, realized I was barely interested in the present, turned the chair around, and began looking at the front of the house and the hills behind it. I asked myself what I was looking for, what I wanted, would it not be enough to sit here looking at that hill that is so beautiful, as that novel said, what was it called? To raise three pavilions, Lord, one for You, one for Moses, and one for Elijah, and loaf without a past and without a future. Perhaps that is what paradise is like.

But the diabolical power of paper got the better of me. After a while I began daydreaming about the house, imagining myself as the hero of a My Children's Library story, standing before the Castle of Ferlac or Ferralba, looking for the crypt or the granary in which the forgotten parchment must lie. You press the centre of the sculpted rose on a coat of arms, the walls open, and a spiral staircase appears...

I could see the dormer windows on the roof, and below them the second-floor windows of my grandfather's wing, all now open to illuminate my wanderings. Without being aware of it I was counting them. In the middle was the balcony, and to the left of it three windows: the dining room, my grandparents' bedroom, my parents' bedroom. To the right, the kitchen, the bathroom, and Ada's room. Symmetrical. I could not see, on the far left, the windows of my grandfather's study or of my little room, because they were at the end of the hall, past the point where the façade meets the left wing, and their windows face the side of the house.

I was gripped by an uneasy feeling, as if my sense of symmetry had been disturbed. On the far left, the hall ends with my room and my grandfather's study, but on the right it ends just after Ada's room. So the hall is shorter on the right than on the left.

Amalia was walking by, and I asked her to describe the windows of her wing. "That's easy," she said. "On the ground floor that's where we eat, and that little window would be the bathroom, your dear grandfather had it put in special for those of us who didn't care to use the bushes like the rest of the farmers, goodness knows. As for the others, them two windows you see there belong to the storage room where we keep all the tools and such, and there's the entrance to it on the side. On the second floor, there's my window, and then the other two are my poor parents' bedroom and their dining room, I leave them like they used to be and never open them out of respect."

"So the last window is their dining room, and that room ends where your wing meets my grandfather's wing," I said. "It sure does," Amalia confirmed. "The rest is part of the owner's wing."

It all sounded so natural that I did not ask her anything more. But I walked around to the right side of the house, near the threshing floor and the henhouse. I could immediately see the rear window of Amalia's kitchen, then the wide, ramshackle door I had passed some days ago that led into the farm-equipment storage room I had already visited. Entering it now, I realized it was too long: it extended beyond the point where the right wing met the central wing; in other words, the storage room continued beneath the last part of my grandfather's wing, all the way to the back wall that faced the vineyard, as was clear from a little window that offered a glimpse of the foot of the hill.

Nothing extraordinary, I told myself, but what is there on the second floor above that extension, if Amalia's rooms end where the two wings meet? In other words, what up there corresponds to the area of the left wing occupied by my grandfather's study and my little room?

I returned to the threshing floor and looked up. There were three windows in that space, just as there were on the opposite side (two in my grandfather's study and one in my room), but the shutters of all three were closed. Above them, the regular dormer windows of the attic, which, as I already knew, ran without interruption around the entire house.

I called Amalia, who was busying herself in the garden, and asked her what was behind those three windows. Not a thing, she said, as if that were the most natural answer in the world. What do you mean not a thing? If there are windows, there must be something behind them, and it isn't Ada's room; her window faces onto the courtyard. Amalia tried to cut me off: "That was your dear grandfather's affairs, I don't know a thing."

"Amalia, don't treat me as if I were stupid. How do you get in there?

"You don't, there's nothing to get to any more. The hellcats took it all away by now."

"I told you not to treat me as if I were stupid. You have to be able to get up there either through one of your rooms or some other goddamn way!"

"Don't curse, please, the only thing God has damned is the devil. What do you want me to say, your good grandfather made me swear never to breathe a word about that business, and I will not break an oath or else the devil really will carry me off."

"But what did you swear, and when?"

"I swore that same evening, when later that night the Black Brigades came and your dear grandfather said to me and my mother, Swear that you don't know a thing and haven't seen a thing, and in fact I won't actually let you see what we're fixing to do, me and Masulu—who was my poor father—because if the Black Brigades come and put your feet to the fire you won't be able to help yourselves and you'll say something, so it's better if you don't know a thing, because they are a nasty bunch and can make a person talk even after they've cut his tongue out."

"Amalia, if the Black Brigades were still around, this must have been more than forty years ago. My grandfather and Masulu are both dead, the men in the Black Brigades are probably all dead, the oath you swore no longer holds!"

"Your dear grandfather and my poor father are long dead it's true, it's always the best that go first, but I don't know about those others because they're a wretched sort that never dies."

"Amalia, the Black Brigades are gone, the war ended back then, nobody will put your feet to the fire."

"If you say so then for me it's gospel, but Pautasso was in the Black Brigades, and I sure remember him, reckon he was less than twenty at the time, and he's still around these parts, lives in Corseglio and once a month comes to Solara for his business, he started a brick factory in Corseglio and made a mint, and there's still people in this town who never forgot what he done and when they see him coming they go the other way. Maybe he can't put a body's feet to the fire any more, but an oath is an oath and not even the parish priest can help that."

"So even though I'm still sick, and my wife believes that you are helping me get better, you won't tell me this thing, even if not knowing it may harm me."

"May the Lord strike me down if I would harm a hair on your head, Signorino Yambo, but an oath is an oath, am I right?"

"Amalia, whose grandson am I?"

"Your dear grandfather's, like the word says."

"And I am my grandfather's universal heir, the owner of everything you see here. Okay? And if you don't tell me how to get up there, it's as if you're stealing what's mine."

"May the Lord gobble me up this very second if I ever tried to steal a thing of yours, why I never heard such nonsense, I've spent all my born days killing myself to keep this house pretty as a picture for you!"

"And furthermore, since I am my grandfather's heir, and it's as if everything I'm saying now were being said by him, I solemnly release you from your oath. Okay?"

I had put forth three persuasive arguments: my health, my property rights, and my direct descent, with all the privileges of primogeniture. Unable to resist, Amalia yielded. Does Signorino Yambo carry more weight than the priest and the Black Brigades, or not?

Amalia led me up to the second floor of the central wing, then to the right, past Ada's room, towards the armoire that smells of camphor where the hall ends. She asked me to help her move the armoire, at least a little, and showed me that behind it was a walled-up doorway. At one time that had been the entrance to the chapel, because when that great-uncle who left everything to my grandfather still lived here, he kept a working chapel in the house, not large, but big enough to hear mass on Sundays with his family, and the priest would come from the village. When the house was taken over by my grandfather, who though fond of his Nativity scene was not a churchgoer, the chapel was abandoned. The benches were taken out and placed here and there in the large downstairs rooms, and since the chapel was empty I had asked my grandfather to allow me to drag a few bookcases down from the attic, to use for my things—and I often hid out there and did God knows what. Indeed, when the parish priest learned of the arrangement, he asked if he could take away at least the consecrated altar stones, to avoid sacrilege, and my grandfather also let him take a statue of the Madonna, the ampullae, the paten, and the tabernacle.

Late one winter afternoon (there were already Partisans in or around Solara by this time; sometimes the town harboured them and other times the Black Brigade, and that month it was the Black Brigade, while the Partisans were said to be up in the Langhe hills) someone came by to tell my grandfather that he needed to hide four boys whom the Fascists were hunting. They may not have been Partisans yet, from what I could gather, but deserters who were making their way through those parts precisely in order to join the resistance up in the mountains.

My parents and sister and I were not home, having gone away for two days to visit my mother's brother, who had evacuated to Montarsolo. Only my grandfather, Masulu, Maria, and Amalia were there, and my grandfather had made the women swear never to speak of what was taking place, indeed had sent them straight to bed. Except that Amalia only pretended to go to bed, then went to spy on them from somewhere. When the boys arrived, around eight, my grandfather and Masulu took them to the chapel, gave them some food, then went to get bricks and buckets of mortar, and the two of them, though no masons, walled up that door by themselves and then put that piece of furniture, which had been elsewhere, in front of it. They had just finished when the Black Brigades arrived.

"If you'd seen them faces. Luckily the one in charge was a refined person, wore gloves no less, and acted the gentleman with your grandfather, which no doubt they was told he owned land, and dog does not eat dog. Oh, they poked around here and there, even went up to the attic, but you could tell they was in a rush and was doing it just so they could say they did—they still had a lot of farmhouses to go to and likely figured one of us farm folk was apt to be hiding our own. They didn't find a thing, the one with the gloves apologized for the bother, said Long live Il Duce, and your grandfather and my father which they was smart as tacks said Long live Il Duce right back, and amen."

How long had those four stowaways remained up there? Amalia did not know, she had played deaf and dumb and knew only that for some days she and Maria had had to prepare baskets with bread, salami, and wine, and then at a certain point no more. When we came home, my grandfather simply told us that the flooring in the chapel had been giving way, he had had some provisional reinforcements put in, and the masons had closed up the entrance to make sure that none of us children went poking around in there and got hurt.

Okay, I said to Amalia, we have explained the mystery. But if they went in, the stowaways had to come out, and Masulu and my grandfather somehow got food in to them for several days. So even after the door was walled up, there must still have been an access point somewhere.

"I swear to you I didn't even ask myself if they was going in or out or through what hole. Whatever your dear grandfather did was fine by me. He closed it up? Well then he closed it up, and for me that chapel wasn't there any more, in fact it don't exist even now, and if you didn't make me talk it would be like I forgot it. Maybe they got the food through the window, hoisted up baskets with a rope, and they all left through the window too, during the night. Right?"

"No, Amalia, because in that case one window would have been left open, and instead it's clear that they were all closed from the inside."

"I always did say you was the smart one. What do you know, I never thought of that. Well then, how did my father and your dear grandfather get them out?"

"That, said the Bard, is the question."

"Who?"

Forty-five years late, perhaps, but Amalia had put her finger on the problem. I, however, had to solve it myself. I looked all over the house trying to find a hidden door, a hole, a grate, thoroughly searching the rooms and halls of both floors of the central wing once again, and combing both floors of Amalia's wing like a Black Brigadier. Nothing.

You did not have to be Sherlock Holmes to come to the only conclusion possible: there was a way into the chapel from the attic. The chapel had its own stairway, but the entry point in the attic had been concealed. From the Black Brigades, but not from Yambo. Imagine my coming home from our trip, my grandfather telling us that the chapel was no longer there, and my being satisfied with that, especially since I apparently kept some of my dearest possessions there. Attic scout that I was, I must have known the passageway well and no doubt continued to go into the chapel, indeed with more pleasure than before, because it had become my hideaway, and once I was there no one could find me.

Nothing left to do but go back up to the attic and explore the right wing. At that moment a thunderstorm was gathering, so it was less hot than usual. That would facilitate what was no trifling task: everything that had been piled up against the walls had to be moved away, and this was the farm wing and contained not collector's items but rather junk—old doors, beams salvaged from some renovation, coils of old barbed wire, large broken mirrors, bundles of old blankets held together with twine and oilcloth, unusable kneading troughs and settles, worm-eaten for centuries and piled one on top of the other. I moved it all, as boards fell on me and rusty nails scratched me, but I saw no secret passageways.

Then I realized I should not be looking for a door, because there could be no doors in those walls: they were exterior walls on all four sides. If there was no door, there had to be a trapdoor. Foolish not to have thought of that first, that was how it always happened in My Children's Library. I should be examining not the walls, but the floor.

Naturally, the floor was worse than the walls, and I had to climb over or walk on all manner of things: more boards tossed here and there, frames for long lost beds and cots, bundles of iron construction rods, an ancient ox yoke, even a saddle. And amid all that, clots of dead flies, which had come in the previous year seeking shelter from the first cold snaps but had not survived. To say nothing of the spiderwebs that ran from one wall to the other, like the once luxurious drapery of a haunted house.

Flashes of lightning from quite nearby were lighting up the dormer windows, and the attic was getting darker—though in the end it did not rain; the storm unburdened itself elsewhere. *The Alchemist's Tower, The Castle Mystery, The Pretty Prisoners of*

Casabella, The Morande Mystery, The North Tower, The Iron Man's Secret, The Old Mill, The Acquaforte Mystery... Christ, I was in the middle of an actual storm, a bolt of lightning could have brought the roof down on me, but I was seeing it all through the eyes of an antiquarian book dealer. *The Antiquarian's Attic*—I could have written a new story and signed it Bernage or Catalany.

Luckily, at a certain point I stumbled: beneath a layer of shapeless junk there was a sort of step. I cleared the area, scraping my hands, and there was the prize for the intrepid boy: a trapdoor. The one my grandfather, Masulu, and the fugitives had used, the one I too must have used who knows how often, reliving adventures that had already been imagined over so many sheets of paper. What a wonderful childhood.

The trapdoor was not large and came up easily, though I raised a cloud of fine powder in the process, since nearly fifty years of dust had accumulated in those cracks. What does one find beneath a trapdoor? A ladder, elementary, my dear Watson, and not a particularly taxing one, either, even for my limbs, now stiffened by two hours of tugging and bending—no doubt I took it in a single bound back then, but I am pushing sixty, and there I was behaving like a child still able to chew his toenails. (I swear I have never thought about this before, but it seems normal that, while in bed in the dark, I might try to bite my big toe, just to see if I could.)

In brief, I went down. The darkness was nearly total, barely striped by a few slivers of light from the shutters, which no longer closed properly. In the dark that space seemed immense. I went at once to open the windows: the chapel, predictably, was as large as my grandfather's study and my room put together. I saw the dilapidated remains of a gilded wooden altar, against which four mattresses were still leaning: no doubt the beds of the fugitives, though I found no other traces of them, which indicated that the chapel had been occupied afterwards, at least by me.

Along the wall in front of the windows I saw some shelves of unfinished wood, full of printed matter, newspapers and magazines, in piles of unequal heights, as if each pile were a separate collection. In the middle of the room, a long table with two chairs. Next to what should have been the entry door (marked by the crude masonry put up in an hour by my grandfather and Masulu, with mortar overflowing between the bricks—after all, they had been able to trowel it smooth only from the outside, not the inside) I found a light switch. I tried it without hope, and indeed nothing came on, though several bulbs hung from the ceiling at regular intervals, each beneath a white plate. Perhaps over the course of fifty years the mice had gnawed through the wiring, assuming they had been able to get through the trapdoor—and mice have ways. Or my grandfather and Masulu might have destroyed it all when they were walling up the door.

At that hour, the daylight sufficed. I felt like Lord Carnarvon setting foot in Tutankhamun's tomb after millennia, and the challenge was to avoid getting stung by some mysterious scarab that had been lying in wait all that time. Everything in there had remained as I must have left it after my last visit. Indeed, I did not want to open the windows too much, just enough to see, so as not to disturb that sleeping atmosphere.

I did not yet dare even look at what was on the shelves. Whatever was there, it was mine and only mine, otherwise it would have remained in my grandfather's study and been shoved into the attic by my aunt and uncle. At this point, why bother trying to remember? Memory is a stopgap for humans, for whom time flies and what has passed is past. I was enjoying the marvel of beginning *ab ovo*. I was doing again the things I had once done, passing like Pipino from old age into early youth. From then on, I should have retained only what was to happen to me later, which after all would have been the same as what had happened to me back then.

In the chapel, time had stopped, or rather, no, it had gone backwards, like a clock whose hands have been turned back to the day before, and no matter that yesterday's four o'clock looks like today's, you simply have to know (and I alone knew) that it is the four o'clock of yesterday, or a hundred years ago. That is how Lord Carnarvon must have felt.

If the Black Brigade were to discover me here now, I was thinking, they would assume I was in the summer of 1991, whereas I (I alone) would know I am in the summer of 1944. And even that officer with the gloves would have to doff his hat, for he would be entering Time's Temple.

11. Up There at Capocabana

I spent many days in the chapel, and when I left in the evenings I would take a bundle of things and spend all night looking through them in my grandfather's study, beneath the green lamp, with the radio on (as I now believed), to fuse what I was listening to with what I was reading.

The shelves of the chapel contained the comic books and comic albums of my childhood, not bound, but nicely arranged in ordered piles. These items had not belonged to my grandfather, and their dates started in 1936 and finished around 1945.

Perhaps, as I had already imagined from my conversations with Gianni, my grandfather was a man from another era and had preferred that I read Salgari or Dumas. So I, to reassert the rights of my imagination, had kept my comics beyond the range of his control. But since some of them went back to 1936, before I started school, that meant that someone else, if not my grandfather, had bought them for me. Maybe there had been some kind of conflict between my grandfather and my parents—"why do you let your son look at that trash?"—but my parents, having read some of those things as children themselves, had indulged me.

Indeed, the first pile contained several years' worth of *Il Corriere dei Piccoli,* the illustrated children's weekly, and the issues from

1936 bore the inscription "Anno XXVIII"—not of the Fascist Era, but of that publication. So *Il Corriere dei Piccoli* had been around in the early years of the century, no doubt gladdening my parents' childhoods—they may even have enjoyed reading it to me more than I enjoyed having it read to me.

In any case, paging through the *Corrierino* (I instinctively began using that diminutive) was like reliving the tensions I had experienced in the preceding days. Without in any way distinguishing one from the other, the *Corrierino* spoke of Fascist glories and of fantasy worlds inhabited by grotesque fairy-tale characters. It offered me stories and serious cartoons of absolute Fascist orthodoxy alongside panelled pages that were, by all appearances, American in origin. The only concession to tradition: in strips that had originally used speech balloons, the content had been eliminated, or had been retained merely as decoration: all the stories in the *Corrierino* had captions—long prose captions for the serious ones, nursery rhymes for the funny ones.

Here follows the adventure / of Signor Bonaventure: this was a story, which certainly touched a chord, about a gentleman with improbably wide-legged white trousers, who, thanks to some completely accidental intervention, always receives a million-lira reward (this in the days of a thousand lire a month) and yet by the next episode is indigent again, awaiting another stroke of luck. Perhaps he was a squanderer, like the oh-so-content Signor Pampurio, who—in each new instalment—wants to move to a new apartment. I concluded from the style and the artists' signatures that both of these strips were of Italian origin, like the strips about Formichino and Cicalone (a diminutive ant and a chatty cicada), Signor Calogero Sorbara (who is always preparing to go on a trip), Martin Muma (who is light as a feather and flies on the wind), and Professor Lambicchi (who invented an amazing superpaint that brings his portraits to life, so that his house is always being invaded by troublesome figures from the past, now a furious Orlando Paladino, now one of the kings from a deck of cards, irritated and bitter about having been removed from his throne in the Land of Make-Believe).

CORRIERE dei PICCOLI

	REGNO	ESTERO
ANNO	L. 19.-	L. 32.-
SEMESTRE	L. 10.-	L. 17.-

SUPPLEMENTO ILLUSTRATO
del CORRIERE DELLA SERA
SI PUBBLICA OGNI SETTIMANA

UFFICI DEL GIORNALE:
VIA SOLFERINO, N° 28.
MILANO.

PER LE INSERZIONI RIVOLGERSI ALL'AMMINISTRAZIONE DEL «CORRIERE DELLA SERA» - VIA SOLFERINO, 28 - MILANO

Anno XXXI - N. 42 — 15 Ottobre 1939-XVII — Centesimi 40 il numero

1. Nella tattica, che inizia
hanno presso San Sulpizio,
colonnelli e capitani
stan studiando i vari piani.

2. Un reparto "nazionale"
(Marmittone n'è il caporale)
deve entrar nell'intricato
campo avverso trincerato.

3. Le difese formidabili
sono affatto insormontabili.
Non si vede che una via:
passar sotto, in galleria.

4. Marmittone e i suoi soldati,
zappatori diventati,
incominciano lo scavo,
e ciascun si mostra bravo.

5. Si lavora, scava, sterra,
come talpe, sotto terra:
dei lavori ha Marmittone
la suprema direzione.

6. "...Siamo, sotto, metri venti
e mi sembran sufficienti;
or pian piano si risale
in iscavo verticale."

7. Giunti all'ultimo diaframma
si delinea questo dramma:
che a sboccar vanno bel bello
dove dorme il Colonnello.

8. Or rimugina, in prigione,
l'accaduto Marmittone:
"...Certamente era sbagliato
il disegno del tracciato".

But indisputably American were the surreal landscapes of Felix the Cat, those colonial rascals the Katzenjammer Kids, Happy Hooligan, and Jiggs and Maggie (with those Chrysler Building interiors in which figures emerged from their picture frames on the wall).

It was hard to believe that the *Corrierino* had brought me the adventures of the soldier Marmittone (dressed exactly like my Soldiers of Cockaigne!) who, thanks to unlucky genes or to the stupidity of decorated generals with risorgimento moustaches, always ended up in prison.

Not much of a warrior or Fascist, this Marmittone. And yet he was allowed to cohabit with other strips that told, in an epic rather than grotesque tone, of young heroic Italians fighting to civilize Ethiopia (in "The Last Ras", the Abyssinians who had resisted our invasion were dubbed marauders) or, as in *The Hero of Villahermosa,* protecting the flanks of Franco's troops against the ruthless Republicans in their red shirts. Of course this last strip failed to inform me that although some Italians were battling alongside the Falangists, others were fighting on the other side, in the International Brigades.

Next to the *Corrierino* collection was a stack of *Il Vittorioso,* another weekly, along with some of its large colour albums, dating from 1940 on. At around eight years of age then, I must have demanded *grown-up* literature, with speech balloons.

Total schizophrenia there too, with the reader going from delightful episodes in Zoolandia, among characters such as Giraffone the giraffe, Aprilino the fish, and Jojò the monkey, or from the mock-heroic adventures of Pippo, Pertica, and Palla, or of Alonzo Alonzo (Alonzo for short), who was arrested for giraffe theft, to celebrations of Italy's past glories and to stories directly inspired by the ongoing war.

The ones that affected me most were those about Romano the Legionnaire, because of the engineer-like precision of the machines of war, the aeroplanes, the tanks, the torpedo boats and submarines.

Made sharper by having revisited the conflict in the pages of my grandfather's newspapers, I was now able to match up the dates. For example, the story "Towards I.E.A." began on February 12, 1941. Just a few weeks before, the English had mounted an offensive in Eritrea, and on February 14 they would occupy Mogadishu in Somalia, but despite that Ethiopia still seemed to be solidly in our hands, so it was a good time to move our hero (who till then had been fighting in Libya) to the East African front. Sent on a secret mission to deliver a confidential message to the Duke of Aosta, then commander in chief of the Italian East Africa forces, he travelled from North Africa across the Anglo-Egyptian Sudan. Strange, given that radios existed then and that, as it turned out, the message was in no way confidential (its contents: "Resist and Triumph"); it was as if the Duke of Aosta were simply amusing himself. In any case, Romano travelled with his friends and had various adventures with savage tribes, English tanks, aerial dogfights, and whatever else allowed the artist to make sheet metal shine.

By the time of the March issues, the English had already penetrated deep into Ethiopia, and the only person who seemed unaware of that was Romano, who entertained himself along his route by hunting antelopes. On April 5, Addis Ababa fell, the Italians were regrouping in Galla-Sidamo and Amhara, and the Duke of Aosta was fleeing towards Amba Alagi. Romano continued on straight as an arrow, even taking time to capture an elephant. He and his readers probably thought he was still on his way to Addis Ababa, though by this time the Emperor, deposed exactly five years earlier, had returned. It is also true that in the April 26 issue, a rifle shot shattered Romano's radio, but that meant that up until then he had one, and so it was unclear why he was not up-to-date on current events.

In mid May, the seven thousand soldiers at Amba Alagi, out of provisions and munitions, surrendered, and the Duke of Aosta was taken prisoner with them. The readers of *Il Vittorioso* might not have known that, but the poor Duke of Aosta at least should have noticed; instead, Romano meets him on June 7 in Addis Ababa, finding him fresh as a daisy and radiating optimism. Indeed, the Duke reads Romano's message and affirms: "Of course, and we will resist until victory is achieved."

Obviously, these panels had been drawn months earlier, and despite the course of events the editors of *Il Vittorioso* lacked the courage to cut the series short. They went forward believing that Italy's children had remained unaware of all the dismal news—and perhaps they had.

The third stack was my collection of *Topolino,* a weekly dedicated primarily to the exploits of Mickey Mouse (a.k.a. Topolino) and Donald Duck, though it also included stories about brave Balilla Boys, such as "The Submarine Cabin Boy". I was able to trace, through the volumes of *Topolino,* the transition that began around December of 1941, when Italy and Germany declared war on the United States—I went to double-check my grandfather's newspapers, and indeed that was how it had happened; I had thought that at a certain point the Americans had tired of Hitler's pranks and entered the war, but no, it was Hitler and Mussolini who had declared war on the Americans, perhaps thinking they could dispose of them in a matter of months with the help of the Japanese. Since it would clearly have been difficult simply to dispatch a platoon of SS or Blackshirts to occupy New York, we had, for several years already, been waging war in comic books, from which the speech balloons had disappeared, replaced by captions beneath each picture. Then—as I must have seen happen in various comics—the American characters simply began to vanish, replaced by Italian imitations, and in the end—and this, I think, was the last, most painful barrier to fall—the famous mouse was killed. The same adventures continued as if nothing had happened, but from one week to the next, without any notice, the protagonist ceased to be Topolino and became a certain Toffolino, who was a human, not a mouse, although he still had four fingers, like all Disney's anthropomorphic animals, and his friends, though also humanized, continued to go by their original names. How had I taken it, back then, this crumbling of a world? Perhaps with utter calm, given that the Americans, from one moment to the next, had become bad. But was I even aware, back then, that Topolino was American? My life must have been a roller coaster of dramatic turns, but given all the exciting dramatic turns in the stories I was reading, the dramatic turns in the history I was living must have seemed unexceptional.

After *Topolino* I found several years' worth of *L'Avventuroso*, and that was completely different. The first issue was October 14, 1934.

I could not have bought it myself, since at the time I was not yet three, and I do not think my parents would have bought it for me, as its stories were not at all suitable for children—they were American comics conceived for an audience of adults, if not necessarily grown-ups. So they must have been issues I had sought out later, perhaps swapping other comics for them. But there was no doubt that I was the one who, several years later, had acquired some of the large-format albums with brilliantly coloured covers, on which appeared, like movie previews, various scenes from the story that unfolded inside.

Both the weekly issues and the albums of *L'Avventuroso* must have opened my eyes to a new world, beginning on the first page of the first issue with an adventure called "The Destruction of the World". The hero was Flash Gordon, who thanks to a scheme

C. C. Postale - Anno I - N. 1 - Firenze, 14 Ottobre 1934-XII.
Centesimi 30
CASA EDITRICE NERBINI - FIRENZE
l'avventuroso
grande settimanale d'Avventure
CASA EDITRICE NERBINI
LA DISTRUZIONE DEL MONDO!!
LA FINE DEL MONDO!!
UNO STRANO PIANETA PRECIPITA VERSO LA TERRA – SOLO UN MIRACOLO PUO' SALVARCI- DICE LA SCIENZA!–
XTRA
IN AFRICA IL TAN-TAN-ROMBO INCESSANTE ANNUNZIATORE DI MORTE.
IN ARABIA SI PREGA E S'IMPLORA LA SALVEZZA DALL'INEVITABILE DISASTRO.
POSIZIONE DEL PIANETA RISPETTO ALLA TERRA.
NEW YORK LA POPOLAZIONE E' PRESA DAL PANICO E GUARDA CON ORRORE IL BOLLETTINO.–
LO SCIENZIATO DR. ZARRO LAVORA GIORNO E NOTTE PERFEZIONANDO UNO STRUMENTO CON IL QUALE SPERA SALVARE IL MONDO – IL SUO CERVELLO E' STANCO DAL LAVORO SNERVANTE.–
A BORDO DI UN VELIVOLO TRANSOCEANICO, VI SONO UN UFFICIALE DI POLIZIA, GORDON FLASCE, E DALE ARDEN PASSEGGIERA..
UNA METEORA, STACCATASI DAL PIANETA, TAGLIA NETTAMENTE UN'ALA ALL'APPARECCHIO E PRECIPITA.–
FLASCE RIESCE A PRENDERE LA PASSEGGIERA E GETTARSI FUORI CON IL PARACADUTE DISCENDENDO AL SUOLO
ATTERRATO PRESSO L'OSSERVATORIO DEL DR. ZARRO FLASCE SI LIBERA DEL PARACADUTE
CHE VI PRENDE? ABBASSATE L'ARMA! SIAMO AMICI!
SIETE SPIE! VOLETE RUBARE IL MIO SEGRETO PER DIRLO AL MONDO.. NON LO SAPRANNO MAI.. VENITE CON ME!
QUESTA ENIGMATICA FIGURA SI PARA DINANZI A LORO!
ORA ENTRATE NEL RAZZO! IO INTENDO CON QUESTO DIRIGERMI VERSO IL PIANETA CHE MINACCIA LA TERRA E SVIARNE IL SUO CORSO! MORIREMO, MA SAREMO MARTIRI DELLA SCIENZA–! ORA PARTIREMO!–
MA.. VOI SIETE PAZZO!
CON UN ROMBO ASSORDANTE IL RAZZO DEL DR. ZARRO SI INALZA NEL CIELO, PORTANDOSI FLASCE GORDON E DALE ARDEN!
E SI DIRIGE SOTTO IL CONTROLLO DELLO SCIENZIATO, VERSO IL PIANETA DISTRUTTORE!–
IL RAZZO DEL DR. ZARRO SI AVVICINA VELOCEMENTE AL PIANETA.
NON POSSO! NON POSSO PARLO! MORIREMO!
DOBBIAMO DOBBIAMO SALVARE LA TERRA! PASSATEMI IL COMANDO!
FLASCE! ATTENZIONE! IMPAZZISCE!..
NO! IO NON VOGLIO MORIRE! CAPITE?!
FERMATEVI! LO UCCIDETE.. IO......

concocted by a certain Dr. Zarkov had landed on the planet Mongo, controlled by a cruel dictator, Ming the Merciless, whose name and features were diabolically Asiatic. Mongo: glass skyscrapers that rose from space platforms, underwater cities, kingdoms stretching through the trees of an immense forest, and characters ranging from the maned Lion Men to the Hawk Men and the Blue Magic Men of Queen Azura, all of them dressed with an easy syncretism, either in outfits that suggested a cinematic Middle Ages, like so many Robin Hoods, or in barbaric loricae and helmets, or occasionally (at court) in the uniforms of cuirassiers or uhlans or dragoons from turn-of-the-century operettas. And all of them, the good and the bad, were incongruously equipped not only with blades and arrows but also with prodigious ray guns, just as their conveyances ranged from scythed chariots to needle-nosed interplanetary rockets in colours as loud as Luna Park bumper cars.

Gordon was beautiful and blond, like an Aryan hero, but the nature of his mission must have astounded me. Prior to that, what heroes had I encountered? In my schoolbooks and my Italian comic books, the valiant men who fought for Il Duce and yearned to die on command; in my grandfather's nineteenth-century adventure novels, if I was already reading them by that time, the outlaws who fought against society, nearly always for personal gain or out of natural wickedness—except perhaps for the Count of Monte Cristo, who, however, still wanted revenge for wrongs done to himself, not to the community. In the end, even the Three Musketeers, though basically on the side of good and not without a sense of justice, did what they did out of esprit de corps, the king's men against the cardinal's men, or for some gain, or for a captain's commission.

Gordon was different, he fought for liberty against a despot, and though at the time I may have thought that Ming resembled the terrible Stalin, the red ogre of the Kremlin, I could not have helped but recognize in him certain traits of our own house dictator, who held unquestioned power of life and death over his faithful. And so Flash Gordon must have provided me with my first image of a hero—of course I understood that now, following my recent rereadings, not back then—fighting some kind of war of liberation in an Absolute Elsewhere, blowing up fortified asteroids in distant galaxies.

Looking through the other albums, in a crescendo of mysterious flames that had me burning through one issue after another, I discovered heroes my schoolbooks had never mentioned. Tim Tyler and his pal Spud, in the light-blue shirts of the Ivory Patrol, scoured the jungle amid a symphony of pale colours, no doubt in part to keep unruly tribes in check, but primarily to stop the ivory poachers and slave traders who preyed on colonial populations (so many white bad guys against good guys with black skin!), in thrilling pursuit of both traffickers and rhinos, chases in which rifles did not go *bang bang* or even *pum pum,* as in our own strips, but rather *crack crack,* and that *crack* must somehow have imprinted itself in the most secret recesses of those frontal lobes I was trying to unhinge, because I still felt those sounds as an exotic promise, a finger pointing me towards a different world. Once again, more than the images it was the sounds, or better yet their alphabetical transcriptions, that had the power to suggest the presence of a trail that was still eluding me.

Arf arf bang crack blam buzz cai spot ciaf ciaf clamp splash crackle crackle crunch deleng gosh grunt honk honk cai miaow mumble pant plop pwutt roaaar dring rumble blomp sbam buizz schranchete slam puff puff slurp smack sob gulp sprank blomp squit swoom bum thump plack clang tomp smash trac uaaaagh vrooom giddap yuk spliff augh zing slap zoom zzzzzz sniff…

Noises. I saw all of them, paging through comic after comic. I had been brought up since I was little on the *flatus vocis.* Among the various noises, *sffft* came to mind, and my forehead beaded with sweat. I looked at my hands: they were shaking. Why? Where had I read that sound? Or perhaps it was the only one I had not read, but heard?

TRATTO PER MEZZO DI MILIONI DI RADIO E DI ALTOPARLANTI
DALI QUELLA DI TUTTO IL POPOLO FLITTONICO CHE ERA PIENA
DI SPERANZA DOPO LA FUGA DEI DETENUTI POLITISI!
STURM!
KAPUT
DRRRR
SCIAZZ
BAU... BAU..
MIAOOOUUHH!
AHI! FLIT!
AHI FLIT!
AIUTO!
DEMOKRATEN
AUG!
CRACK
CRACK
BWOOM!
SOCK
BONG
BONG
DUE GIOR-
NI DOPO -
KRAK!
AWRK
SLAM!
CUCCU
SDLAN
DLEN
SMACK

I felt more at ease when later I encountered the albums of the Phantom, the do-good outlaw, sheathed in an almost homoerotic way in his red tights, his face barely covered by a black mask that revealed the feral whites of his eyes, but not the pupils, rendering him all the more mysterious. The beautiful Diana Palmer must have been driven wild with love and must have felt with a shiver, on those occasions when she kissed him, the heroic musculature beneath those tights he never took off (sometimes, wounded by a gunshot, he was treated by his uncivilized acolytes with bandages, always over his tights, which were no doubt water-repellent, seeing as they remained form-fitting even when he emerged from long swims in the steamy South Seas).

But those rare kisses were enchanted moments, for Diana would somehow be quickly whisked away, either because of a misunderstanding, or an aspiring rival, or her other obligations as a beautiful international traveller, and he would be unable to follow her and make her his bride, fettered as he was by an ancestral oath, condemned to his personal mission: to protect the people of the Bengali jungles from the mischief of Indian pirates and white adventurers.

Thus it was that after, or while, encountering cartoons and songs that taught me how to subjugate the fierce, barbaric Abyssinians, I met a hero who lived in brotherhood with the Bandar Pygmies and fought with them against the evil colonialists—and Guran, the

Bandar witch doctor, was much more cultured and wise than the unsavoury pale-skinned figures whom he helped defeat, not as a faithful Dubat, but rather as a full-fledged partner in that benevolently vengeful mafia.

Then there were other heroes, ones that did not seem particularly revolutionary (if these past few days allowed me to imagine my political growth in such terms), such as Mandrake the Magician, who, though he treated his Negro servant, Lothar, as a friend, seemed to use him more as a bodyguard and faithful slave. Mandrake—or "Mandrache", as he was called in early Italian versions—defeated bad guys with his magic powers and could with a gesture turn an adversary's pistol into a banana. He was a bourgeois hero, with no black or red uniform, though he was always impeccable in his tailcoat and top hat. Another bourgeois hero was Secret Agent X-9, in his trench coat, jacket and tie, who pursued not the enemies of some regime, but rather robber barons and gangsters, protecting the taxpayers with small, graceful pocket revolvers, which at times seemed surpassingly delicate, even in the hands of carefully made-up blondes in silk dresses, with feather-trimmed necklines.

Another world, one that ought to have ruined the language that my school was trying so hard to make me use correctly, since the anglicizing translations resulted in rough-hewn Italian. But what did it matter? Clearly I was encountering heroes in those ungrammatical albums who differed from the ones put forward by the official culture, and perhaps in those garish (yet so mesmerizing!) cartoons I had been initiated into a different vision of Good and Evil.

There was more. Next to that stack was an entire series of Golden Albums with the early exploits of Mickey Mouse, which unfolded in an urban setting that was obviously not mine (but I do not know if I understood at the time whether it was a small city or a great American metropolis). *The Plumber's Helper* (oh, the ineffable Mr. Piper!), *Mickey Mouse and the Treasure Hunt, Mickey Mouse and the Seven Ghosts, Clarabelle's Treasure* (here it was, finally,

identical to the reprint edition in Milan, but with the colours ochre and brown), *Mickey Mouse in the Foreign Legion*—not because he was a soldier or a cut-throat, but because he had agreed out of a sense of civic duty to get involved in international espionage, which led to terrifying adventures in the Legion where he was persecuted by the treacherous Trigger Hawkes and the perfidious Peg-Leg Pete: *Mickey Mouse, he's our guy / in the desert he will die…*

The issue I had read most often, judging by the perilous state of my copy, was *Mickey Mouse Runs His Own Newspaper:* it was unthinkable that the regime would have allowed an article about freedom of the press, but clearly the state censors did not consider animal stories to be realistic or dangerous. Where had I heard

"That's the press, baby, the press, and there's nothing you can do about it"? That must have been later. In any case, with scant resources Mickey Mouse manages to set up his newspaper, the *Daily War Drum*—the first issue is full of typographical errors—and continues fearlessly to publish *all the news that's fit to print,* despite unscrupulous gangsters and corrupt politicians who want to stop him by any means necessary. Who had ever spoken to me, before that time, of a free press, capable of resisting all censorship?

Some of the mysteries of my childhood schizophrenia began to resolve themselves. I had been reading schoolbooks and comic books, and it was probably through the comics that I had laboriously constructed a social conscience. That was why, no doubt, I had saved those shards of my shattered history, even after the war, when I was able to get my hands on American newspapers (brought over perhaps by soldiers), whose colourful Sunday comics introduced me to other heroes, such as Li'l Abner and Dick Tracy. I doubt our pre-war editors would have dared publish them, as their attitude was too outrageously modern and suggested what the Nazis called degenerate art.

Later, having grown older and wiser, was I drawn to Picasso thanks to a nudge from Dick Tracy?

I was certainly not nudged in that direction by the earlier comics, with the exception of Flash Gordon. The reproductions, sometimes made directly from American publications, and without paying royalties, were poorly printed, the lines often blurred, the colours dubious. Nor, needless to say, by those pages in which the Phantom, poorly aped by a home-grown artist after the ban on imports from enemy countries, began sporting green tights and a new personal history. Nor by the cleverly drawn autarkic heroes, probably invented to compete with the pantheon of *L'Avventuroso,* though they were still generally likeable—the massive Dick Fulmine, for instance, with his jutting Mussolini jaw, who pummelled bandits who were clearly of non-Aryan origin, such as the Negro Zambo, the South American Barreira, and, later, the evil criminal Flattavion, a mephistophelized Mandrake, whose name suggested cursed if unspecified races, and who possessed, in lieu of the American magician's topper and tails, a big shabby hat and a rustic cape. "Take your best shot, my little lovebirds," shouted Fulmine at his enemies in their newsboy caps and their rumpled jackets, and down rained the avenging blows. "This man's a fiend," the renegades would say, until Fulmine's fourth arch-enemy, White Mask, would emerge from the darkness to strike Fulmine on the nape of the neck with a mallet or a sack of sand, and Fulmine would crumple, saying "Da . . . !" But all was not lost, because, though he might be chained in a dungeon with water rising menacingly, he could flex his muscles and break his bonds, and before long he had captured and delivered to the commissioner (a little round-headed man whose unistache was more bankerly than Hitlerian) the entire gang, neatly packaged.

Water rising in a dungeon must have been a topos of comics everywhere. I felt something like a live coal in my chest as I picked up a Juventus album, *The Five of Spades: The Final Episode of Death's Standard-Bearer.* A man in riding clothes, with a cylindrical red mask that covers his head and extends into a scarlet cape, stands, legs apart, arms stretched above him, each limb chained to the crypt walls, as water from some underground source pours into the room, destined to submerge him, little by little.

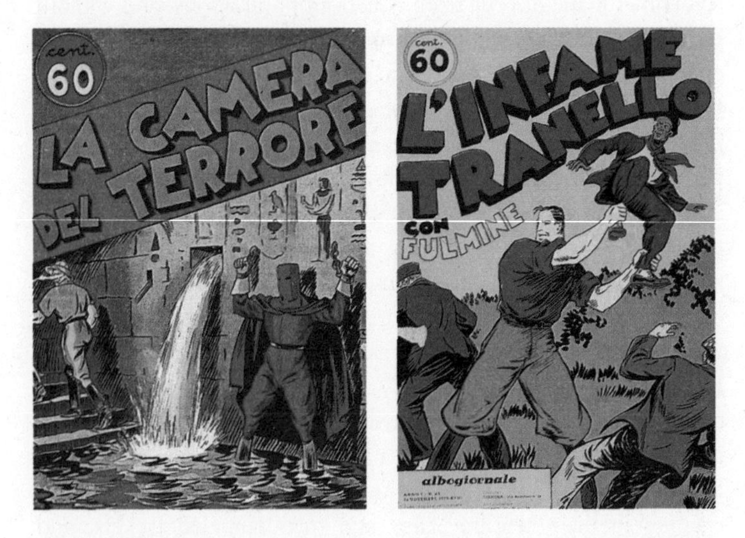

But in the back of those same albums were other serialized stories, in a more intriguing style. One was called *On China's Seas,* and its protagonists were Gianni Martini and his brother, Mino. It might have seemed odd to me that two young Italian heroes would be having adventures in a region where we had no colonies, among Oriental pirates, villains with exotic names, and gorgeous women with even more exotic names, such as Drusilla and Burma. But I certainly would have noticed the difference in the style of the drawings. From the few American strips I had, obtained perhaps from soldiers in 1945, I soon learned that the story was originally called *Terry and the Pirates.* The Italian version was from 1939, which meant that the Italianization of foreign stories had begun as early as that. I also noticed, in my small collection of foreign materials, that during those years the French had translated Flash Gordon as Guy l'Éclair.

I could no longer tear myself away from those covers and those stories. It was like being at a party and feeling as though you recognized everyone, experiencing déjà vu with every face but being unable to say when you first met these people, or who they were, constantly feeling the urge to exclaim, How's it going old buddy, extending your hand but then instantly withdrawing it for fear of making a blunder.

It is awkward, revisiting a world you have never seen before: like coming home, after a long journey, to someone else's house.

I had not been reading them in any order, neither by date nor series nor character. I was jumping around, going backwards, skipping from the heroes of the *Corrierino* to those of Walt Disney, when it occurred to me to compare a patriotic story with Mandrake's battle against the Cobra. And in turning back to the *Corrierino*, to the story of the last ras, which pits Mario, the heroic Vanguard Youth, against Ras Aitù, I saw an illustration that made my heart stop, and I felt something quite like an erection—or rather something more preliminary, what those who suffer from *impotentia coeundi* must feel. Mario flees from Ras Aitù, taking with him Gemmy, a white woman, the Ras's wife or concubine, who has by now understood that Abyssinia's future lies in the saving, civilizing hands of the Blackshirts. Aitù, enraged by the betrayal of that evil woman (who has, of course, finally become good and virtuous), orders that the house in which the two fugitives are hiding be set on fire. Mario and Gemmy succeed in climbing onto the roof, and from there Mario notices a giant euphorbia. "Gemmy," he says, "grab hold of me and close your eyes!"

It is inconceivable that Mario would have wicked intentions, especially at such a moment. But Gemmy, like every cartoon heroine, was dressed in a soft tunic, a sort of peplos that bared her shoulders and arms and part of her bosom. As the four panels devoted to their escape and their dangerous leap documented, peploses, especially silky ones, rise first up the ankle, then up the calf, and if the woman is hanging onto the neck of a Vanguard Youth, and is afraid, her hold cannot help but become a convulsed embrace, with her cheek, no doubt perfumed, pressed to his sweaty neck. Thus, in the fourth illustration, Mario was clinging to one of the euphorbia's branches, concerned only with not falling into the hands of the enemy, but Gemmy, now safe, was forgetting herself, and her left leg, as if the skirt had a slit, protruded, naked up to her knee, exposing her lovely calf, ennobled and tapered by a stiletto heel, whereas only the ankle of her right leg was exposed—but it was lifted coquettishly, so that her calf formed a right angle with her provocative thigh, and her gown (perhaps as a result of the scorching winds coming off the ambas) clung damply to her body, clearly revealing her callipygian curves and the entire shapely length of her legs. The artist could not possibly have been unaware of the erotic effect he was creating, and no doubt he drew on various models from the movies, or on Flash Gordon's women, who were always sheathed in skintight garments studded with precious stones.

Whether that was the most erotic image I had ever seen I could not say, but surely (since the date of the *Corrierino* was December 20, 1936) it was the first. Nor could I guess whether, at four years of age, I had had a physical reaction—a blush, an adoring gasp—but surely that image had for me been the first revelation of the eternal feminine, and indeed I wonder whether after that I was

NON VI RESTA CHE SCEGLIERE,
ME O LA MORTE - SE FOSTE INTEL-
LIGENTE NON CI PENSE-
RESTE DUE VOLTE!

LO ZIO E' STATO FERITO!
VERA-MENTE?

..QUINDI RIENTRA CON DALE NEL

able to rest my head on my mother's bosom with the same innocence as before.

A leg emerging from a long, soft, nearly transparent gown, bringing into relief the body's curves. If that had been one of my primordial images, had it left a mark?

I started going back over pages and pages that I had already examined, my eye now peeled for the most trivial wear in each margin, for the pale prints of sweaty fingers, creases, dog-ears in the upper corners of the pages, slight surface abrasions in places over which I may have run my fingers more than once.

And I found a series of bare legs slipping through the slits of many dresses: slitted the attire of the women on Mongo, including Dale Arden and Ming's daughter, Aura, and the odalisques that gladdened the imperial balls; slitted the voluptuous negligees of the ladies into whom Secret Agent X-9 was always bumping; slitted the tunics of the sinister girls of the Sky Band that the Phantom eventually defeated; slitted, one guessed, the black dress of the seductive Dragon Lady in *Terry and the Pirates*... Certainly I fantasized about those lascivious women, while the ones in the Italian magazines revealed legs void of mystery between knee-length skirts and enormous cork heels. *Oh as for me, it's their legs*... Which were the ones who awoke the first urges in me—those belonging to lovely milliners' assistants and domestic beauties on bicycles, or those of women from other planets and remote megalopolises? It seemed obvious that unattainable beauties would have attracted me more than the girl, or woman, next door. But who could say for sure?

If I daydreamed about my next-door neighbour or about the girls who played in the park near my house, that remained my secret, about which the publishing industry neither received, nor offered, any news.

Done with the stacks of comics, I pulled out several scattered issues of a women's magazine, *Novella,* which my mother must have read. Long love stories, a few refined illustrations featuring slender ladies and gentlemen with Britannic profiles, and photos of actors and actresses. All of it rendered in a thousand shades of brown—even the text was brown. The covers were a gallery of the beauties of the period, immortalized in extreme close-ups, and at the sight of one my heart suddenly withered, as if licked by a tongue of flame. I could not resist the urge to bend down to that face and touch my lips to its lips. I felt no physical sensation, but that is what I must have done furtively in 1939, at seven, already no doubt in the grip of certain agitations. Did that face resemble Sibilla? Paola? Vanna, the lady with the ermine? Or the others Gianni had sneeringly mentioned: Cavassi, or the American at the London book fair, or Silvana, or the Dutch girl I made three trips to Amsterdam to see?

Maybe not. Certainly I must have formed, out of all those images that had transported me, my ideal figure, and were I to have all the faces of all the women I have loved in front of me, I could extract from them an archetypal profile, an Ideal I have never realized but have pursued my whole life. What did Vanna's face and Sibilla's have in common? Perhaps more than appeared at first glance, perhaps the mischievous crinkle of a smile, the way they let their teeth show when they laughed, the gesture with which they straightened their hair. Simply the way they moved their hands would have been enough...

There was something different about the woman I had just kissed in effigy. Had I met her in person I would not have thought her worth a look. It was a photograph, and photos always look dated, lacking the Platonic lightness of a drawing, which keeps you guessing. In her I had kissed, not the image of a love object, but rather the overweening power of sex, the blatancy of lips marked by garish make-up. It had not been a hesitant, nervous kiss, but rather a primitive way of acknowledging the presence of flesh. I probably forgot the episode quickly, as a dark, forbidden event, while Abyssinian Gemmy seemed to me an unsettling but sweet figure, a distant, graceful princess—to look at, not to touch.

But how did it happen that I had saved those copies of my mother's magazine? When I returned to Solara in late adolescence, already in high school, I must have begun to salvage evidence of what even then felt like the distant past, thus devoting the dawn of my youth to retracing the lost steps of my childhood. I was already condemned to the salvaging of memory, except that back then it was a game, with all my madeleines at my disposal, and now it was a desperate struggle.

In the chapel I had in any case understood something about my discovery of the flesh and the way it both frees and enslaves. Well, that was one way to escape the thralldom of marching, uniforms, and the asexual empire of the Guardian Angels.

Was that all? Except for the Nativity scene in the attic, for example, I had found no clues to my religious feelings, and it seemed to me impossible for a child not to have harboured some, even in a secular family. And I had not found anything to shed light on what had happened from 1943 on. It may have been precisely between 1943 and 1945, after the chapel had been walled shut, that I had stashed within it the most intimate evidence of a childhood that was already blurring in the soft focus of memory: I was assuming the toga of manhood, becoming an adult in the maelstrom of the darkest years, and I had decided to conserve in a crypt a past to which I would devote my adult nostalgia.

Among the many *Tim Tyler's Luck* albums, I finally stumbled on one that made me feel I was on the cusp of some final revelation. It had a multicoloured cover and was entitled *The Mysterious Flame of Queen Loana*. There lay the explanation for the mysterious flames that had shaken me since my reawakening, and my journey to Solara was finally acquiring a meaning.

I opened the album and encountered the most insipid tale ever conceived by the human brain. It was a ramshackle story, no part of which held water: events were repetitive, characters fell instantly in love, for no reason, and Tim and Spud find Queen Loana sort of charming and sort of evil.

Tim and Spud and two friends, while travelling in Central Africa, stumble on a mysterious kingdom in which an equally mysterious queen is the guardian of an ultra-mysterious flame that grants long life, immortality even, considering that Loana, still beautiful, has been ruling over her savage tribe for two thousand years.

Loana enters the picture at a certain point, and she is neither alluring nor unsettling: she reminded me of certain parodies from early variety shows that I had recently seen on television. For the rest of the story, until she hurls herself out of lovesickness into a bottomless abyss, Loana goes hither and thither, pointlessly enigmatic, through an incredibly slipshod narrative that lacks both charm and psychology. She wants only to marry one of Tim and Spud's friends, who resembles (two peas in a pod) a prince she loved two thousand years before, whom she had killed and petrified when he refused her charms. It is unclear why Loana needs a modern double (especially one who does not love her either, having in fact fallen in love at first sight with her sister), considering that she could use her mysterious flame to bring her mummified lover back to life.

I noticed there, as I had in other comics, that neither the femmes fatales nor the satanic males (think of Ming with Dale Arden) ever sought to ravish, rape, imprison in their harems, or know carnally the objects of their lust. They always sought to marry them. Protestant hypocrisy of American origin, or an excess of bashfulness imposed on the Italian translators by a Catholic government waging a demographic battle?

As for Loana, a variety of catastrophes ensue, the mysterious flame is extinguished for ever, and for our protagonists it is goodbye immortality, which must not be such a big deal, given that they have dragged their feet so much in its pursuit and that in the end having lost the flame seems to matter very little to them—and to think they started all that hullabaloo to find it. Perhaps the authors ran out of pages, had to end the album somehow, and could no longer quite recall how or why they had begun.

In short, an incredibly dumb story. But apparently it had come across my path just as Signor Pipino had. You read any old story as a child, and you cultivate it in your memory, transform it, exalt it, sometimes elevating the blandest thing to the status of myth. In effect, what seemed to have fertilized my slumbering memory was not the story itself, but the title. The expression *the mysterious flame* had bewitched me, to say nothing of Loana's mellifluous name, even though she herself was a capricious little fashion plate dressed up as a *bayadère*. I had spent all the years of my childhood—perhaps even more—cultivating not an image but a sound. Having forgotten the "historical" Loana, I had continued to pursue the oral aura of other mysterious flames. And years later, my memory in shambles, I had reactivated the flame's name to signal the reverberation of forgotten delights.

The fog was still, as always, within me, pierced from time to time by the echo of a title.

Poking around haphazardly, I picked out a clothbound album, in landscape format. As soon as I opened it I saw that it was a collection of stamps. Clearly mine, as it bore my name at the beginning, with the date, 1943, when I presumably began collecting. The album seemed almost professionally done, with removable pages, organized alphabetically by country. The stamps were attached with hinges, though some—Italian stamps from those years, the discovery of which on envelopes or postcards may well have inaugurated my philatelic period—were thickened, their backs rough, crusted with something. I deduced that I had started out by attaching them to some cheap notebook using gum arabic. Apparently I had later learned how it was done and had tried to salvage that first draft of a collection by submerging the notebook pages in water. The stamps had come off, but had retained the indelible signs of my foolishness.

That I later learned how it was done was evidenced by a book underneath the album, a copy of Yvert and Tellier's 1935 catalogue, which I had probably found amid my grandfather's junk. That catalogue was clearly obsolete for the serious collector of 1943, but evidently it had become precious to me, and I had learned from it not the current prices or latest issues, but the method, the technique of cataloguing.

Where had I obtained stamps in those years? Had my grandfather passed them on to me, or could a person buy envelopes of assorted stamps in stores, as they do today in the stalls between Via Armorari and the Cordusio in Milan? I probably invested all of my scant capital with some stationer in the city, one who specialized in selling to budding collectors, and so those stamps that to me seemed straight from fairy tales represented currency. Or perhaps, in those years of war, with the curtailment of international trade—and domestic, too, eventually—materials of some value found their way onto the market, and at low prices, sold perhaps by some retiree in order to be able to buy butter, a chicken, a pair of shoes.

For me, that album must have been, more than a material object, a receptacle of oneiric images. I was seized with a burning fervour at the sight of each figure. Forget the old atlases. Looking through that album I imagined the clear blue seas, framed in purple, of Deutsch-Ostafrika; I saw the houses of Baghdad, framed by a tangle of Arabian-carpet lines, against a night-green background; I admired a profile of George V, sovereign of the Bermudas, in a pink frame against a blue field; the face of the bearded pasha or sultan or rajah of the Bijawar State—perhaps one of Salgari's Indian princes—subdued me with its shades of terracotta; certainly the little pea-green rectangle from the Labuan Colony was rich in Salgarian echoes; perhaps I was reading about the war that was started over Gdansk as I was handling the wine-coloured stamp marked *Danzig;* on the stamp of the state of Indore, I read FIVE RUPEES in English; I daydreamed about the strange native pirogues outlined against the

ZANZIBAR
COOK ISLANDS
NEW GUINEA
TWO POUNDS
LIECHTENSTEIN
Danzig
QUARTER ANNA
FIVE RUPEES
BIJAWAR STATE
BRITISH CENTRAL AFRICA
LABUAN
POSTAGE & REVENUE

purple backdrop of some part of the British Solomon Islands. I invented tales involving a Guatemalan landscape, the Liberian rhinoceros, another primitive boat, which filled a large stamp from Papua (the smaller the state, the larger the stamp, I was learning), and I wondered where Saargebiet was, and Swaziland.

During the years when we seemed to be penned in by insuperable barriers, pinched between two clashing armies, I travelled the wide world through the medium of stamps. When even the train connections were interrupted—when the only way to get to the city from Solara would have been by bicycle—there I was, soaring from the Vatican to Puerto Rico, from China to Andorra.

A new flutter of tachycardia seized me at the sight of two stamps from Fiji (how had I pronounced that name?). They were no prettier or uglier than the others. One showed a native, the other bore a map of the Fiji islands. Perhaps I had gone to great lengths to trade for them and so held them dearer than the others; perhaps I was struck by the map's precision, like a chart of treasure islands; perhaps I had encountered the unheard-of names of those territories for the first time upon those little rectangles. I seem to recall Paola telling me that I had a fixation: I wanted to go to Fiji some day, and I would scour the travel agency brochures, and then in the end put the trip off because it involved going to the other side of the globe, and to go for less than a month made no sense.

I kept staring at those two stamps, and I began spontaneously to sing a song I had listened to days before: "Up There at Capocabana". And along with the song came back the name Pipetto. What was it that tied the stamps to the song, and the song to the name, just the name, of Pipetto?

The mystery of Solara was that at every turn I would approach a revelation, and then I would come to a stop on the edge of a cliff, the chasm invisible before me in the fog. Like the Gorge, I said to myself. What was the Gorge?

12. Blue Skies Are on the Way

I asked Amalia if she knew anything about a gorge. "Of course I do," she replied. "The Gorge . . . I hope you haven't got it into your head to go there, because it was bad enough when you was little, but now that you're no spring chicken, you'll break your neck. Don't think I won't call Signora Paola, hmph."

I reassured her. I just wanted to know what it was.

"The Gorge? Just look out of your bedroom window, you'll see that hill far off with a little town sitting on top, that's San Martino, an itty-bitty town more like it, a village of a hundred souls, nasty people if you want to know, with a bell tower as tall as the town is wide, and they're always telling stories about how they've got the body of Saint Antoninus, which it looks like a carob pod, with a face as black as a cow pie, and fingers that stick out from under his robe like twigs, and my poor pa used to say that a hundred years ago they pulled some nobody out of the ground who already stank, put some who-knows-what on him, and set him up under glass to make a little money off the pilgrims, but nobody ever goes there anyhow, you know what people couldn't give about Saint Antoninus, which he isn't even from these parts, they probably picked him by closing their eyes and poking the calendar."

"But the Gorge?"

"The Gorge—well the only way to get to San Martino is a road that goes straight up, which even cars nowadays have a hard time with it. Not one of them roads like decent folk have that winds up the hill and gets to the top eventually. If only. No, it goes straight up, or well-nigh straight, that's why it's such a chore. And do you know why? Because on the side where the road goes up, there's a few trees and vineyards which they had to put in reinforcements to be able to go up there and tend them without sliding down towards the valley on their hind parts, but on every other side it's like the ground just fell away, a mess of briars and scrub and stones, no place to put your feet, and that's the Gorge, and folks have even got themselves killed there, took their chances without knowing what a nasty beast it was. And it's bad enough in the summer, but when the fog sets in, well you're better off taking a rope and hanging yourself from an attic beam than wandering around the Gorge, at least you'll die quicker. And then even if you've got the stomach for it, there's hellcats up there."

It was the second time Amalia had spoken of hellcats, but she tried to dodge all my questions about them, and I could not tell whether it was out of reverential awe or because when you came down to it she herself did not know what they were. I gathered they were witches, who looked like solitary old hags but who would gather at night in the steepest vineyards and in blighted places like the Gorge to cast evil spells with black cats, goats, or vipers. Mean as poison, they entertained themselves by cursing whoever crossed them and ruining their harvest.

"One time, one turned herself into a cat and snuck into a house not far from here and carried off a baby. So one of the neighbours, worried sick for his own baby, spent the night by the crib with an axe, and when the cat showed up he chopped one of its paws clean off. Then he had a bad thought and went to the house of an old woman who lived down the road and he saw that there wasn't any hand sticking out of her sleeve, and he asked how come and she started making excuses, she'd hurt herself with the sickle cutting weeds, but he said Let me take a look, and she didn't have a hand. That cat was her, and so the townsfolk took her and burned her."

"Is that true?"

"True or not, that's how my grandmother used to tell it, even though that one time my grandfather came in shouting Hellcats, hellcats, he was coming home from the tavern with his umbrella over his shoulders, and every now and then someone would grab the handle and wouldn't let go, but my grandmother said, Hush up you good-for-nothing, yes, that's what you are, you were soused as a herring and wobbling from one side of the path to the other getting that handle caught in the tree branches, hellcats nothing, and then she thrashed him good. I don't know if all them yarns are true, but once upon a time there was a priest up in San Martino who could ward off spirits, and like all priests he was a Freemason, and he got along just fine with them hellcats, but if you give money to the church, he'd ward them off and you could rest easy for a year. For a year, see, and then more money."

But the problem with the Gorge, Amalia explained, was that when I was twelve or thirteen, I used to go up there with a band of delinquents like myself to make war on the San Martino kids, trying to surprise them by climbing up that side. If she happened to see me headed that way, she would carry me back home over her shoulders, but I was like a grass snake, and nobody ever knew what hole I had disappeared into.

That must be why, as I was thinking of a cliff and a chasm, the Gorge had come to mind. Though here again, merely the word. By midmorning I was no longer thinking about the Gorge. Someone had called from town, saying that a package was waiting for me. I went down to pick it up. It was from the studio, proofs of the catalogue. I took the opportunity to visit the pharmacist: my pressure was back up to 170. All those emotions in the chapel had done it. I decided to take it easy for the day, and the proofs were a good excuse. As it turned out, it was the proofs themselves that threatened to hike my pressure up to 180, and perhaps did.

The sky was overcast, and it was quite nice in the yard. Stretched out comfortably, I began looking through the proofs. The pages had not yet been laid out, but the text was impeccable. We were going into the autumn season with a fine selection of valuable books. Well done, Sibilla.

I was about to skip over what seemed an innocuous edition of the works of Shakespeare, when I balked at the title: *Mr. William Shakespeares Comedies, Histories, & Tragedies. Published according to the True Originall Copies.* I nearly had a heart attack. Beneath the Bard's portrait, the publishers and the date: "London, Printed by Isaac Iaggard and Ed. Blount. 1623." I checked the collation, the measurements (34.2 by 22.6 centimetres, very generous margins): shiver my timbers, hell's bells, *saccaroa*—this was the unobtainable 1623 folio!

Every antiquarian, I think every collector, daydreams at some point about the ninety-year-old lady. A little old lady with one foot in the grave and no money to pay for her medications, who comes to you saying she wants to sell some of her great-grandfather's books that have been sitting in her cellar. You go to take a look, just to make sure, and find a dozen or so volumes of little value before suddenly noticing a large, poorly bound folio, its parchment cover utterly worn out, its headcaps gone, its joints failing, its corners eaten away by rats, heavily stained. You are struck by the two columns of Gothic script, you count the lines, forty-two, you race to the colophon...It is Gutenberg's forty-two-line Bible, the first book ever printed in the world. The last copy on the market (the others are all on display in famous libraries) fetched I forget how many millions of dollars—billions of lire—recently at a New York auction, secured, I believe, by some Japanese bankers, who immediately locked it away in a safe. A new copy, still in circulation, would be priceless. You could ask whatever you wanted for it, a gazillion lire.

You look at the little old lady, you know that if you gave her just ten million she would be perfectly happy, but your conscience nags at you: you offer her a hundred, two hundred million, enough to put her back on her feet for the few years she has left. Then naturally, once you get back home, hands trembling, you have no idea what to do. In order to sell the book, you would have to mobilize the great auction houses, and they would take a big chunk of the profits and the other half would go to taxes, so you would prefer to hold on to it, but you could never show it to anyone, because if word got around then half the world's thieves would be at your door, and what pleasure would there be in having that prodigious thing and not being able to make other collectors green with envy. Forget insurance, the cost would make you faint. What should you do? Loan it to the city, let them keep it, say, in a room in the Castello Sforzesco, under bulletproof glass, with four armed gorillas to guard it day and night? Then if you wanted to look at *your* book you would have to wade through a crowd of idlers who all want to see the rarest thing in the world up close. And then what do you do, elbow the next guy and say *that's my book*? Is it worth it?

It is then that you think not of Gutenberg but of Shakespeare's first folio. It would bring a few billion less, but it is well known only to collectors, so it would be easier either to keep it or to sell it. The first folio of Shakespeare. Every bibliophile's number two dream.

How much was Sibilla asking for it? I was dumbstruck: a million, as if it were any old book. Was it possible that she did not know what she had in her hands? And when had it come into the studio, and why had she not said anything? I'll fire her, I'll fire her, I murmured furiously.

I called her to ask if she realized what item 85 in the catalogue was. She sounded taken aback: it was seventeenth-century, not much to look at, indeed she was quite pleased to have already sold it, right after she sent me the proofs, for only twenty thousand lire less than the asking price, so now she was taking it out of the catalogue since it was not even the sort of thing you would leave in and mark SOLD, just to show what good pieces you had. I was about to tear into her, when she burst out laughing and told me I should watch my blood pressure.

It was a joke. She had inserted that entry to see if I was reading the proofs carefully, and if my scholarly memory was still in good shape. She laughed impishly, proud of her hoax—which among other things echoed certain celebrated pranks we fanatics like to play, and certain catalogues have themselves become collectible precisely because they offered impossible or non-existent books and even experts had been fooled.

"Such a practical joker," I finally said, but by now I was lying down. "You'll pay for that. But the rest of the entries are perfect, no need for me to send them back, I don't have any corrections. Let's go forward, thanks."

I relaxed: people do not realize it, but to somebody like me, in the state I am in, even an innocent joke could bring on the big one.

By the time I finished speaking with Sibilla, the sky had turned the colour of a bruise: another storm was coming, a real one this time. With the light as it was, I was relieved of the obligation or the temptation to go into the chapel. But the attic would still be lit by the dormers, and I could spend at least an hour browsing there.

I was rewarded with another box, unlabelled, thrown together by my aunt and uncle, full of illustrated magazines. I brought the box downstairs and began leafing through them casually, as one does in a dentist's office.

I looked at the pictures in some of the movie magazines, lots of actor photos. There were of course Italian films, these, too, utterly and openly schizophrenic: on one hand, propaganda flicks such as *The Siege of Alcazar* and *Luciano Serra, Pilot;* on the other, films with gentlemen in tuxedos, dissipated women in snow-white bed jackets, and luxurious decor, such as white telephones beside voluptuous beds—at a time when, I imagine, all phones were still black and attached to walls.

But there were also photos from foreign films, and I felt a few slight twinges of flame on seeing the sensual face of Zarah Leander, or of Kristina Söderbaum from *Goldene Stadt*.

Last, many stills from American movies—Fred Astaire and Ginger Rogers dancing like dragonflies, the John Wayne of *Stagecoach*. In the meantime I had reactivated what I thought of by now as my radio, hypocritically ignoring the gramophone that made it sing, and I had picked out some records whose titles resonated with me. My God, Fred Astaire was dancing with and kissing Ginger Rogers, but in the same years Pippo Barzizza and his orchestra were playing melodies I knew, because they were a part of everyone's musical education. It was jazz, no matter how Italianized; the record called "Serenità" was an adaptation of "Mood Indigo", another one that had been pirated as "Con stile" was "In the Mood", and "Tristezze di San Luigi" (Luigi IX or Luigi Gonzaga?) was "St. Louis Blues". None had lyrics, except for the ham-fisted ones of "Tristezze di San Luigi", so as not to give away their very un-Aryan origins.

In short, between jazz, John Wayne, and the chapel comics, my childhood had been spent learning that I was supposed to curse the English and defend myself against the evil Negroes who wanted to defile the Venus de Milo, and at the same time I was lapping up messages from the other side of the ocean.

From the bottom of the box, I plucked a packet of letters and postcards addressed to my grandfather. I wavered for a moment, because it seemed sacrilegious to pry into his personal secrets. Then I told myself that my grandfather was, after all, the recipient, not the author, of those writings, that the authors were others, to whom I owed no consideration.

I read through those missives not expecting to learn anything of significance, and yet I did: in replying to my grandfather, those people, probably friends whom he trusted, made references to things he had written to them, and a more accurate portrait of my grandfather emerged. I began to understand what he had thought, what kind of friends he had spent time with or cultivated prudently from a distance.

But it was only after having seen the little bottle that I was able to reconstruct my grandfather's political "physiognomy". It took me a while, because the account Amalia gave me had to be handled with care, but my grandfather's ideas had come through clearly in some of the letters, and some writers had made allusions to his past. Finally, one correspondent, to whom my grandfather, in 1943, had recounted the final chapter of the oil story, congratulated him on his feat.

So. I was leaning against the windows, with the desk in front of me and the bookshelves behind it. Only then did I notice, atop the bookcase directly across from me, a little bottle, roughly ten centimetres in height, an old medicine or perfume flacon, made of dark glass.

Curious, I climbed up on a chair to reach it. The top was screwed tight and still bore the red traces of ancient sealing wax. I peered into it and shook it, but it no longer seemed to contain anything. I opened it, with some difficulty, and inside I glimpsed little spots of some dark substance. What little odour it still released from within was decidedly unpleasant, like some putrid thing that had dried up decades ago.

I called Amalia. Did she know anything about it? Amalia lifted her eyes and her arms towards the heavens and began to laugh. "Ah, the castor oil, so it was still up there!"

"Castor oil? A purgative, I think…"

"Of course it was, and sometimes they gave it to you young'uns too, just a teaspoon, to make you move your bowels when something had got stuck in your little bellies. And two teaspoons of sugar right after, to kill the taste. But they gave your dear grandfather a mite more than that, at least three times what's in this little bottle here!"

Amalia, who had heard Masulu tell the story many times, began by saying that my grandfather had sold newspapers. No, he sold books, not papers, I said. And she insisted (or so I understood) that first he sold papers. Then I realized what the misunderstanding was. In those parts, they still call the man who sells the newspaper the "newspaper man". So when she said "newspaper man", I understood "newspaper vendor". But she was just repeating what she had heard others say, and my grandfather really had been a newspaperman: that is, a journalist.

As I pieced together from his correspondence, he had been one until 1922, writing for some socialist daily or weekly. In those times, with the march on Rome looming, the squadristi were going around patting subversives on the back with truncheons. But when they really wanted to punish someone, they forced him to drink a healthy dose of castor oil, to purge him of his skewed ideas. Not a teaspoonful—at least a quarter-litre. And so it happened that the squadristi one day barged into the offices of the newspaper where my grandfather worked: considering he must have been born around 1880, he would have been at least forty in 1922, whereas his persecutors were no-good youths, much younger than he. They smashed everything, including the small printing press. They threw the furniture out of the windows, and before leaving the building and nailing two planks over the door, they grabbed the two editors who were present, and after caning them as much as necessary, gave them the castor oil.

"I don't know if you know this, Signorino Yambo, but when they make a body drink that stuff there, if the poor creature manages to get home on his own two feet, I reckon I don't have to tell you where he'll be spending the next few days, which words just can't describe it, a creature shouldn't be treated that way."

I gathered, from advice contained in a letter from a Milanese friend, that from that moment on (given that the Fascists were to rise to power a few months later) my grandfather had decided to leave journalism and the active life, had opened his dusty old bookshop, and had held his tongue for twenty years, speaking or writing of politics only among trusted friends.

But he never forgot who poured that oil into his mouth, while accomplices pinched his nose shut.

"It was a fellow named Merlo, your dear grandfather knew it all along, and in twenty years he never lost track of him."

Indeed certain of the letters gave news of Merlo's activities. He had made a career of sorts as a centurion in Il Duce's militia, in charge of provisioning, and he must have lined his own pockets in the process, because he bought himself a country house.

"I'm sorry, Amalia, I understand the story about the oil, but what was in that little bottle?"

"Oh, don't ask, Signorino Yambo, that was a nasty business..."

"You have to tell me, Amalia, if I'm to understand what happened. Please make an effort."

And then, because it was me asking, Amalia tried to explain. My grandfather had returned home, his flesh weak from the oil but his spirit still unbroken. For the first two evacuations, he had no time to think about what he was doing, and his will went out with the rest. By the third or fourth evacuation, he decided to defecate into a pot. And into that pot drained the oil mixed with that other business that comes out after a person takes a purgative, as Amalia explained. My grandfather emptied a flacon of his wife's rosewater, washed it out, then transferred into it both the oil and that other business. He screwed the cap on and sealed the whole thing with wax, so none of that liquor would evaporate and it would retain its bouquet, as wines do.

He had been keeping the little bottle in his house in the city, but when we all took refuge in Solara, he brought it and put it in his study. It was clear that Masulu knew his story and shared his feelings, because every time he came into his study (Amalia was peeking or eavesdropping) he would glance at the bottle, then at my grandfather, and make a gesture: he would stick his hand out, palm down, then turn his wrist so that his palm faced up, and say in a menacing tone: "*S'as gira,*" *if it turns,* meaning if things ever change. And my grandfather, especially in later years, would reply, "It's turning, it's turning, my dear Masulu, they've already landed in Sicily..."

And eventually July 25, 1943 came around. The Fascist Grand Council had put Mussolini on the ropes the evening before, the king had fired him, and two carabinieri had taken him who knows where in an ambulance. Fascism was finished. I could bring those moments back to life by going through the newspaper collection. Banner headlines, the fall of a regime.

It was fascinating to see the newspapers from the days that followed. They reported with satisfaction on the crowds that pulled the statues of Il Duce down from their pedestals and hacked the Fascist emblem off the façades of public buildings, and on the regime leaders who slipped into civvies and out of sight. Dailies that had, until July 24, assured us of the splendid steadfastness of the Italian people's support for their Duce were by July 30 rejoicing in the dissolution of the Chamber of Fasces and Corporations and in the

Anno ... - N. 177 - Italia Impero e Colonie cent. 20 — Milano — Lunedì, 26 luglio 1943

CORRIERE DELLA SERA

Le dimissioni di Mussolini

Badoglio Capo del Governo

UN PROCLAMA DEL SOVRANO

Il Re assume il comando delle Forze Armate - Badoglio agli Italiani: "Si serrino le file intorno a Sua Maestà vivente immagine della Patria,,

L'annunzio alla Nazione

Sua Maestà il Re e Imperatore ha accettate le dimissioni dalla carica di Capo del Governo, Primo Ministro segretario di Stato, presentate da Sua Eccellenza il cavaliere Benito Mussolini ed ha nominato Capo del Governo, Primo Ministro segretario di Stato Sua Eccellenza il cavaliere Maresciallo d'Italia Pietro Badoglio. *(Stefani)*

La parola di Vittorio Emanuele

Sua Maestà il Re e Imperatore ha rivolto agli Italiani il seguente proclama:

ITALIANI,

Assumo da oggi il comando di tutte le Forze Armate.

Nell'ora solenne che incombe sui destini della Patria ognuno riprenda il suo posto di dovere, di fede e di combattimento: nessuna deviazione deve essere tollerata, nessuna recriminazione può essere consentita.

Ogni italiano si inchini dinanzi alle gravi ferite che hanno lacerato il sacro suolo della Patria.

L'Italia, per il valore delle sue Forze Armate, per la decisa volontà di tutti i cittadini, ritroverà nel rispetto delle istituzioni che ne hanno sempre confortata l'ascesa, la via della riscossa.

ITALIANI,

Sono oggi più che mai indissolubilmente unito a voi dalla incrollabile fede nell'immortalità della Patria.

Firmato: VITTORIO EMANUELE.

Controfirmato: BADOGLIO.

Roma, il 25 luglio 1943.

Precisa e chiara consegna

Sua Eccellenza il Maresciallo d'Italia Pietro Badoglio ha rivolto agli Italiani il seguente proclama:

ITALIANI,

Per ordine di Sua Maestà il Re e Imperatore assumo il Governo militare del Paese, con pieni poteri.

La guerra continua. L'Italia, duramente colpita nelle sue provincie invase, nelle sue città distrutte, mantiene fede alla parola data, gelosa custode delle sue millenarie tradizioni.

Si serrino le file attorno a Sua Maestà il Re e Imperatore, immagine vivente della Patria, esempio per tutti.

La consegna ricevuta è chiara e precisa: sarà scrupolosamente eseguita, e chiunque si illuda di poterne intralciare il normale svolgimento, o tenti turbare l'ordine pubblico, sarà inesorabilmente colpito.

Viva l'Italia. Viva il Re.

Firmato: Maresciallo d'Italia PIETRO BADOGLIO.

Roma, 25 luglio 1943.

VIVA L'ITALIA

Manifestazioni a Roma

La folla al canto dell'inno di Mameli si riversa sotto il Quirinale

Soldato del Sabotino e del Piave

L'esultanza di Milano

release of political prisoners. The manager of the paper, it is true, had changed from one day to the next, but the rest of the staff must have consisted of the same people as before: they were adapting, or else many of them, after biting their tongues for years, were finally getting sweet revenge.

And my grandfather's hour, too, had come. "It has turned," were his lapidary words to Masulu, who understood that it was time to set certain wheels in motion. He called on two sturdy young fellows who helped him in the fields, Stivulu and Gigio, their faces red from the sun and Barbera, muscles out to here—especially Gigio, who when a wagon fell into a ditch was the one called on to pull it out single-handed—and he unleashed them on the nearby towns, while my grandfather went down to the public telephone in Solara and gleaned some information from his friends in the city.

Finally, on the 30th of July, Merlo was located. His country house or estate was in Bassinasco, not too far from Solara, and that was where he had snuck off to, quietly. He had never been a bigwig and might have hoped he would be forgotten.

"We'll go on the second of August," my grandfather said, "because it was on precisely that date twenty-one years ago that that man gave me the oil, and we'll go after supper, first because it will be cooler, and second because by then he will have finished eating like a priest, and that's the best time to help him with his digestion."

They took the carriage and left at sunset for Bassinasco.

When they knocked at Merlo's house, he came to the door with a checkered napkin still tucked in his collar and asked who they were and were not, since naturally my grandfather's face meant nothing to him. They pushed him backwards, Stivulu and Gigio sat him down and held his arms behind his back, and Masulu pinched his nose shut with his thumb and index finger, which were all he needed to uncork a demijohn.

My grandfather calmly recounted the story of twenty-one years before, as Merlo shook his head, as if to say they had the wrong man, he had never been involved in politics. My grandfather, his explanation complete, then reminded his host that before pouring the oil down his throat, Merlo and his friends had encouraged him by means of a caning to say, through his pinched nose, *alalà*. He himself, being a peaceful man, did not wish to use his cane for that, and so if Merlo would be kind enough to cooperate and say that *alalà* right away, they could avoid an embarrassing scene. So Merlo, with nasal emphasis, shouted *alalà,* which, after all, was one of the few things he had learned to do.

Then my grandfather stuck the bottle in his mouth, making him swallow all the oil along with whatever amount of faecal matter was dissolved in it, the whole solution nicely aged at the proper temperature, vintage 1922, controlled denomination of origin.

They left Merlo on his knees, his face against the brick floor, trying to vomit, but his nose had been held shut long enough for the potion to make its way into the lower reaches of his stomach.

That evening, on his return, my dear grandfather was more radiant than Amalia had ever seen him before. And it seems that Merlo was so shaken up that even after September 8—when the king asked for an armistice and fled to Brindisi, Il Duce was liberated by the Germans, and the Fascists returned—he did not go to Salò to join Mussolini's new Italian Social Republic, but stayed home instead and worked in his garden. He too must be dead by now, the wretched man, Amalia said, and she thought that even had he wanted to avenge himself by telling the Fascists, he had likely been so terrified that night that he would have been unable to recall the faces of those men who had entered his house—and who knows how many others he had made drink oil? "Some of them folks must have kept an eye on him all them years, too, and I reckon he gulped down more than one little bottle, I'm telling you and you can believe it, and that's the sort of business that can make a man lose his taste for politics."

That, then, is who my grandfather was, and it explained those underlined newspapers and Radio London. He was waiting for the turn.

I found a copy, dated July 21, of a paper in which the end of the regime was hailed, in a single exultant message, by the Democratic Christian Party, the Action Party, the Communist Party, the Socialist Party, and the Liberal Party. If I saw that, and surely I did, I must have instantly understood that for those parties to come out of the woodwork overnight meant they had existed before, underground, somewhere. Perhaps that was how I began to understand what democracy was.

My grandfather also kept broadsheets from the Republic of Salò, and one of them, *Il Popolo di Alessandria* (what a surprise! there was Ezra Pound's byline!), contained vicious cartoons against the king, whom the Fascists hated not only for having had Mussolini arrested but also for having asked for an armistice before fleeing South to join the hated Anglo-Americans. The cartoons were also furious with his son, Umberto, who had followed him. They depicted the two in perpetual flight, kicking up little clouds of dust, the king short, nearly a dwarf, and the prince tall as a beanpole, the one nicknamed Stumpy Quickfoot and the other the Fairy Heir. Paola told me I had always favoured republics, and it seems I received my first lesson from the very people who had made the king emperor of Ethiopia. The ways of providence, as they say.

I asked Amalia if my grandfather had told me the story of the oil. "Why of course! First thing the next day. He was tickled pink! He sat on the edge of your bed as soon as you woke up, told you all of it and showed you the bottle."

"And what did I do?"

"And you, Signorino Yambo, I remember it like it was yesterday, clapped your hands and yelled Hooray, Grandpa, you're better than gudòn."

"Than gudòn? What was that?"

"How should I know? But that's what you was yelling, like it was yesterday."

It was not gudòn, but Gordon. I was celebrating in my grandfather's act the revolt of Gordon against Ming, tyrant of Mongo.

13. The Pallid Little Maiden

I had followed my grandfather's adventure with all the enthusiasm of a reader of comic books. But in my chapel collections there was nothing between the middle of 1943 and the end of the war. Only, from 1945, the strips I had collected from the liberators. Maybe comics were no longer published during those years or never made it to Solara. Or maybe after September 8 of '43 I witnessed real events that were so fantastic—what with the Partisans, the Black Brigades coming to our house, the arrival of clandestine broadsheets—that they outstripped anything I could have read in comics. Or maybe I felt too old for comics by then, and those were the very years I moved on to spicier fare, such as *The Count of Monte Cristo* and *The Three Musketeers*.

In any case, up until that point, Solara had not given me back anything that was truly and uniquely mine. What I had rediscovered were the things I had read, which countless others had also read. All my archaeology boiled down to this: except for the story of the unbreakable glass and a charming anecdote about my grandfather (but not about me), I had not relived my own childhood so much as that of a generation.

Up until that point, the songs had made the clearest statements. I went into the study to turn the radio back on, selecting songs at random. The first song the radio offered me was another of those light-hearted farces that accompanied the bombardments:

Last night it happened, as I was walking by,
that a crazy young guy
suddenly asked me if I
would join him for a drink, so off we went,
and with a strange accent
he began to tell his tale:
"I know a little lady,
her hair as blond as gold,
and yet my love for her cannot be told...
My grandma used to say
that way back in her day
young lovers talked this way:
I would love to kiss
your hair so long and black,
your rosy lips,
your eyes that all deception lack...
But with my sweet beloved
I can never be so bold,
because her hair's as blond as gold!"

The second song was definitely older, and more of a tear-jerker—it must have made my mother cry:

Oh pallid little maiden,
who lived across the hall on the fifth floor,
no night goes by that I don't dream of Naples,
and I left twenty years ago or more.

...My little son
in a yellowed Latin book of mine
discovered—can you guess?—a pansy...
Why did a teardrop tremble in my eye?
Oh who knows, who knows why...

And myself? The comic books in the chapel told me that I had been exposed to revelations of sex—but what about love? Had Paola been the first woman in my life?

It was strange that nothing in the chapel dated from the period between my thirteenth and eighteenth years, for during those five years—that was before the disaster—I still went to the house regularly.

I suddenly recalled having glimpsed three boxes that had not been on the shelves, but up against the altar. I had paid them little mind, caught up as I was in the multihued allure of my collections, but perhaps they were worth a look.

The first box was full of photographs of my childhood. I expected some great revelation, but no. I felt only a powerful, religious emotion. Having seen the photos of my parents in the hospital and the one of my grandfather in his study, I was able to identify them, even at different ages, by their clothes, recognizing them as younger or older depending on the length of my mother's skirt. That child in the sun hat poking the snail on the rock must have been me; that toddler solemnly holding my hand was Ada; Ada and I were the creatures in white outfits, almost a tailcoat for me, almost a bridal gown for her, on the occasion of a first communion or confirmation; I was the second Balilla Boy on the right, standing in line with my little musket clasped to my chest, one foot forward; and there I was, a little older, standing next to a black American soldier who had a sixty-four-tooth smile, perhaps the first liberator I had met and had myself immortalized with after April 25.

Only one of the photos truly moved me: a snapshot (which had been enlarged, you could tell by the blurriness) showing a little boy leaning slightly forward, embarrassed, as a tiny girl tipped up on little white shoes, put her arms around his neck, and kissed him on the cheek. Mamma or Papà must have caught us unawares, as Ada, tired of posing, spontaneously rewarded me with sisterly affection.

I knew the boy was me and the girl was her, and I could not help being affected by the sight, but it was as if I had seen it in a movie, and I was moved as a stranger might be before an artistic representation of brotherly love. The way one is moved by Millet's *Angelus,* Hayez's *The Kiss,* or a pre-Raphaelite Ophelia floating upon a blanket of jonquils, water lilies, and asphodels.

Were they really asphodels? How should I know, once again it was the word flexing its muscle, not the image. People say our brains have two hemispheres: the left, which presides over rational relationships and verbal language, and the right, which deals with emotions and the visual universe. Perhaps my right hemisphere was paralysed. And yet it was not, because there I was dying of consumption in my quest for something or other, and a quest is a passion, not a dish served cold like revenge.

I put away the photos, which only made me nostalgic for the unknown, and took out the second box.

It contained holy cards, many of Domenico Savio, a pupil of Don Bosco's, whose ardent piety the painters revealed by depicting him in creased trousers that sagged beneath his knees, as if he kept them bent all day, lost in prayer. Then a little volume with a black binding and red edges, like a breviary: *The Provident Young Man,* by Don Bosco himself. An 1847 edition, in rather bad shape—who knows who had passed it down to me. Edifying readings and collections of hymns and prayers. Many of them exalting purity as the highest virtue.

Other pamphlets, too, contained ardent exhortations to purity, invitations to abstain from wicked spectacles, dubious company, and dangerous readings. It seemed that of all the commandments the sixth was the most important, not committing impure acts, and many of the teachings were rather transparently directed against the illicit touching of one's own body, to the point of advising young readers to lay themselves down at night in a supine fashion, their hands crossed over their chests, so that their bellies would not press into the mattress. Warnings against contact with the opposite sex were rare, as if the likelihood of that were remote, impeded by strict social conventions. The prime enemy, though the word was generally avoided in favour of cautious circumlocutions, was masturbation. One little handbook explained that the only animals that masturbate are fish: it must have been alluding to external insemination; many fishes spill their spermatozoa and their eggs into the water, which then takes care of the fertilization—meaning that those poor creatures were not sinning by spilling their seed in improper vessels. Nothing about apes, for whom onanism is a calling. And silence regarding homosexuality, as if allowing oneself to be touched by a seminarian were no sin.

I also picked up a very worn copy of Don Domenico Pilla's *Little Martyrs*. It is the story of two pious youths, a boy and a girl, who suffer the most horrible tortures at the hands of anticlerical, Satan-worshipping Freemasons who, out of hatred for our blessed religion, want to initiate the youths into the joys of sin. But crime does not pay. The sculptor Bruno Cherubini, who had carved the Statue of Sacrilege for the Masons, is wakened at night by the apparition of his partner in debauchery, Volfango Kaufman. After their last orgy, Volfango and Bruno had made a pact: the first to pass on would return to tell the other what awaited in the great beyond.

Dinanzi a lui era comparso uno spaventoso fantasma avvolto in un ampio lenzuolo.

Thus Volfango emerges post-mortem from the mists of Tartarus, wrapped in a shroud, his eyes bulging from his Mephistophelian face. His incandescent flesh glows with a sinister light. The ghost identifies himself and declares: "Hell exists, and I'm there!" And he tells Bruno, "If you want proof, extend your right hand"; the sculptor obeys and the spectre lets fall a droplet of sweat that passes through Bruno's hand from one side to the other, like molten lead.

The dates of the book and the pamphlets, even when given, told me nothing, because I could have read them at any age, and so I was unable to determine whether it was during the last years of the war or after my return to the city that I had gone in for pious practices. Was it a reaction to the war's events, a way of dealing with the tempests of puberty, or a series of disappointments that had sent me into the welcoming arms of the Church?

The only real scraps of myself were in the third box. On the very top, several issues of *Radiocorriere* from '47 and '48, with certain programmes marked and annotated. The handwriting was unquestionably mine, and hence those pages told me what I alone had wanted to hear. The underlined entries, except for a few late-night programmes devoted to poetry, were mostly chamber and concert music. They were brief entr'actes between one programme and another, early in the morning, in the afternoon, or late in the evening: three études, a nocturne, on a good day an entire sonata. Strictly for diehard fans, scheduled in the off-hours. After the war, then, back in the city, I had eagerly awaited those musical events, slowly becoming an addict, glued to the radio, which I turned down low so as not to disturb the rest of my family. My grandfather had some classical records, but who can say he did not buy them later, precisely to encourage my new passion? Before that, I had noted down like a spy the rare occasions when I could listen to my music, and who knows how angry I felt, going into the kitchen for a long-awaited date and being prevented from listening by shuffling busybodies or nattering salesmen, by women tidying up or rolling out sheets of dough for pasta.

Chopin was the composer I had underlined most emphatically. I carried the box into my grandfather's study, turning on both the record player and the station panel of my Telefunken, and began my latest quest to the strains of the Sonata in B-flat Minor, opus 35.

Beneath the *Radiocorriere* were several notebooks from my final three years of high school, '47 to '50. I must have had a truly great philosophy teacher, because the better part of what I know on the subject was right there, in my notes. Then there were drawings and cartoons, jokes I had shared with my schoolmates, and our end-of-the-year class pictures, all of us lined up in three or four rows with our teachers in the centre. Those faces told me nothing, and I even had trouble recognizing myself and had to proceed mainly by elimination, latching onto the last tufts of Ciuffettino's quiff.

Mixed in with the school notebooks was another, which began with the date 1948, but the handwriting gradually changed as I turned the pages, so perhaps it contained texts from the subsequent three years as well. They were poems.

Poems so bad they could have been no one's but mine. Teenage acne. I think everyone writes poems when they are sixteen; it is a phase in the passage from adolescence to adulthood. I do not remember where I read that there are two kinds of poets: the good poets, who at a certain point destroy their bad poems and go off to run guns in Africa, and the bad poets, who publish theirs and keep writing more until they die.

Perhaps that is not really how things go, but my poems were bad. Not dreadful or repulsive, which might suggest some genius provocateur, but pathetically obvious. Was it worth it to come back to Solara to discover that I was a hack? But at least I could be proud of one thing: I had sealed away those abortions in a box, in a chapel with a walled-up door, and had dedicated myself to collecting other people's books. I must have been, at eighteen, admirably lucid, critically incorruptible.

But although I had buried them, I had in fact kept them, so I must have retained some attachment to those poems, even after the acne had passed. As records. Some people who rid themselves of a tapeworm save the head in an alcohol solution and others do likewise with stones removed from their gall bladders.

The first poems were sketches, fleeting revelations in the face of nature's charms, the sort every budding poet writes: winter mornings that hinted amid the frost at a sly desire for April, jumbles of lyrical reticence about the mysterious colour of an August evening, many (too many) moons, and only one moment of humility:

Tell me, moon in the sky, what do you do?
I go about my life,
my dull, colourless life,
because I am a heap
of earth, and lifeless valleys,
and tedious extinct
volcanoes.

By God, perhaps I had not been such a fool after all. Or maybe I had just discovered the Futurists, who wanted to kill off moonlight. But right after that I read a few verses about Chopin, his music and his unhappy life. Think about it, at sixteen no one writes poems about Bach, who lost it only on the day his wife died, telling the vultures, when they asked him what he wanted in the way of obsequies, to ask her. Chopin seems made to order for bringing sixteen-year-olds to tears: his departure from Warsaw with Constantia's ribbon over his heart, death looming at the Valldemossa monastery. Only when you get older do you realize he wrote some good music, before that you just cry.

The next poems were about memory. With milk still on my lips, I was already worrying about gathering remembrances that had barely had any time to fade. One poem declared:

I build myself memories.
I stretch

life into this mirage.
With every passing moment,
with every instant,
I gently turn a page
with my unsteady hand.
And memory is that wave
that ripples the waters briefly
and disappears.

Very short lines, no doubt I learned that from the Hermetics.

A lot of poems about hourglasses, which spin time into a thin filament and deposit it into the intense granaries of memory, a hymn to Orpheus (!) in which I warned him that *you cannot enter twice / the kingdom of remembrance / and hope to find unspoiled / the unexpected freshness / of the first theft.* Advice to myself: *I should not have wasted / a single moment*... Marvellous, all it took was one overflowing artery and I wasted everything. To Africa, to Africa, to run guns.

In addition to the rest of my lyric offal, I was writing love poems. So, I was in love. Or was I rather, as often happens at that age, in love with love? In any case I wrote about a "she", however impalpable:

Creature contained
within that transient mystery
that keeps you far from me,
perhaps you were born merely
to live these verses, yet
you do not know it.

Troubadouric enough, and with hindsight equally chauvinist. Why would she have been born merely to live my poor verses? If she did not exist, I was a monogamous pasha turning the fair sex into flesh for my imaginary harem, and that can only be called masturbation, even if one ejaculates with a quill pen. But what if the Contained Creature was real and truly had not known? Then I was a dunce, but who was she?

I saw no images before me, just words, and I felt no mysterious flame, if only because Queen Loana had disappointed me. But I felt something, to the point of being able to anticipate certain lines as I gradually went on reading: *one day you will disappear / and perhaps it was a dream.* A poetic figment never disappears, you write it down to make it eternal. If I feared she might melt away, it was because the poem was a poor stand-in for something that I had been unable to approach. *Incautiously I built / upon the transient sands of moments spent / in the presence of a face, simply a face. / But I do not know if I regret the instant / in which you damned me to construct a world.* I was constructing a world for myself, but in order to welcome someone else.

Indeed, I read a description that was too detailed to have referred to a fictional creation:

As she passed blithely by through the May air,
her hair in a new style,
a student standing near me
(older, taller, and blond)
said grinning to his friends
that the adhesive bandage on his neck
covered a syphiloma.

And farther on a yellow jacket appeared, like a vision of the Angel of the Sixth Trumpet. The girl existed, and I could never have invented the syphiloma sleazeball. And what of this one, among the last in the love section?

An evening just like this,
three days before Christmas,

I was deciphering love
for the first time.
An evening just like this,
the snow crushed flat along the avenues,
and I was making noise beneath a window
hoping to be seen by a certain someone
throwing snowballs,
and thinking that sufficed
to place myself in the upper ranks of men.
So many seasons now
have changed the cells and tissues of my body
that I may not persist even in memory.

Only you, only you,
gone off to who knows where (where have you gone?),
as I still find you in the muscle of
my heart,
and with the same amazement as three days
before Christmas.

To this Contained Creature, who was clearly real, I had devoted my three most formative years. Then (*where have you gone?*) I lost her. And perhaps during the period when I lost my parents and grandfather and was moving to Turin, I decided to put that behind me, as the final two poems suggest. Though they had been slipped into the notebook, they were not handwritten but typed. I doubt we used typewriters in high school. So these final two poetic efforts must have dated from the beginning of my college years. Strange to find them here, since everyone told me I stopped coming to Solara at the very beginning of that period. But perhaps after my grandfather's death, as my aunt and uncle were settling everything, I had come back to the chapel, to put a final seal on memories I was renouncing, and had left these two pages as a kind of testament and farewell. They sound like a farewell, as if I were settling my accounts, with my poetry and my soft adulteries alike, by leaving everything behind.

The first began:

Oh the pale dames of Renoir
The balcony ladies of Manet
The outdoor tables on the boulevards
And the white parasol in the landau
Faded with the last cattleya
at Bergotte's final breath...

Let's look each other in the eyes:
Odette de Crecy
Was a great whore.

The second was entitled "The Partisans". It was all that remained of my memories from '43 until the end of the war:

Talino, Gino, Ras, Lupetto, Sciabola
may you come down together some spring day
singing the wind is whistling the storm is howling
for how I long to have them back, those summers
of sudden rifle shots up high in the hills
breaking the silence of the midday sun
of afternoons spent waiting,
of news that made the rounds in quiet voices:
the Decima retreats, the Badogliani
are coming down tomorrow, the roadblock's gone,
the road to Orbegno is impassable,
they're carrying the wounded off in gigs,
I saw them going by the Oratorio,
Sergeant Garrani locked himself inside
the City Hall...

Then suddenly the dreadful racket,
the hellish noise, the tapping on the wall
of the house, a voice in the alley...
And the night, silence and occasional shots,
from San Martino, and the final sweeps...

I'd like to dream about those endless summers
that fed on certainty like blood,
about those days in which
Talino, Ras and Gino may have looked
into the face of truth.

But I cannot, for there remains
my own roadblock
on the road to the Gorge.
And so I close the notebook
of memory. By now they're gone,
the clear nights in which
the Partisan in the woods
watched the little birds so they wouldn't sing,
so Sleeping Beauty could remain asleep.

These verses remained a puzzle. Evidently I had experienced a period that seemed heroic to me, at least as long as I saw others as the protagonists. While trying to settle all the enquiries into my childhood and adolescence, I had tried, on the threshold of adulthood, to call back certain moments of exaltation and certainty. But I was blocked (the last roadblock of that war fought outside my door) and I had surrendered in the face of—what? Something I could not or would not call back to mind, something that had to do with the Gorge. The Gorge, once again. Had I seen the hellcats there and had that encounter taught me that I must blot out everything? Or, since I was by then aware that I had lost the Contained Creature, had I turned other days, and the Gorge, into an allegory of that loss—thus explaining why I was putting away everything I had been, up to that moment, in the chapel's inviolable coffer?

Nothing else remained, at least not at Solara. I could only infer that after that renunciation, I had decided to devote myself, already a student, to old books, to turn my attention to someone else's past, one that would not have anything to do with me.

But who was that Creature who, fleeing, had convinced me to file away both my high school years and my time at Solara? Had I, too, had my pallid little maiden, a sweet girl who lived across the hall on the fifth floor? If that was the case, it was just another song and nothing more, a song everyone has sung at one time or another.

The only person who might have known anything about it was Gianni. If you fall in love, and for the first time, you at least confide in your desk mate.

Some days ago I had not wanted Gianni to clear away the fog of my memories with the calm light of his own, but on this point I could call upon nothing but his memory.

It was already evening when I phoned him, and we talked for several hours. I began in a roundabout way, talking about Chopin, and I learned that in those days the radio really had been our only source for the great music for which we were developing a passion. In the city, it was not until our fifth and final year of high school that a friends-of-music society had been formed: from time to time it offered a violin or piano concert, a trio at most, and in our class there were only four of us who went, almost furtively, because the other rascals, though not yet eighteen, were always trying to get into the brothel, and they looked at us as if we were light in the loafers. Okay, we had shared some thrills, I could risk it. "In the third year of high school, did I start thinking about a girl?"

"So you've forgotten about that too, then. Every cloud has a silver lining. Why should you care, so much time has passed... Come on, Yambo, think of your health."

"Don't be an ass, I've discovered certain things here that intrigue me. I have to know."

He seemed to hesitate, then lifted the lid off his memories, growing quite animated, as if he had been the one in love. And indeed that was nearly the case, because (so he told me) up to that time he had remained immune to love's torments, and my confidences intoxicated him as if the affair had been his own.

"And besides, she really was the most beautiful girl in her class. You had high standards, you did. You fell in love, yes, but only with the most beautiful girl."

"*Alors, moi, j'aime qui?... Mais cela va de soi! / J'aime—mais c'est forcé—la plus belle qui soit!*"

"What's that?"

"I don't know, it came to me. But tell me about her. What was her name?"

"Lila, Lila Saba."

Nice name. I let it melt in my mouth like honey. "Lila. Nice. And so, how did it happen?"

"In the third year of high school, we were still pimply boys in knickerbockers. The girls our age, sixteen or so, were already women, and they wouldn't even look at us. They would rather flirt with the college students who came to wait for them by the gate. You saw her once and were smitten. A Dante and Beatrice kind of thing, and I'm not just saying that, because that was the year they made us study *La Vita Nuova* and *clear cool sweet waters,* and those were the only things you learned by heart, because they were about you. In short, you were thunderstruck. You spent a week walking around in a daze with a lump in your throat, not touching food, to the point where your parents thought you were ill. Then you wanted to find out what her name was, but you didn't dare ask around for fear that everyone would notice how you felt. Fortunately Ninetta Foppa was in your class, a nice, squirrel-faced girl who lived near you, and you had played together since you were kids. So when you ran into her on the stairs, after chatting about other things, you asked her the name of the girl you had seen her with the day before. Then at least you knew her name."

"Then what?"

"I'm telling you, you turned into a zombie. And since you were quite religious at that time, you went to see your spiritual director, Don Renato, one of those priests who rode around on a moped wearing a beret, who everyone said was broad-minded. He even allowed you to read the books in the Index, since it was important to exercise one's critical faculties. I wouldn't have had the guts to go and tell something like that to a priest, but you just had to tell someone. You know, you were like that guy in the joke who gets shipwrecked on a desert island, alone with the most beautiful and famous actress in the world, and the inevitable happens, but the guy still isn't happy and can't be content until he persuades her to dress up as a man and to draw on a moustache with charred cork, and then he takes her by the arm and says, 'Gustavo, you'll never guess who I laid'..."

"Don't be vulgar, this is a serious matter for me. What did Don Renato say?"

"What do you expect a priest to say, even a broad-minded one? That your feeling was noble and beautiful and natural, but that you shouldn't spoil it by transforming it into a physical relationship, because it was important to remain pure until marriage, and therefore you should keep it secret in the depths of your heart."

"And me?"

"And you, like a pea-brain, you kept it secret in the depths of your heart. In my opinion, it was partly because you had an insane fear of approaching her. But the depths of your heart weren't enough, so you came and told me everything, and I even had to be your accomplice."

"Why, if I never approached her?"

"The situation was that you lived right behind the school. When you got out all you had to do was turn the corner and you were home. The girls, one of the principal's rules, were let out after the boys. So there was no way you could ever see her, unless you planted yourself like a dumb-ass in front of the high school steps. Basically, both us and the girls had to cross the grounds, which let out into a square, Largo Minghetti, and from there we all went our separate ways. She lived right on Largo Minghetti. So you would come out, pretend to accompany me to the edge of the grounds, all the while waiting for the girls to come out, then you would go back and pass her as she was coming down the stairs with her friends. You would pass her, look at her, and that's it. Every damn day."

"And I was satisfied."

"Oh no you weren't. Then you began to get up to all kinds of mischief. You got involved with charity drives so the principal would let you go from class to class selling tickets of some kind, and in her class you would somehow contrive to spend an extra half-minute at her desk, perhaps trying to find the right change. You managed to bring on a toothache, because your parents' dentist was also on Largo Minghetti and his windows faced the balcony of her house. You would complain of terrible pains, and the dentist wouldn't know what else to do, so just to be safe he'd start drilling. You got yourself drilled a bunch of times for nothing, but you would arrive a half-hour early so you could stay in the waiting room and peep out of the window at her balcony. Of course, did she ever come out—not once. One evening it was snowing and a group of us went to the cinema, also on Largo Minghetti, and you started a snowball fight and started screaming like a wild man, we thought you were drunk. You were hoping she would hear the ruckus and come to the window, and just think what a fine figure you'd have cut. Some old hag came to the window instead, shouted that she was calling the police. And then, your stroke of genius. You organized the revue, the extravaganza, the high school's big show. You risked failing your exams that year because you were thinking of nothing but the revue, the script, the musical numbers, the stage design. And finally the great occasion: three shows so that the entire school, families included, could come to the main hall and see the greatest show on earth. She came two nights in a row. The pièce de résistance was Signora Marini. Signora Marini was the natural sciences teacher, skinny as a rail, flat as a board, kept her hair in a bun and always wore big tortoiseshell glasses and a black smock. You were as skinny as she was, and it was easy for you to dress up as her. In profile, you were her spitting image. As soon as you walked out on stage, they started clapping like Caruso never heard. Now, during class Signora Marini was always taking cough drops out of her handbag and she'd slide them from one cheek to the other for half an hour. When you opened your handbag, you pretended to put a lozenge in your mouth and then you stuck your tongue in your cheek, well, let me tell you, it brought the house down, a single roar that lasted a good five minutes. With a flick of your tongue you had hundreds of people in spasms. You had become a star. But it was clear that what excited you was that she was there and had seen you."

"Didn't I think at that point that I could make a move?"

"Sure, and your promise to Don Renato?"

"So except when I was selling her tickets, I never spoke to her?"

"A few times. For instance, they used to take the whole school to Asti to see Alfieri's tragedies, the matinée was just for us, and four of us managed to commandeer a box. You looked for her in the other boxes and in the orchestra, and you saw that she had ended up in overflow seating in the back, where she couldn't see anything. So during the intermission you contrived to cross her path, said hi, asked her if she liked the play, and when she lamented that she couldn't see very well, you told her that we had a lovely box with one seat still empty, if she wanted to join us. She did, and she watched the remaining acts leaning forward, while you sat behind her on one of those little sofas. You couldn't see the stage any more, but you stared at the back of her neck for two hours. Almost an orgasm."

"And then?"

"And then she thanked you and rejoined her friends. You had been nice and she was thanking you. As I said, they were already women, they didn't give a crap about us."

"Even though I had been the star of the big show at school?"

"Right, and do you think women fell in love with Jerry Lewis? They thought he was clever, and that's it."

Okay, Gianni was telling me the banal story of a high school romance. But it was in telling me the rest of the story that he helped me understand something. I had spent my third year of high school in a state of delirium. Then summer vacation came, and I suffered like a dog because I did not know where she was. When she returned in the autumn, I continued my silent rituals of adoration (and meanwhile, as I now knew and Gianni did not, I continued to write my poems). It was like being with her day by day, and by night, too, I would guess.

But in the middle of our second year Lila Saba vanished. She left the school and, as I later learned from Ninetta Foppa, the city too, with her whole family. It was a murky affair, even Ninetta knew little about it, just scraps of gossip. Her father was in some trouble, fraudulent bankruptcy or something. He had left everything in the lawyers' hands, and while waiting for things to get straightened out had taken a job overseas—and things never got straightened out, because the family never came back.

No one knew where they had fetched up, some said Argentina, some Brazil. South America, in a period when for us Lugano was the ultima Thule. Gianni made an effort: it seemed that Lila's best friend was a certain Sandrina, but this Sandrina, out of loyalty, was not talking. We were sure she was in correspondence with Lila, but she was a tomb—and after all, who were we that she should tell us anything.

I spent the year and a half before graduation constantly on edge—and sad—I was a mess. I thought only about Lila Saba, and where she might be.

Then, Gianni said, I seemed to forget about it completely when I went off to college; between my freshman year and the time I finished my degree I had two girlfriends, and after that I met Paola. Lila should have remained a nice adolescent memory, the sort everyone has. Instead, I had looked for her the rest of my life. I even thought of going to South America, hoping to meet her on the streets of, who knows, Tierra del Fuego or Pernambuco. In a moment of weakness I had confessed to Gianni that in every woman I had an affair with I was always looking for Lila's face. I wanted to see her again at least once before I died, no matter how she had turned out. You would spoil your memories, Gianni would say. That did not matter, I was unable to leave that account unsettled.

"You spent your life looking for Lila Saba. I used to say it was just an excuse to meet other women. I didn't take you very seriously. I realized it was serious only in April."

"What happened in April?"

"Yambo, that's what I don't want to tell you, because that's what I told you a few days before your incident. I'm not saying there was any direct connection, but just to be on the safe side let's drop it, besides, I don't think it's a big deal..."

"No, now you have to tell me everything, otherwise my blood pressure will go up. Spit it out."

"Well, I went back home at the beginning of April, to take flowers to the cemetery, as I sometimes do, and because I felt a little nostalgic for our old city. Nothing has changed since we left it, so it makes me feel young to go back. While there I ran into Sandrina, like us she's pushing sixty, but she hasn't really changed much. We went for a coffee and talked about the old days. We talked and talked, and I asked her about Lila Saba. Didn't you know, she said—and how the hell could I have known?—didn't you know Lila died right after we graduated? Don't ask how or why, she said, I sent letters to her in Brazil, and her mother sent them back and told me what had happened, imagine, the poor thing, dead at eighteen. And that was it. Basically, even for Sandrina it was ancient history."

For forty years I had been all worked up over a ghost. I had made a clean break with my past at the beginning of college; of all my memories, hers was the only one I had been unable to put behind me, and without knowing it I had been spinning my wheels in a tomb. How poetic. And excruciating.

"But what was Lila Saba like?" I asked, persisting. "At least tell me what she was like."

"What do you want me to say? She was pretty, I liked her, too, and when I'd tell you that you'd act all proud, the way a man gets when someone tells him what a pretty wife he has. She had blond hair almost down to her waist, a face somewhere between angelic and devilish, and when she laughed you could see her two front teeth..."

"There must be some photograph of her around, our class photos!"

"Yambo, the high school, our old high school, burned down in the sixties, walls, desks, files, and all. There's a new one now, it's hideous."

"Her friends, Sandrina, someone must have photos..."

"Could be, I'll check if you want, though I'm not really sure how to go about asking. Beyond that, what can you do? Not even Sandrina after nearly fifty years remembers what city she moved to, said it had some weird name, wasn't one of the famous ones like Rio—you want to lick your finger and go through every Brazilian phone book looking for Sabas? You might find a thousand. Or maybe the father changed his name when they fled. And say you go there, who will you find? Her parents must be dead, too, by now, or else addlebrained, as they would no doubt be past ninety. You're going to say, Excuse me I was just passing by and I'd like to see a photo of your daughter Lila?"

"Why not?"

"Come on, why keep chasing after these fantasies? Let the dead bury their dead. You don't even know what cemetery her headstone's in. And besides, her name wasn't even Lila."

"What was her name?"

"Oops, I should have shut up. Sandrina mentioned it to me in April, and I told you right away because it was such an odd coincidence, but I immediately saw that the news hit you harder than it should have. Much too hard, if I may say, because it truly is only a coincidence. But fine, I'll spit this out too. Lila was a nickname for Sibilla."

A profile I had seen in a French magazine when I was a child, a face I encountered on the school stairs as a boy, and then other faces that perhaps all had some common thread, Paola, Vanna, the pretty Dutchwoman, and so on, all the way to Sibilla, the living one, who is getting married soon, and so I will lose her too. A relay race across the years, a quest for something that had ceased to exist even before I had stopped writing my poems.

I recited:

I am alone, leaning in the fog
against an avenue's trunk...
And nothing in my heart
except your memory,
pallid and colossal
and lost in the cold lights and far away
from every place among the trees.

This is beautiful because it is not mine. A colossal but pallid memory. Among all the treasures of Solara, not a single photo of Lila Saba. Gianni can call her face to mind as if it were yesterday and I—the only one with the right—cannot.

14. The Hotel of the Three Roses

Does anything remain for me to do in Solara? It is now clear that the most important episode of my adolescence played out elsewhere, in the city in the late forties, and in Brazil. Some of those places (the house I grew up in, the high school) no longer exist, and the more distant places, where Lila spent the last years of her brief life, may not, either. The last documents that Solara was able to offer me were my poems, which have given me a glimpse of Lila without letting me see her face. Again I find a wall of fog before me.

That was what I thought this morning. I felt I had one foot already out of the door, but I wanted to say a last goodbye to the attic. I was convinced there was nothing more for me to find up there, but I was spurred on by an impossible desire to find some final trace.

I went back over those now familiar spaces: here the toys, there the armoires full of books...I noticed that, between the two armoires, one unopened box remained. More novels, including a few classics by Conrad and Zola, along with popular fiction like the adventures of the Scarlet Pimpernel by the Baroness Orczy...

There was also an Italian detective novel from the thirties, *The Hotel of the Three Roses,* by Augusto de Angelis. Once again I had found a book that was telling my story:

Rain fell in long strands, which in the glare of headlights looked like silver. The pervasive, smoky fog stuck its needles in your face. The infinite theory of umbrellas flowed in waves over the pavements. Cars in the middle of the road, a few carriages, brimming trams. By six in the evening it was pitch dark, in those early days of December in Milan.

Three women were hurrying along, jerkily, as if in gusts, cutting as best they could through the ranks of pedestrians. All three were dressed in black, in pre-war fashion, with little hats of mesh and beads…

And the three were so similar one to the other that, had it not been for the differently coloured ribbons—mauve, violet, black—knotted under their chins, passers-by would have thought they were hallucinating, certain they were seeing the same person three times over. They turned onto Via Ponte Vetero from Via dell'Orso, and when they came to the end of the brightly lit pavement, all three leapt into the darkness of Piazza del Carmine…

The man, who was following them but seemed reluctant to catch up to them, stopped when they had crossed the piazza, and remained standing in front of the church façade, in the rain…

He looked annoyed. He stared at the small black entryway… He waited, still staring at the small entry to the church. Every so often some black shadow crossed the piazza and disappeared through the doors. The fog thickened. A half-hour passed and more. The man seemed resigned… He had leaned his umbrella against the wall, so it would dry, and he rubbed his hands with a slow, rhythmic motion that accompanied an interior monologue…

He took Via Mercato out of Piazza del Carmine, and then Via Pontaccio, and when he found himself before a large glass-paned door, beyond which appeared an enormous, brightly lit lobby, he opened it and went in. On the glass panes it said in large letters: HOTEL OF THE THREE ROSES…

That was me: in the pervasive fog I had glimpsed three women, Lila, Paola, and Sibilla, who in the haze appeared indistinguishable, and who had suddenly disappeared into the darkness. Pointless to look for them now, especially as the mist was thickening. The solution lay elsewhere, perhaps. Better to turn onto Via Pontaccio, enter the brightly lit lobby of a hotel (but would the lobby not open onto the scene of the crime?). Where was the Hotel of the Three Roses? Everywhere, for me. *A rose by any other name.*

At the bottom of the box was a layer of newspapers, and beneath the newspapers, two much older tomes, in large format. One was a Bible with Doré engravings, but in such poor condition as to be little more than fodder for street vendors. The other had a binding that was no more than a hundred years old, in half leather, the spine blank and worn, the marbled boards faded. As soon as I opened it, I was fairly sure it was a seventeenth-century volume.

The typesetting and the two columns of text put me on full alert, and I raced at once to the title page: *Mr. William Shakespeares Comedies, Histories, & Tragedies.* Portrait of Shakespeare, *printed by Isaac Iaggard…*

Even for one in normal health, a stroke of luck like this was heart-attack material. There was no doubt, and this time it was not

Mr. WILLIAM
SHAKESPEARES
COMEDIES,
HISTORIES, &
TRAGEDIES.
Published according to the True Originall Copies.

LONDON
Printed by Isaac Iaggard, and Ed. Blount. 1623

one of Sibilla's jokes: this was the First Folio of 1623, complete, with a few faint water stains and ample margins.

How had that book come into my grandfather's hands? Probably through a bulk acquisition of nineteenth-century material, from the perfect little old lady who never quibbled over the price, because it was like selling cumbersome junk to the second-hand man.

My grandfather had not been an expert on antiquarian books, but neither had he been uneducated. He would certainly have realized that he was dealing with a volume of some value, and was probably pleased to have the collected works of Shakespeare but had not thought to consult auction catalogues, which he did not have. Thus, when my aunt and uncle threw everything into the attic the First Folio wound up there as well, and had lain there for forty years, just as it had lain in wait somewhere else for more than three centuries.

My heart was racing like crazy, but I paid it no mind.

Now here I am, in my grandfather's study, touching my treasure with trembling hands. After so many gusts of grey, I have entered the Hotel of the Three Roses. It is not Lila's photo, but it is an invitation to return to Milan, to the present. If Shakespeare's portrait is here, Lila's portrait will be there. The Bard will guide me towards my Dark Lady.

With this First Folio I am living out an adventure story that is rather more exciting than all the castle mysteries I experienced between the walls of the Solara house, during nearly three months of high blood pressure. Excitement is muddling my thoughts, my face is blazing with heat.

This is surely the greatest stroke of my life.

Part Three

ΟΙ ΝΟΣΤΟΙ

15. You're Back at Last, Friend Mist!

I am travelling through a tunnel with phosphorescent walls. I am rushing towards a distant point that appears as an inviting grey. Is this the death experience? Popular wisdom suggests that those who have it and then come back say just the opposite, that you go through a dark, vertiginous passageway, then emerge in a triumph of blinding light. The Hotel of the Three Roses. So either I am not dead, or they lied.

I am nearing the mouth of the tunnel, and the vapours that gather thickly beyond it are filtering in. I simmer in them, barely aware that I am now moving through a delicate tissue of hovering fumes. This is fog: not read, not described by others—real fog, and I am in it. I have returned.

Around me the fog rises, painting the world with a soft insubstantiality. If I could make out the outlines of houses, I would see the fog stealing in to nibble away a roof, starting at the edges. But it has already swallowed everything. Or perhaps this is fog over fields and hills. I am not sure whether I am floating or walking, but even the ground is only fog. Like tramping over snow. I plunge into the fog, fill my lungs with it, breathe it back out, roll in it like a dolphin, the way I used to dream of swimming through cream... The friendly fog welcomes me, circles me, coats me, breathes me, caresses my cheeks and then slips between my collar and my chin and stings my neck—and it tastes of something gone sour, of snow, of a drink, of tobacco. I move as I do beneath the arcades in Solara, where you can never see the whole sky, the arcades low like the arched ceilings of wine cellars. *Et, comme un bon nageur qui se pâme dans l'onde, / tu sillonnes gaiement l'immensité profonde / avec une indicible et mâle volupté.*

Several silhouettes approach. They seem at first like many-armed giants. They give off a weak heat and the fog melts around them, as if they were being lit by a feeble streetlamp, and I shrink away for fear that they will hurl themselves upon me, dominate me, I go through them the way you can with ghosts, and they disperse. It is like being in a train and watching the signal lights approach in the darkness and then seeing them swallowed by darkness, vanishing.

Now the mocking figure from the Thermogène ad comes forward, a satanic clown sheathed in a green and blue unitard, squeezing something to his chest, a flabby mass, like human lungs, and spewing flames from his unseemly mouth. He crashes into me, licking me like a flame-thrower, then goes away, leaving a thin wake of heat that for a few moments lightens that *fumifugium.* A globe rolls up to me with a huge eagle atop it, and after the bird comes the ashen face of the Presbitero pencil man, with a hundred pencils bristling from his head like hair standing on end from fear... I know them, they were my companions when as a child I lay in bed with fever, feeling immersed in royal soup, in a purulence of yellow wellsprings that boiled around me as I cooked in their broth. Now, as in those nights, I am lying in the darkness of my room when suddenly the doors of the dark old wardrobe open and out comes a crowd of Uncle Gaetanos. Uncle Gaetano had a triangular head, with a sharp chin and curly hair that formed two excrescences at his temples, a consumptive face, gloomy eyes, and one gold tooth at the centre of

FERNET-BRAN

a rotten set. Like the pencil man. The Uncle Gaetanos came forth at first in pairs, then multiplied, dancing around my room with marionette-like motions, bending their arms geometrically, sometimes wielding a two-metre ruler like a cane. They would return with every seasonal flu, every measles or scarlet fever, to plague those late afternoons when my temperature would rise, and I feared them. Then they would go away as quickly as they had come—perhaps they went back into the wardrobe, and later, as I convalesced, I would open it fearfully and examine the interior inch by inch, but I never found the hidden passage from which they had emerged.

When I was well, I would, on occasion, meet Uncle Gaetano along the avenue on Sunday at noon, and he would smile at me with his gold tooth, caress my cheek, say "Good lad", and move on. He was a nice old guy, and I never understood why he came to haunt me when I was sick, nor did I dare ask my parents what was so ambiguous, so oily, so subtly threatening about Uncle Gaetano's life, his very being.

What was it I had said to Paola when she held me back from being run over by a car? That I knew that cars run over chickens, that the driver hits the brakes to avoid them and black smoke comes out and then two men in dustcoats with big black goggles have to start it again with a crank. At the time I did not know, now I do, that these men appeared after Uncle Gaetano during my bouts of delirium.

Those men are here, I meet them suddenly in the mist.

I barely dodge them, their car is anthropomorphically hideous, and out they jump, wearing masks and trying to grab me by my ears. My ears are now extremely long, astronomically asinine, flaccid and hairy, they could stretch to the moon. Watch out, because if you're a bad boy, never mind Pinocchio's nose, you'll get Meo's ears! Why was that book not in Solara? I was living inside *Meo's Ears*.

I have regained my memory. Except that now—when it rains it pours—my memories are wheeling around me like bats.

The fever has been going down since the last quinine pill: my father is sitting by my little bed reading me a chapter of *The Four Musketeers*. Not the three, the four. A parody that had all of Italy glued to the radio, because it was tied in to an advertising contest: every box of Perugina chocolates contained a colourful card depicting one of the characters from the programme, and people collected them in albums, competing for various prizes.

But only those lucky enough to get the rarest figure, the Fierce Saladin, would win a Fiat Balilla, and the entire country was getting drunk on chocolate (or giving it away to whomever—relatives, lovers, neighbours, employers) in their efforts to capture the Fierce Saladin.

In the tale to which you're listening, / you'll see gloves and feathered hats, / swords, and duels, and sneak attacks, / lovely ladies, and lovers trysting... They even published it as a book, full

of witty illustrations. Papà would read and I would fall asleep to visions of Cardinal Richelieu surrounded by cats, or of the Beautiful Sulamite.

Why was it that in Solara (when? yesterday? a thousand years ago?) there were so many traces of my grandfather and none of Papà? Because my grandfather had dealt in books and magazines, and books and magazines were things I read, paper, paper, paper, whereas Papà worked all day and never got involved in politics, perhaps in order to keep his job. When we were in Solara, he would somehow manage to visit us on the weekends, spending the rest of his time in the city amid the bombardments, and he would appear at my bedside only when I was sick.

Bang crack blam splash crackle crackle crunch grunt pwutt roaar rumble blomp sbam buizz schranchete slam sprank blomp swoom bum thump clang tomp trac uaaaagh vroom augh zoom...

When they were bombing the city, we could see the distant flashes from our windows in Solara, could hear the rumbling of something like thunder. We would watch the spectacle, always knowing that Papà might be trapped in a collapsing building, never being able to find out for sure until Saturday, when he was supposed to return. Sometimes they would bomb on Tuesday. We would wait for four days. The war had made us fatalists, a bombing was like a storm. We kids kept playing calmly through Tuesday evening, Wednesday, Thursday, and Friday. But were we really calm? Were we not beginning to be marked by anxiety, by the stunned and relieved melancholy that grips whoever passes alive through a field strewn with corpses?

Only now do I sense that I loved my father, and I see his face again, marked by a life of sacrifice—he worked hard to acquire the car in which he would be crushed, perhaps so that he could feel independent of my grandfather, a bon vivant without financial worries, who was, moreover, haloed with heroism, thanks to his political past and his revenge on Merlo.

Papà is here beside me, he is reading the spurious adventures of D'Artagnan, who was shown in the book wearing knickerbockers, like a golfer. I can smell the scent of Mamma's breast, when I would go and stretch out in bed and she, so many years after she had suckled me, would put away her *Filotea* and sing in soft tones a hymn to the Virgin, which to me was the chromatic ascent from the Prelude to *Tristan*.

How is it that now I remember? Where am I? I pass from foggy vistas to the most vivid images of domestic scenes, and I see an all-encompassing silence. I sense nothing outside me, everything is within. I try to move a finger, a hand, a leg, but it is as if I had no body. As if I were floating in nothingness and gliding towards abysses that call out to the Abyss.

Has someone drugged me? Who? Where do I last remember being? A person usually recalls on waking what he did before he went to sleep, even that he closed the book and laid it on the nightstand. But sometimes it happens that you wake up in a hotel, or even in your own house after returning from a long trip, and you look for the light on the left when it is on the right, or you try to get out of bed on the wrong side, believing you are still in the other place. I recall it as if it were last night, before I went to sleep Papà was reading me *The Four Musketeers,* I know that must be fifty years ago, but I am struggling to recall where I was before waking up here.

Was I not in Solara with the First Folio of Shakespeare in my hands? And then? Amalia put LSD in my soup and now I am hovering here, in a fog teeming with figures who emerge from every cranny of my past.

Silly me, how simple it is... In Solara I had a second incident, they thought I was dead, they buried me, and I have awakened inside the tomb. Buried alive, a classic scenario. But in such cases you become agitated, you move your limbs, bang against the walls of your zinc box, gasp for air, panic. But this is different, I do not feel like a body, I am supremely calm. I am experiencing only these memories that assail me, taking pleasure in them. That is not how you awaken in a tomb.

Then I must be dead and the afterlife is this calm, dull zone in which I will relive my past life eternally, and tough luck if it was terrible (that will be hell), otherwise it will be paradise. Oh come on! Say you were born hunchbacked, blind, and deaf-mute, or that the ones you loved died like flies around you, parents, wife, five-year-old son—does that mean that your afterlife will be nothing but the repetition, varied but continuous, of all you suffered in your earthly life? That hell is not *les autres,* but the trail of death we leave alive? Not even the cruellest of gods could imagine such a fate for us. Unless Gragnola was right. Gragnola? I think I knew him once, but my memories are shoving one another around and I have to put them in order, line them up, otherwise I will lose myself in the fog again and the Thermogène clown will come back.

Maybe I am not dead. If I were, I would feel no worldly passions, no love for my parents or anxiety about the bombings. To die is to remove oneself from the cycle of life and from the beating of one's heart. No matter how hellish hell might be, I would be able to observe from sidereal distances what I myself have been. Being flayed in boiling pitch is not hell. You reflect on the evil you have done, you can never again free yourself from it, and you know it. But you would be pure spirit. Whereas I not only remember but also experience nightmares, affection, and delight. I cannot feel my body, but I still remember it, and I suffer as if I had it still. The way someone who has had a leg amputated can still feel it ache.

Try again. I had a second incident, this one more severe than the first. I got too worked up, first at the thought of Lila, and then, later, when I found the First Folio. No doubt my blood pressure soared to vertiginous heights. I fell into a coma.

On the outside, Paola, my daughters, everyone who loves me (and Gratarolo, tearing out his hair for letting me go when perhaps he should have kept me under tight control for at least six months), is watching me as I lie in a deep coma. Their machines are saying that my brain shows no signs of life, and they are despairing over whether to pull the plug or wait, maybe for years. Paola is holding my hand, Carla and Nicoletta have put some records on, having read that even in a coma a sound, a voice, any sort of stimulus might suddenly wake you up. And they could go on like this for years while I remained hooked up to a tube. Anyone with an ounce of dignity would say, Let's end this right now, so that those poor women can at last feel hopeless but free. And I am able to think that they should pull the plug, but I am unable to say so.

Yet brains in deep comas, as everyone knows, show no signs of activity, whereas I think, I feel, I recall. But that is just what people on the outside believe. The encephalogram flatlines according to science, but what does science know of the body's stratagems? Maybe my brain waves are flat on their screens and I am thinking with my guts, with the tips of my toes, with my testicles. They believe I no longer have cerebral activity, but I still have interior activity.

I am not saying that when the brain flatlines, the soul is still in operation, somewhere. I am saying only that their machines record my cerebral activity up to a certain point. Below this threshold I am still thinking, and they do not know it. If I can wake up again to tell my tale, someone might get a Nobel in neurology and those machines could be tossed on the scrap heap.

To be able to re-emerge from the fog of the past, to show myself again, alive and powerful, to those who loved me and to those who wished me dead. "Look at me, I am Edmond Dantès!" How many times does the Count of Monte Cristo appear to someone who has given him up for dead? To his former benefactors, to his beloved Mercedes, to those who brought about his downfall: "Look at me, I have returned, I am Edmond Dantès."

Or else to be able to escape this silence, drift incorporeally above the hospital room, see the people crying beside my motionless body. To attend one's own funeral and at the same time be able to fly, no longer hindered by the flesh—two universal wishes granted at once. Instead I dream, imprisoned in my immobility…

In truth, I nurse no grudges. If I have reason to be upset, it is because I feel fine and cannot say so. If only I could move a finger, an eyelid, send a signal, maybe in Morse code. But I am all thought and no action. No sensation. I might have been here a week, a month, a year, and I feel no heartbeat, no pangs of hunger or thirst, no desire to sleep (should this continual wakefulness frighten me), I do not even know if I excrete (perhaps tubes take care of everything), or sweat, or even breathe. For all I know, outside me and around me there may not even be any air. I suffer at the thought of Paola, Carla, and Nicoletta suffering, thinking me out of commission, but the last thing I ought to do is give in to this suffering. I cannot take on the pain of the entire world—may I be granted the gift of fierce selfishness. I live with myself and for myself, and I can remember that which, after my first incident, I had forgotten. For now, and perhaps for ever, this is my life.

So then, nothing to do but wait. If they revive me, it will be a surprise for everyone. But I may never wake up, and I must prepare myself for this uninterrupted reliving of the past. Or perhaps I will last only a little longer, then go out—in which case I must take full advantage of these moments.

If I were suddenly to cease to think, what would happen next? Would some other kind of afterlife kick in that would resemble my ultra-private present life, or would it be darkness and unconsciousness for ever?

I would be a fool to waste whatever time has been granted me in pondering such questions. Someone, or perhaps chance, has given me the opportunity to remember who I am. I must take it. If I turn out to have something to be penitent for, I will do penance. But in order to repent, I must first remember what it is I have done. As for the sleaziness I know about, Paola, or the widows I cheated, will have forgiven me already. And in the end, after all, if hell exists, it is empty.

In the attic in Solara, before entering this sleep, I found a tin frog that was linked to the name Angelo Bear and to the phrase "Dr. Osimo's candies". Those were words. Now I see.

Dr. Osimo, with his egg-bald head and pale blue glasses, is the pharmacist on Corso Roma. Whenever Mamma takes me with her on her errands and stops by the pharmacy, Dr. Osimo, even if she is buying nothing more than a roll of absorbent gauze, opens a towering glass container full of fragrant white orbs and gives me a packet of milk candies. I know I must not eat them all right away, must make them last at least three or four days.

On our previous outing I noticed—I am less than four—nothing out of the ordinary about Mamma's belly, but one day after our last visit to Dr. Osimo, I am sent downstairs and entrusted to Signor Piazza. Signor Piazza lives in a great room that resembles a forest, full of animals that look alive: roosters, foxes, cats, eagles. I have been told that he takes animals, but only when they die of their own accord, and rather than burying them he stuffs them with straw. Now I am sitting in his house, and he is entertaining me by explaining the names and traits of the various animals, and I spend who knows how much time in that marvellous necropolis, wherein death seems gentle, Egyptian, and exudes perfumes I smell only there, probably a blend of chemical solutions and the odour of dusty feathers and tanned hides. The most beautiful afternoon of my life.

When someone comes to retrieve me and I go back up the stairs at home, I learn that during my sojourn in the kingdom of the dead my baby sister has been born. The midwife found her in a cabbage and brought her. All I can see of my baby sister, through the whiteness of lace, is a single flushed purple ball featuring a black hole out of which piercing shrieks emerge. That does not mean she is sick, they tell me: when a baby sister is born she does that because that is her way of saying how happy she is that she now has a mamma and a papà and a little brother.

I am exceedingly agitated, and I offer at once to give her one of Dr. Osimo's milk candies, but they explain that when a baby sister is first born she has no teeth and can only suck milk from her mamma. It would have been great to throw those little white balls and make them go into that black hole. Maybe I would have won a goldfish.

I run to the toy chest and take out the tin frog. She might have just been born, but a green frog that croaks when you squeeze its belly cannot fail to entertain her. But no, and I put the frog away too, and slink off. What good, then, is a new baby sister? Would it not have been better to remain among Signor Piazza's dead old birds?

The tin frog and Angelo Bear. In the attic they had popped into my mind at the same time because Angelo Bear, too, became linked to my sister, when she later became an accomplice in my games—and a glutton for milk candies.

"Stop it, Nuccio, Angelo Bear can't take it any more." Who knows how many times I asked my cousin to end the torture. But he was bigger than I was, and had been sent by the priests to a boarding school where he spent his days chafing in a uniform, and so when he came back to the city he let loose. At the end of a long battle of the toys he captured Angelo Bear, tied him to the foot of the bed, and subjected him to unspeakable floggings.

Angelo Bear, how long had I had him? The memory of his arrival disappears into the time that Gratarolo described, before we learn to organize our personal memories. Angelo, my yellowish plush friend, had movable arms and legs, like a doll's, so he could sit or walk or raise his arms to the sky. He was large and impressive, with two twinkling, bright brown eyes. Ada and I had elected him king of the toys, of the soldiers as well as the dolls.

Age, as it wore him down, rendered him even more venerable. He gained a halting authority all his own, which only increased over time, as one by one, like a veteran of many battles, he lost an eye, then an arm.

Turned upside down, the footstool would become a boat, a pirate ship, or a Vernian craft with its square stem and stern: Angelo Bear sat beside the helmsman, and in front of him, setting a course for adventure in distant lands, were Captain Potato and the Soldiers of Cockaigne, who were more important, because of their size, though also more comical, than their earnest brothers-in-arms, the clay soldiers, who by this time were more disabled than Angelo, several having lost heads or limbs, leaving only wire hooks sticking out of the compressed, friable, and now faded substance of their flesh, like so many Long John Silvers. While that glorious vessel sailed out of the Bedroom Sea, traversed the Hallway Ocean, and made land in the Kitchen Archipelago, Angelo towered above his Lilliputian subjects, but the disproportion, rather than bothering us, merely emphasized his Gulliverian majesty.

Over time—thanks to his generous service, his proclivity for all manner of acrobatics, and Cousin Nuccio's rage—Angelo Bear lost his second eye, his second arm, and finally his legs. As Ada and I grew, tufts of straw began falling out of his mutilated torso. Our parents somehow got the notion that his mangy body had become a host for bugs, and perhaps bacterial cultures, and so, with the appalling threat to toss him in the garbage while we were at school, they goaded us into getting rid of him.

By this point, for both Ada and myself, our beloved plantigrade was a painful sight: so frail, unable to stand on his own, exposed to that slow disembowelment and that indecorous spillage of internal organs. We had accepted the idea that he had to die—should indeed be considered already deceased—and thus that he should have an honourable burial.

We are up early in the morning, and Papà has just turned on the boiler, the central unit that distributes heat to all the radiators in the house. We have formed a slow, hieratic cortège. Beside the boiler, the ranks of surviving toys, marshalled under the command of Captain Potato. They stand in orderly rows, at attention, to bestow the honours of war, as befits the defeated. I proceed, bearing the cushion on which is laid the nearly departed, followed by each member of my family, including the cleaning woman, all united in mournful veneration.

With ritual compunction I am now introducing Angelo Bear into the maw of that fiery Baal. Angelo, now no more than a sack of straw, goes up in a single burst of flame.

It was a prophetic ceremony, because not long afterwards the boiler itself was extinguished. Originally it had fed upon anthracite, and then, when that ran out, upon egg-shaped lumps of coal dust, but as the war went on those were rationed, too, and we had to rehabilitate an old kitchen stove, much like the one we would later use in Solara, that could swallow wood, paper, cardboard, and a type of briquette made of a compressed, wine-coloured substance that burned poorly but slowly and gave the appearance of flame.

The death of Angelo Bear does not grieve me, nor does it bring on a surge of nostalgia. Perhaps it did in the years that immediately followed, and perhaps I felt it again, at sixteen, when I began devoting myself to the recovery of the recent past, but not now. Now I do not live in the stream of time. I am, blessedly, in the eternal present. Angelo is before my eyes, the day of his obsequies and also the days of his triumphs. I can move from one memory to the other, and I experience each as the *hic et nunc*.

If this is eternity, it is splendid—why did I have to wait until I was sixty before deserving it?

And Lila's face? Now I should be able to see it, but it is as though memories were coming to me of their own accord, one at a time, in an order they have chosen. I simply must wait. I have nothing else to do.

I am sitting in the hall, beside the Telefunken. There is a play on. Papà is following the whole thing, and I am in his lap, thumb in my mouth. I do not understand such things—family tragedies, affairs, redemptions—but those distant voices lead me towards sleep.

When I go to bed I ask that my bedroom door be left open, so that I can see the hall light. I have become enormously shrewd at a tender age, have figured out that the Wise Men's gifts, on the eve of Epiphany, are bought by our parents. Ada does not believe it, I cannot strip a little girl of her illusions, and on the night of January 5, I try desperately to stay awake to hear what happens out there. I hear them arranging the gifts. The next morning I will feign joy and wonder at the miracle, because I am a manipulative bastard and do not want this game to end.

I am a sharp one, I am. I have figured out that babies are born from their mother's bellies, but I keep it to myself. Mamma talks about female matters with her friends (*so-and-so is in a delicate, ahem, condition,* or *that one has adhesions there, ahem, on her ovaries*), one of them shushes her, warns her there is a child around, and Mamma says it does not matter, because at that age we are so slow on the uptake. I peek from behind the door and penetrate life's secrets.

From the small circular door of Mamma's dresser, I have purloined a book: *It Isn't True that Death,* by Giovanni Mosca, a well-mannered, ironic elegy on the joys of cemetery life and the pleasures of lying beneath a cosy blanket of earth. I like this invitation to demise, perhaps it is my first encounter with death, before Valente's green stakes. But one morning, chapter five, sweet Maria, who in a moment of weakness has known a gravedigger, feels a wing-beat in her belly. Up to that point, the author has been quite modest, has merely referred to an unhappy love and a creature yet to come. But now he allows himself a realistic description that terrifies me: "Her belly, from that morning on, came to life with flutters and flaps, like a cageful of sparrows.... The baby was moving."

This, with its unbearable realism, is the first time I have ever read about a pregnancy. I am not surprised by what I learn, which confirms what I have gathered on my own. But I am frightened by the thought that someone might catch me in the act of reading that forbidden text, and learn that I have learned. I feel sinful, because I have violated a prohibition. I place the book back in the dresser, trying to hide every trace of my intrusion. I know a secret, and I feel guilty for knowing it.

This happens long before I kiss the face of the lovely diva on the cover of *Novella,* and it is part of the revelation of birth, not of sex. Like certain primitive peoples who, they say, never managed to establish a direct correlation between the sexual act and pregnancy (and nine months is a century, as Paola would say), I, too, went a long time before grasping the mysterious link between sex, that adult activity, and babies.

Not even my parents worry that I might feel distressing sensations. It seems their generation felt them late, or else they have forgotten their childhoods. They are leading me and Ada by the hand, they run into an acquaintance, Papà says we are on our way to see *Goldene Stadt,* and the acquaintance grins mischievously at us little ones and whispers that the movie is "a little saucy". Papà replies nonchalantly, "I guess we'll have to wipe their chins." And me with my heart in my throat watching Kristina Söderbaum's clinches.

In the hallway at Solara, as I was thinking of the expression "races and peoples of the earth", a hairy vulva came to mind. Indeed, here I am, with a few friends, around the time of middle school perhaps, in someone's father's study, where we are looking at Biasutti's *Races and Peoples of the Earth.* We flip the pages quickly until we reach a page with a photo of Kalmyk women, *à poil,* their sexual organs visible, or rather their fur. Kalmyk women, women who sell by themselves.

I am in the fog again. It reigns supreme in the dark of the blackout, as the city contrives to vanish from the celestial sight of enemy aircraft, and does in any case vanish from my sight as I observe it from the ground. I advance through that fog, like the boy in that picture in my first-grade reader, holding Papà's hand, and he is wearing the same Borsalino hat as the man in the picture, though his coat is less elegant, shabbier, and slope-shouldered, raglan-style—

and mine is even more threadbare, with the buttonholes on the right, a sign that it is made of reversed material from one of Papà's old overcoats. In his right hand he holds not a walking stick but an electric flashlight, though not the kind with batteries. It recharges with friction, like a bicycle headlamp, and as he presses four fingers on a kind of trigger, it buzzes softly and lights up the sidewalk enough to see a step, a corner, the edge of an intersection, and then his fingers loosen their grip, and the light vanishes. We walk another ten paces or so, on the basis of what little we have seen, as in blind flight, then he turns it back on for a moment.

Shadows pass each other in the fog. Sometimes a greeting is whispered, or a *pardon me,* and it seems right that they are whispered, though if you think about it the bombardiers can see light but cannot hear sounds, so we could go around singing in that fog at the top of our lungs. But no one does, and it is as though our silence encourages the fog to protect our steps, to render us invisible, us and the streets.

Are such strict blackouts really helpful? Perhaps they merely comfort us, especially since when they want to bomb they come during the day. It is the middle of the night and the sirens have sounded. Mamma, crying, wakes us up—she is crying not out of fear of the bombs, but over her babies' ruined sleep—slips little overcoats over our pyjamas and takes us down to the shelter. This is not in our house, which has nothing more than a cellar reinforced with a few beams and sandbags, but in the house behind ours, which was built in '39, in anticipation of the conflict. We get there not by crossing the courtyards, which are separated by walls, but by going around the block, hurriedly, trusting in the fact that the sirens sound when the planes are still fairly far away.

The air-raid shelter is lovely, its cement walls grooved by rivulets of water, its lights dim but warm. All the grown-ups are sitting on benches and jabbering, and we kids are running around in the middle. We hear the muffled sound of anti-aircraft artillery;

everyone is convinced that if a bomb falls on this block of flats the shelter will withstand it. It is not true, but it helps. The building guard, who is my elementary school teacher, Maestro Monaldi, mills around with a self-absorbed air, mortified because he is a centurion in the militia but did not have time to don his uniform, with his squadrista decorations. At this time, anyone who had been part of the March on Rome was like a veteran of the great Napoleonic battles—it was only after September 8, 1943 that my grandfather explained to me how the march had been a procession of petty thieves armed with walking sticks, and if the king had given the order, a few companies of infantry could have stopped them in their tracks. But the king was Stumpy Quickfoot, and betrayal was in his blood.

In any event, Maestro Monaldi now walks among his fellow tenants, calms them, pays attention to the pregnant ladies, explains that there are small sacrifices that must be endured for the final victory. The all-clear signal sounds, families swarm out into the street. One man—no one knows him, he took refuge with us because the alarm caught him while he was on the road—lights a cigarette. Maestro Monaldi grabs him by the arm and asks him sarcastically whether he knows that we are at war and that there is a blackout.

"Even if there was still a bomber up there, he couldn't see the light of one match," the man replies, and he begins to smoke.

"Oh, you're sure, are you?"

"Of course I'm sure. I'm a pilot and I fly bombers. You ever bombed Malta?"

A real hero. Maestro Monaldi flees, seething with rage. Amused comments from some of his fellow tenants: I always said he was a stuffed shirt, the ones in charge are always like that.

Maestro Monaldi and his heroic compositions. I see myself in the evening, with Papà and Mamma hovering over me. The next day we are to have an in-class composition as part of the Culture Competitions. "No matter what the topic is," Mamma says, "it will have something to do with Il Duce and the war. So you need to prepare some nice phrases that will make an impression. For example, faithful and incorruptible guardians of Italy and its civilization is a phrase that always works well, no matter what the subject."

"And what if the topic turns out to be the wheat battle?"

"You can work it in anyhow, use your imagination."

"Remember that our soldiers redden the burning sands of Marmarica with their blood," Papà suggests. "And don't forget that our civilization is new, heroic, and blessed. That always makes a good impression. Even if it is the wheat battle."

They want a son who gets good marks. A fine goal. If a good mark depends on knowing the parallel postulate, one studies the geometry text. If it depends on being able to talk like a Balilla Boy, one memorizes what a Balilla Boy is supposed to think. Regardless of whether it is right or not. My parents did not know this, but even Euclid's fifth postulate holds only for flat surfaces, so ideally flat that they do not exist in reality. The Fascist regime was the flat surface to which everyone by this time had adapted—ignoring the curvilinear vortices in which the parallels clash or hopelessly diverge.

I see again a brief scene that must have taken place some years earlier. I ask:

"Mamma, what's a revolution?"

"It's when the workers go to the government and chop the heads off all the office workers, like your father."

Just two days after I wrote my composition, the Bruno episode occurred. Bruno, two cat eyes, pointy teeth, and mouse-grey hair with two bare spots, as if from alopecia or impetigo. They were scab scars. Poor kids always had scabs on their heads, the result of less-than-clean environments combined with poor nutrition. In our elementary school class, De Caroli and I were the rich kids, or so people thought; in fact, our families belonged to the same social class as the teacher, in my case because my father was an office worker and wore a tie and my mother wore a pretty hat (making her not a woman but a lady), and in De Caroli's because his father owned a small fabric store. The others were all from lower classes and still spoke dialect at home with their parents and thus made spelling and grammatical errors, and the poorest of them all was Bruno. The black smock of Bruno's uniform was torn, he did not wear the white collar, or when he did it was dirty and threadbare, and it goes without saying that he did not have a blue bow like respectable boys. He had scabs, and so his head had been shaved—that was the only cure the family knew for that or for lice—and the bare spots were from scabs that had already healed. Stigmata of inferiority. The teacher was, all things considered, a good man, but since he had been a squadrista he felt obliged to set a manly example, and he could give a mighty cuffing. Though never to me or De Caroli, because he knew we would tell our parents, who were his equals. (And because my mother and the headmaster's sister-in-law were cousins, and you never know.) Since he and I lived on the same block, he offered to accompany me home every day after school, together with his son, to save my father the trouble of coming to meet me.

With Bruno, on the other hand, cuffings were daily, because he was lively and so behaved badly, and came to school in a greasy smock. Bruno was always being sent to stand behind the blackboard, our pillory.

One day Bruno came to school after an unexcused absence, and the teacher was rolling up his sleeves when Bruno started crying and between sobs gave us to understand that his father had died. The teacher was moved, because even squadristi had hearts. Of course for him social justice meant charity, so he took up a collection from us all. Even our parents must have had hearts, because the next day everyone came in with a few coins, some cast-off clothes, a jar of marmalade, a kilo of bread. Bruno had his moment of solidarity.

But that same morning, as we marched in the courtyard, he started crawling on all fours, and we all thought that such behaviour in the wake of his father's death was truly disgraceful. The teacher shouted that he lacked the most basic sense of gratitude. Orphaned two days earlier, now the beneficiary of his classmates' generosity, and already delinquent: with the family he came from, he would never be redeemed.

A deuteragonist in that little drama, I had a moment of doubt. I had felt something similar the morning after the composition, when I woke unsettled, wondering if I really loved Il Duce or if I was just a hypocritical boy writing that I did. Watching Bruno go around on all fours, I understood that it was a spasm of dignity, a way of reacting to the humiliation that our clammy generosity had inflicted on him.

I understood it better days later, during one of those Fascist Saturday rallies, when all the Balilla Boys lined up in uniform—ours looked brand-new, Bruno's looked like his school smock, and his blue neckerchief was poorly knotted—to recite the Oath. The centurion said, "In the name of God and Italy, I swear to carry out the orders of Il Duce and to serve with all my strength and, if need be, with my blood, the cause of the Fascist Revolution. Do you all swear it?" While the rest of us shouted "I swear!", Bruno, who was close enough for me to hear him perfectly, shouted "Pierre!" He was rebelling. It was the first act of revolt I had ever witnessed.

Was he rebelling of his own accord, or because his father, like the father of Italy's boy-in-the-world, had been a drunkard and a socialist? Regardless, I now understand that Bruno was the first to teach me how to react to the rhetoric that was suffocating us.

Between the composition of my tenth year and the chronicle of my eleventh, at the end of fifth grade, I had been transformed by Bruno's lesson. He was a revolutionary anarchist, I a budding sceptic, and his Pierre became my unbreakable glass.

It is clear now, in the coma's silence, that I understand better all that has happened to me. Is this the illumination others achieve when they come to the brink, at which point, like Martin Eden, they understand everything, but as they know, they cease to know? I, who am not yet on the brink, have an advantage over those who die. I understand, I know, and I even remember (now) that I know. Does that make me one of the lucky?

16. The Wind Is Whistling

I would like to remember Lila.... What was Lila like? From the soot of this half-sleep rise other images, but none of her...

And yet under normal conditions a person ought to be able to say, I want to remember last year's vacation. If he has retained any trace, he remembers. I cannot. My memory is proglottidean, like the tapeworm, but unlike the tapeworm it has no head, it wanders in a maze, and any point may be the beginning or the end of its journey. I must wait for the memories to come of their own accord, following their own logic. That is how it is in the fog. In the sunlight, you see things from a distance and you can change directions purposefully in order to meet up with something particular. In the fog, something or someone approaches you, but you do not know who until it is near.

Maybe this is normal, you cannot have everything in a single moment, memories come in a sequence, as on a skewer. What was it Paola said about the magic number seven that psychologists talk about? It is easy to remember up to seven elements from a list, but any more is too many. Not even seven. Who are the seven dwarfs? Happy, Dopey, Sleepy, Grumpy, Bashful, Doc... And then? You can never remember the seventh. And the seven kings of Rome?

Romulus, Numa Pompilius, Tullus Hostilius, Servius Tullius, Tarquin the Elder, Tarquin the Proud...and the seventh? Ah, Sneezy.

I think my earliest memory is of a doll dressed as the lead drummer in a military band, in a white uniform and a kepi, and when you wound him up with a little key he would beat out his rat-a-tat-tat. Is that it, or did I revise it to that over the years, harnessing my parents' reminiscences? Might it not be the fig scene, me at the base of a tree and a farmer named Quirino clambering up a ladder to pick me the best fig—except that I could not yet pronounce the word *fig* and said *sig*?

Last memory: in Solara looking at the First Folio. Will Paola and the others realize what it was I was holding in my hands when I was sleep-struck? They should give it to Sibilla, immediately, because if I remain like this for years they will not be able to bear the expenses, will have to sell the studio, and then Solara, and even that might not be enough, whereas with the First Folio they could pay for my everlasting hospitalization, with ten nurses, and that way they could just come to see me once a month and then get back to their own lives.

Another figure from an ad is approaching, grinning at me and making an obscene gesture with a large aspirin. It is as if he were running into me and wrapping himself around me and then dissolving in the mist.

The drummer boy with the kepi passes by. I seek refuge in my grandfather's arms. I smell the odour of pipe as I put my cheek against his waistcoat. My grandfather smoked a pipe and smelled of tobacco. Why was his pipe not at Solara? My damned aunt and uncle must have thrown it out, thinking it unimportant, its bowl gnawed away by the flames of many matches—thrown it out with his pens, his blotters, who knows what, a pair of eyeglasses, a holey sock, and his last tin of tobacco, still half full.

The fog is clearing. I remember Bruno crawling on all fours, but not Carla's birth, my graduation day, or my first encounter with Paola. Before I remembered nothing, now I remember everything about the earliest years of my life, but I cannot recall when Sibilla first entered my studio looking for work—or when I wrote my last poem. I am unable to recall Lila Saba's face. If I could do that, all this sleep would be worth it. I cannot recall that face I looked for everywhere throughout my adult life, because I still cannot remember my adult life, nor that which, on the threshold of adulthood, I tried to forget.

I must wait, or else prepare myself to wander eternally among the pathways of my first sixteen years. That could be enough; if I relived each moment, each event, then I could endure in this state for another sixteen years. Long enough, I would be seventy-six, a reasonable lifespan...and Paola all the while wondering if she should pull the plug.

But does not telepathy exist? I could concentrate on Paola and think intensely about sending her a message. Or I could try it with the fresh, clear mind of a child: "Message for Sandro, message for Sandro, this is Grey Eagle of Fernet Branca, Grey Eagle here, please respond. Over..." If only he could transmit back: "Roger, Grey Eagle, I hear you loud and clear..."

I get bored in the city. There are four of us in short pants playing in the street in front of the house, where one car per hour goes by, and goes slowly. They allow us to play down here. We are playing with marbles, a poor man's plaything, good even for those who have no other toys. Some are clay, the brown ones, and some are glass, and those are either transparent with colourful arabesques in the centre or milky with red veins. First game, *the pit:* we shoot the marbles from the middle of the street, with a precise blow from the index finger flicked across the thumb (though the better players flick the thumb across the index finger), into a shallow pit, dug out against the pavement. Some may get their marble in on the first shot, otherwise the game proceeds by turns. Second game, *spanna cetta,* which in Solara we called *cicca spanna:* you try to get close to the first marble, like bocce, but not closer than a span, measured with four fingers.

How I admire those who can spin a top. Not the rich-kid tops, made of metal with multicoloured stripes, which are charged by pumping a knobbed rod several times and then released so that the wheel makes colourful swirls, but rather the wooden peg top, the *pirla* or *mongia,* a sort of rounded cone, a pot-bellied pear that tapers to a nail point, its body scored with spiral grooves. You wrap it with a string that fits into the grooves, then you give the free end a yank, unspooling the string, and the *mongia* spins. Not everyone can do it, and I have never got the hang of it because I have been spoiled by the more expensive, easier tops—the other kids make fun of me.

We cannot play today because several gentlemen, wearing jackets and ties, are pulling weeds with hand hoes along the pavement. They work with scant enthusiasm, slowly, and one of them begins talking to us, telling us about various marble games. He says that as a boy he used to play *the ring:* you traced a ring on the pavement with chalk or in the dirt with a stick, you put marbles inside it, then using a larger marble you tried to knock marbles out of the circle, and whoever knocked the most out won. "I know your parents," he told me. "Tell them Signor Ferrara said hello, the man with the hat shop."

I reported this back home. "Those are Jews," Mamma said. "They make them do odd jobs." Papà raised his eyes towards the sky and said, "Hmph!" Later I went to my grandfather's store and asked him why the Jews were doing odd jobs. He told me to be polite if I encountered them, because they were good people, but for the moment he was not going to tell me the rest of the story because I was too young. "Keep quiet and don't go around talking about it, especially to your teacher." One day he would tell me everything. *S'as gira.*

At the time I simply wondered how it was that Jews sold hats. The hats I saw on posters pasted up along the walls, or in magazine ads, were high-class and elegant.

I still had no reason to worry about the Jews. It was only later, in Solara in 1938, that my grandfather showed me a newspaper announcing the racial laws, but in '38 I was six and did not read the papers.

Then one day Signor Ferrara and the others were no longer seen weeding the pavements. I thought then that they must have been allowed to go back home, having done their little penance. But after the war, I overheard someone tell Mamma that Signor Ferrara had died in Germany. By war's end I had learned a great deal, not only how babies are born (including the preliminaries of nine months beforehand), but also how Jews die.

Life changed with my evacuation to Solara. In the city I had been a melancholy boy who played with his schoolmates for a few hours a day. The rest of the time I was curled up with a book or roaming around on my bike. The only enchanted moments were those spent in my grandfather's shop: as he talked with a customer, I would rummage and rummage, dazzled by endless revelations. But in this way my solitude increased, and I lived alone with my imaginings.

At Solara, where I could walk to the town school by myself and romp through the fields and vineyards, I was free, and uncharted territory opened up before me. And I had many friends with whom I roamed. Our main goal was to build ourselves a fort.

Now, once more, I can see my whole life at the Oratorio, like a film. No longer proglottidean, but rather a logical sequence...

A fort did not have to be like a house with a roof, walls, and a door. It was usually a pit or a ditch, over which we would build a covering of branches and leaves, such that an embrasure of sorts remained, allowing us to control a valley or at least a clearing. Walking sticks were aimed and fired like machine-guns. As at Giarabub, only hunger could defeat us.

We had begun going to the Oratorio because at one end of the soccer field, atop a rise nestled against the low surrounding wall, we had identified the ideal site for a fort. All twenty-two players in the Sunday match could be gunned down. At the Oratorio we were basically free—they rounded us up only around six for catechism and benediction, but the rest of the time we did as we pleased. There was a rudimentary merry-go-round, a few swings, and a little playhouse where I trod the boards for the first time, in *The Little Parisian.* It was there that I gained that mastery of the footlights that years later would make me memorable in Lila's eyes.

Older boys also came by, and even young men—ancient to us—who played Ping-Pong or cards, though not for money. That good man Don Cognasso, the Oratorio's director, required of them no profession of faith; rather, it was enough that they came there instead of caravanning towards the city on bicycles, even at the risk of being caught in a bombardment, to attempt the climb up to the Casa Rossa, the bordello famous throughout the province.

It was at the Oratorio, after September 8 of '43, that I first heard about the Partisans. Before, they were just boys who were trying to avoid either the Repubblica Sociale's new draft or the Nazi round-ups, which meant being sent off to work in Germany. Later people began to call them rebels, because that was what they were called in official communiqués. It was only after several months, when we found out that ten of them had been executed—including one from Solara—and when we heard via Radio London that special messages were being directed to them, that we began to call them partisans, or patriots, as they preferred. In Solara, people rooted for the Partisans, because the boys all grew up in those parts, and when they came around, and although they all now went by nicknames—Hedgehog, Ferruccio, Lightning, Bluebeard—people still used the names they had known them by before. Many were youths I had seen at the Oratorio, playing hands of scopa in flimsy, threadbare jackets, and now they reappeared wearing brimmed berets, cartridge belts over their shoulders, sub-machine guns, a belt with two grenades attached—some even had holstered pistols. They wore red shirts, or jackets from the English army, or the pants and leggings of the king's officers. They were beautiful.

By 1944 they were already appearing in Solara, as they made quick incursions at moments when the Black Brigades were elsewhere. On occasion the Badogliani came down, with their blue neckerchiefs; people said they backed the king and still charged into battle shouting *Savoy.* On occasion it would be the Garibaldini, with their red neckerchiefs, singing songs against the king and Badoglio: *the wind is whistling, and the storm is howling, / our shoes are tattered, yet still we must press on / until our victory in a red Spring, / when the sun of the coming day will dawn.* The Badogliani were better armed—it was said that the English sent aid to them but not to the others, who were all communists. The Garibaldini had sub-machine guns, like the Black Brigades', captured in occasional clashes or in some surprise attack on an armoury, and the Badogliani had the latest models of the English Sten gun.

The Sten gun was lighter than the machine-gun, with a hollow stock, like a wire outline, and a magazine that stuck out not downward but to one side. One of the Badogliani once let me fire a round. Most of the time they fired to keep in practice, or to impress girls.

Once the San Marco Fascists showed up, singing *San Marco! San Marco! / what does it matter if we die.*

People said that they were nice kids from good families and maybe they had picked the wrong side, but they were polite with the locals and well-mannered when they courted women.

The men in the Black Brigades, on the other hand, had been freed from prisons or reform schools (some were as young as sixteen), and all they wanted was for everyone to fear them. But times were hard, and we had to be suspicious of even the San Marco unit.

I am going into town with Mamma for mass and we are joined by the lady from the villa a few kilometres away, who is always spewing venom about her tenant farmer, who steals part of her share. And since her tenant farmer is a Red, she has become a Fascist, at least in the sense that the Fascists are against the Reds. We come out of church and two officials from the San Marco unit have spotted the ladies, who are no longer terribly young, but who still have their figures—and besides, of course, soldiers catch as catch can. They approach under the pretext of asking for some information, since they are not from these parts. The two women treat them politely (after all, here are two handsome young men) and ask how it feels to be so far from home. "We're fighting to restore this country's honour, my dear ladies, the honour that certain traitors have tarnished," one of the two replies. And our neighbour comments: "How good of you, not like the gentleman I was just talking about."

One of the two smiles oddly and says, "We would be much obliged to know the name and address of that gentleman."

Mamma went pale, then red, but handled it well: "Oh, well, Lieutenant, my friend is referring to a fellow from Asti who used to come around here in recent years, and now, who knows where he is now, they say he was taken to Germany."

"Serves him right," says the lieutenant, smiling, not pressing it. Mutual salutations. On the way home, Mamma, through clenched teeth, tells that thoughtless woman that in these times you better be careful how you talk because it doesn't take much to get someone stood up against a wall.

Gragnola. He frequented the Oratorio. He insisted his name was pronounced Gràgnola, but everyone called him Gragnòla, a word that brought to mind a hail of gunfire. He replied that he was a peaceful man, and his friends answered back: "Come off it, we know..." It was whispered that he had connections to the Garibaldini brigades up in the mountains—he was even a great leader, someone said, and risked more by living in town than by hiding out, because if he were ever discovered, he would be shot at the drop of a hat.

Gragnola acted with me in *The Little Parisian,* and after that he took a liking to me. He taught me how to play three-seven. He seemed to feel uncomfortable with the other adults there, and he spent long hours chatting with me. Perhaps it was his pedagogical calling, because he had been a teacher. Or perhaps he knew he was saying such outrageous things that if the others heard him they would take him for the anti-Christ, and so he could only trust a kid.

He showed me the clandestine broadsheets that were circulating on the sly. He would never let me take one because, he said, anyone caught with them got shot. That was how I learned of the Ardeatine massacre, in Rome. "Our comrades stay up in the hills," Gragnola used to tell me, "so these things won't happen any more. Those Germans, they should all be *kaputt*!"

L'ITALIA LIBERA

ORGANO DEL PARTITO D'AZIONE

LA LOTTA CONTRO IL NAZISMO UNICA POSSIBILITA' DI RINASCITA

Quanto ci costa l'occupazione tedesca

Il posto dell'Italia nella guerra di liberazione

I volontari della libertà

Avanti!

GIORNALE DEL PARTITO SOCIALISTA ITALIANO DI UNITÀ PROLETARIA

Sulla fossa dei 500 fucilati di Roma la Nazione raccoglie un monito di lotta!

Esecrazione

Il riconoscimento sovietico del Governo Badoglio

He would tell me how the mysterious parties who made themselves known through those broadsheets had existed before the advent of Fascism, then had survived clandestinely, abroad, with their top leaders working as bricklayers, and sometimes they were identified by Il Duce's henchmen and flogged to death.

Gragnola had been a teacher, I did not know of what, in trade schools, going to work every morning on his bicycle and returning home in mid-afternoon. But he had to stop—some said because he was devoting himself heart and soul by then to the Partisans, others murmured that he was unable to continue because he was consumptive. Gragnola indeed had the look of a consumptive, an ashen face with two sickly pink cheekbones, hollow cheeks, a persistent cough. He had bad teeth, limped, was slightly hunchbacked, or rather had a curved spine, with shoulder blades that jutted out, and his jacket collar stood apart from his neck, so that his clothes seemed to hang on him like sacks. On stage, he always had to play the bad guy or the lame caretaker of a mysterious villa.

He was, everyone said, a well of scientific knowledge and had often been invited to teach at the university, but had refused out of fondness for his students. "Horseshit," he later told me. "Yambin, I only taught in the poor kids' school, as a substitute, because with this foul war I never even graduated college. When I was twenty they sent me off to *break the back of Greece,* I was wounded in the knee, and never mind that because you can barely tell, but somewhere in that mud I came down with a nasty sickness and I've been spitting up blood ever since. If I ever got my hands on Fat Head, I wouldn't kill him because unfortunately I'm a coward, but I would kick his ass until it was out of commission for what little time I hope he has left to live, the Judas."

I once asked him why he came to the Oratorio, since everyone said he was an atheist. He told me that he came because it was the only place he could see people. And besides he was not an atheist but an anarchist. At that time I did not know what anarchists were, and he explained that they were people who wanted freedom, with no masters, no kings, no state, and no priests. "Above all no state, not like those communists in Russia where the state tells them even when they have to use the crapper."

He told me about Gaetano Bresci, who in order to punish the first King Umberto for having ordered the massacre of the workers in Milan, left America where he was living in peace, with no return ticket, after his anarchist group chose him by lottery, and went off to kill the king. After he did, he was killed in prison, with officials saying he had hung himself out of remorse. But an anarchist never has remorse for actions undertaken in the people's name. He told me about legendary anarchists who had to emigrate from country to country, hounded by police everywhere, singing "Addio Lugano Bella".

Then he went back to bad-mouthing the communists, who had done in the anarchists in Catalonia. I asked him why he associated with the Garibaldini, who were communists, if he was against the communists. He replied that, number one, not all of the Garibaldini were communists, there were socialists and even anarchists among them, and number two, the enemies at the moment were the Nazi-Fascists, and it was no time for splitting hairs. "First we'll win together, we'll settle our differences later."

Then he added that he came to the Oratorio because it was a good place. Priests were like the Garibaldini, they were an evil breed, but there were some respectable men among them. "Especially in these times when who knows what's going to happen to these kids, who until the past year were being taught that *books and muskets make perfect Fascists.* At the Oratorio, at least, they don't let them go to the dogs, and they teach them to be decent, even if they do make too much fuss about jerking off, but that doesn't matter because you all do it anyway, and at most you confess it later. So I come to the Oratorio and I help Don Cognasso to get the kids to play. When we go to mass, I sit quietly in the back of the church, because Jesus Christ I respect even if I don't God."

One Sunday, at two in the afternoon when there were just a few of us at the Oratorio, I told him about my stamps, and he said that once upon a time he had collected them, too, but when he came back from the war he lost interest and threw them all out. He had twenty or so left and would be happy to give them to me.

I went to his house and was amazed by my windfall: it included the two Fiji stamps I had gazed at with such longing in the pages of the Yvert and Tellier.

"So you have the Yvert and Tellier, too?" he asked, impressed.

"Yeah, but it's an old one..."

"They're the best."

The Fiji Islands. That was why I had been so fascinated by those two stamps back at Solara. After Gragnola's gift, I took them home to put them on a new page of my album. It was a winter evening, Papà had come home the day before, but he had left again that afternoon, going back to the city until the next visit.

I was in the kitchen of the main wing, which because we had just enough wood for the fireplace was the only heated room in the house. The light was dim. Not because the blackout meant much in Solara (who would have ever bombed us?), but because the bulb was muted by a lampshade from which hung strings of beads, like necklaces one might offer the primitive Fijians as gifts.

I was sitting at the table tending my collection, Mamma was tidying up, my sister was playing in the corner. The radio was on. We had just heard the end of the Milanese version of *What's Happening in the Rossi House,* a propaganda programme from the Republic of Salò that featured the members of a single family discussing politics and concluding, of course, that the Allies were our enemies, that the

Partisans were bandits resisting the draft out of sloth, and that the Fascists in the north were defending Italy's honour alongside their German comrades. But there was also, on alternate evenings, the Roman version, in which the Rossis were a different family, with the same name, living in a Rome now occupied by the Allies, realizing in the end how much better things had been when things were worse, and envying their northern neighbours, who still lived free beneath Axis flags. From the way my mother shook her head, you could tell that she did not believe it, but the programme was lively enough. Either you listened to that or you turned the radio off.

But later—at which point my grandfather would come in, too, having held out in his study until then with the help of a foot warmer—we were able to tune in to Radio London.

It began with a series of kettledrum beats, almost like Beethoven's Fifth, then we heard Colonel Stevens's winning "Buona sera", with his accent reminiscent of the dubbed voices of Laurel and Hardy. Another voice we had grown accustomed to, thanks to the regime radio, was that of Mario Appelius, who concluded his exhortations to victory with "God curse the English!" Stevens did not curse the Italians, in fact he called on them to rejoice with him in the defeat of the Axis, talking to us evening after evening as if to say, "See what he's been doing to you, your Duce?"

But his chronicles were not only about battles in the field. He described our lives, people like us, glued to the radio to listen to the Voice of London, overcoming our fear that someone might be spying and get us thrown in jail. He was telling our story, the story of his listeners, and we trusted him because he described exactly what we were doing, all of us, the local pharmacist and even—Stevens said—the cop on the corner, who knew the score and was biding his time. That was what he said, and if he was not lying about that, we could trust him about the rest. We all knew, even us kids, that his report was propaganda, too, but we were drawn to an understated propaganda, without heroic phrases and calls to death. Colonel Stevens made the words we were fed each day seem excessive.

I do not know why, but I saw this man—who was nothing but a voice—as Mandrake: elegant in his tailcoat, his neat moustache only slightly more grizzled than the magician's, able to turn every pistol into a banana.

After the colonel finished, the special messages began, as mysterious and evocative as a Montserrat stamp, for the Partisan brigades: *Messages for Franchi, Happy is not happy, The rain is past, My beard is blond, Giacomone kisses Muhammad, The eagle flies, The sun also rises…*

I see myself still adoring the Fiji stamps when suddenly, between ten and eleven, the sky starts buzzing, and we turn out all the lights and run to the window to await Pipetto's passage. We heard it every night, at more or less the same time, or that was how legend had it by then. Some said it was an English reconnaissance plane, some, an American plane that came to drop packages, food and arms for the Partisans in the mountains, perhaps not far from us, on the slopes of the Langhe.

It is a starless, moonless night, we cannot see lights in the valley nor the silhouettes of the hills, and Pipetto is passing above us. No one has ever seen him; he is only a noise in the night.

Pipetto has passed, everything has gone as usual again this evening, and we return to the radio's last songs. Out in that night bombs might be falling on Milan, packs of German shepherds might be chasing the men Pipetto helps through the hills, but the radio, with that saxophone-in-heat voice, is singing *Up there at Capocabana, at Capocabana the woman is queen, and she reigns supreme,* and I picture a languid diva (maybe I had seen her photo in *Novella*). She glides softly down a white staircase whose steps light up at the touch of her feet, surrounded by young men in white tailcoats who tip their top hats and kneel adoringly as she passes. With Capocabana (it was actually Capocabana, not Copacabana), the sexy singer is sending me a message every bit as exotic as that of my stamps.

Then the transmissions end, with various anthems to glory and revenge. But we must not turn it off now, as Mamma knows.

After the radio has given the impression of falling silent until the next day, we hear a heartfelt voice come through, singing:

You'll come back
To me...
It's written in the stars, you see,
you'll come back.
You'll come back,
it's a fact
that I am strong because I do
believe in you.

I had just listened to that song again at Solara, but there it was a love song: *You'll come back to me / because you are my heart's one dream, / its only dream. / You'll come back, / because I / without all your languid kisses / won't survive.* So the song I had heard all those evenings had been a wartime version, which to the hearts of many must have sounded like a promise, or an appeal to someone far away who in that moment might have been freezing in the steppes or facing a firing squad. Who was airing that song at that time of night? A nostalgic employee, before closing down the broadcast booth, or someone obeying an order from a higher-up? We did not know, but that voice carried us to the threshold of sleep.

It is nearly eleven, I close my stamp album, it is bedtime. Mamma has prepared the brick, an actual brick, by placing it in the oven until it is too hot to touch, then wrapping it in woollen cloths and slipping it under the covers, where it warms the entire bed. It feels good to rest your feet on it, especially as it relieves the itching of chilblains, which in those years (cold, vitamin deficiencies, hormonal tempests) made all our fingers and toes swell up, and sometimes turned into agonizing, suppurating sores.

A hound is baying from some farm in the valley.

Gragnola and I talked about everything. I would tell him about the books I was reading, and he would discuss them passionately: "Verne," he would say, "is better than Salgari, because he's scientific. Cyrus Smith manufacturing nitroglycerin is more real than that Sandokan tearing his chest with his fingernails just because he's fallen for some bitchy little fifteen-year-old."

"You don't like Sandokan?" I asked.

"He seemed a little Fascist to me."

I once told him I had read *Heart* by De Amicis, and he told me to throw it away because De Amicis was a Fascist. "Didn't you notice," he said, "how they're all against old Franti, who comes from a poor family, and yet they fall over each other trying to please that Fascist teacher. And what are the stories about? About good Garrone, who was an ass-kisser, about the little Lombard lookout, who dies because some wretch of a king's officer has sent the kid to watch for the enemy, about the Sardinian drummer boy who gets sent into the middle of a battle, at his age, to carry messages, and then that repulsive captain, who after the poor kid loses a leg throws himself onto him with open arms and kisses him three times over his heart, things you would just never do to a kid who's just been crippled, and even a captain in the Piedmontese army ought to have a little common sense. Or Coretti's father, stroking his son's face with his palm still warm from shaking hands with that butcher, the king. Up against the wall! Up against the wall! It's men like De Amicis who opened the road to Fascism."

He taught me about Socrates and Giordano Bruno. And Bakunin, about whose work and life I had known very little. He told me about Campanella, Sarpi, and Galileo, who were all imprisoned or tortured by priests for trying to spread scientific principles, and about some who had cut their own throats, like Ardigò, because the bosses and the Vatican were keeping them down.

Since I had read the Hegel entry ("Emin. Ger. phil. of the *pantheist school*") in the *Nuovissimo Melzi,* I asked Gragnola about him. "Hegel wasn't a pantheist, and your Melzi is an ignoramus. Giordano Bruno might have been a pantheist. A pantheist believes that God is everywhere, even in that speck of a fly you see there. You can imagine how satisfying that is, being everywhere is like being nowhere. Well, for Hegel it wasn't God but the State that had to be everywhere, therefore he was a Fascist."

"But didn't he live more than a hundred years ago?"

"So? Joan of Arc, also a Fascist of the highest order. Fascists have always existed. Since the age of... since the age of God. Take God—a Fascist."

"But aren't you one of those atheists who says God doesn't exist?"

"Who said that—Don Cognasso, who can never grasp the most trifling thing? I believe that God does, unfortunately, exist. It's just that he's a Fascist."

"But why is God a Fascist?"

"Listen, you're too young for me to give you a theology lecture. We'll start with what you know. Recite the ten commandments for me, seeing as the Oratorio makes you memorize them."

I recited them. "Good," he said. "Now pay attention. Among those ten commandments are four, think about it, only four that promote good things—and even those, well, let's review them. Don't kill, don't steal, don't bear false witness, and don't covet your neighbour's wife. This last one is a commandment for men who know what honour is: on the one hand, don't cuckold your friends, and on the other try to preserve your family, and I can live with that; anarchy wants to get rid of families too, but you can't have everything all at once. As for the other three, I agree, but common sense should tell you that much at a bare minimum. And even then you have to weigh them, we all tell lies sometimes, perhaps even for good ends, whereas killing, no, you shouldn't do that, ever."

"Not even if the king sends you off to war?"

"There's the rub. Priests will tell you that if the king sends you off to war you can, indeed you should, kill. And that the responsibility lies with the king. That's how they justify war, which is a nasty brute, especially if Fat Head is the one who sends you off. But notice that the commandments don't say it's okay to kill in war. They say don't kill, period. And then..."

"Then?"

"Let's look at the other commandments. I am the Lord thy God. That's not a commandment, otherwise there would be eleven. It's a prologue. But it's a sham of a prologue. Try to picture it: some guy appears to Moses, or actually he doesn't even really appear, a voice comes from who knows where, and then Moses goes and tells his people that they have to obey the commandments because they come from God. But who says they come from God? That voice: 'I am the Lord thy God.' And what if he wasn't? Imagine if I stop you on the street and say I'm a plain-clothes carabiniere and you have to pay me a ten-lira fine because no one's allowed on that street. If you're smart you'll say back: and how can I be sure that you're a carabiniere, maybe you're someone who makes his living by screwing people over. Let me see your papers. And instead God persuades Moses that he's God because he says so and that's that. It all begins with false witness."

"You don't believe it was God who gave the commandments to Moses?"

"No, actually I do believe it was God. I'm just saying he used a trick. He's always done that: you have to believe in the Bible because it's inspired by God, but who tells you the Bible's inspired by God? The Bible. See the problem? But let's move on. The first commandment says you shall have no other God before him. That's how the Lord prevents you from thinking, for instance, about Allah, or Buddha, or maybe even Venus—and let's be honest, it couldn't have been bad to have a piece of tail like that as your goddess. But it also means you shouldn't believe in philosophy, for instance, or in science, or get any ideas about man descending from apes. Just him, that's it. Now pay attention, because the other commandments are all Fascist, designed to force you to accept society as it is. Remember the one about keeping the Sabbath day holy.... What do you think of it?"

"Well, basically it says to go to mass on Sunday—what's wrong with that?"

"That's what Don Cognasso tells you, and like all priests he doesn't know the first thing about the Bible. Wake up! In a primitive tribe like the one Moses took out for a walk, this meant that you have to observe the rites, and the purpose of the rites—from human sacrifices on up to Fat Head's rallies in Piazza Venezia—is to addle people's brains! And then? Honour thy father and mother. Oh hush, don't tell me it's good for children to obey their parents, that's fine for children, who need guidance. But honour thy father and mother means respect the ideas of your elders, don't oppose tradition, don't presume to change the tribe's way of life. See? Don't cut off the king's head, though God knows if we have a head on our own shoulders we have to, especially with a king like that dwarf Savoy, who betrayed his army and sent his officers to their death. And now you can see that even Don't steal isn't quite as innocent a commandment as it seems, because it orders you not to touch private property, which belongs to the person who got rich by stealing from you. If only it ended there. There are three commandments left. What does Thou shalt not commit impure acts mean? The Don Cognassos of the world would have you believe its only purpose is to keep you from wagging that thing that hangs between your legs, and to drag in the stone tablets for the occasional wank seems a bit much. What's a guy like me supposed to do, a failure? That beautiful woman my mother didn't make me beautiful, and I'm a gimp to boot, and I've never touched a woman who's a woman, and they want to deny me even that release?"

At that time I knew how babies were born, but my ideas about what led up to that were vague. I had heard my friends talking about wanks and other kinds of touching, but I never dared do further research. Still, I did not want to make a bad impression on Gragnola. I nodded silently, solemnly.

"God could have said, for instance, You can screw, but only to make babies, especially since at that time there weren't enough people in the world. But the ten commandments don't say that: on the one hand, you can't covet your friend's wife and on the other you can't commit impure acts. So, then, when is screwing allowed? I mean really, you're trying to make a law that works for the whole world—when the Romans, who weren't God, made laws it was stuff that still makes sense today—and God tosses down a Decalogue that doesn't tell you the most important things? You'll probably say: Sure, but the prohibition against impure acts forbids screwing outside of marriage. Are you sure that was really the case? What were impure acts for the Hebrews? They had very strict rules, for example they couldn't eat pork, nor cows that had been killed in certain ways, and from what I'm told not even whitebait. So the impure acts are all the things that the people in power have prohibited. Which are? All the things that the people in power have defined as impure acts. Just look around, Fat Head claimed it was impure to speak ill of Fascism, and he'd send you off to confinement if you did. It was impure to be a bachelor, so you paid the bachelor tax. It was impure to fly a red flag. And so on and so on and so on. And now we come to the last commandment: Don't covet other people's stuff. But have you ever asked yourself why this commandment exists, when you've already got Don't steal? If you covet a bike like the one your friend has, is that a sin? No, not if you don't steal it from him. Don Cognasso will tell you that this commandment prohibits envy, which is certainly an ugly thing. But there's bad envy, which is when your friend has a bicycle and you don't, and you hope he breaks his neck going down a hill, and there's good envy, which is when you want a bike like his and work your butt off to be able to buy one, even a used one, and it's good envy that makes the world go round. And then there's another envy, which is justice envy, which is when you can't see any reason why a few people have everything and others are dying of hunger. And if you feel this fine sort of envy, which is socialist envy, you get busy trying to make a world in which riches are better distributed. But that's exactly what the commandment prohibits you from doing: Don't covet more than you have, respect the rule of property. In this world there are those who own two fields of grain just because they inherited them, and there are those who toil in those fields for a crust of bread, and the ones toiling must not covet the owner's fields, otherwise the state will be ruined and we'll have a revolution. The tenth commandment prohibits revolution. Therefore, my dear boy, don't kill and don't steal from poor kids like yourself, but go ahead and covet what other people have taken from you. That's the sun of the coming day, and that's why our comrades are staying up there in the mountains, to get rid of Fat Head, who rose to power funded by agrarian landowners and by Hitler's toadies, Hitler who wanted to conquer the world so that that guy Krupp who builds Berthas this long could sell more cannons. But you, how could you ever understand about these things, you who grew up memorizing oaths of obedience to Il Duce's orders?"

"No, I understand, even if not everything."

"I sure hope so."

That night I dreamed of Il Duce.

One day we went walking through the hills. I had thought Gragnola was going to tell me about the beauties of nature, as he had done in the past, but on that day he pointed out only dead things, dried cow dung with flies buzzing around it, a vine infected with downy mildew, a row of processionary caterpillars that were going to kill a tree, some potato plants with eyes larger than the tubers, which were now inedible, an animal carcass in a ditch, so putrefied that you could no longer tell whether it was a marten or a hare. And he smoked one Milit after another, excellent for TB, he would say, they disinfect your lungs.

"You see kid, the world is dominated by evil things. Indeed, by Evil with a capital E. And I'm not just talking about the evil of man killing his fellow man for a few coins, or the evil of the SS hanging our comrades. I'm talking about Evil itself, the thing that rotted my lungs, that makes a crop go bad, or that lets a hailstorm reduce a man who owns a small vineyard and nothing else to misery. Have you ever asked yourself why Evil exists in the world, and especially

death, when people like living so much, and one fine day death comes and carries them off, rich and poor alike, even babies? Have you ever heard anyone talk about the death of the universe? I read and I know: the universe, I mean the whole thing, the stars, the sun, the Milky Way, is like an electric battery that runs and runs, but all the while it's running down, and one day it will run out. End of the universe. The Evil of evils is that the universe itself has been condemned to death. Since birth, you might say. So what kind of world is that, where Evil exists? Wouldn't a world without Evil be better?"

"Well, yeah," I philosophized.

"Of course, you could say that the world was born by mistake, the world is a sickness afflicting the universe, which even before we came along wasn't feeling so great, and one fine day the open sore that is our solar system appears, and us with it. But the stars, the Milky Way, and the sun don't know they're bound to die, so it doesn't bother them. We, on the other hand, who have been born out of this sickness of the universe, we have the bad luck to be bright boys and to understand that we're bound to die. So not only are we victims of Evil, but we know it. Cheery stuff."

"But it's atheists who say that the world wasn't made by anyone, and you say you're not an atheist..."

"I'm not because I can't bring myself to believe that all these things we see around us—the way trees and fruits grow, and the solar system, and our brains—came about by chance. They're too well made. And therefore there must have been a creating mind. God."

"So then?"

"So then, how do you reconcile God with Evil?"

"Off the top of my head I'm not sure, let me think about it..."

"Ah yes, let me think about it, he says, as if the greatest minds haven't been thinking about it for century upon century..."

"And what did they end up with?"

"Diddly-squat. Evil, they said, was brought into the world by the rebel angels. Oh really? God sees and foresees all, and he didn't know the rebel angels were going to rebel? Why did he create them if he knew they were going to rebel? That's like somebody making car tyres that he knows will blow out after two kilometres. He'd be a prick. But no, he went ahead and created them, and afterwards he was happy as a clam, look how clever I am, I can even make angels.... Then he waited for them to rebel (no doubt drooling in anticipation of their first false step) and then hurled them down into hell. If that's the case, he's a monster. Other philosophers had a different idea: Evil doesn't exist outside of God, it's inside him, like a sickness, he spends eternity trying to free himself of it. Poor guy, maybe that's how it is. But since I know I'm tubercular, I would never bring children into the world, so as not to create other wretches, because TB is passed from father to son. And yet God, knowing he's got the sickness he's got, is going to make you a world that at best will be dominated by Evil? That's sheer wickedness. And further, one of us might have a child without meaning to, might get a little reckless one night and not use a rubber, but God made the world because that's exactly what he wanted to do."

"What if it just slipped out of him, like sometimes pee does?"

"You think you're being funny, but that's exactly what other sharp minds have thought. The world slipped out of God like piss slips out of us. The world is the result of his incontinence, like a man with an enlarged prostate."

"What's a prostate?"

"It doesn't matter, pretend I gave a different example. What matters is that the world slipped out of Him, that God just wasn't able to hold it in, and that all this is the result of the Evil he carries inside him—that's the only way to excuse God. We're in shit up to our eyes, but he's no better off himself. Then, however, all the pretty things they tell you at the Oratorio start falling like overripe fruit, things about God as the Good, as the perfect being who created the heavens and the earth. He created the heavens and the earth precisely because he was profoundly imperfect. That's why he made the stars like batteries that can't be recharged."

"But hang on, maybe God did create a world where those of us in it are destined to die, but say he did it as a test, to make us earn paradise, and therefore eternal happiness."

"Or burn in hell."

"The ones who yield to the devil's temptations."

"You talk like theologians, who are all in bad faith. Like you, they say that Evil exists, but that God has given us the greatest gift in the world, which is our free will. We are free to do what God tells us to do or what the devil tempts us to do, and if we end up in hell it's just because we haven't been created as slaves but as free men, and it just so happens we've used our freedom badly, which is our own doing."

"Exactly."

"Exactly? But who told you that freedom is a gift? In other words, be careful not to confuse things. Our comrades in the mountains are fighting for freedom, but it's freedom from other men who wanted to turn them into so many little machines. Freedom is a beautiful thing between one man and another; you don't have the right to make me do and think what you want me to. And besides, our comrades were free to decide whether to go up into the mountains or to hide out somewhere. But the freedom that God granted me, what kind of freedom is that? The freedom to go to paradise or to hell, with no middle ground. You're born and you're forced to play a hand of briscola, and if you lose you suffer for all eternity. And what if I didn't want to play this game? Fat Head, who among all his evil deeds actually did a few good things too, banned gambling houses, because those are places where people are tempted and end up ruining their lives. And don't tell me people are free to go there or not. Better not to lead them into temptation. But here God has created us free and incredibly weak, exposed to temptation. You call that a gift? It's as if I were to throw you down that escarpment and tell you, Don't worry, you're free to grab onto some shrub and haul yourself back up, or you can let yourself roll down until you've been reduced to the kind of minced meat they eat in Alba.

You might ask: But why did you throw me down when I was doing just fine up there? And I would answer: To see how strong you were. A fine lark. You didn't want to prove how strong you were, you were just happy not to fall."

"Now you're confusing me. What is it you believe, then?"

"It's simple, it just never occurred to anyone before: God is evil. Why do priests say God is good? Because he created us. But that's precisely why he's evil. God doesn't have evil the way we have a headache. God *is* Evil. Maybe, seeing as he's eternal, he wasn't evil billions of years ago. Maybe he became that way, like kids who get bored in the summer and start tearing the wings off flies, to pass the time. Notice how if you think that God is evil, the whole question of Evil becomes crystal clear."

"They're all bad, then, even Jesus?"

"Ah, no! Jesus is the only evidence that at least us men are capable of being good. To tell the truth, I'm not sure Jesus was God's son, because it doesn't make sense to me that a good guy like that could be born from such an evil father. I'm not even sure that Jesus really existed. Maybe we invented him ourselves, and that in itself would be a miracle, that our minds could come up with such a beautiful idea. Or maybe he did exist, was the best of men, and said he was the son of God with the best of intentions, to convince us that God was good. But if you read the Gospels closely, you'll realize that in the end even Jesus realized that God was bad: he gets scared in the olive grove and asks, Let this cup pass from me, and zilch, God doesn't listen; on the cross he shouts Father why hast thou forsaken me, and zilch, God turns his back. But Jesus showed us what a man can do to offset God's wickedness. If God is evil, then we at least have to try to be good, forgive each other, refrain from doing each other harm, heal the sick, and turn the other cheek. We've got to help each other, seeing as God doesn't help us. Do you see how great Jesus' idea was? Imagine how much it must have irritated God. Forget the devil, Jesus was the only true enemy of God, and he's the only friend us poor wretches have."

"You must be some kind of heretic, like the ones they burned..."

"I'm the only one who understands the truth, but unless I want to get burned I can't go around speaking it, so you're the only one I've told. Swear you won't tell anyone."

"I swear," I said, tracing a cross over my lips with my finger.

I noticed that Gragnola always wore a long, thin leather sack that hung from his neck, beneath his shirt.

"What's that, Gragnola?"

"A lancet."

"Were you studying to be a doctor?"

"I was studying philosophy. I was given the lancet in Greece by a doctor in my regiment, before he died. 'I don't need this any more,' he told me. 'That grenade has opened my belly. What I need now is one of those kits, like women have, with a needle and thread. But this hole is past stitching up. Keep this lancet to remember me by.' And I've worn it ever since."

"Why?"

"Because I'm a coward. With the things I do and the things I know, if the SS or the Black Brigades catch me, they'll torture me. If they torture me, I'll talk, because evil scares me. And I'll be sending my comrades to their deaths. This way, if they catch me, I'll cut my throat with the lancet. It doesn't hurt, only takes a second, *sffft*. I'll be screwing them all: the Fascists because they won't learn a thing, the priests because I'll be a suicide and that's a sin, and God because I'll be dying when I choose and not when he chooses. Put that in your pipe and smoke it."

Gragnola's speeches left me sad. Not because I was sure they were evil, but because I feared they were good. I was tempted to discuss them with my grandfather, but I did not know how he would react. He and Gragnola might not have understood each other, though they were both anti-Fascists. Grandfather had resolved his problems with Merlo, and with Il Duce, in an amusing way. He had saved the four boys in the chapel, pulling one over on the Black Brigades, and that was it. He was not a churchgoer, but that did not mean he was atheist—if he were, why would he have set up the Nativity scene? If he believed in God, it was a jolly God, who would have had a good laugh seeing Merlo trying to vomit his guts out—Grandfather had saved God the trouble of sending Merlo to Hell, since after all that oil he would surely have been sent merely to purgatory, where he could relieve himself in peace. Gragnola, on the other hand, lived in a world made wretched by an evil God, and the only times I saw him smile with any tenderness were when he was talking to me about Socrates or Jesus. Both of whom, I would remind myself, were killed, so I did not see what there was to smile about.

And yet he was not mean, he loved the people around him. He had it in only for God, and that must have been a real chore, because it was like throwing rocks at a rhinoceros—the rhinoceros never even notices and continues going about its rhino business, and meanwhile you are red with rage and ripe for a heart attack.

When was it that my friends and I began the Great Game? In a world where everyone was shooting at everyone else, we needed an enemy. And we chose the kids up in San Martino, that village on the peak above the plunging Gorge.

The Gorge was even worse than Amalia had described it. You really could not climb up it—and forget coming down—because you would lose your footing at every step. Where there were no brambles, the earth fell away beneath you, you might see a thicket of acacia or blackberry with an opening right in the middle and think you had found a path, but it would be just a random patch of stony ground, and after ten steps you would start to slip, then fall to one side and tumble at least twenty metres. Even if you survived the fall without breaking any bones, the thorns would scratch your eyes out. On top of that, it was said to be thick with vipers.

The people of San Martino had a mad fear of the Gorge, in part because of the hellcats, and anyone who would enshrine St. Antoninus, a mummy that looked like something risen from the grave to curdle a new mother's milk, would believe in hellcats. They made ideal enemies, since in our minds they were all Fascists. In reality that was not the case, it was just that two brothers from San Martino had joined the Black Brigades, while their two younger brothers remained in the village, the ringleaders of the bunch up there. But still, the town was attached to its sons who had gone off to war, and in Solara it was whispered that the people of San Martino were not to be trusted.

Fascists or not, we used to say that the boys of San Martino were no better than animals. The fact is that if you live in such an accursed place, you have to get up to some mischief every day, just to feel alive. They had to come down to Solara for school, and we who lived in town used to watch them as if they were gypsies. Many of us would bring a snack, bread and marmalade, and they were lucky if they had been given a wormy apple. In short, they had to do something, and on several occasions they bombarded us with rocks as we approached the gate of the Oratorio. We had to make them pay. So we decided to go up to San Martino and attack them while they played ball in the church piazza.

But the only way to San Martino was by the road that went straight up, with no bends, and from the church piazza you could see if anyone was coming. Thus we thought we could never take them by surprise. Until Durante, a farmer's kid with a head as big and dark as an Abyssinian's, said Yes we could, if we climbed the Gorge.

Climbing the Gorge required training. It took us a season, starting out with ten metres the first day, memorizing each step and each crevice, trying to place our feet in the same places on the way down as we had on the way up, and the next day we worked on the next ten metres. We could not be seen from San Martino, so we had all the time we wanted. It was important not to improvise, we had to become like those animals who made their homes on the slopes of the Gorge—the grass snakes, the lizards.

Two of my friends got sprains, one almost killed himself and skinned the palm of his hand badly trying to stop his fall, but by the end of it we were the only people in the world who knew how to climb the Gorge. One afternoon we risked it: we climbed for more than an hour and arrived out of breath, emerging from a dense thicket at the very base of San Martino, where between the houses and the precipice was a walkway with a wall along it to prevent the locals from falling over the precipice in the dark. Our path reached the wall at the very point where a gap opened, a breach, wide enough for us to slip through. Beyond that was a lane that ran past the door to the rectory, then opened right into the church piazza.

When we burst into the piazza, they were in the middle of a game of blindman's bluff. A masterstroke: the blindman could not see at all, of course, and the others were jumping here and there in their efforts to avoid him. We launched our munitions, hitting one kid directly on the forehead, and the others fled into the church seeking the priest's aid. That would suffice for the moment, and back down the lane we ran, through the gap, and down the Gorge. The priest arrived in time to see our heads disappearing into the shrubs, and he hurled some terrible threats at us, and Durante shouted "Hah!" and clapped his left hand against his right bicep.

But by now the San Martino boys had wised up. Seeing that we had come up the Gorge, they placed sentinels at the breach. It is true that we could get almost right up to the wall before they were aware of us, but only almost: the last few metres were in the open, through blackthorn scrub that slowed our progress, giving the sentinel enough time to raise the alarm. They were ready at the end of the lane with sun-baked balls of mud, and they launched them at us before we could gain the walkway.

It seemed a shame to have worked so hard learning to climb

the Gorge only to have to give it all up. Until Durante said, "We'll learn to climb it in the fog."

Since it was early autumn, there was as much fog in those parts as a person could want. On foggy days, if it was the good stuff, the town of Solara disappeared beneath it, even Grandfather's house disappeared, and the only thing that rose above all that grey was the San Martino bell tower. Being up in that tower was like being in a dirigible above the clouds.

Already on such days we would have been able to get as far as that wall, where the fog began to thin, and those kids could not spend the whole day looking down into nothing, especially once darkness had fallen. And when the fog really got bullish, it spilled over the wall and flooded the church piazza.

Climbing the Gorge in the fog was much harder than climbing it in sunlight. You really had to learn every step by heart, be able to say such and such a rock is here, watch out for the edge of a dense thorn thicket there, five steps (five, not four or six) farther to the right the ground drops suddenly away, when you reach the boulder there will be a false path just to your left and if you follow it you will fall off a cliff. And so on.

We made exploratory trips on clear days, then for a week we practised by repeating the steps in our heads. I tried to make a map, as in the adventure books, but half my friends could not read maps. Too bad for them, I had it printed in my brain and could have traversed the Gorge with my eyes closed—and going on a foggy night was essentially the same thing.

After everyone had learned the route, we continued training for several days, in the thickest fog, after sunset, in order to see if we would be able to gain the wall before they had sat down for supper.

After many test runs, we attempted our first expedition. Who knows how we made it to the top, but we did, and there they were, in the piazza, which was still free of fog, shooting the breeze—because in a place like San Martino either you hang out in the piazza or you go to bed after eating your soup of stale bread and milk.

We entered the piazza, gave them a proper pelting, jeered them as they fled to their houses, and then climbed back down. Going down was harder than going up, because if you slip going up you have a chance to grab a shrub, but if you slip going down you are finished, and before you come to a stop your legs are bleeding and your pants are ruined for ever. But we made it down, victorious and exultant.

After that we risked other incursions, and they were unable to post sentinels even when it was just dark, because most of them were afraid of the dark, on account of hellcats. We who attended the Oratorio could not have cared less about hellcats, because we knew that half a Hail Mary would basically paralyse them. We kept that up for several months. Then we got bored: the climb was no longer a challenge, in any weather.

No one back home ever learned the story of the Gorge, otherwise I would have received a thorough thrashing, and whenever we went up after dark I would say that I was going down to the Oratorio for a rehearsal. But everyone at the Oratorio knew, and we peacocked around because we were the only ones in the whole town who had mastered the Gorge.

It was noon on a Sunday. Something was happening, everyone already knew: two German trucks had arrived in Solara, searched half the town, and then taken the road up towards San Martino.

A thick fog had settled in early that morning, and daytime fog is worse than night fog because it is light out but you have to move around as if it were dark. You could not even hear the church bells, as if that grey worked as a silencer. Even the voices of numb sparrows in the tree branches came to us as if through cotton wool. Some guy's funeral was supposed to be held that day, but the people in the procession would not venture onto the cemetery road, and the gravedigger sent word that he would not be burying anyone that day, lest someone make a mistake when lowering the coffin and cause him to fall into the grave himself.

Two men from town had followed the Germans to find out what they were up to, had seen them make their way slowly, headlamps on but penetrating less than a metre, as far as the beginning of the ascent towards San Martino, and then stop, not daring to go on. Certainly not with their trucks, because they had no idea what was on either side of that steep incline, and they did not want to roll off some precipice—they may even have expected treacherous curves. Nor did they dare to attempt it on foot, not knowing what was where. Someone, however, had explained to them that the only way up to San Martino was by that road, and in that weather no one could possibly get down any other way, because of the Gorge. So then they placed trestles at the end of the road and waited there, headlamps on and guns levelled, so as not to let anyone pass, while one of them yelled into a field telephone, perhaps asking for reinforcements. Our informers said they heard him repeat *volsunde, volsunde* a number of times. Gragnola explained at once that they were certainly asking for *Wolfshunde*, that is, German shepherds.

The Germans waited there, and around four in the afternoon, with everything still a thick grey but also still light, they caught sight of someone coming down, on a bicycle. It was the parish priest of San Martino, who had been taking that road for who knows how many years and could even come down using his feet as brakes. Seeing a priest, the Germans held their fire, because, as we later learned, they were looking not for cassocks but for Cossacks. The priest explained more with gestures than words that some fellow was dying on a farm near Solara and had called for extreme unction (he showed them the necessaries in a bag attached to the handlebars), and the Germans believed him. They let him pass, and the priest came to the Oratorio to whisper with Don Cognasso.

Don Cognasso was not the sort to get involved in politics, but he knew what was what, and without saying more than a few words he told the priest to tell Gragnola and his friends what there was to tell, because he himself would not and could not get mixed up in such matters.

A group of young men quickly gathered around the card table, and I slipped in behind the last few, crouching a little to avoid notice. And I listened to the priest's story.

There was a detachment of Cossacks with the German troops. We had not known that, but Gragnola was informed. They had been taken prisoner on the Russian front, but for reasons of their own the Cossacks had it in for Stalin, so that many had been convinced (motivated by money, by hatred of the Soviets, by a desire not to rot in prison camp, or even by the chance to leave their Soviet paradise, taking horses, carts, and family with them) to enrol as auxiliaries. Most were fighting in eastern areas, like Carnia, where they were extremely feared for their toughness and ferocity. But there was also a Turkistani division in the Pavia region—people called them Mongols. Former Russian prisoners, if not actually Cossacks, were roaming around in Piedmont too, with the Partisans.

Everyone by now knew how the war was going to end, and what is more the eight Cossacks in question were men with religious principles. After having seen two or three towns burned and poor people hung by the dozen, and more, after two of their own number had been executed for refusing to shoot at old people and children, they had decided they could no longer remain with the SS. "Not only that," explained Gragnola, "but if the Germans lose the war, and by now they've lost, what will the Americans and the English do? They'll capture the Cossacks and give them back to the Russians, their allies. In Russia, these guys are *kaputt.* So they're trying to join the Allies now, so that after the war they'll be given refuge somewhere, beyond the clutches of that Fascist Stalin."

"Indeed," the priest said, "these eight have heard about the Partisans who are fighting with the English and Americans, and they're trying to reach them. They have their own ideas and are well informed: they don't want to join the Garibaldini, but rather the Badogliani."

They had deserted who knows where, then headed towards Solara simply because someone had told them that the Badogliani were in those parts. They had walked many kilometres on foot, off the roads, moving only at night and so taking twice as long, but the SS had managed to stay hot on their heels, and it was a miracle that they had managed to reach us, begging food at the occasional farm, always on the verge of running into people who might be spies, communicating as best they could, since they all spoke a smattering of German but only one knew Italian.

The day before, realizing the SS was onto them and was about to catch up with them, they had gone up to San Martino, thinking that from there they could fight off a battalion for a few days, and after all they might as well die bravely. And also because someone had told them that a certain Talino lived up there who knew someone who might be able to help them. At this point they were a desperate bunch. They reached San Martino after dark and found Talino, who however told them there was a Fascist family who lived there, and in a village that small, secrets lasted no time. The only thing he could think to do was have them seek refuge in the rectory. The priest took them in, not for political reasons, nor even out of the goodness of his heart, but because he saw that letting them wander about would be worse than hiding them. But he could not keep them long. He did not have enough food for eight men, and he was scared out of his wits, because if the Germans came they would waste no time in searching every house, including the rectory.

"Boys, try to understand," the priest said. "You've all read Kesselring's manifesto too, they've put it up everywhere. If they find those men in any of our houses, they'll burn the town, and even worse, if one of them shoots at the Germans, they'll kill us all."

Unfortunately, we had indeed seen Field Marshal Kesselring's manifesto, and even without it we knew that the SS did not mince such matters, and that they had already burned several towns.

"And so?" Gragnola asked.

"So, seeing that this fog has by the grace of God descended upon us, and seeing that the Germans don't know the area, someone

Following the well-known appeal directed by Field Marshal Kesselring to the Italians, the same Field Marshal has now imparted to his own troops the following orders:

1. Initiate the most vigorous action against the armed bands of rebels, against the saboteurs and criminals who by their deleterious conduct in any way hinder the prosecution of the war or disturb order and public safety.

2. Establish a percentage of hostages in those localities where armed bands continue to exist and execute said hostages each time an act of sabotage occurs in those localities.

3. Undertake acts of reprisal, including the burning of dwellings located in areas from which gunshots have been fired against German military individuals or units.

4. Hang in public piazzas those elements held responsible for homicides, and the leaders of armed bands.

5. Hold responsible the inhabitants of those towns where interruptions of telegraphic or telephonic lines occur, as well as acts of sabotage related to traffic flow (scattering of broken glass, nails, or other materials on the road surfaces, damaging of bridges, obstruction of roads).

Field Marshal Kesselring

from Solara has to come up and get those blessed Cossacks, lead them back down, and take them to the Badogliani."

"And why someone from Solara?"

"Imprimis because, to be frank, if I speak about this with anyone in San Martino, word will begin to get around, and in these times the fewer words getting around the better. In secundis, because the Germans have closed the road and no one can get out by that route. Hence the only thing left is to go through the Gorge."

Hearing mention of the Gorge, everyone said, What, do we look crazy, in fog like this, how come that Talino fellow can't do it—things of that kind. But the damn priest, after reminding them that Talino was eighty and could not come down from San Martino even on the sunniest of days, added—and I say it was in revenge for the frights we boys from the Oratorio had given him: "The only people who know how to get through the Gorge, even in fog, are your boys. Seeing as they learned that deviltry for their roguish ends, let them for once use their talents for the good. Bring the Cossacks down with the help of one of your boys."

"Christ," Gragnola said, "even if that's true, what would we do once we got them down, keep them in Solara so that on Monday morning they can be found among us instead of with you, so that then they can burn our town instead?"

Among the group were Stivulu and Gigio, the two men who went with my grandfather to make Merlo take the castor oil, and it was clear that they too had connections to those in the Resistance. "Calm down," said Stivulu, the sharper of the two, "the Badogliani are as we speak in Orbegno, and neither the SS nor the Black Brigades have ever laid a hand on them there, because they stick to the high ground and control the entire valley with those English machine-guns, which are fantastic. From here to Orbegno, even in this fog, for somebody like Gigio who knows the road, if he could use Bercelli's truck, which has got headlamps on it made special for fog, that's a two-hour trip. Let's go ahead and say three because it's already getting dark. It's five now, Gigio gets there by eight, he warns them, they come down a little way and wait by the Vignoletta crossroad. Then the truck's back here by ten, let's go ahead and say eleven, and it hides in that cluster of trees at the foot of the Gorge, near that little chapel of the Madonna. One of us, after eleven, goes up the Gorge, gets the Cossacks in the rectory, brings them down, loads them into the truck, and before morning those fellows are with the Badogliani."

"And we're going through all this rigmarole and risking our necks for eight Mamelukes or Kalmyks or Mongols or whatever, who were with the SS up until yesterday?" asked a man with red hair, whose name, I think, was Migliavacca.

"Hey buddy, these guys have changed their minds," Gragnola said, "and that's already a fine thing, but they're also eight strongmen who know how to shoot, so they're useful, the rest is horseshit."

"They're useful for the Badogliani," snapped Migliavacca.

"Badogliani or Garibaldini, they're all fighting for freedom, and as everybody's always saying, the accounts will be settled later, not sooner. We've got to save the Cossacks."

"You're right, too. And after all, they're Soviet citizens and so belong to the great fatherland of socialism," said a man named Martinengo, who had not quite kept up with all the turning of coats. But these were months when people were doing all sorts of things, like Gino, who had been in the Black Brigades, and one of its more fanatical members, then ran off to join the Partisans and returned to Solara wearing a red neckerchief. But he was impulsive, and came back when he should have stayed away, to meet a girl, and the Black Brigades caught him and executed him in Asti one day at dawn.

"In short, it can be done," Gragnola said.

"There's just one problem," said Migliavacca. "Even the priest said that only the kids know how to climb the Gorge, and I wouldn't involve a kid in such a delicate situation. Questions of judgement aside, they're likely to go around blabbing about it."

"No," said Stivulu. "For example, take Yambo here, none of

you even noticed him, but he's heard everything. If his grandfather heard me saying this he'd kill me, but Yambo knows the Gorge like the back of his hand, and he's got a good head on his shoulders, and what's more he's not the kind to wag his tongue. I'd stake my life on it, and besides everyone in his family is on our side, so we're not running any risks."

I broke out into a cold sweat and started to say it was late and I was expected at home.

Gragnola pulled me aside and rattled off a slew of fine words. That it was for freedom, that it was to save eight poor wretches, that even boys my age could be heroes, that after all I'd climbed the Gorge many times and this time wouldn't be any different from the others, except there would be eight Cossacks coming down behind me and I would have to be careful not to lose them along the way, that in any case the Germans were way over there waiting at the base of the road like dumb-asses with no idea where the Gorge was, that he would come with me even though he was sick, because you cannot turn your back when duty calls, that we would not go at eleven but rather at midnight, when everyone in my house was already asleep and I could slip out unnoticed, and the next day they would see me back in my bed as if nothing had happened. And so on, hypnotizing me.

Finally I said yes. After all, it was an adventure I would later be able to tell stories about, a Partisan thing, a coup unlike any of Flash Gordon's in the forests of Arboria. Unlike any of Tremal-Naik's in the Black Jungle. Better than Tom Sawyer in the mysterious cave. The Ivory Patrol had never ventured into such a jungle. In short, it would be my moment of glory, and it was for the Fatherland—the right one, not the wrong one. And no peacocking around with a bandolier and a Sten gun, but unarmed and bare-handed like Dick Fulmine. In short, all my reading was coming in handy. And if I did have to die, I would finally see the blades of grass as stakes.

But since I had a good head on my shoulders, I immediately set a few things straight with Gragnola. He was saying that with eight Cossacks in tow, we risked losing them along the way, and so we should get a nice long rope to tie everyone together, as mountain climbers do, and that way each could follow the next even without seeing where he was going. I said no, if we were roped together like that and the first one fell, he would pull everyone else down with him. What we needed were ten pieces of rope: each of us would hold tight to the end of the rope of the person in front of us as well as the end of the rope of the person behind us, and if we felt one of them falling, we would immediately let go of our end, because it was better one should fall than all of us. You're sharp, Gragnola said.

I asked him excitedly if he was going to come armed, and he said no, in the first place because he would never hurt a fly, but also because if there were, God forbid, an engagement, the Cossacks were armed, and finally, in the event that he was unlucky enough to get caught, they might not put him up against the wall right away if he were unarmed.

We went and told the priest we were in agreement, and to have the Cossacks ready by one in the morning.

I went home for dinner around seven. The rendezvous was for midnight by the little chapel of the Madonna, and it took forty-five minutes of brisk walking to get there. "Do you have a watch?" Gragnola asked. "No, but at eleven, when everyone goes to bed, I'll wait in the dining room where there's a clock."

Dinner at home with my mind aflame, after dinner a show of listening to the radio and looking at my stamps. The trouble was that Papà was there too, because with the fog he had not dared drive back to the city, and was hoping he would be able to leave in the morning. But he went to bed quite early, and Mamma with him. Did my parents still make love in those years, when they were in their forties? I wonder now. I think that the sexuality of our parents remains a mystery for all of us, and that Freud invented the primal scene. I cannot imagine them letting us see them. Though I do recall a conversation my mother had with some of her friends, near the beginning of the war, when she was not much past forty (I once

heard her say with forced optimism: "Besides, life begins at forty"): "Oh, in his day my Duilio did his part..." When? Until Ada was born? And then they stopped having sex? "Who knows what Duilio's doing behind my back, alone in the city, with the company secretary," my mother sometimes joked with my grandfather. She was kidding. But might my poor Papà have held someone's hand during the bombardments, to lift his spirits?

At eleven, the house was immersed in silence, and I was in the dining room, in the dark. Every now and then I would light a match to check the clock. At 11:15 I slipped out, heading through the fog towards the little chapel of the Madonna.

Fear grips me. Now or then? I am seeing images that have nothing to do with this. Maybe there really were hellcats. They were waiting for me behind a wispy thicket, which I could not see in the fog: there they were, at first alluring (who said they would be toothless old women? maybe they had slits), but later they were going to point their sub-machine guns at me and dissolve me in a symphony of reddish holes. I am seeing images that have nothing to do with this...

Gragnola was there, and complained that I was late. I realized he was trembling. Not I. I was now in my element.

Gragnola handed me the end of a rope, and we began climbing up the Gorge.

I had the map in my head, but Gragnola kept saying oh God I'm falling, and I would reassure him. I was the leader. I knew how to make my way through the jungle among Suyodhana's thugs. I moved my feet as if following the score of a piece of music, that must be how pianists do it—with their hands, I mean, not their feet—and I did not miss a step. But he, even though he was following me, kept stumbling. And coughing. I often had to turn around and pull him by the hand. The fog was thick, but from half a metre away we could see each other. If I pulled the rope, Gragnola would emerge from dense vapours, which seemed to dissipate all at once, and appear suddenly before me, like Lazarus throwing off his shroud.

The climb lasted a good hour, but that was about average. The only time I warned Gragnola to be careful was when we reached the boulder. If instead of going around it and rejoining the path, you mistakenly went to the left, feeling pebbles beneath your feet, you would end up in the ravine.

We reached the top, at the gap in the wall, and San Martino was a single invisible mass. We go straight, I told him, down the lane. Count at least twenty steps and we will be at the rectory door.

We knocked at the door as we had agreed: three knocks, a pause, then three more. The priest came to let us in. He was a dusty pale colour, like the clematis along the roads in the summer. The eight Cossacks were there, armed like bandits and scared as children. Gragnola talked with the one who spoke Italian. He spoke it quite well, though with a bizarre accent, but Gragnola, as people do with foreigners, spoke to him in infinitives.

"You to go ahead of friends and to follow me and child. You to say to your men what I say, and they to do what I say. Understand?"

"I understand, I understand. We are ready."

The priest, who was about to piss himself, opened the door and let us out into the lane. And in that very moment we heard, from the end of the village where the road came in, several Teutonic voices and the yelp of a dog.

"God damn it all to hell," Gragnola said, and the priest did not even blink. "The toadies made it up here, they've got dogs, and dogs don't give a rat's ass about fog, they go by their noses. What the hell do we do now?"

The leader of the Cossacks said, "I know how they do. One dog every five men. We go just the same, maybe we meet ones without dog."

"*Rien ne va plus*," said Gragnola the learned. "To go slow. And to shoot only if I say. To prepare handkerchiefs or rags, and other ropes." Then he explained to me: "We'll hurry to the end of the lane and stop at the corner. If no one's there, we'll go right over the wall and be gone. If anyone comes and they've got dogs, we're fucked. If it comes to it, we'll shoot at them and the dogs, but it depends how many they are. If on the other hand they don't have dogs, we'll let them pass, come up behind them, bind their hands and stick rags in their mouths, so they can't yell."

"And then leave them there?"

"Yeah, right. No, we take them with us into the Gorge, there's nothing else for it."

He quickly explained all that again to the Cossack, who repeated it to his men.

The priest gave us some rags, and some cords from the holy vestments. Go, go, he was saying, and God protect you.

We headed down the lane. At the corner we heard German voices coming from the left, but no barks or yelps.

We pressed flat against the wall. We heard two men approaching, talking to each other, probably cursing the fact that they could not see where they were going. "Only two," Gragnola explained with signs. "Let them pass, then on them."

The two Germans, who had been sent to comb that area while the others took the dogs around the piazza, were going along almost on tiptoe, with their rifles pointed, but they could not even see that a lane was there, and so they passed it. The Cossacks threw themselves on the two shadows and showed that they were good at what they did. In a flash the two men were on the ground with rags in their mouths, each one held by two of those demoniacs, while a third tied their hands behind them.

"We did it," Gragnola said. "Now you, Yambo, toss their rifles over the wall, and you, to push the Germans behind us two, down where we go."

I was terrified, and now Gragnola became the leader. Getting through the wall was easy. Gragnola passed out the ropes. The problem was that except for the first and the last in line, each person had to have both hands occupied, one for the front rope and the other for the back rope. But if you have to push two trussed Germans, you cannot hold a rope, and for the first ten steps the group went forward by shoving, until we slipped into the first thickets. At that point Gragnola tried to reorganize the rope system. The two who were leading the Germans each tied his rope to his prisoner's gun belt. The two who were following each held onto his collar with his right hand, and with his left hand held onto the rope of the man behind him. But just as we were preparing to set off again, one of the Germans tripped and fell onto the guard in front of him, taking the one behind with him, and the chain was broken. The Cossacks hissed things under their breath that must have been curses in their language, but they had the good sense to do so without shouting.

One German, after the initial fall, tried to get back up and distance himself from the group. Two Cossacks began groping their way after him and might have lost him—except that he did not know where he was going either, and after a few steps he slipped and fell forward, and they had him again. In the confusion his helmet had fallen off. The leader of the Cossacks made it clear that we should not leave it there, because if the dogs came they could follow the scent and would track us down. Only then did we realize that the second German was bareheaded. "God damn those bastards," murmured Gragnola, "his helmet fell off him when we took him in the alley. If they get there with their dogs, they'll have the scent!"

Nothing for it. And indeed we had gone only a few metres farther when from above we heard voices, and dogs barking. "They've reached the alley, the animals have sniffed the helmet, and they're saying we've come this way. Stay calm and quiet. First, they have to find the gap in the wall, and if you don't know it, it's not easy. Second, they have to come down. If their dogs are cautious and go slow, they'll go slow too. If the dogs go fast, they won't be able to keep up and will fall on their asses. They don't have you, Yambo. Go as fast as you can, let's move."

"I'll try, but I'm scared."

"You're not scared, just nervous. Take a deep breath and move."

I was about to piss myself like the priest, but at the same time I knew everything depended on me. My teeth were clenched, and in that moment I would rather have been Giraffone or Jojo than Romano the Legionnaire; Horace Horsecollar or Clarabelle Cow than Mickey Mouse in the House of Seven Ghosts; Signor Pampurio in his apartment than Flash Gordon in the swamps of Arboria, but when you are on the dance floor there is nothing to do but dance. I started down the Gorge as fast as I could, replaying each step in my mind.

The two prisoners were slowing us down, because with the rags in their mouths they had a hard time breathing and paused every minute. After at least fifteen minutes we came to the boulder, and I was so sure of where it was that I touched it with my outstretched hand before I could even see it. We had to stay close together as we went around it, because if anyone veered right they would come to the ledge and the ravine. The voices above us could still be heard distinctly, but it was unclear whether that was because the Germans were yelling louder to incite their reluctant dogs, or whether they had made it past the wall and were approaching.

Hearing their comrade's voices, the two prisoners began trying to jerk away, and when not actually falling they were pretending to fall, trying to roll off to the side, unafraid of injuring themselves. They had realized that we could not shoot them, because of the noise, and that wherever they ended up the dogs would find them. They no longer had anything to lose, and like anyone with nothing to lose, they had become dangerous.

Suddenly we heard machine-gun fire. Not being able to come down, the Germans had decided to fire. But for one thing, they had almost a hundred and eighty degrees of the Gorge before them and no idea which way we had gone, so they were firing all over the place. For another, they had not realized how steep the Gorge was, and they were firing almost horizontally. When they fired in our direction, we could hear the bullets whistling over our heads.

"Let's move, let's move," Gragnola said, "they still won't get us."

But the first Germans must have begun climbing down, getting an idea of the slope of the terrain, and the dogs must have begun heading in a more precise direction. Now they were shooting down, and more or less at us. We heard some bullets murmur through nearby bushes.

"No fear," said the Cossack, "I know the *Reichweite* of their *Maschinen.*"

"The range of those machine-guns," Gragnola offered.

"Yes, that. If they do not come more far down and we go fast, then the bullets will not reach to us any more. So quick."

"Gragnola," I said with huge tears in my eyes, longing for Mamma, "I can go quicker but the rest of you can't. You can't drag these two with us, there's no point in me running down like a goat if they keep holding us up. Let's leave them here, or I swear I'm taking my life in my own hands."

"If we leave them here they'll get loose in a flash and call down the others," Gragnola said.

"I kill them with the butt of machine-gun, that makes no noise," hissed the Cossack.

The idea of killing those two poor men froze me, but I snapped out of it when Gragnola growled: "It's no good, goddamnit, even if we leave them here dead, the dogs will find them, and the others will know which way we've gone," and in the excitement he was no longer speaking in infinitives. "There's only one thing to do, make them fall in some direction that isn't ours, so the dogs will go that way and we might gain ten minutes or even more. Yambo, to the right here, isn't there that false path that leads to the ravine? Good, we'll push them down there, you said that anyone going that way won't notice the ledge and will fall easily, then the dogs will lead the Germans to the bottom. Before they can recover from that blow we're in the valley. A fall from there will kill them, right?"

"No, I didn't say that a fall there would definitely kill them. You'll break bones, if you're unlucky you might hit your head..."

"Goddamn you, how come you said one thing and now you're saying another? So maybe their ropes will come loose as they're falling, and when they come to a stop they'll still have enough breath to yell and warn the others to be careful!"

"Then they must fall when they are already dead," commented the Cossack, who knew how things worked in this dirty world.

I was right next to Gragnola and could see his face. He had always been pale, but he was paler now. He stood there gazing upwards, as if seeking inspiration from the heavens. In that moment, we heard a *frr frrr* of bullets passing near us at the level of a man's head. One of the Germans shoved his guard and both fell to the ground, and the Cossack started complaining because the first one was head-butting him in the teeth, gambling everything and trying to make noise. That was when Gragnola made his decision and said, "It's them or us. Yambo, if I go right, how many steps before the ledge?"

"Ten steps, ten of mine, maybe eight for you, but if you push your foot out in front of you you'll feel it start to slope away, and from that point to the ledge it's four steps. To be safe take three."

"Okay," Gragnola said, turning to the Cossack, "I'll go forward, two of you push these two toadies, hold them tight by the shoulders. Everybody else stays here."

"What are you going to do?" I asked, my teeth chattering.

"You shut up. This is war. Wait here with them. That's an order."

They disappeared to the right of the boulder, swallowed by the *fumifugium*. We waited several minutes, heard the skittering of stones and several thuds, then Gragnola and the two Cossacks reappeared, without the Germans. "Let's move," Gragnola said, "now we can go faster."

He put a hand on my arm and I could feel him trembling. Now that he was closer I could see him again: he was wearing a sweater that was snug around his neck, and now the lancet case was hanging over his chest, as if he had taken it out. "What did you do with them?" I asked, crying.

"Don't think about it, it was the right thing. The dogs will smell the blood and that's where they'll lead the others. We're safe, let's go."

And when he saw that my eyes were bulging out: "It was them or us. Two instead of ten. It's war. Let's go."

After nearly half an hour, during which we kept hearing angry shouts and barking from above, but not coming towards us, indeed getting farther away, we reached the bottom of the Gorge, and the road. Gigio's truck was waiting nearby, in the cluster of trees. Gragnola loaded the Cossacks on it. "I'm going with them, to make sure they reach the Badogliani," he said. He was trying not to look at me, was in a hurry to see me leave. "You go on from here, get back home. You've been brave. You deserve a medal. And don't think about the rest. You did your duty. If anyone is guilty of anything, it's me only."

I returned home sweating, despite the cold, and exhausted. I took refuge in my little room and would have been happy to spend a sleepless night, but it was worse than that, I kept dozing off from exhaustion for a few minutes at a time, kept seeing Uncle Gaetanos dancing with their throats cut. Maybe I was running a fever. I have to confess, I have to confess, I kept telling myself.

The next morning was worse. I had to get up more or less at the usual hour, to see Papà off, and Mamma could not understand why I was so addle-brained. Several hours later Gigio showed up and quickly conferred with my grandfather and Masulu. As he was leaving I signalled him to meet me in the vineyard, and he could not hide anything from me.

Gragnola had escorted the Cossacks to the Badogliani, then returned, with Gigio and the truck, to Solara. The Badogliani had told them they should not go around at night unarmed: they had learned that a detachment of Black Brigades had reached Solara to assist their comrades. They gave Gragnola a musket.

The trip to and from the Vignoletta crossroads took a total of three hours. They returned the truck to Bercelli's farm, then set out walking on the road to Solara. They thought it was all over, heard no noises, and were walking calmly. From what they could tell in that fog, it was nearly dawn. After all that tension, they were trying to cheer each other up, slapping each other on the back, making noise. And so they failed to notice that the Black Brigades were crouching in a ditch, and they were caught not more than two kilometres from town. They had weapons on them when they were taken and could not explain them away. They were thrown into the back of a van. There were only five of the Fascists, two up front, two in back facing them, and one standing on the front running board, to help see better in the fog.

They had not even bound them, though the two who were guarding them were sitting with sub-machine guns across their laps, while Gigio and Gragnola had been thrown down like sacks.

At a certain point Gigio heard a strange noise, like fabric tearing, and felt a viscous liquid spray him in the face. One of the Fascists heard a gasp, turned on a flashlight, and there was Gragnola with his throat cut, lancet in hand. The two Fascists started cursing, stopped the van, and with Gigio's help dragged Gragnola to the side of the road. He was already dead, or nearly, spilling blood everywhere. The other three had come over too, and they were all blaming each other, saying he could not croak like that because command needed to make him talk, and they would all be arrested for having been so stupid, failing to tie up the prisoners.

While they were yelling over Gragnola's body, they forgot Gigio for a moment and he, in the confusion, thought Now or never. He took off to one side, crossing the ditch, knowing there was a steep slope beyond it. They fired off a few shots, but he had already rolled to the bottom like an avalanche, and then hidden among some trees. In that fog, he would have been a needle in a haystack, nor were the Fascists too interested in making a big deal out of it, because it was obvious by that point that they had to hide Gragnola's body and go back to their command pretending not to have taken anyone that night, so as to avoid trouble with their leaders.

That morning, after the Black Brigades had left to meet up with the Germans, Gigio had taken a few friends to the site of the tragedy, and after searching the ditches awhile, they found Gragnola. The priest of Solara would not allow the corpse in the church, because Gragnola had been an anarchist and by now it was known that he was a suicide too, but Don Cognasso said to bring him to the little church at the Oratorio, since the Lord knew the proper rules better than his priests.

Gragnola was dead. He had saved the Cossacks, got me back safely, and then died. I knew perfectly well how it had happened, he had foretold it too many times. He was a coward and feared that if they tortured him he would talk, would name names, sending his comrades to the slaughterhouse. It was for them he had died. Just like that, *sffft,* as I was sure he had done with the two Germans—a kind of Dantesque poetic justice, perhaps. The courageous death of a coward. He had paid for the only violent act of his life, and in the process purged himself of that remorse he was carrying within him and would no doubt have found unbearable. He had screwed them all: Fascists, Germans, and God in a single stroke. *Sffft.*

And I was alive. I could not forgive myself for that.

Even in my memories the fog is thinning. I now see the Partisans entering Solara in triumph, and on April 25 comes the news of Milan's liberation. People swarm the streets, the Partisans shoot into the air, they arrive perched on the fenders of their trucks. A few days later I see a soldier, dressed in olive drab, bicycling up the drive between the rows of horse-chestnut trees. He lets me know he is Brazilian, then goes happily off to explore his exotic surroundings. Were there Brazilians, too, with the Americans and British? No one had ever told me that. *Drôle de guerre.*

A week passes, and the first detachment of Americans arrives. All blacks. They are settling in with their tents in the Oratorio courtyard, and I make friends with a Catholic corporal, who shows me an image of the Sacred Heart that he always carries in his breast pocket. He gives me some newspapers with L'il Abner and Dick Tracy strips, and a few pieces of what he calls "chewing gum", which I make last a long time, taking the wad out of my mouth at night and putting it in a glass of water, as old folks do with their dentures. He gives me to understand that in exchange he would like to eat spaghetti, and I invite him home, certain that Maria will fix him agnolotti with hare sauce. But as we arrive, the corporal sees another black man sitting in our yard, a major. He excuses himself and leaves, stunned.

The Americans, looking for decent lodgings for their officers, had approached my grandfather, and we had put a nice room in the left wing at their disposition, the very room Paola later made into our bedroom.

Major Muddy is a portly man, with a Louis Armstrong smile, and he manages to communicate with my grandfather; it helps that he knows some French, at that time the only foreign language that educated people in those parts knew, and it is French that he speaks with Mamma and with the other ladies who live nearby. They come for tea to see the liberator—even that Fascist lady who hated her tenant farmer. All of them in the yard around a little table decked out with the good china, beside the dahlias. Major Muddy says "mersì bocou" and "Oui, màdam, moi ossì j'aime le champeign." He behaves with the polite hauteur of a black man who is finally being received in a white family's house, and a nice house at that. The ladies whisper to themselves, My, such a gentleman, and to think they painted them as drunken savages.

The news of the German surrender arrives. Hitler is dead. The war is over. In Solara there is a huge party in the streets, people hugging each other, some dancing to the sounds of an accordion. Grandfather has decided to return at once to the city, even though summer has just begun, because by now everyone has had enough of the country.

I emerge from the tragedy, amid a crowd of radiant people, with the images of the two Germans falling into the ravine and of Gragnola, virgin and martyr—out of fear, out of love, and out of spite.

I lack the courage to go to Don Cognasso and confess... and besides, confess what? That which I did not do, nor even see, but only guessed at? Not having anything to ask forgiveness for, I cannot even be forgiven. It is enough to make a person feel damned for ever.

17. The Provident Young Man

Oh such grief I feel, such misery, / To think, My Lord, that I offended Thee... Did they teach me that at the Oratorio, or did I sing it after going back to the city?

In the city, lights come back on at night, people take to the streets again even in the evenings, to drink beer or eat gelato in the recreational clubs along the river, and the first open-air movie theatres arrive. I am alone, missing my Solara friends, and I have not yet reconnected with Gianni, whom I will see again only when high school begins. I go out with my parents in the evening, ill at ease, because I no longer hold their hands but they will not yet leave me alone for long. I had more freedom at Solara.

We often go to the movies. I discover new ways to fight a war in *Sergeant York* and *Yankee Doodle Dandy,* where James Cagney's tap-dancing opens my eyes to the existence of Broadway. "*I'm a Yankee Doodle Dandy*..."

I first encountered tap in the old Fred Astaire films, but Cagney's style is more violent, liberating, assertive. Astaire's was a divertissement, Cagney's feels to me like a duty, in fact it is even patriotic. A patriotism expressed through tap-dancing is a revelation, metal-tipped shoes instead of grenades in hand and a flower between our teeth. Then there was the allure of the stage as model of the world and of destiny's inexorability: The show must go on. I learn about a new world through musicals, which are arriving late.

Casablanca. Victor Laszlo singing the Marseillaise... So I had at least met with tragedy on the side of right.... Rick Blaine shooting Major Strasser... Gragnola was right, war is war. Why did Rick have to abandon Ilsa Lund? Does that mean we are not supposed to love? Sam is certainly Major Muddy, but who is Ugarte? Is he Gragnola, the lost and luckless coward who in the end will be taken by the Black Brigades? No, with that sarcastic sneer Gragnola is more like Captain Renault, who will in the end go off into the fog with Rick to join the Resistance in Brazzaville, cheerfully facing his destiny with a friend...

Gragnola however cannot follow me into the desert. With Gragnola, I experienced not the beginning but the end of a beautiful friendship. And I have no letters of transit to get me out of my memories.

The news-stands are full of papers with new mastheads and provocative magazines featuring cover girls with plunging necklines or blouses so tight they outline the nipples. Ample bosoms dominate movie posters. My world is reborn in the shape of a breast. But also a mushroom. I see the photo of the bomb falling on Hiroshima. The first images of the Holocaust appear. Not yet the heaps of corpses we will see later, but the first photos of the liberated, with hollow eyes, skeletal chests showing each rib, enormous elbows joining the two sticks of each arm. Until now my news of the war has been indirect, sums (ten planes shot down, this many dead and that many prisoners), rumoured executions of Partisans in the area, but except for the night in the Gorge I have never been exposed to the sight of a debased corpse—and not even that night, actually, since the last time I saw the two Germans they were still alive, and the rest I witnessed only in nightmares. I scan the photos for the face of Signor Ferrara, who knew how to play marbles, but even if he were there I would not recognize him now. *Arbeit macht frei.*

Corriere Lombardo

E' ESPLOSA LA BOMBA ATOMICA

Il mondo è sbigottito
Che cosa accadrà?

Paravento?

Sblocco dei tessili e delle calzature

Il Comando alleato ordina di riprendere i lanci

Gli esseri viventi polverizzati a Hiroshima

"Il sole è battuto"

Una voce clandestina esorta all'insurrezione

La Germania non arrivò prima perché esperti italiani sabotarono le ricerche

Londra dice:
"Principio o fine della nostra civiltà"

Provvedimenti del Governo

Clausura di tecnici nella "città segreta"

Tagliato in due dal mare

At the movies we laugh at the funny faces of Abbott and Costello. Bing Crosby and Bob Hope arrive, along with Dorothy Lamour in her obligatory sarong, travelling towards Zanzibar or Bali (*Road to*...), and everyone thinks, and has since 1944, that life is beautiful.

Each day at noon I ride my bike to a black marketeer who always sets aside, for us kids, two rolls of white bread, our first white bread after several years of chewing yellowish, poorly baked sticks, made from a thready fibre (bran, they said), that sometimes contained pieces of string or even cockroaches. I ride my bike to claim this symbol of our renascent wealth, and I stop in front of the news-stands. Mussolini's corpse hung upside down in Piazza Loreto, along with Claretta Petacci's, her skirt safety-pinned between her legs by some pious hand to spare her that final indignity. Celebrations honouring the Partisans who had been killed. I did not know they had shot and hung so many. The first death tolls appear for the war that has just ended. Fifty-five million, they say. What does Gragnola's death matter in the face of such slaughter? Might God truly be evil? I read about the Nuremberg trials, all of them hung but Göring, who poisons himself with cyanide that his wife passed him during their final kiss. The Villarbasse massacre signals the return of open violence—now you can kill people again for merely personal reasons. The killers are arrested, executed by firing squad one morning. Executions continue in peacetime. Leonarda Cianciulli is convicted of turning her victims into soap during the war. Rina Fort beats her lover's wife and children to death with an iron bar. A newspaper describes the whiteness of her bosom, which had so overwhelmed her lover, a skinny man with teeth as rotten as Uncle Gaetano's. The first films to which my parents take me reveal a post-war Italy that is home to disquieting "segnorine"—every evening beneath the streetlamp's glow, as before. Alone through city streets I go...

It is Monday, market morning. Cousin My-eye shows up around noon. What was his real name? Ada came up with "My-eye"—according to her, he said "my eye" instead of "may I", which seems impossible to me. Cousin My-eye was an extremely distant relative, but he had known us in Solara and could never come into the city, he said, without saying hello. Everyone knew he expected an invitation to lunch, because he could not afford to go to a restaurant. I never figured out what kind of work he did, other than looking for work.

I can see Cousin My-eye at the table, sipping his ditalini in broth, not leaving a drop, with his tan, hollow face, what little hair he had left combed carefully back, the elbows of his jacket worn. "You know, Duilio," he would say each Monday, "I don't want a fancy job. Just an office job, with a state-run company, the minimum salary. A drop is all I ask. But every day that drop, and every month thirty drops." He made a Bridge-of-Sighs gesture, mimed the drop that would land on his nearly bald head, and beamed at the thought of that beneficent torture. One drop, he repeated, but every day.

"Today I almost got it, I went to talk with Carloni, you know, the fellow from the agriculture consortium. A bigwig. I had a letter of recommendation—nowadays, you know, without a recommendation you're nobody. When I went out this morning, at the station, I bought a paper. I don't follow politics, Duilio, I just asked for any old paper, and then I didn't even read it because I had to stand on the train and I was holding on to keep from falling. I folded it up and put it in my pocket, like a person does with a paper—even if you haven't read it, it's still good the next day for wrapping something. I go to see Carloni, he greets me all friendly, he opens the letter, but I can see him eyeing me over the page. Then he sends me on my way with a few words, says we won't be hiring any time soon. As I'm leaving I realize that the paper I've got in my pocket is *L'Unità*. Now Duilio, you know I agree with the government, I always do, I just asked for any old paper, I didn't even realize what I was getting. But that man saw a communist paper in my pocket and sent me on my way. If I had folded the paper the other way, at this very moment I might... When you're born unlucky... It's fate."

The city has a new dance hall, and its star is my Cousin Nuccio, finally free of boarding school: he is a young man now, or, how should I say, a dandy (he already seemed terribly adult to me back when he was flogging Angelo Bear). To the great pride of his relatives, a local weekly even runs a caricature of him that shows him bent into a thousand contortions (like an Uncle Gaetano, only less disjointed), doing that dance craze, the boogie-woogie. I am still too young, would not dare, and could not enter that hall, whose rituals feel to me like an affront to Gragnola's cut throat.

We have come back at the very beginning of summer, and I am bored. I ride my bike at two in the afternoon through the nearly deserted city. I wear myself out with open spaces in order to bear the tedium of those muggy days. Or perhaps it is not the mugginess, but rather a great melancholy I carry inside me, the one passion of my fevered, lonely adolescence.

I ride my bike, without a break, between two and five in the afternoon. In three hours you can circumnavigate the city several times, you need only vary your route: speed through the city centre towards the river, then take the ring road, head back in where it crosses the provincial road that goes south, pick it up again with the cemetery road, veer left before the train station, go through the city centre again but this time on secondary roads, straight and empty, enter the big market piazza, too wide, surrounded by arcades that are always sunny, no matter where the sun is, and that at two in the afternoon are more deserted than the Sahara. The piazza is empty, you can bike across it without worrying about anyone watching you or waving to you from afar. Because even if someone you knew were walking over in that far corner, he would look too small, as would you to him, just shapes haloed by sunlight. Then you wind around the piazza in wide concentric circles, like a vulture with no carrion in sight.

I am not wandering at random, I have a goal, but I pass it by, often and on purpose. I have seen, at the train station newsstand, an edition, perhaps several years old, judging by what looks to be a pre-war price, of Pierre Benoît's *Atlantida.* Its attractive cover depicts a large hall full of stone guests and promises a tale like no other. It is cheap; in my pocket I have the exact sum and no more. Occasionally I risk it: I stop at the station, rest my bike on the pavement, go in, and contemplate the book for fifteen minutes. It is in a display case, so I cannot open it to get a sense of what it might offer me. On the fourth visit, the vendor begins eyeing me suspiciously, and he can watch me all he wants, because there is no one else in that concourse—no one arriving, no one leaving, no one waiting.

The city is nothing but space and sunlight, a track for my bike with its pitted tyres, and the book in the station is the only guarantee that, through fiction, I will be able to return to some less desperate reality.

Around five o'clock, that long seduction—between me and the book, between the book and me, between my desire and the resistance of infinite space—that amorous pedalling through the vacuous summer, that excruciating concentric escape, comes to an end: I have made my decision, I withdraw my capital from my pocket, purchase *Atlantida,* and head home to curl up and read it.

Antinea, the gorgeous femme fatale, appears dressed in an Egyptian *klaft* (what is a *klaft*? it must be some magnificent and tempting thing, veiling and revealing at the same time) that flows down around her thick, wavy hair, so black it is blue, until the two points of its heavy, golden fabric reach down to her slim hips.

"She wore, beneath a black veil that glittered with gold, a flimsy, loosely fitting tunic, barely held closed by a white muslin sash embroidered with irises made of black pearls." Beneath those garments, a slender girl with long black eyes and a smile unheard of among the women of the Orient. You cannot see her body through those diabolically sumptuous vestments, but her tunic is audaciously open on the side (ah, the slit), her delicate bosom is exposed, her arms are bare, and mysterious shadows can be glimpsed beneath the veils. A temptress, bitterly virginal. For her, a man could die.

I close the book, embarrassed, when my father comes home at seven, but he thinks I am simply trying to conceal the fact that I am reading. He remarks that I read too much and am ruining my vision. He tells my mother I should get out more, go for a nice bike ride.

I dislike the sun, and yet I did not mind it at all at Solara. They observe that I often squint, crinkling my nose: "You act like you can't see, but it's not true," they scold. I am waiting for the fogs of autumn. Why should I love the fog, since it was in the fog of the Gorge that my night of terror was consummated? Because even there it was the fog that protected me, leaving me with the ultimate alibi: it was foggy, I saw nothing.

With the first foggy days, I rediscover my ancient city, and those exaggerated, sleepy spaces are erased. The voids disappear and out of that milky greyness, in the light of the streetlamps, outcroppings, corners, and sudden façades emerge from nowhere. Comfort. As during the blackouts. My city was made, conceived, designed by generation after generation to be seen in this penumbral light as you walk, sticking close to the walls. Then it becomes beautiful and protective.

Was it that year or the next that saw the appearance of *Grand Hotel,* the first comic book for adults? The first image of that first photo-romance led me towards temptation, but I fled.

That was tame compared to something I later came across in my grandfather's shop: a French magazine that as soon as I opened it made me burn with shame. I filched it, slipping it in my shirt and leaving.

I am home, stretched out in my bed on my stomach, and as I flip through the pages I press my crotch into the mattress, just as they advise you not to do in the devotional handbooks. On one page: a photo, fairly small but immensely evident, of Josephine Baker, topless.

I stare at her shadowed eyes so as not to look at her breasts, then my gaze shifts, they are (I believe) the first breasts of my life—the ample, flaccid things on the *à poil* Kalmyk women were something else entirely.

A wave of honey surges through my veins, I feel an acrid aftertaste in the back of my throat, a pressure on my forehead, a swoon in my loins. I stand up frightened and moist, wondering what terrible disease I have contracted, delighted by that liquefaction into primordial soup.

I believe it was my first ejaculation: more forbidden, I think, than cutting a German's throat. I have sinned again—that night in the Gorge was the mute witness to the mystery of death, and this moment is the interloper penetrating the forbidden mysteries of life.

I am in a confessional. A fiery Capuchin entertains me at length on the virtues of purity.

He tells me nothing I have not already read in those little handbooks at Solara, but perhaps his words were what sent me back to Don Bosco's *Provident Young Man:*

Even at your tender age the devil is laying snares to rob you of your soul.... It will aid greatly in preserving you from temptation should you remain far from opportunities, from scandalous conversations, from public spectacles, from which no good can come.... Endeavour to keep busy at all times; when you do not know what to do, adorn altars, straighten images or small pictures.... If afterwards the temptation persists, make the sign of the Holy Cross, kiss some blessed object and say: Saintly Aloysius, let me not offend my God. I give you this saint's name because the Church has declared him the special protector of youth...

Above all else, flee the company of persons of the opposite sex. Understand well: I mean to say that young men should not ever enter into any familiarity with girls.... The eyes are windows through which sin makes its way into our hearts... thus you must never stop to gaze upon that which is contrary in the slightest to modesty. Saint Aloysius Gonzaga did not want even his feet to be seen as he put himself to bed or rose from it. He did not permit his own mother to look him in the eyes.... He spent two years with the queen of Spain as a page and never once gazed upon her face.

Imitating Saint Aloysius is not easy, or rather the price of fleeing temptation seems rather exorbitant, given that the young fellow, having scourged himself bloody, would put pieces of wood beneath his sheets, to torture himself even in his sleep. He hid riding spurs beneath his clothes because he had no hair shirts; he sought his displeasure wherever he stood, or sat, or walked... But the exemplar of virtue my confessor proposes to me is Domenico Savio, whose trouser legs were misshapen from too much kneeling but whose penances were less bloody than Saint Aloysius's, and he also exhorts me to contemplate, as an example of holy beauty, Mary's exquisite face.

I try to become infatuated with a sublime and sublimated femininity. I sing in the boys' choir, in the apse of the church or at other sanctuaries during Sunday field trips:

Thou risest at dawn full of beauty
to gladden the earth with each ray.
The sky puts its night stars away,
for none is so lovely as Thee.

Lovely Thou art as the sun,
white as the light of the moon,
and the loveliest star
is but a far candle to Thee.

Thine eyes are more lovely than oceans,
the colour of lilies Thy brow,
Thy cheeks are two roses, kissed
by the Son, and Thy lips are a flower.

Perhaps I am preparing myself, though I am not yet sure, for my encounter with Lila, who must be equally unreachable, equally splendid in her empyrean, her beauty *gratia sui,* free from the flesh, able to dwell in the mind without stirring the loins, with eyes that gaze elsewhere, above and beyond me, rather than fixing slyly on me like Josephine Baker's.

It is my duty to pay, by means of meditation, prayer, and sacrifice, for my sins and the sins of those around me. To devote myself to the defence of faith, as the first magazines and the first wall posters begin telling me about the Red Menace, about Cossacks waiting to water their horses at the holy-water fonts in Saint Peter's. I wonder, confused, how in the world the Cossacks, who were Stalin's enemies and had even fought alongside the Germans, have now become communism's messengers of death, and whether they will also want to kill all the anarchists like Gragnola. These Cossacks look to me very like that evil Negro who was raping the Venus de Milo, and perhaps they were drawn by the same artist, reinventing himself for a new crusade.

Spiritual exercises, in a little monastery out in the countryside. A rancid smell from the refectory, strolls through the cloister with the librarian, who advises me to read Papini. After dinner we all go into the choir of the church, and illuminated by a single candle we recite the Exercise for a Good Death.

The spiritual director reads us the passages on death from *The Provident Young Man:* We do not know where death will surprise us—you do not know if it will take you in your beds, as you work, in the street or elsewhere; a burst vein, a catarrh, a rush of blood, a fever, a sore, an earthquake, a bolt of lightning—any could be enough to deprive you of your life, and it could happen a year from now, a month, a week, an hour, or perhaps just as you finish reading this passage. In that moment, we will feel our head darkened, our eyes aching, our tongue parched, our jaws closed, heavy our chest, our blood cold, our flesh worn, our heart broken. When we have breathed our last, our body, dressed in a few rags, will be thrown into a ditch, and there the mice and the worms will gnaw away all our flesh, and nothing of us will remain save a few bare bones and some fetid dust.

Then the prayer, a long invocation recounting each of the last throes of a dying man, the pangs in his every limb, the first tremors, the rising pallor leading to the *facies hippocratica* and the death rattle. Each description of the fourteen stages of our final passage (only five or six come clearly to mind) concludes, after defining the body's attitude and the moment's anguish, with *merciful Jesus, have pity on me.*

When my motionless feet shall warn me that my time on this earth is nearing its end, merciful Jesus, have pity on me.

When my numb, tremulous hands shall no longer be able to grasp you, my blessed Crucifix, and against my will shall let you fall onto the bed of my suffering, merciful Jesus, have pity on me.

When my eyes, darkened and stricken with horror by death's imminence, shall fix their enfeebled and moribund glances on You, merciful Jesus, have pity on me.

When my pale, leaden cheeks shall inspire compassion and terror in onlookers, and my hair, damp with death's sweat, shall stand erect, announcing the nearness of my end, merciful Jesus, have pity on me.

When my imagination, agitated by terrible, fearsome spectres, shall be immersed in mortal sorrows, merciful Jesus, have pity on me.

When I shall have lost the use of all my senses, and the entire world shall have vanished from me, and I shall moan in death's final, anguished throes, merciful Jesus, have pity on me.

Singing psalms in the dark thinking about my own death. It was just what I needed, to stop me thinking about other people's. I relive that exercise not with terror, but with a serene consciousness of the fact that all men are mortal. That lesson in Being-towards-Death prepared me for my destiny, which is everyone's destiny. In May, Gianni told me the joke about that doctor who advises a terminally ill patient to take sand baths. "Do they help, doctor?" "Not really, but you'll get accustomed to being underground."

I am getting accustomed.

One evening the spiritual director stood in front of the altar balustrade, illuminated—like all of us, like the entire chapel—by that single candle that haloed him in light, leaving his face in darkness. Before dismissing us, he told us a story. One night, in a convent school, a girl died, a young, pious, beautiful girl. The next morning, she was stretched out on a catafalque in the nave of the church, and the mourners were reciting their prayers for the deceased, when all of a sudden the corpse sat up, eyes wide and finger pointing at the celebrant, and said in a cavernous voice, "Father, do not pray for me! Last night I had an impure thought, a single thought—and now I am damned!"

A shudder travels through the audience and spreads to the pews and the vaults, seeming almost to make the candle flame flicker. The director exhorts us to go to bed, but no one moves. A long line forms in front of the confessional, everyone intent on giving in to sleep only after the merest hint of sin has been confessed.

In the menacing comfort of dark naves, fleeing the evils of the century, I spend my days in icy ardours, in which even Christmas carols, and what had been the comforting crèche of my childhood, become the birth of the Child into the horrors of the world:

Sleep, do not cry, oh my sweet Jesus,
sleep, do not cry, my beloved Redeemer…
Oh beautiful child, hasten to shut
your sweet-natured eyes in horror extreme.
That's why they sting, the straw and the hay,
Because your bright eyes are shimmering still.
Hasten to close them, so sleep at least may
offer its remedy for every ill.
Sleep, do not cry, oh my sweet Jesus,
sleep, do not cry, my beloved Redeemer…

One Sunday, Papà, a soccer fan and a bit disappointed in that son of his who spends his days ruining his eyes over books, takes me to a match. It is a minor contest, the stands are nearly empty, speckled with the colours of the few onlookers, blotches on white stands that are scorching hot in the sun. The game is stopped by a referee's whistle, one captain protests the call, the other players move around the field aimlessly. Two colours of jerseys in disarray, bored athletes milling about a green field, a scattered mess. Everything stalls. What happens unreels now in slow motion, as in a parochial movie theatre when the sound suddenly cuts off with a *miaow,* movements become more careful, then jerk frame by frame to a stop on a single image, which dissolves on the screen like melting wax.

And in that moment I experience a revelation.

I realize now that it was a painful sense that the world is purposeless, the lazy fruit of a misunderstanding, but in that moment I was able to translate what I felt only as: "God does not exist."

I leave the match in the grip of lacerating regrets and run straight to confession. The fiery confessor from my previous visit now smiles, indulgent and benevolent, asks me how I got such a silly notion in my head, mentions the beauty of nature, which points to a creative and ordering will, then talks at length about the *consensus gentium:* "My child, the greatest writers, Dante, Manzoni, Salvaneschi, have believed in God, and great mathematicians like Fantappiè, and you want to be lesser?" The consensus of people, for the moment, calms me. It must have been the match's fault. Paola told me I never went to soccer matches, at most I would watch the finals of the World Cup on television. I must have had it in my head, from that day on, that going to a match meant losing my soul.

But there are other ways to lose it. My schoolmates begin telling stories in whispers and giggles. They drop hints, they share magazines and books stolen from home, they speak about the mysterious Casa Rossa, which we are not yet old enough to visit, they empty their wallets at the cinema on comedies featuring scantily clad

women. They show me a photo of Isa Barzizza in skimpy panties, on stage in a variety show. I cannot refuse to look without seeming like a pharisee, so I look, and as we know anything can be resisted except temptation. I enter the movie house furtively, early in the afternoon, hoping not to run into anyone who knows me: in *The Two Orphans* (with Totò and Carlo Campanini), Isa Barzizza and several other convent girls, in defiance of the mother superior's orders, bathe naked.

The girls' bodies cannot be seen, they are shadows behind the shower curtains. They throw themselves into their ablutions as if it were a dance. I should go to confession, but those transparencies remind me of a book I once clapped shut in Solara, fearful of what I was reading: Hugo's *The Laughing Man*.

I do not have it in the city, but I am sure my grandfather has a copy in his shop. I find it, and while my grandfather converses with someone I curl up at the foot of the bookshelf and turn feverishly to the forbidden page. Gwynplaine, horribly mutilated by *comprachicos* who turned his face into a freak-show mask, cast off from society, finds himself suddenly recognized as Lord Clancharlie, heir to an immense fortune and a peerage. Before he fully understands what is happening to him, he is taken, wearing the splendid garb of a gentleman, to an enchanted palace, and the series of marvels he discovers there (alone in that resplendent desert), the fugue of rooms and chambers, makes not only his head spin, but also the reader's. He wanders from room to room until he comes to an alcove where he sees, upon a bed, near a tub of water ready for a virginal bath, a naked woman.

Not literally naked, notes Hugo slyly. She was dressed. But in a chemise so long and sheer as to make her appear merely wet. And here follow seven pages describing how a naked woman looks, and how she looks to the Laughing Man, who until then had loved, chastely, only a blind girl. The woman looks to him like a dozing Venus amid an immensity of sea foam, and as she sleeps her slow movements draw and erase enticing curves with the vague dynamics of water vapour forming clouds in the blue sky. Hugo remarks: "A woman naked is a woman armed."

Suddenly the woman, Josiane, the queen's sister, awakes, recognizes Gwynplaine, and makes a frenzied effort to seduce him, one the wretch is by this point unable to resist, except that she has brought him to the brink of desire without yet yielding herself. She launches into a series of fantasias more disconcerting than her nakedness, presenting herself as virgin and as prostitute, eager to enjoy not only the pleasures his deformity promises, but also the thrill of defying the world and the court, prospects which intoxicate her: Venus on the verge of a double orgasm, from both the private possession and the public exhibition of her Vulcan.

Gwynplaine is ready to yield, but a message arrives from the queen, who informs her sister that the Laughing Man has been recognized as the legitimate Lord Clancharlie and that she is to marry him. Josiane declares, "So be it," rises, points to the door, and (shifting from the *tu* to the *vous*) tells the man with whom she had wanted to couple wildly: "Begone." She explains: "Since you are my husband, begone.... You have no right to be here. This is my lover's place."

Sublime corruption—not of Gwynplaine, of Yambo. Not only does Josiane offer me more than Isa Barzizza had promised from behind her curtain, but she wins me over with her shamelessness: "You are my husband, begone, this is my lover's place." Could sin possibly be so heroically overpowering?

Are there, in the world, women like Lady Josiane and Isa Barzizza? Will I ever meet them? Will I remain thunderstruck by them—*sffft*—just punishment for my fantasies?

There are, at least on the screen. On another afternoon, furtively, I went to see *Blood and Sand*. The adoration with which Tyrone Power presses his face into Rita Hayworth's belly persuades me that some women are armed even when they are not naked. As long as they are brazen.

To be intensely educated about the horror of sin and then to be conquered by it. I tell myself that it must be prohibition that kindles fantasy. Thus I decide that, if I am to escape temptation, I must avoid

the suggestions of an "education in purity": both are the devil's stratagems, and each sustains the other. This intuition, however heterodox, hits me like a whip.

I withdraw into a world all my own. I cultivate music, always glued to the radio in the afternoon hours, or the early morning, and sometimes they play a symphony in the evening. My family would prefer to listen to other things. "Enough with these dirges," complains Ada, impervious to the muses. One Sunday morning I encounter Uncle Gaetano, now an old man, on the street. He has lost even his gold tooth, or maybe he sold it during the war. He asks benevolently after my studies, and Papà has told him that these days I am obsessed with music. "Ah, music," he says with delight, "how well I understand you, Yambo, I adore music. And all kinds, you know? Any sort, as long as it's music." He reflects for a moment, then adds: "As long as it's not classical. Then I turn it off, of course."

I am an exceptional creature exiled among philistines. I sequester myself ever more proudly in my solitude.

In my high school's first-year reader, I stumble on the verses of several contemporary poets. I discover that one can be illumined by immensity, encounter the evil of living, be pierced by a ray of sunlight. I do not fully understand it, but I like the idea that *this is the one thing we can tell you now: what we are not, what we do not desire.*

In my grandfather's shop I find an anthology of the French symbolists. My ivory tower. I merge into a shadowy and profound unity, seeking everywhere *de la musique avant toute chose,* listening to silences, noting the inexpressible and determining vertigos.

But to confront such books freely, one must first be freed from many interdictions, so I choose the spiritual director Gianni told me about, the broad-minded priest. Don Renato had seen *Going My Way,* with Bing Crosby, in which American Catholic priests play piano in their clergyman suits and sing *too-ra-loo-ra-loo-ral, too-ra-loo-ra-li* to adoring girls.

Don Renato cannot dress like the Americans, but he belongs to the new generation of priests who wear berets and ride mopeds. He does not play the piano, but he has a small collection of jazz records and loves good literature. I tell him that I was advised to read Papini, and he tells me that Papini was most interesting not after he converted, but before. Broad-minded. He loans me *The Failure,* perhaps thinking that temptations of the spirit may save me from temptations of the flesh.

It is the confession of someone who was never a baby and who had the unhappy childhood of a thoughtful, peevish old toad. That is not me, my childhood was (*nomen omen*) sunny. But in Solara, in a single haunted night, I lost that. The peevish toad about whom I am now reading is saved by his thirst for knowledge and loses himself in volumes "with green, ragged spines, with huge, wide, crinkled pages, reddish from moisture, often ripped in half or ink-stained." That is me, not only as a child in the attic at Solara but also in the life I later chose. I never emerged from books: I know it now in the continuous wakefulness of this sleep, but I first grasped it in the moment I am presently recalling.

This man, a failure since birth, not only reads, he also writes. I could write, too, could add my own monsters to those that scuttle with their ragged claws across the silent sea floors. That man ruins his eyes over pages on which he sets down his obsessions in muddy ink from inkwells whose bottoms are thick with sludge, like Turkish coffee. He ruined them as a boy, reading by candlelight; he ruined them in the penumbra of libraries, his eyelids reddening. He writes with the help of strong lenses, dogged by fears of going blind. If not blind, then paralytic—his nerves are shot, he has pains and numbness in one leg, his fingers twitch involuntarily, his head shakes badly. He writes with his thick glasses nearly touching the page.

I can see fine, I ride my bike, I am no toad—I may already have my irresistible smile, but what good does it do me? I do not complain that others do not smile at me; it is because I find no reason to smile at others...

I am not like the failure, but I would like to become so. To fashion from his bibliomaniacal fury an opportunity for my own non-monastic escape from the world. To build a world that is all mine. But I am not moving towards a conversion, if anything, I am coming back from one. Seeking an alternative faith, I become enamoured of the decadents. Brothers, sad lilies, I pine for beauty.... I become a Byzantine eunuch watching the great white barbarians go by and composing indolent acrostics; I install, by means of science, the anthem of spiritual hearts into the work of my patience, scour atlases, herbals, and rituals.

I can still think of the eternal feminine, as long as I am dazzled by artifice and by some sort of sickly pallor. I read, and am aroused—above the neck:

This dying girl whose garments he was touching inflamed him as did the most ardent of females. There was no bayadère *on the banks of the Ganges, no odalisque from the baths of Istanbul, no naked Bacchante who ever existed whose embrace could have made his bone marrow boil as much as the touch, the simple touch of that fragile, febrile hand whose sweat he could feel through the glove that covered it.*

I do not even have to confess to Don Renato. It is literature, I am permitted its company, even if it speaks to me of perverse nudities and androgynous ambiguities. They are far enough from my experience that I can yield to their seduction. It is word, not flesh.

Towards the end of my second year of high school, I stumble on *À rebours,* by Huysmans. His hero, Des Esseintes, comes from a long line of grim, muscular warriors with yataghan moustaches, but ancestral portraits reveal a gradual impoverishment of the stock, sapped by too much inbreeding: his forebears already appear weakened by an excess of lymph in the blood, exhibit feminine traits and anaemic, nervous faces. Des Esseintes is marked from birth by these atavistic evils: his is a dismal childhood, fraught with scrofula and stubborn fevers, and his mother, long, silent, and pale, always entombed in a dark room in one of their châteaux, in the faint glow of a lampshade that shields her from excessive light and noise, dies when he is seventeen. Left to himself, the boy looks through books on rainy days and in nice weather goes for walks in the country. "His greatest pleasure was going down into the gorge as far as Jutigny," a village at the foot of the hill. Into the Gorge. He stretches out in the fields, listens to the muffled sound of the watermills, then climbs to the top of a ridge from where he can see the Seine valley,

with its river disappearing into the distance, merging with the blue of the sky, and the churches and towers of Provins, which seem to tremble in the sun, in the golden dustiness of the air.

He reads and daydreams, relishing his solitude. As an adult, disappointed by life's pleasures and by the pettiness of men of letters, he dreams of a refined retreat, a private desert, a snug, still ark. Thus he builds his completely artificial hermitage where, in the aquarial half-light of window-panes that cut him off from the dull spectacle of nature, he transforms music into flavour and flavour into music, revels in the halting Latin of the Decadence, runs his pallid fingers over dalmatics and semi-precious stones, and has the shell of a living tortoise set with sapphires, occidental turquoise, hyacinths from Compostela, aquamarines, and slate-grey rubies from Södermanland.

The chapter I love most of all is the one in which Des Esseintes decides to leave his house for the first time to visit England. He is prompted by the foggy weather he sees around him, the vault of heaven that stretches uniformly in all directions like a grey pillow-case. In order to feel in tune with the place he is going to, he selects a pair of socks the colour of dead leaves, a mouse-grey suit with lava-grey checks and sable-brown dots, then he dons a derby, takes a collapsible suitcase, a carpetbag, a hatbox, umbrellas and canes, and sets out for the station.

Already exhausted when he reaches Paris, he travels around the rainy city in a carriage to pass the time until his departure. Gaslights flicker through the fog, ringed by yellowish haloes, putting him in mind already of an equally rainy, colossal, and vast London, with its cast-iron smell, its smoky mist, its rows of docks, and cranes, and capstans, and bales.... Then he enters a tavern of sorts, a pub frequented by the English, its walls lined with casks emblazoned with royal arms, its tables laden with Palmers biscuits, savoury cakes, mince pies, and sandwiches, and he looks forward to the array of exotic wines on offer there: *Old Port, Magnificent Old Regina, Cockburn's Very Fine....* Around him sit the English: pale clerics, men with tripe-butcher faces, others with collars of whiskers similar to those of certain large apes, tow-headed men. He abandons himself, in that fictive London, to the sound of foreign voices and the honks of tugboats on the river.

He leaves in a daze, the sky having now settled down around the bellies of the houses, the arcades of Rue de Rivoli reminding him of the gloomy tunnel carved out beneath the Thames, then enters another tavern, where he sees beers spilling forth from pumps that rise from the bar and robust Anglo-Saxon women with paddle-sized teeth and long hands and feet attacking a "rump-steak pie"—meat cooked in a mushroom sauce and cloaked in a crust, like a pastry. He orders an "oxtail" soup, a "haddock", some "roast beef", and two pints of "ale"; he nibbles on some "Stilton"; he chases it all with a glass of "brandy".

As he asks for the bill, the tavern door opens and the people who enter bring with them the odour of wet dog and fossil coal. Des Esseintes wonders why he should bother crossing the Channel: he has in effect already been to London, has smelled the smells, tasted the foods, seen the typical decor—he has gorged himself on British life. He has his driver take him back to the Sceaux station, and he returns, with his suitcases, his bags, his travelling rugs and his umbrellas, to his familiar refuge, "feeling all the physical exhaustion and moral fatigue of a man returning home following a long, perilous journey."

That is how I become: even on spring days I can be wrapped in a uterine fog. But only illness (and the fact that life refuses me) could fully justify my refusal of life. I must prove to myself that my escape is good, is virtuous.

Thus I find that I am ill. I have heard it said that heart disease manifests itself through the violet colour of the lips, and during those very years my mother is showing signs of heart trouble. Not serious, perhaps, but the whole family gets more caught up in it than we should, to the point of hypochondria.

One morning, when I look in the mirror, my lips seem purple. I go down to the street and start sprinting like a madman: I gasp for breath, I feel an abnormal throbbing in my chest. So, I have a bad heart. Consecrated to death, like Gragnola.

Heart disease becomes my absinthe. I track its progress, watching my lips grow ever darker, my cheeks ever gaunter, as the first blooms of teen acne lend my face a morbid flush. I will die young, like Saint Aloysius Gonzaga and Domenico Savio. But my spirit has asserted itself, and I have slowly reformulated my Exercise for a Good Death: little by little I have given up hair shirts for poetry.

I live in a dazzling crepuscular light:

The day will come: I know
that this my ardent blood
will of a sudden slow,
and that my pen, not dry,
will clatter down on wood…
it's then that I will die.

I am dying, no longer because life is evil, but because in its madness it is banal, monotonously repeating its rituals of death. A secular penitent, a logorrhoeic mystic, I convince myself that the most beautiful island is the one that has not been found, that sometimes appears, but only in the distance, between Tenerife and La Palma:

Their vessels sail along that blessed shore:
the dense green sacred forest scents the air;
over the nameless flowers, huge palms soar;
cardamom weeps, the rubber trees perspire…

The unfound isle, announced by fragrances,
like courtesans... But like vain semblances,
when pilots sail too near it vanishes,
turning that shade of blue that distance is.

Faith in the ungraspable allows me to close my penitential parenthesis. Life as a provident young man had promised me, as a reward, she who was lovely as the sun and pale as the light of the moon. But a single impure thought could snatch her away from me for ever. The Unfound Isle, however, since it is unattainable, remains for ever mine.

I am educating myself for my encounter with Lila.

18. Lovely Thou Art as the Sun

Lila too was born from a book. I was entering my third year of high school, on the verge of turning sixteen, when I began reading, in my grandfather's shop, *Cyrano de Bergerac,* by Rostand. Why I did not find it in Solara, in the attic or in the chapel, I do not know. Perhaps I had read and reread it so many times that it finally fell apart. I could recite it now from memory.

Everyone knows the story, indeed if someone even after my incident had asked me about *Cyrano,* I think I could have said what it was about, that it was a melodrama of exaggerated Romanticism that touring companies still put on every so often. I could have said what everyone knows. But not the rest, which, as I am rediscovering only now, is linked to my growing up, to my first amorous tremors.

Cyrano is a marvellous swordsman and an ingenious poet, but he is ugly, oppressed by that monstrous nose (*Of which much could be said, it is so ample, / By varying one's tone. Thus, for example: / Aggressive: "Why, if I had such a beak, / I'd amputate the eyesore as we speak!" / Friendly: "When drinking wine, you must quite hate it; / Perhaps a punch bowl could accommodate it?" / Descriptive: "It's a crag, a cliff, a cape! / A cape? No, more peninsular in shape!"*).

Cyrano loves his cousin Roxane, a *précieuse* of divine beauty

(*I love—who else?—the fairest of them all!*). She may well admire him for his bravura wit, but he, because of his ugliness, would never dare declare himself. Only once, when she asks to meet him, does he entertain hopes that something might develop, but his disappointment is cruel: she confesses that she loves the beautiful Baron Christian, who has just joined the Gascony Cadets, and she begs her cousin to protect him.

Cyrano makes the ultimate sacrifice and decides to woo Roxane by speaking to her through Christian's lips. He supplies Christian, who is handsome and passionate but uneducated, with the sweetest declarations of love, writes enflamed letters for him, and one night takes his place beneath Roxane's balcony to whisper his celebrated encomium to the kiss—but it is Christian who then climbs up to reap the reward of that bravura. *Then climb up here to pluck this peerless flower...this taste of a heart...this hum of a bee...this instant of infinity...* "Climb, you brute," says Cyrano, prodding his rival, and as the couple kisses he weeps in the shadows, savouring his feeble victory: *For on those lips to which she's been misled / Roxane is kissing the words that I just said.*

When Cyrano and Christian go off to war, Roxane comes after them, more in love than ever, won over by the letters Cyrano has sent her each day, and she confides to her cousin her realization that she loves, in Christian, not his physical beauty but rather his passionate heart and exquisite spirit. She would love him even if he were ugly. Cyrano then understands it is he whom she loves, but just as he is about to tell all, he learns that Christian has been shot. As Roxane kneels weeping over the poor man's corpse, Cyrano understands that he can never tell.

Years pass, Roxane has withdrawn into a convent, thinking always of her lost love and rereading each day his last letter, stained with his blood. Cyrano, her faithful friend and cousin, visits her every Saturday. But this Saturday he has been attacked, by political enemies or envious literati, and has a bloody bandage on his head, which he conceals from Roxane beneath his hat. Roxane shows him, for the first time, Christian's last letter, which Cyrano reads aloud, but Roxane realizes that darkness has fallen, and wonders how he can decipher those faded words when, in a flash, it all becomes clear: he is reciting, from memory, *his* last letter. She had loved, in Christian, Cyrano. *And so for fourteen years he played his role: the old friend bringing cheer by being droll!* No, Cyrano says, trying to deny it, it is not true: *No, no, my dear beloved—I never loved you!*

But by now our hero is reeling, and his faithful friends, arriving to reproach him for leaving his bed, reveal to Roxane that he is on the point of death. Cyrano, leaning against a tree, acts out his final duel against the shadows of his enemies, then falls. After he says that the one thing he will take, unsullied, up to heaven is his *panache* (and this is the last word of the play), Roxane leans over him and kisses him on the brow.

This kiss is barely mentioned in the stage directions, no character refers to it, an insensitive director might even overlook it, but to my sixteen-year-old mind it became the central scene, and not only did I see Roxane leaning over him, but I also, with Cyrano, savoured for the first time (her face so close) the perfume of her breath. This kiss *in articulo mortis* repaid Cyrano for that other kiss, the stolen one, which so moves everyone in the audience. This final kiss was beautiful because Cyrano received it just as he was dying, and Roxane was thus escaping him once more, but that is precisely what I, now one with the protagonist, was so proud of. I was expiring happily, without having touched my beloved, leaving her in her heavenly state of uncontaminated dream.

With Roxane's name in my heart, all I needed was a face to go with it. The face was Lila Saba's.

As Gianni had told me, I saw her coming down the stairs one day at our high school, and Lila became mine for ever.

Papini wrote about his fear of blindness and his greedy myopia: "I see everything blurred, as if in a fog that, for now, is very light, yet general and continuous. At a distance, in the evening, figures blur: a man in a cape might look to me like a woman; a small still flame, like a long line of red light; a boat going downriver, like a black patch on the current. Faces are patches of light; windows, dark patches on houses; trees, dense, dim patches rising from the shadows; and three or four first-magnitude stars, at most, shine in the sky for me." That is what is happening to me now, in this hyperalert sleep of mine. Since reawakening into memory's favour (a few seconds ago? a thousand years?), I have seen my parents in vivid detail, and Gragnola and Dr. Osimo and Maestro Monaldi and Bruno, seen every feature of their faces, smelled them, heard their voices. Everything around me is clear except for Lila's face. As in those photos where the face is pixelated, to protect the identity of the underage defendant, or of the axe murderer's innocent wife. I can make out Lila's slim outline in her black smock, her smooth stride as I follow her like a spy, can see the back of her hair lilt with each step, but I have yet to see her countenance.

I am still struggling against a roadblock, as if I were afraid of not being able to withstand that light.

I can see myself writing my poems for her, *Creature contained within that transient mystery,* and I am beside myself, not only at the memory of my first love, but also with the anguish of not being able, now, to recall her smile, those two front teeth Gianni mentioned—which he, damn him, knows and remembers.

I must remain calm, must give my memory whatever time it needs. This is enough for now; if I am breathing, my breath must be growing calm, for I can sense that I have reached the place. Lila is a step away.

I can see myself entering the girls' class to sell those tickets, I can see Ninetta Foppa's ferret eyes, Sandrina's rather plain profile, then here I am in front of Lila, ready with some clever remark as I rummage for her change but fail to find it, so as to prolong my stay before an icon whose image keeps breaking up, like a TV screen gone tilt.

I feel the boundless pride in my heart that evening in the theatre, as I pretend to place Signora Marini's cough drop in my mouth. The theatre erupts, and I experience an unspeakable feeling of limitless power. The next day I try to explain it to Gianni. "It was," I tell him, "the amplifier effect, the miracle of the megaphone: with a minimal expenditure of energy you cause an explosion, you feel yourself generate immense force with little effort. Down the road I might become a tenor who drives crowds wild, a hero who leads ten thousand men to their deaths to the strains of the Marseillaise, but I couldn't possibly ever again feel anything as intoxicating as last night."

I now feel exactly that. I am there, my tongue moving back and forth against my cheek, I hear the roar coming from the hall, I have a rough idea of where Lila is sitting, because before the show I peeked out between the curtains, but I cannot turn my face in her direction, because that would ruin everything: Signora Marini, as the lozenge travels around her cheeks, must remain in profile. I move my tongue, I babble something in a mother-hen voice (making as little sense as Signora Marini herself), focusing on Lila whom I cannot see, but who can see me. I experience this apotheosis as a carnal embrace, compared to which my first *ejaculatio praecox* over Josephine Baker was a bland sneeze.

It must have been after that incident that I said to hell with Don Renato and his advice. What good is it to keep that secret in the depths of my heart if it means we cannot both be intoxicated by it? And besides, if you love someone, you want that person to know everything about you. *Bonum est diffusivum sui.* Now I will tell her everything.

It was a question of meeting her not as she left the school but as she was arriving home, alone. On Thursdays the girls had an hour of gym, and she came home around four. I worked day after day on my opening lines. I would say something witty to her, like Fear not, this is no robbery, she would laugh, then I would say that something strange was happening to me, something I had never felt before, that perhaps she could help me.... Whatever could it be, she would wonder, we barely know each other, perhaps he likes one of my girlfriends and is afraid to approach her.

But then, like Roxane, she would understand everything in a flash. *No, no, my dear beloved—I never loved you.* Now that was a good technique. Tell her I do not love her, and please excuse the oversight. She would understand my witticism (was she not a *précieuse*?) and might lean towards me and say something like Don't be a fool, but with unhoped-for tenderness. Blushing, she would touch her fingers to my cheek.

In short, my opening was to be a masterpiece of wit and subtlety, irresistible—because I, since I loved her, could not imagine that she did not share my feelings. I had it wrong, like all lovers; I had given her my heart and asked her to do as I would have done, but that is how things have gone for millennia. Were it otherwise, literature would not exist.

Having chosen the day, the hour, having created all the conditions for the happy knock of Opportunity, I found myself standing in front of the gate to her house at ten minutes to four. At five minutes to four, I felt that too many people were passing by, and I decided to wait inside the gate, at the foot of the stairs.

After several centuries, which passed between five to four and five past four, I heard her come into the foyer. She was singing. A song about a valley—I can recall only a vague tune, not the words. The songs in those years were terrible, unlike those of my childhood. They were the idiotic songs of the idiotic post-war: "Eulalia Torricelli from Forlì", "The Firemen of Viggiù", "Nice Apples, Nice Apples", "Gascony Cadets"—at best they were sticky declarations of love, such as "Go Celestial Serenade" or "I Could Fall Asleep in These Arms of Yours". I hated them. At least Cousin Nuccio danced to American rhythms. The idea that she might like such things may have cooled me off for a moment (she *had* to be as exquisite as Roxane), though I doubt I was thinking clearly at the time. Indeed, I was not even listening, I was simply awaiting her appearance, and I spent at least ten full seconds suffering through a nervous eternity.

I stepped forward just as she reached the stairs. If someone else were telling me this story, I would remark that we could use some strings at this point, to heighten the anticipation, to create atmosphere. But at the time all I had was that miserable song I had just overheard. My heart was beating with such violence that on this occasion, for once, I could have reasonably concluded I was ill. Instead I felt charged with a wild energy, ready for the supreme moment.

She appeared before me, then stopped, surprised.

I asked her: "Does Vanzetti live here?"

She said no.

I said Thank you, excuse me, I was mistaken.

And I left.

Vanzetti (who the hell was he?) was the first name that, in the grip of panic, popped into my head. Later, that night, I convinced myself that it was good that it had happened that way. It was the ultimate stratagem. Because if she had begun to laugh, had said, What's got into you, you're very sweet, I'm flattered, but you know, I've got other things on my mind—what would I have done then? Was I going to forget her? Would such a humiliation have caused me to think her a fool? Would I have stuck to her like flypaper for the days and months to come, pleading for a second chance, becoming the laughing stock of the school? By keeping quiet, on the other hand, I had held on to everything I already had, and I had lost nothing.

She did in fact have other things on her mind. There was a college boy, tall and blondish, who sometimes came to wait for her at the school gate. His name was Vanni—whether that was his first or last name I do not know—and one time when he had a Band-Aid on his neck he really did say to his friends, with a cheerfully corrupt air, that it was only a syphiloma. Then one day he arrived on a Vespa.

Vespas had only recently come out. As my father used to say, only spoiled kids had them. For me, having a Vespa was like going to the theatre to see dancing girls in panties. It was on the side of sin. Some of my friends mounted theirs by the school gate, or showed up on them in the evenings in the piazza, where everyone shot the breeze for hours on the benches in front of a fountain that was usually sick, some of them recounting things they had heard about the "houses of tolerance", or about Wanda Osiris in the magazines—and whoever had heard something gained in the eyes of the others a morbid charisma.

The Vespa, in my eyes, was the transgression. It was not a temptation, since I could not even conceive of possessing one myself, but rather the evidence, both plain and obscure, of what could happen when you went off with a girl sitting sidesaddle on the rear seat. Not an object of desire, but the symbol of unsatisfied desires, unsatisfied through deliberate refusal.

That day, as I went back from Piazza Minghetti towards the school, in order to walk past her and her friends, she was not with her group. As I quickened my pace, fearing that some jealous god had snatched her from me, something terrible was happening, something much less holy, or, if holy, hellishly so. She was still there, standing at the bottom of the school stairs, as if waiting. And here (on his Vespa) came Vanni. She mounted behind him and clung to him, as if she were used to it, passing her arms beneath his and pressing them to his chest, and off they went.

It was already the period when the skirts of the war years, which had risen to just above the knee, or to the knee for flared skirts—the kind that graced the girlfriends of Rip Kirby in the first American post-war comics—were giving way to long, full skirts that reached to mid-calf.

These were not more prim than the shorter ones, indeed they had a perverse grace of their own, an airy, promising elegance, all the more so if they were flapping gently in the breeze as the girl vanished clutching her centaur.

That skirt was a modest, mischievous undulation in the wind, a seduction through an ample, intermediary flag. The Vespa faded regally into the distance, like a ship leaving a wake of singing foam, of capering, mystic dolphins.

She faded into the distance that morning on the Vespa, and for me the Vespa became even more a symbol of torment, of useless passion.

And once again, her skirt, the oriflamme of her hair—but seen, as always, from the back.

Gianni had told me about it. Through an entire play, in Asti, I had looked only at the back of her neck. But Gianni had failed to remind me—or I had not given him a chance—of another theatre evening. A touring company came to our city to put on *Cyrano*. It was my first opportunity to see it staged, and I convinced four of my friends to reserve seats in the gallery. I looked forward to the pleasure, and pride, of being able to anticipate the lines at crucial moments.

We arrived early, we were in the second row. A little before it started, a group of girls took their seats in the first row, right in front of us: Ninetta Foppa, Sandrina, two others, and Lila.

Lila was sitting right in front of Gianni, who was next to me, so I was looking at the back of her neck once again, though if I tilted my head I could make out her profile (not now, her face remains solarized). Rapid greetings, oh you too, what a nice coincidence, and that was all. As Gianni said, we were too young for them, and if I had been a star with the lozenge in my mouth, I was an Abbott and Costello kind of star, at whose jokes one laughs, but with whom one does not fall in love.

For me, though, it was enough. Following *Cyrano,* line by line, with her in front of me, multiplied my vertigo. I no longer remember the actress who played Roxane on stage, because my Roxane was right before my eyes. I felt I could tell when she was moved by the drama (who is not moved by *Cyrano,* written to wring tears from the stoniest heart?) and I was utterly convinced that she was moved not *with* me, but *over* me, *because of* me. I could ask for nothing more: myself, Cyrano, and her. The rest was the anonymous crowd.

When Roxane bent down to kiss Cyrano's brow, I became one with Lila. In that moment, even if she did not know it, she could not help but love me. And after all, Cyrano had waited years and years before Roxane finally understood. I, too, could wait. That evening, I rose to within a few steps of the Empyrean.

To love a neck. And a yellow jacket. That yellow jacket in which she appeared one day at school, luminous in the spring sun—and about which I waxed poetic. From that day on, I could never see a woman in a yellow jacket without feeling a call, an unbearable nostalgia.

Because now I understand what Gianni was telling me: throughout my life I sought, in all my affairs, Lila's face. I waited all my life to play the final scene of *Cyrano* with her. The shock that may have led to my incident was the revelation that such a scene had been denied me for ever.

I see now that it was Lila who, when I was sixteen, gave me hope that I might forget that night at the Gorge, opening me to a new love for life. My poor poems had taken the place of the Exercise for a Good Death. With Lila near me—not mine, but in my sight—my last years of high school would have been (what to call it?) an ascent, and I could gradually have made peace with my childhood. But after her abrupt disappearance, I lived in a precarious limbo until college, and then—when the very emblems of that childhood, my parents and grandfather, disappeared for good—I renounced any attempt at a benevolent rereading. I repressed, starting over from scratch. On the one hand, I escaped into a comfortable, promising field of study (I even did my thesis on the *Hypnerotomachia Poliphili,* not on the history of the Resistance), and on the other, I met Paola. But if Gianni was right, an underlying dissatisfaction remained. I had repressed everything except Lila's face, which I continued to look for in the crowd, hoping to meet her again by going, not backwards, as one must do with the dead, but forward, in a quest I now know to have been vain.

The advantage of this sleep of mine, with its sudden, labyrinthine short-circuits—such that, though I recognize the chronology of different periods, I can travel through them in both directions, having done away with time's arrow—the advantage is that I can now relive it all, no longer encumbered by any forward or backwards, in a circle that could last for geological ages, and in this circle, or spiral, Lila is always and once more beside me as I, the beguiled bee, dance timidly around the yellow pollen of her jacket. Lila is present, along with Angelo Bear, Dr. Osimo, Signor Piazza, Ada, Papà, Mamma, and Grandfather, along with the aromas and odours of the cooking of those years, comprehending with balance and pity even the night in the Gorge, and Gragnola.

Am I being selfish? Paola and the girls are waiting out there, and it is thanks to them that for forty years I have been able to keep searching for Lila, in the background, without losing touch with reality. They made me come out of my enclosed world, and even if I did wander amid incunabula and parchments, I still produced new life. They are suffering and I am feeling blessed. But what can I do about that now, I cannot return to the outside world, and so I might as well take pleasure in this suspended state. So suspended that I suspect that between now and the moment when I first awoke here, although I have relived nearly twenty years, sometimes moment by moment, only seconds have elapsed—as in dreams, where one can sometimes doze for a moment and in a flash experience an epic.

Perhaps I am, indeed, in a coma, but am dreaming within it, not remembering. I know that in some dreams we have the impression of remembering, and we believe the memories to be authentic, then we wake and are forced to conclude, reluctantly, that those memories were not ours. We dream false memories. For example, I recall having dreamed on several occasions of returning at last to a house I had not visited for some time, but to which I had for some time intended to return, because it was a sort of secret pied-à-terre where I had once lived, and I had left many of my belongings there. In the dream I remembered every piece of furniture perfectly and every room in the house, and the only irritation was that I knew that there should have been, beyond the living room, in the hall that led to the bathroom, a door that opened into another room, yet the door was no longer there, as if someone had walled it up. Thus I would awake full of longing and nostalgia for my hidden refuge, but would soon realize that the memory belonged to the dream, that I could not remember that house because—at least in my life—it had never existed. Indeed I have often thought that in our dreams we take over other people's memories.

But has it ever happened to me that, in a dream, I dreamed about another dream, as I would be doing now? There is the proof that I am not dreaming. And besides, in dreams memories are unfocused, imprecise, whereas I can now recall, page by page and image by image, everything I read at Solara during the past two months. Those memories really happened.

But who can say that everything I remembered in the course of this sleep really happened? Maybe my mother and my father had different faces, maybe Dr. Osimo never existed, nor Angelo Bear, and I never lived through the night in the Gorge. Worse, I dreamed even that I woke up in a hospital, that I lost my memory, that I had a wife named Paola, two daughters, and three grandkids. I never lost my memory, am some other man—God knows who—who by some accident finds himself in this state (coma or limbo), and all these figures have been optical illusions caused by the fog. Otherwise why would everything I believed I was remembering till now have been dominated by fog, which was nothing if not the sign that my life was but a dream. That is a quotation. And what if all the other quotes, those I offered the doctor, Paola, Sibilla, myself, were nothing but the product of this persistent dream? Carducci and Eliot never existed, nor Pascoli nor Huysmans, nor all the rest of what I took for my encyclopaedic memory. Tokyo is not the capital of Japan. Not only did Napoleon not die on St. Helena, he was never born, and if anything exists outside of me it is a parallel universe in which who knows what is happening or has happened. Perhaps my fellow creatures—and myself—are covered in green scales and have four retractile antennae above our single eye.

I cannot prove that this is not, in fact, the case. But had I conceived an entire universe within my brain, a universe that contains not only Paola and Sibilla but also the *Divine Comedy* and the atom bomb, I would have to have drawn on a capacity for invention exceeding that of any individual—still assuming that I am an individual, and human, and not a madrepore of linked brains.

But what if Someone is projecting a film directly into my brain? Perhaps I am a brain in some kind of solution, in a culture broth, in that glass container where I saw the dog testicles in formalin, and someone is sending stimuli into me to make me believe that I once had a body, and that others existed around me—when only my brain and the Stimulator exist. But if we were brains in formalin, could we imagine that we were brains in formalin or claim that we were not?

If that were the case, I would have nothing to do but await further stimuli. The ideal viewer, I would experience this sleep as an endless evening at the movies, believing the movie was about me. Or perhaps what I am dreaming now is only movie number 10,999, and I have already dreamed more than ten thousand others: in one, I identified with Julius Caesar, I crossed the Rubicon and suffered like a butchered hog after being stabbed those twenty-three times; in another, I was Signor Piazza and I stuffed weasels; in another, I was Angelo Bear, wondering why they were burning me after so many years of honourable service. In one I could be Sibilla, wondering, distraught, whether I might one day remember our affair. In this moment, I would be a provisional *I*; tomorrow I might be a dinosaur beginning to suffer as the ice age cometh to kill me; the day after tomorrow I will live the life of an apricot, a sparrow, a hyena, a twig.

I cannot let myself go, I want to know who I am. One thing is certain. The memories that surfaced at the beginning of what I believe to be my coma are obscure, foggy, and arranged in patchwork fashion, with breaks, uncertainties, tears, missing pieces (why can I not remember Lila's face?). Those of Solara, however, and those of Milan after I woke up in the hospital, are clear, they follow a logical sequence, I can put them back in chronological order, can say that I ran into Vanna in Largo Cairoli before buying the dog testicles from that stall in the Cordusio market. Sure, I could be dreaming about having vague memories and clear memories, but on the evidence of this difference I am going to make a decision. In order to survive (odd expression for someone like me who may already be dead) I must decide that Gratarolo, Paola, Sibilla, my studio, all of Solara with Amalia and the stories of Grandfather's castor oil, were memories of real life. That is how we do it in normal life, too: we could suppose we have been deceived by some evil genius, but in order to be able to move forward we behave as if everything we see is real. If we let ourselves go, if we doubt that a world exists around us, we will stop acting, and within the illusion produced by the evil genius we will fall down the stairs or die of hunger.

It was in Solara (which exists) that I read my poems about a Creature, and it was in Solara that Gianni told me over the phone that the creature had existed and her name was Lila Saba. So, even within my dream, Angelo Bear might be illusory, but Lila Saba is real. And besides, if I were only dreaming, why would the dream not be generous enough to restore Lila's face to me as well? In dreams the dead can even bring you lottery numbers, so why should Lila, of all people, be denied me? If I am unable to remember everything it is because beyond the dream there exists some blockage that is somehow preventing me from getting to the other side.

Of course, none of my muddled arguments hold. I could perfectly well be dreaming that a blockage exists, the Stimulator could be refusing (out of malice or pity) to send me Lila's image. People you know appear in dreams, you know who they are, yet you may not see their faces...None of the things I might convince myself of stands up to a logical proof. But the very fact that I can appeal to logic proves I am not dreaming. Dreams are illogical, and one does not bemoan that fact in dreams.

I am deciding therefore that things are a certain way, and I would sure like to see someone come along to contradict me.

If I could manage to see Lila's face, I would be convinced that she existed. There is no one I can ask for help, I have to do it all myself. I cannot beseech anyone outside of me, and both God and the Stimulator—if they even exist—are outside of the dream. Communications with the outside have been interrupted. Perhaps I could turn to some private deity, one who I know is weak, but who should at least be grateful to me for having given her life.

Who else but Queen Loana? I know, I am falling back on my paper memory again, but I am not thinking of the Queen Loana of the comic strip, but rather of my own, longed for in rather more ethereal ways, the custodian of the flame of resurrection, who can bring petrified cadavers back from any distant past.

Am I crazy? This, too, is a reasonable hypothesis: I am not comatose, but trapped in a lethargic autism, believing myself in a coma, believing that what I have dreamed is not real, believing I have the right to make it real. But how can a madman form a reasonable hypothesis? And besides, one is crazy only with respect to norms established by others, but no one else is here, the only measuring rod is me and the only real thing the Olympus of my memories. I am imprisoned in my Cimmerian isolation, in this ferocious egotism. And if such is my condition, why make distinctions between Mamma, Angelo Bear, and Queen Loana? My ontology is out of joint. I have the supreme power to create my own gods, and my own mothers.

And thus now I pray: "O good Queen Loana, in the name of your hopeless love, I do not ask that you reawaken your millenary victims from their stony sleeps, but merely that you restore to me a face...I, who from the nethermost pit of my enforced sleep have seen what I have seen, ask that you uplift me higher, towards a semblance of health."

Is it not the case with those who are miraculously healed that it is simply their expression of faith in the miracle that heals them? And thus I strongly will Loana to save me. I am so focused on this hope that, if I were not already in a coma, I would have a stroke.

And at last, great God, I saw. I saw like the apostle, I saw the centre of my Aleph from which shone forth not the infinite world, but the jumbled notebook of my memories.

Or rather, I certainly saw, but the first part of my vision was so blinding that afterwards it was as if I had been plunged back into a foggy sleep. I do not know whether within a dream you can dream of sleeping, but there is no doubt that, if I am dreaming, I am also dreaming that I have now awoken and can remember what I saw.

I was at my high school standing at the foot of the stairs, which rose white towards the neoclassical columns that framed the main entrance. I was as though carried away in spirit and I heard a powerful voice telling me: "What you shall see, feel free to write it in your book, because no one will read it, because you are only dreaming that you are writing it!"

And at the top of the stairs appeared a throne and upon the throne sat a man with a golden face and a ghastly Mongol smile, his head crowned with flame and emerald, and everyone raised their chalices to praise him: Ming the Merciless, Lord of Mongo.

And in the midst of the throne and around the throne were four Creatures, the lion-faced Thun, and the hawk-winged Vultan, and Barin, Prince of Arboria, and Azura, the Witch Queen of the Blue Magic Men. And Azura was descending the stairs wrapped in flame, and she resembled a great harlot mantled in purple and crimson, adorned with gold, precious stones, and pearls, drunk on the blood of the men who have come from the Earth, and when I saw her I was amazed with great amazement.

And Ming sitting on his throne said he wanted to judge the men of the earth, and he sneered lubriciously at the sight of Dale Arden, ordering her to be fed to the Beast from the Sea.

And the Beast had a horrible horn on its forehead, gaping jaws with sharpened teeth, predatory claws, and a tail like a thousand scorpions, and Dale did weep and call for help.

And coming to Dale's aid were the knights of the undersea world of Corelia, now climbing the stairs astride their beaked monsters that had only two legs and a long ocean-fish tail...

And the Blue Magic Men loyal to Gordon, in their gold and coral chariot pulled by green griffins with long, scale-crested necks...

And the Lancers of Fria astride their Snow Birds, whose beaks were contorted like golden cornucopias, and finally there came, in a white coach, alongside the Queen of the Snows, Flash Gordon, who shouted to Ming that the great tournament of Mongo was set to begin, and that he would pay for all his crimes.

And at Ming's signal, the Hawk Men dropped from the sky to fight Gordon, obscuring the clouds like swarms of grasshoppers, as the Lion Men with their nets and clawed tridents fanned out through the open area at the foot of the staircase, trying to capture Vanni and other students who had appeared in another swarm, this time of buzzing Vespas, and the battle was uncertain.

And uncertain of that battle, Ming gave another signal and his rocket ships were rising high into the sun and launching towards the Earth when, at Gordon's signal, other rocket ships belonging to Dr. Zarkov were launched and a majestic agon was under way, amid hissing death rays and tongues of fire, and the stars of the heavens seemed to fall upon the earth, and rocket ships were penetrating the heavens and rolling liquefied like a book being rolled up, and the day of Kim's Great Game arrived, and wrapped in more multicoloured flames Ming's other celestial rocket ships began crashing to the ground, crushing the Lion Men in the clearing. And the Hawk Men plummeted, swathed in flames.

And Ming the Merciless, Lord of Mongo, unleashed a fierce, bestial scream and his throne was overturned and tumbled down the stairs of the high school, crushing his fearful courtiers.

And the tyrant was dead, and gone were the beasts come from far and wide, and as an abyss opened beneath Azura's feet, which were sinking in a swirl of sulphur, there arose, in front of the high-school staircase and above the high school, a City of Glass, and of other precious stones, lifted by rays of all the colours of the rainbow, and it was twelve thousand furlongs in height, and its walls of jasper resembled pure glass and were one hundred and forty-four cubits thick.

And in that moment, after a time that was made both of flames and also of vapours, the fog rarefied, and now I saw the staircase, free of all monsters, white in the April sun.

I have returned to reality! Seven trumpets are playing, and they are from Maestro Pippo Barzizza's Orchestra Cetra, Maestro Cinico Angelini's Orchestra Melodica, and Maestro Alberto Semprini's Orchestra Ritmo Sinfonica. The doors of my high school are open, held wide by the Molièrian doctor from the Cachet Fiat aspirin ad, who is knocking with a baton to announce the parade of archons.

And here they are coming down the stairs on both sides of the staircase, the male students first, arranging themselves like rows of angels for the descent of all seven heavens, wearing striped jackets and white pants, like so many Diana Palmer suitors.

And at the foot of the stairs Mandrake the Magician now appears, nonchalantly twirling his cane. He climbs, tipping his top hat in greeting, the steps lighting up one by one as he goes, and he is singing I'll build a stairway to Paradise, with a new step ev'ry day! I'm gonna get there at any price, Stand aside, I'm on my way!

Mandrake now points his cane upwards, to signal the descent of the Dragon Lady, sheathed in black silk, and at every step the students kneel and hold out their hats as a gesture of adoration, as she sings, with that saxophone-in-heat voice, Sentimental this autumn evening sky, infinitely gentle this rose from days gone by, the signs all point to love much to my heart's delight, that's all it's dreamin' of, an hour of joy tonight an hour with you.

And coming down after her, having returned at last to our planet, Gordon, Dale Arden, and Dr. Zarkov, intoning Blue skies, smilin' at me, nothin' but blue skies do I see, Bluebirds, singin' a song, nothin' but bluebirds all day long.

And following him is George Formby, with his horsy smile and his ukulele, strumming along to It's in the air this funny feeling everywhere that makes me sing without a care today, as I go on my way, it's in the air, it's in the air... Zoom zoom zoom zoom high and low, zoom zoom zoom zoom here we go...

Down come the Seven Dwarfs, rhythmically reciting the names of the seven kings of Rome, all but one; and then Mickey Mouse and Minnie, arm in arm with Horace Horsecollar and Clarabelle Cow, bedecked with diadems from her treasure, to the rhythms of "Pippo Pippo doesn't know". Then come Pippo, Pertica and Palla, Cip and Gallina, and Alvaro the Corsair, with Alonzo Alonzo (Alonzo for short), who was once arrested for giraffe theft; and then, arm in arm like old pals, Dick Fulmine, Zambo, Barriera, White Mask, and Flattavion, shouting out *the Partisan in the woods;* and then all the kids from *Heart,* Derossi first, then the Little Lombard Lookout and the Sardinian Drummer Boy, then Coretti's father, his hand still warm from the King's touch, all singing *Addio Lugano Bella,* as the anarchists, unfairly chased away, leave, and Franti, bringing up the rear, repentant, whispers Sleep, do not cry, oh my sweet Jesus.

Fireworks burst forth, the sunny sky a blaze of golden stars, and the Thermogène man with his hot compresses tumbles down the stairs with fifteen Uncle Gaetanos, their heads all bristling with Presbitero pencils, their joints coming unjointed in a mad tap-dance, *I'm a Yankee Doodle Dandy;* kids and adults swarm out of My Children's Library, Gigliola di Collefiorito, the Wild Rabbit tribe, Signorina di Solmano, Gianna Preventi, Carletto di Kernoel, Rampichino, Editta di Ferlac, Susetta Monenti, Michele di Valdarta and Melchiorre Fiammati, Enrico di Valneve, Valia and Tamarisco, the airy ghost of Mary Poppins looming over all of them, and all of them sporting military caps, like the Paul Street boys, and long Pinocchio noses. The Cat and the Fox and the gendarme are tap-dancing.

Then, at a nod from the psychopomp, Sandokan appears. He is dressed in a tunic of Indian silk, snugged at the waist with a blue sash studded with precious stones, and his turban is pinned with a diamond the size of a hazelnut. The butt of an exquisitely crafted pistol sticks out from his belt, and his scimitar's scabbard is encrusted with rubies. In his baritone voice, he sings Mailù, under the Singapore sky, its golden stars dreamily high, we fell in love, you and I, and he is followed by his young "tigers", yataghans between their teeth, thirsty for blood, singing the praises of Mompracem, our flotilla, which laughed at England in Souda and Malta, in Alexandria and in Gibraltar...

Now here comes Cyrano de Bergerac, his sword sheathed, who with a sweeping gesture addresses the crowd in a nasal baritone: "Maybe you know my cousin? She's truly one of a kind... So modern and so pretty, her equal you won't find. She does the boogie-woogie, and speaks some English too; you'll find that she can murmur, quite graciously, *for you.*"

Gliding smoothly after him is Josephine Baker, but this time *à poil,* like the Kalmyk women from *Races and Peoples of the Earth,* except for a skirt of bananas around her waist, softly crooning Oh such grief I feel, such misery, to think, My Lord, that I offended Thee.

Then comes Diana Palmer singing *Il n'y a pas, il n'y a pas d'amour heureux,* Yanez de Gomera trilling Iberically O *Maria la O, I've got kisses for you, O Maria la O, please let me adore you, a single look from you and there's nothing I can do,* and then the executioner of Lille, who sobs *blond is your hair, made of strands of gold, sweet are your lips and fair,* before decapitating Milady de Winter with a single blow, *sffft,* causing her adorable head, marked by a fleur-de-lis branded on her brow, to roll to the bottom of the stairs, almost to my feet, as the Four Musketeers croon in falsetto, *She gets too hungry for dinner at eight, she likes the theatre and never comes late, she never bothers with people she'd hate, that's why Milady is a tramp!* Down comes Edmond Dantès intoning *This time my friend, it's on me, it's on me,* and Abbé Faria, coming after him wrapped in his sackcloth shroud, points and says, *That's him, that's him, yes, yes, that's the man,* as Jim, Dr. Livesey, Lord Trelawney, Captain Smollett, and Long John Silver (dressed up as Peg-Leg Pete, hitting every step once with his foot and three times with his prosthesis) challenge his right to Captain Flint's treasure, and Ben Gunn smiling like Trigger Hawkes with his canine teeth and saying *Cheese!* With the clack of Teutonic boots, Comrade Richard descends the stairs, his tap shoes clattering to the rhythm of *New York, New York, it's a wonderful town! The Bronx is up and the Battery's down,* and the Laughing Man, on the arm of Lady Josiane, who is as naked as only an armed woman can be, is articulating *I got rhythm, I got music, I got my girl, who could ask for anything more?*

And stretching along the staircase now, thanks to a staging miracle concocted by Dr. Zarkov, is a long shimmering monorail, on which La Filotea arrives, rises to the summit, then passes into the entry of the school.... And emerging out of it as if from a happy apiary, and retracing its route towards the bottom of the stairs, come Grandfather, Mamma, Papà leading a tiny Ada by the hand, Dr. Osimo, Signor Piazza, Don Cognasso, the parish priest of San Martino, and Gragnola, his neck wrapped in a brace that supports even the back of his head, like Erich von Stroheim's, that almost even straightens his back, and all of them harmonizing:

The whole family sings along from the dusk until the dawn,
Slow and soft, soft and slow, sings the Trio Lescano,
Some are fans of Boccaccini, some are fond of Angelini,
For others Rabagliati's voice is for ever their first choice.
Mamma loves a melody, but her daughter fills with glee
When Maestro Petralìa plays a tune in the key of G.

And, as Meo glides over everyone, his long ears catching the wind, splendidly asinine, all the kids from the Oratorio burst chaotically in, wearing the uniforms of the Ivory Patrol, pushing Fang, the lithe black panther, ahead of them, exotically psalming "They're off, the caravans of Tigrai."

Then, after firing a few shots at passing rhinos, they raise their

weapons and their hats to salute her: Queen Loana.

She appears in her chaste bra, a skirt that almost reveals her navel, a white veil over her face, a feather rising from her headdress, and an ample cape wavering in a light wind, sashaying gracefully between two Moors dressed in the style of Incan emperors.

She is descending towards me like a Ziegfeld dancer, smiling at me, giving me an encouraging nod and pointing towards the door of the school, where the figure of Don Bosco now stands.

Don Renato follows behind him in his clergyman suit, chanting, mystically and broad-mindedly, *Duae umbrae nobis una facta sunt, infra laternam stabimus, olim Lili Marleen, olim Lili Marleen.* The saint, with a cheerful expression, his vestments splashed with mud and his feet encumbered by his Salesian shoes with the tip and tap of each step, holds before him, as if it were Mandrake's top hat, *The Provident Young Man,* and he seems to me to be saying *Omnia munda mundis,* and your bride awaits you, and it was given her to wear a splendid, wholesome byssus, whose splendour shall be like to priceless gems, and I am come to tell you what shall happen shortly...

I have their consent... The two holy men position themselves on opposite sides of the bottom step and nod indulgently up towards the main entry, out of which the girls are now coming from their classes, bearing a great transparent veil in which they wrap themselves, assembled in the shape of a white rose. Backlit and nude, they raise their hands to reveal the profile of their virginal breasts. The hour has come. At the end of this radiant apocalypse, Lila will appear.

What will she be like? I tremble and anticipate.

She will appear as a girl of sixteen, lovely as a rose opening in all its freshness to the first rays of a beautiful dewy morning, in a long cerulean gown, draped from waist to knees with silver reticella

lace, which though echoing the colour of her irises will fall well short of equalling their ethereal azure, their soft and languid splendour, and a copious profusion of blond hair, downy and lustrous, checked only by a crown of flowers; she will be a creature of eighteen, diaphanously white, her flesh animated by a light rosy hue, the skin around her eyes imbued with a faint aquamarine cast, through which can be glimpsed, upon her forehead and at her temples, tiny veins of the palest blue, and her fine blond hair will fall upon her cheek, her eyes, a tender blue in colour, will seem suspended in some moist, scintillating substance, and her smile will be that of a little girl at both corners of whose mouth, in serious moods, a slight, trembling wrinkle forms; she will be a seventeen-year-old girl, slender and elegant, with a waist so narrow a single hand would suffice to encircle it, with skin like a newly opened flower and a mass of hair tumbling down in picturesque disorder, like gold rain on the white corset covering her breast, a bold forehead will rule the perfect oval of her face, her complexion will have the white opacity, the velvet freshness of a camellia petal lit by dawn's rays, her pupils, black and dazzling, will barely leave room, in each corner of those long-lashed eyes, for the blue transparency of her eyeballs.

No. Her tunic audaciously open on the sides, her arms bare, with mysterious and suggestive shadows beneath her veils, she will slowly unfasten something beneath her hair, letting the long silks that wrapped her like a shroud fall suddenly to the ground, and my gaze will travel up and down her body, robed now only in a clinging white garb, belted at the waist with a two-headed serpent made of gold, as she crosses her arms over her chest, and I will be driven mad by her androgynous form, by that flesh as white as the pith of the elderberry, that mouth with its predatory lips, that blue bow just beneath her chin, a missal angel whom some perverse minotaur has dressed as a mad virgin, on whose flat chest small but definite breasts rise distinctly, pointedly, the lines of her waist widening slightly at her hips, then disappearing into the too-long legs of a Luca di Leyda Eve, the gaze of her green eyes ambiguous, her mouth large and her smile disturbing, her hair the flaxen colour of old gold, all of her head belying the innocence of her body; passionate chimera, supreme achievement of art and sensuality, bewitching monster, she will be revealed in all her secret splendour, arabesques will radiate from lozenges of lapis lazuli, rainbow lights and prismatic blazes will glide over inlays of mother-of-pearl, she will be like Lady Josiane, her veils melting away in the heat of the dance, her brocades falling to the ground, until she is clad only in fashioned gold, in translucent gems, a gorget cinching her waist like a corselet, its superb clasp, a marvellous jewel, flashing its rays into the crevice between her breasts, her hips wrapped in a band that hides her upper thighs, against which slaps a gigantic pendant, a spilling river of carbuncles and emeralds, her belly arching from her now naked torso with its navel's hollow like an onyx seal, with its milky sheen, and in the ardent light radiant around her head every facet of every jewel will catch fire, the stones will come to life, accenting her body with their incandescent traces, stinging her neck, her legs, her arms with their sparks, now the deep red of embers, now the violet of gas jets, now the azure of burning alcohol, now the whiteness of starlight, and she will appear pleading for me to flog her, holding out an abbess's hair shirt and seven silk ropes for scourging the seven deadly sins, with seven knots in each rope for the seven ways of falling into mortal sin, and the drops of blood that blossom on her flesh will be roses, and she will be slender as a temple candle, her eyes pierced by love's swords, and my desire will be to place my heart upon that pyre in silence, will be that she, paler than a winter dawn, paler than candle wax, her hands clasped over her smooth chest, remain august beneath her robes, and red from the blood of the dead hearts that bleed for her.

No, no, what wicked literature am I letting myself be seduced by, I am no longer a prurient adolescent.... I would simply like her as she was, as I loved her then, just a face above a yellow jacket. I would like the most beautiful woman I have ever been able to conceive, but not that supreme beauty which has led others astray. I would be happy even were she frail and sick, as she must have been in her final days in Brazil, and still I would tell her, You are the most beautiful of creatures, I would never trade your broken eyes or your pallor for the beauty of all the angels in heaven! I would like to see her rise midstream, alone and still as she gazes out to sea, a creature transformed by magic into a strange and beautiful seabird, her long slender bare legs delicate as a crane's, and without importuning her with my desire I would leave her to her remoteness, the faraway princess.

I do not know whether it is the mysterious flame of Queen Loana that is burning in my crumpled-parchment lobes, whether some elixir is attempting to wash the browned pages of my paper memory, still marred by the many stains that render illegible that part of the text that still eludes me, or whether it is I who am trying to drive my nerves to the point of unbearable exertion. If I could tremble in this state, I would be trembling, I feel as storm-tossed in here as if I were bobbing out there on a squalling sea. But I also feel on the verge of orgasm, as my brain's corpora cavernosa swell with blood, as something gets ready to explode—or blossom.

Now, as on that day in the foyer, I am finally about to see Lila, who will descend still modest and mischievous in her black smock, lovely as the sun, white as the moon, nimble and unaware of being the centre, the navel of the world. I will see her lovely face, her well-drawn nose, that glimpse of her two front teeth between her lips, she an angora rabbit, Matù the cat mewing and rippling his soft fur, a dove, an ermine, a squirrel. She will descend like the first frost, and will see me, and will gently extend her hand, not in invitation but simply to keep me from fleeing once again.

I will finally learn how to perform for evermore the final scene of my *Cyrano,* I will see what I have looked for all my life, from Paola to Sibilla, and I will be reunited. I will be at peace.

Careful. This time I must not ask her "Does Vanzetti live here?" I must finally seize the Opportunity.

But a faint, mouse-coloured *fumifugium* is spreading from the top of the stairs, veiling the entrance.

I feel a cold gust, I look up.

Why is the sun turning black?

Sources of Citations and Illustrations

p. 23, drawing by the author
p. 60, Dante, *Inferno,* Canto XXXI
p. 61, Giovanni Pascoli, "Il bacio del morto" ("The Dead Man's Kiss"), from *Myricae,* Livorno: Raffaello Giusti, 1891
p. 61, Giovanni Pascoli, "Nebbia" ("Fog"), from *Canti di Castelvecchio* (*Songs of Castelvecchio*), Bologna: Zanichelli, 1903
p. 61, Giovanni Pascoli, "Voci misteriose" ("Mysterious Voices"), from *Poesie varie* (*Selected Poems*), Bologna: Zanichelli, 1928
p. 62, Vittorio Sereni, "L'alibi e il beneficio" ("The Alibi and the Benefit"), from *Gli strumenti umani* (*The Human Instruments*), Turin: Einaudi, 1965. Reproduced by kind permission of the estate of Vittorio Sereni.
p. 67, lyrics by Giancarlo Testoni, "In cerca di te" ("Searching for You"), Metron, 1945. Reproduced by kind permission of IDM Music, Ltd. All rights reserved.
pp. 70–71, cover and two panels from *Il tesoro di Clarabella* (original title: *Race for Riches*), Milan: Mondadori, 1936, © Disney Enterprises, Inc.
p. 91, Giovanni Pascoli, "Nella nebbia" ("In the Fog"), *Primi Poemetti* (*Early Poems*), Bologna: Zanichelli, 1905
p. 93, *La escala de la vida* (*The Stair of Life*), nineteenth-century Catalan print (author's collection)
p. 95, prints from *Zur Geschichte der Kostüme* (*The History of Costume*), Munich: Braun and Schneider, 1861 (author's collection)
p. 97, cover of *La filotea* (*The Filotea*), by Giuseppe Riva, Bergamo: Istituto Italiano d'Arti Grafiche, 1886 (author's collection)
p. 100, *Imagerie d'Épinal,* Pellerin (author's collection)
p. 102, cover of sheet music for "Vorrei volare" (original title: "It's in the Air"), Milan: Carisch, 1940 (author's collection). Reproduced by kind permission of IDM Music, Ltd. All rights reserved.
p. 104, Renée Vivien, "A la femme aimée" ("To the Beloved Woman"), from *Poèmes I* (*Poems I*), Paris: Lemerre, 1923
p. 105 (clockwise):
Alex Pozeruriski, *Après la danse* (*After the Dance*), magazine illustration for *La gazette du Bon Ton,* c. 1915 (in Patricia Frantz Kery, *Art Deco Graphics,* New York: Abrams, 1986)

Janine Aghion, *The Essence of the Mode in the Day,* book illustration, 1920 (in Patricia Frantz Kery, *Art Deco Graphics,* New York: Abrams, 1986)
Julius Engelhard, *Mode Ball,* poster, 1928 (in Patricia Frantz Kery, *Art Deco Graphics,* New York: Abrams, 1986)
Anonymous, *Candee,* advertisement and poster, 1929 (in Patricia Frantz Kery, *Art Deco Graphics,* New York: Abrams, 1986)
p. 106 (clockwise):
George Barbier, *Schéhérazade,* magazine illustration for *Modes et Manières d'Aujourd'hui,* 1914 (in Patricia Frantz Kery, *Art Deco Graphics,* New York: Abrams, 1986)
Charles Martin, *De la pomme aux levres* (*From Apple to Lips*), magazine illustration for *La gazette du Bon Ton,* c. 1915 (in Patricia Frantz Kery, *Art Deco Graphics,* New York: Abrams, 1986)
Georges Lepape, *Vogue* magazine cover, Mar. 15, 1927 (in Patricia Frantz Kery, *Art Deco Graphics,* New York: Abrams, 1986). Reproduced by kind permission of Condé Nast Publications Inc.
George Barbier, *Incantation,* book illustration for *Falbalas et Fanfreluches,* 1923 (in Patricia Frantz Kery, *Art Deco Graphics,* New York: Abrams, 1986)
p. 109, illustration from *Il nuovissimo Melzi,* Milan: Vallardi, 1905 (author's collection)
p. 113, illustration by Alphonse de Neuville for *Vingt mille lieues sous les mers* (*20,000 Leagues under the Sea*), by Jules Verne, Paris: Hetzel, 1869
p. 114, cover of *Il conte di Monte-Cristo* (original title: *Le comte de Monte-Cristo*; English title: *The Count of Monte Cristo*), by Alexandre Dumas, Milan: Sonzogno, 1927, © RCS (author's collection)
p. 115, illustration by Charles Clérice for *Les ravageurs de la mer* (*The Ravagers of the Sea*), by Louis Jacolliot, Paris: Librairie Illustrée, 1894–95 (author's collection)
p. 121, tin of Talmone Cocoa
p. 122, tin of Brioschi Effervescent Powders (author's collection)
p. 124, cigarette packets, from Michael Thibodeau and Jana Martin's *Smoke Gets in Your Eyes,* New York: Abbeville Press, 2000. Copyright © 2000 by Abbeville Press, Inc. Photography by Elliot Morgan/Blink Studio.
p. 125, barber's calendarette, *Sprazzi e bagliori* (*Flashes and Sparkles*), 1929 (author's collection)
p. 126, barber's calendarettes, from Ermanno Detti's *Le carte povere* (*Poor Papers*), Florence: La Nuova Italia, 1989
p. 130 (left to right, top to bottom):
Cover of *Nick Carter: Il gran poliziotto Americano* (*Nick Carter: The Great American Detective*), Milan: Casa Editrice Americana, 1908
Cover of *Cuore,* by Edmondo de Amicis, Milan: Fratelli Treves, 1878
Cover by Domenico Natoli of *Curti Bo e la piccola tigre bionda* (*Curti Bo and the Little Blond Tiger*), by Augusto de Angelis, Milan: 1943, © RCS
Cover by Trancredi Scarpelli of *I promessi sposi* (*The Betrothed*), by Alessandro Manzoni, Florence: Nerbini, no date
Cover of *New Nick Carter Weekly,* Italian edition, Milan: Casa Editrice Americana, no date
Cover by Léo Fontan of *L'aiguille creuse* (*The Hollow Needle*), Paris: Éditions Pierre Lafitte, 1909
Cover of *Il treno della morte* (*The Death Train*), by Carolina Invernizio, Turin, 1905 (author's collection)
Cover of *Il consiglio dei quattro* (original title: The *Council of Justice*), by Edgar Wallace, Milan: Mondadori, 1933 (author's collection)
Cover of *Vidocq: L'uomo dalle cento facce* (*Vidocq: The Man of a Hundred Faces*), by Marc Mario and Louis Launay, Milan: La Milano, 1911
p. 131 (left to right, top to bottom):
Cover by Filiberto Mateldi of *I miserabili* (*Les Misérables*), by Victor Hugo, Turin: Unione Tipografico Editrice Torinese, 1945 (author's collection)
Cover by Gennaro Amato of *I corsari delle Bermude* (*The Bermuda Pirates*), by Emilio Salgari, Milan: Sonzogno, 1938, © RCS (author's collection)

Cover of *Viaggi staordinarissimi di Saturnino Farandola* (original title: *Voyages très extraordinaires de Saturnin Farandoul*; English title: *The Very Extraordinary Voyages of Saturnin Farandoul*), by Albert Robida, Milan: Sonzogno, no date (author's collection)

Cover by Domenico Natoli of *I figli del Capitano Grant* (original title: *Les enfants du capitaine Grant*; English title: *The Children of Captain Grant*), by Jules Verne, Milan: SACSE, 1936 (author's collection)

Cover by Tancredi Scarpelli of *I misteri del popolo* (original title: *Les mystères du peuple*; English title: *The Mysteries of the People*), by Eugène Sue, Florence: Nerbini, 1909 (author's collection)

Cover of *La strana morte del signor Benson* (original title: *The Benson Murder Case*), by S. S. Van Dine (pseudonym of Willard Huntington Wright), Milan: Romanzo Mensile, 1938

Cover of *Senza famiglia* (original title: *Sans famille*; English title: *Nobody's Boy*), by Hector Malot, Milan: Sonzogno, no date, © RCS

Cover by Giorgio Tabet of *Il barone alle strette* (original title: *The Baron at Bay*; U.S. title: *Blue Mask at Bay*), by Anthony Morton (pseudonym of John Creasey), Milan: Romanzo Mensile, 1938, © RCS (author's collection)

Cover by Domenico Natoli of *Il delitto di Rouletabille* (original title: *Le crime de Rouletabille* [*The Crime of Rouletabille*]), by Gaston Leroux, Milan: Sonzogno, 1930, © RCS (author's collection)

p. 132, cover of *Fantômas,* by Marcel Allain and Pierre Souvestre, Florence: Salani, 1912

p. 133 (left), cover of *Rocambole,* by Ponson du Terrail, Paris: Jules Rouff, no date

p. 133 (right), illustration by Giorgio Tabet, from *I sosia del barone* (original title: *Alias the Baron*; U.S. title: *Alias Blue Mask*), by Anthony Morton (pseudonym of John Creasey), Milan: Romanzo Mensile, 1939, © RCS (author's collection)

p. 135, illustration by Attilio Mussino, from *Pinocchio,* by Carlo Collodi (pseudonym of Carlo Lorenzini), Florence: Bemporad, 1911

p. 136, cover of *Le avventure di Ciuffettino* (*The Adventures of Ciuffettino*), by Yambo (pseudonym of Enrico Novelli), Florence: Vallecchi, 1922 (author's collection)

p. 138, covers of *Giornale Illustrato dei Viaggi e delle Avventure di Terra e di Mare* (*Illustrated Journal of Voyages and Adventures by Land and Sea*), Milan: Sonzogno, 1917–20, © RCS (author's collection)

p. 140, covers of My Children's Library books, Florence: Salani (author's collection)

p. 143, illustration from *Otto giorni in una soffitta* (original title: *Huit jours dans un grenier* [*Eight Days in an Attic*]), Florence: Salani (author's collection)

p. 144, cover by Tancredi Scarpelli of *Buffalo Bill: Il medaglione di brillanti,* Florence: Nerbini, no date (author's collection)

p. 145, cover of *Ragazzi d'Italia nel mondo* (*Italy's Boys in the World*), by Pino Ballario, Milan: Prora, 1938 (author's collection)

p. 146, illustration by Newell Convers Wyeth, from *Treasure Island,* by Robert Louis Stevenson, New York: Charles Scribner's Sons, 1911

p. 148 (clockwise):

Cover by Gennaro Amato of *Sandokan alla riscossa* (*Sandokan Fights Back*), by Emilio Salgari, Florence: Bemporad, 1907

Cover by Alberto Della Valle of *I misteri della jungla nera* (*The Mysteries of the Black Jungle*), by Emilio Salgari, Genoa: Donath, 1903

Cover by Alberto Della Valle of *Il corsaro nero* (*The Black Corsair*), by Emilio Salgari, Genoa: Donath, 1908

Cover by Alberto Della Valle of *Le tigri di Mompracem* (*The Tigers of Mompracem*), by Emilio Salgari, Genoa: Donath, 1906

p. 150, illustration by Frederic Dorr Steele from *Collier's,* vol. XXXI, no. 26, Sept. 26, 1903

p. 151, illustrations by Sidney Paget from *Strand Magazine,* 1901–1905

pp. 152–53, Arthur Conan Doyle, "A Study in Scarlet", *Beeton's Christmas Annual,* 1887
p. 153, Arthur Conan Doyle, "The Sign of Four", *Lippincott's Magazine,* Feb. 1890
pp. 153–54, Emilio Salgari, *Le tigri di Mompracem* (*The Tigers of Mompracem*), Genoa: Donath, 1906
p. 157, panel by Bruno Angoletta from *Corriere dei piccoli,* Dec. 27, 1936, © RCS (author's collection)
p. 162 (left), illustration from *Il giornalino di Gian Burrasca* (*The Diary of Hurricane Gian*), by Vamba (pseudonym of Luigi Bertelli), Florence: Bemporad-Marzocco, 1920 (author's collection)
p. 162 (right), cover of *Rocambole: La morte del selvaggio* (original title: *Rocambole: La mort du sauvage* [*Rocambole: The Savage's Death*]), by Ponson du Terrail, Milan: Bietti, no date (author's collection)
p. 165, lyrics by Carlo Prato and Riccardo Morbelli, "Quando la radio" ("When the Radio"), Nuova Fonit-Cetra. Lyrics reproduced by kind permission of IDM Music, Ltd. All rights reserved.
p. 168, record sleeve of *Fiorin Fiorello,* Odeon/EMI, 1939
p. 169, lyrics by Carlo Innocenzi and Alessandro Soprani, "Mille lire al mese" ("A Thousand Lire a Month"), Rome: Marletta, 1938. Lyrics reproduced by kind permission of IDM Music, Ltd. All rights reserved.
p. 172 (left column):
Poster of the Federazione dei Fasci di Combattimento (Federation of Combat Groups)
Lyrics by Salvator Gotta, "Giovinezza" ("Youth")
p. 172 (right column):
Cover of sheet music for "Tulipan" ("Tulips")
Lyrics by Riccardo Morbelli, "Tulipan" ("Tulips"), free adaptation of the original English lyrics of "Tu-li Tulip Time" by Jack Lawrence and María Mendez Grever, Milan: Edizioni Curci, 1940. Cover and lyrics reproduced by kind permission of IDM Music, Ltd. All rights reserved.
p. 173 (left column):
Fiat publicity poster from the 1930s
Lyrics by Vittorio Emanuele Bravetta, "Fischia il sasso" ("The Stone Whistles"). Lyrics reproduced by kind permission of IDM Music, Ltd. All rights reserved.
p. 173 (right column):
Cover of sheet music for "Maramao perché sei morto?" ("Maramao, Why Did You Die?")
Lyrics by Mario Consiglio, "Maramao perché sei morto?" ("Maramao, Why Did You Die?"), Melodi/Sugar, 1939. Cover and lyrics reproduced by kind permission of IDM Music, Ltd. All rights reserved.
p. 176 (clockwise):
Cover of sheet music for "Tango del ritorno" ("Tango of Return"), Milan: Edizioni Joly
Cover of sheet music for "Finestra chiusa" ("Closed Window"), Milan: Edizioni Curci
Cover of sheet music for "Maria la O", Milan: Edizioni Leonardi
Cover of sheet music for "La mia canzone al vento" ("My Song to the Wind"), Milan: Edizioni S.A.M. Bixio. Covers reproduced by kind permission of IDM Music, Ltd. All rights reserved.
p. 181, illustrations by Enrico Pinochi from *Il libro della prima classe elementare* (*The First Grade Reader*), by Maria Zanetti, Rome: Libreria dello Stato, Anno XVI (author's collection)
p. 181, lyrics by Luigi Astore and Riccardo Morbelli, "Baciami piccina" ("Kiss Me Baby"), Milan: Fono Enic. Lyrics reproduced by kind permission of IDM Music, Ltd. All rights reserved.
p. 183, illustration by Angelo Della Torre from *Il libro della IV classe elementare* (*The 4th Grade Reader*), Rome: Libreria dello Stato, Anno XVIII (author's collection)
p. 185 (left column):
Illustration from *Il libro della prima classe elementare* (*The First Grade Reader*), by Maria

Zanetti, Rome: Libreria dello Stato, Anno XVI (author's collection)

Lyrics by Vittorio Emanuele Bravetta, "Inno dei giovani fascisti" ("Young Fascists' Anthem"). Lyrics reproduced by kind permission of IDM Music, Ltd. All rights reserved.

p. 185 (right column):

Cover of sheet music for "Pippo non lo sa" ("Pippo Doesn't Know")

Lyrics by Mario Panzeri, Gorni Kramer, and Nino Rastelli, "Pippo non lo sa" ("Pippo Doesn't Know"), Milan: Melodi, 1940. Cover and lyrics reproduced by kind permission of IDM Music, Ltd. All rights reserved.

p. 186, illustration from *Il libro della IV classe elementare* (*The 4th Grade Reader*), Rome: Libreria dello Stato, Anno XVIII (author's collection)

p. 188, two propaganda postcards by Gino Boccasile, c. 1943–44

p. 189, cover of *Tempo,* June 12, 1950, Milan: Anonima Periodici Italiani

p. 190 (left column):

Cover of sheet music for "La piccinina" ("The Milliner's Assistant"), Milan: Edizioni Melodi, 1939 (author's collection)

Lyrics by Eldo di Lazzaro and Mario Panzeri, "La piccinina" ("The Milliner's Assistant"), Milan: Edizioni Melodi, 1939. Cover and lyrics for "La piccinina" reproduced by kind permission of IDM Music, Ltd. All rights reserved.

Lyrics by Giovanni D'Anzi and Marcello Marchesi, "Bellezze in bicicletta" ("Beauties on Bikes"). Lyrics reproduced by kind permission of IDM Music, Ltd. All rights reserved.

p. 190 (right column):

Fiat poster by Marcello Dudovich, 1934, © 2005 Artists Rights Society (ARS) New York/SIAE, Rome.

Lyrics by Giovanni D'Anzi and Alfredo Bracchi, "Ma le gambe" ("But Their Legs"), Milano: Edizioni Curci

Lyrics by Carlo Buti, "Reginella campagnola" ("Little Country Queen"). Lyrics for "Ma le gambe" and "Reginella campagnola" reproduced by kind permission of IDM Music, Ltd. All rights reserved.

p. 193, propaganda postcard by Enrico Deseta, Rome: Edizioni d'Arte Boeri, 1936

pp. 194–95, lyrics by M. Zambrelli, "Vincere" ("Victory"), 1940. Lyrics reproduced by kind permission of IDM Music, Ltd. All rights reserved.

p. 196, propaganda postcard by Gino Boccasile, *Due popoli, una vittoria* (*Two Peoples, One Victory*)

pp. 196–97, Italian lyrics by Nino Rastelli (free adaptation of the original German lyrics by Hans Leip, 1915), "Lili Marleen", 1943. Lyrics reproduced by kind permission of IDM Music, Ltd. All rights reserved.

pp. 197–98, lyrics by Tito Manlio, "Caro Papà" ("Dear Daddy"), Milan: Accordo, 1941. Lyrics reproduced by kind permission of IDM Music, Ltd. All rights reserved.

p. 199 (left column):

Propaganda postcard by Gino Boccasile, *Tacete!* (*Hush!*), 1943

Lyrics by Vittorio Emanuele Bravetta, "Adesso viene il bello" ("Blue Skies Are on the Way"), Milan: Carisch. Lyrics reproduced by kind permission of IDM Music, Ltd. All rights reserved.

p. 199 (right column):

Propaganda postcard by Gino Boccasile, *Ritorneremo* (*We Will Return*), 1943

Lyrics by Alberto Simeoni and Ferrante Alvare De Torres, "La sagra di Giarabub" ("The Feast of Giarabub"). Lyrics reproduced by kind permission of IDM Music, Ltd. All rights reserved.

pp. 200–201, lyrics by Auro D'Alba, "Battaglioni M" ("The M Battalions"). Lyrics reproduced by kind permission of IDM Music, Ltd. All rights reserved.

p. 202 (left column):

Cover illustration by Achille Beltrame, *La Domenica del Corriere* (*The Sunday Corriere*),

1943, © RCS (author's collection)

Lyrics by Zorro, "La canzone dei sommergibili" ("The Song of the Submarines"), Canzone Marcia, 1941. Lyrics reproduced by kind permission of IDM Music, Ltd. All rights reserved.

p. 202 (right column):

Cover of sheet music for "Signorine non guardate i marinai" ("Young Ladies Take Your Eyes Off Sailor Boys"), Milan: Edizioni Musicali Mascheroni

Lyrics by Vittorio Mascheroni and Marf, "Signorine non guardate i marinai" ("Young Ladies Take Your Eyes Off Sailor Boys"), Milan: Edizioni Musicali Mascheroni. Cover and lyrics reproduced by kind permission of IDM Music, Ltd. All rights reserved.

p. 204 (left column):

Alberto Rabagliati

Lyrics by Giovanni D'Anzi and Alfredo Bracchi, "Non dimenticar le mie parole" ("Don't Forget My Words")

Lyrics by Giovanni D'Anzi and Michele Galdieri, "Ma l'amore no" ("But Love Is Not That Way")

Lyrics by Giovanni D'Anzi and Alfredo Bracchi, "Bambina innamorata" ("Darling How I Love You"). All lyrics reproduced by kind permission of IDM Music, Ltd. All rights reserved.

p. 204 (right column):

Pippo Barzizza

Lyrics by Vittorio Mascheroni and Peppino Mendes, "Fiorin Fiorello" ("Precious Little Flower")

Lyrics by Mario Schisa, Mario Panzeri and Nino Rastelli, "La gelosia non è più di moda" ("Jealousy Has Gone Out of Fashion"). All lyrics reproduced by kind permission of IDM Music, Ltd. All rights reserved.

pp. 214–15, extract from *Il Bertoldo,* Aug. 27, 1937

p. 229, cover illustration by Bruno Angoletta, *Il Corriere dei Piccoli,* Oct. 15, 1939, © RCS (author's collection)

p. 230, panel by Pat Sullivan from *Il Corriere dei Piccoli,* Nov. 29, 1936, © RCS (author's collection)

p. 231 (top), cover illustration by Benito Jacovitti, *Alvaro il corsaro* (*Alvaro the Pirate*), Rome: Edizioni AVE, 1942 (author's collection). Reproduced by kind permission of the Archivio Benito Jacovitti.

p. 231 (bottom), cover illustration by Sebastiano Craveri, *Il carro di trespoli* (*The Trestle Car*), Rome: Edizioni AVE, 1938 (author's collection)

p. 233, panel by Kurt Caesar from "Verso A.O.I." ("Towards I.E.A. [Italian East Africa]"), *Il Vittorioso,* June 7, 1941 (author's collection)

p. 235, first page of the first issue of *L'avventuroso* (*The Adventurous*), Florence: Nerbini, 1934 (author's collection). *Flash Gordon* illustrations by Alex Raymond, © King Features Syndicate, Inc. Reprinted with special permission of King Features Syndicate.

p. 238 (left to right, top to bottom):

Panel by Benito Jacovitti from "Pippo e il dittatore" ("Pippo and the Dictator"), in *Intervallo,* 1945 (author's collection). Panel reproduced by kind permission of the Archivio Benito Jacovitti.

Panel by Lyman Young from "La pattuglia dell'avorio" ("The Ivory Patrol"), Firenze: Nerbini, 1935, © King Features Syndicate, Inc., 1934. Panel reprinted with special permission of King Features Syndicate.

Panel from unknown cartoon

Panel by Elzie Crisler Segar from *Popeye,* © King Features Syndicate, Inc. Panel reprinted with special permission of King Features Syndicate.

Panel by Lyman Young from "Lo spirito di Tambo" ("The Spirit of Tambo"), in *Il giornale di Cino e Franco* (original title: *Tim Tyler's Luck*), Florence: Nerbini, Mar. 22,

1936, © King Features Syndicate, Inc. Panel reprinted with special permission of King Features Syndicate.

Panel by Benito Jacovitti from "Pippo e il dittatore" ("Pippo and the Dictator"), in *Intervallo,* 1945 (author's collection). Panel reproduced by kind permission of the Archivio Benito Jacovitti.

Panel by Lyman Young from "Il coccodrillo sacro" ("The Sacred Crocodile"), in *Il giornale di Cino e Franco* (original title: *Tim Tyler's Luck*), Florence: Nerbini, Sept. 19, 1937, © King Features Syndicate, Inc. (author's collection). Panel reprinted with special permission of King Features Syndicate.

Panel by Walt Disney and Floyd Gottfredson from *Topolino nel paese dei califfi* (English title: *Adventure in an Arabian Country*), Milan: Mondadori, Dec. 10, 1934, © Disney Enterprises, Inc., 1970

Panel by Walt Disney and Floyd Gottfredson from "Topolino nella valle infernale" ("Mickey Mouse in Death Valley"), Milan: Mondadori, May 31, 1930, © Disney Enterprises, Inc., 1970

Panel by Elzie Crisler Segar from *Popeye,* © King Features Syndicate, Inc. Panel reprinted with special permission of King Features Syndicate.

p. 239, panel by Lee Falk and Ray Moore featuring L'Uomo Mascherato (The Phantom), from *Il piccolo Toma* (original title: *Little Tommy*), Florence: Nerbini, July 1, 1938, © King Features Syndicate, Inc. Panel reprinted with special permission of King Features Syndicate.

p. 241 (top): cover by Giove Toppi of *Il mago "900"* (*The Modern Magician*), Florence: Nerbini, no date

p. 241 (bottom): cover by Floyd Gottfredson of *Topolino giornalista* (*Mickey Mouse Runs His Own Newspaper*), Milan: Mondadori, 1936, © Disney Enterprises, Inc.

p. 242, panel detail by Chester Gould from *Dick Tracy* (© Chicago Tribune/New York News Syndicate). Reproduced by kind permission of Tribune Media Services.

p. 244 (left), cover by Vittorio Cossio of *La camera del terrore* (*The Chamber of Terror*), Milan: Albogiornale Juventus, 1939 (author's collection)

p. 244 (right), cover by Carlo Cossio of *L'infame tranello* (*The Infamous Snare*), Albogiornale, 1939 (author's collection)

p. 245, illustration by Milton Caniff from *Terry and the Pirates* (© Chicago Tribune/New York News Syndicate), from the cover of *The Golden Age of the Comics No. 4,* New York: Nostalgia Press, 1970. Reproduced by kind permission of Tribune Media Services.

p. 247 (left to right, top to bottom):

Panel by Pier Lorenzo De Vita, from "L'ultimo Ras" ("The Last Ras"), from *Corriere dei piccoli,* Dec. 20, 1936, © RCS (author's collection)

Panel by Alex Raymond from *Flash Gordon,* 1938, © King Features Syndicate, Inc. (author's collection). Panel reprinted with special permission of King Features Syndicate.

Panel by Lee Falk and Ray Moore from *Nel regno dei Singh* (original title: *The Singh Brotherhood*), Florence: Nerbini, Aug. 1, 1937, © King Features Syndicate, Inc. (author's collection). Panel reprinted with special permission of King Features Syndicate.

Panel by Alex Raymond and Dashiell Hammett from "Agente Segreto X9" ("Secret Agent X9"), in *L'avventuroso,* Oct. 14, 1934, © King Features Syndicate, Inc. (author's collection). Panel reprinted with special permission of King Features Syndicate.

Panel by Alex Raymond from *Flash Gordon,* 1938, © King Features Syndicate, Inc. (author's collection). Panel reprinted with special permission of King Features Syndicate.

Panel by Alex Raymond from *Flash Gordon,* 1938, © King Features Syndicate, Inc. (author's collection). Panel reprinted with special permission of King Features Syndicate.

p. 249, cover of *Novella* with photograph by Braschi, Jan. 8, 1939, Milan: Rizzoli, © RCS (author's collection)

p. 251, Italian cover by Lyman Young of *La Misteriosa Fiamma della Regina Loana* (*The Mysterious Flame of Queen Loana*), Florence: Nerbini, 1935, © King Features Syndicate, Inc., 1934. Reprinted with special permission of King Features Syndicate.
p. 255, various stamps (private collection)
p. 263 (left), still of Fred Astaire and Ginger Rogers, source unknown
p. 263 (right), still of Elsa Merlini from *Ultimo ballo* (*Last Dance*), directed by Camillo Mastrocinque, 1941
p. 268, front page of *Corriere della sera,* July 26, 1943, © RCS
p. 273, lyrics by Lelio Luttazzi, "Il giovanotto matto" ("The Crazy Young Guy"), Milano: Casiroli, 1945. Lyrics reproduced by kind permission of IDM Music, Ltd. All rights reserved.
p. 273, lyrics by Libero Bovio, "Signorinella" ("Little Maiden"), Santa Lucia. Lyrics reproduced by kind permission of IDM Music, Ltd. All rights reserved.
p. 275, photograph (private collection)
p. 277, illustration by Domenico Pilla from *Piccoli martiri* (*Little Martyrs*), no date (author's collection)
p. 294, Cesare Pavese, "Sono solo" ("I Am Alone"), written in 1927, from *Le poesie* (*Poems*), Turin: Einaudi, 1998. Reproduced by kind permission of Einaudi.
p. 296, Augusto De Angelis, *L'albergo delle tre rose,* Milan: Mondadori, 1936
p. 297, title page of the first folio edition of Shakespeare's plays, 1623
p. 303, montage by the author of ads for Fernet Branca bitters (1908), Presbitero pencils (1924), and Thermogène hot compresses (Leonetto Cappiello, 1909)
p. 304, illustration by Attilio Mussino, from *Le orecchie di Meo* (*Meo's Ears*) by Giovanni Bertinetti, Turin: Lattes, 1908 (author's collection)
p. 305, illustrations by Angelo Bioletti, from *I quattro Moschettieri* (*The Four Musketeers*), by Angelo Nizza and Riccardo Morbelli, Perugina/Buitoni, 1935 (author's collection)
p. 310, illustration from *Il conte di Monte-Cristo* (original title: *Le comte de Monte-Cristo*; English title: *The Count of Monte Cristo*), by Alexandre Dumas, Milan: Sonzogno, 1927, © RCS (author's collection)
p. 315, ad for Mineraria briquettes, drawing by Dinelli, c. 1934 (Società Mineraria del Valdarno e Carbonital)
p. 324, montage by the author of cover images from *Novella,* Milan: Rizzoli, 1939, © RCS (author's collection)
p. 326, ad for Cachet Fiat headache pills, drawing by Mario Cussino, 1926
p. 329 (left), publicity poster for Borsalino hats, by Marcello Dudovich, c. 1930, © 2005 Artists Rights Society (ARS) New York/SIAE, Rome.
p. 329 (right), photographs of German concentration camps, 1945
p. 332, propaganda poster from the Repubblica Sociale Italiana, 1944
p. 334, front pages of *L'Italia libera* (Oct. 30, 1943) and *Avanti!* (Apr. 3, 1944) (author's collection)
p. 337, Fijian stamps (private collection)
p. 340, lyrics by Nino Rastelli, "Tornerai" ("You'll Come Back"), Leopardi. Lyrics reproduced by kind permission of IDM Music, Ltd. All rights reserved.
p. 347, photomontage for the ten-year anniversary of the Fascist Revolution, Rome: Istituto Luce, 1932. Reproduced by kind permission of the Istituto Luce.
p. 361, SS poster, 1944
p. 366, montage by the author of Repubblica Sociale Italiana propaganda posters, film stills, and advertising images from the 1940s
p. 380, still from *Casablanca,* directed by Michael Curtiz, Warner Bros., 1942
p. 381 (left), front page of *Corriere Lombardo,* Aug. 8, 1945 (author's collection)
p. 381 (right), publicity poster for *Road to Zanzibar,* directed by Victor Schertzinger, Paramount, 1941
p. 387, Josephine Baker

p. 388, Giovanni Bosco, *Il giovane provveduto* (*The Provident Young Man*), from *Opere edite II* (*Published Works II*), Rome: Libreria Ateneo Salesiano

p. 389, lyrics of "Bella tu sei qual sole" ("Lovely Thou Art as the Sun"), popular hymn

p. 390–91, Giovanni Bosco, *Il giovane provveduto* (*The Provident Young Man*), from *Opere edite II* (*Published Works II*), Rome: Libreria Ateneo Salesiano

p. 392, lyrics by Lorenzo Perosi, "Dormi non piangere" ("Sleep Do Not Cry"), 1912

p. 394, still from *I due orfanelli* (English title: *The Two Orphans*), directed by Mario Mattoli, Excelsa Film, 1947

p. 396, illustration from *L'uomo che ride* (original title: *L'homme qui rit*; English title: *The Man Who Laughs* or *The Laughing Man*), by Victor Hugo, Milan: Sonzogno, no date, © RCS (author's collection)

p. 397, still of Rita Hayworth and Tyrone Power from *Blood and Sand,* directed by Rouben Mamoulian, 20th Century Fox, 1941

p. 398, still of Bing Crosby and Frank McHugh from *Going My Way,* directed by Leo McCarey, Paramount, 1944

p. 400, Jules Barbey d'Aurevilly, *Léa,* from *Œuvres romanesques complètes* (*Complete Novels*), Paris: Pléiade Gallimard, 2002

p. 401, Gustave Moreau, detail of *L'apparition* (*The Apparition*), 1876

p. 404, Sergio Corazzini, from "Il mio cuore" ("My Heart"), from *Dolcezze* (*Sweetnesses*), 1904

pp. 404–405, Guido Gozzano, from "La più bella" ("The Loveliest"), 1913

p. 413, montage by the author of an illustration by Alex Raymond from *Rip Kirby* (© King Features Syndicate, Inc.). Reprinted with special permission of King Features Syndicate; an illustration of a 1950s Schubert pattern (Centro Studi e Archivio della Communicazione, Parma), and a Vespa ad (from *Il libro della communicazione Piaggio* [*The Piaggio Communication Book*]), by Maurizio Boldrini and Omar Calabrese, Siena: Alsaba, 1995

pp. 422–24, 427–28, 430, 432, montages by the author of illustrations by Alex Raymond from *Flash Gordon,* © King Features Syndicate, Inc. All images reprinted with special permission of King Features Syndicate.

p. 434, adaptation by the author of an illustration by Lee Falk and Phil Davis from *Mandrake,* © King Features Syndicate, Inc. Reprinted with special permission of King Features Syndicate.

p. 437, adaptation by the author of an illustration by Milton Caniff from *Terry and the Pirates,* © Chicago Tribune/New York News Syndicate. Reproduced by kind permission of Tribune Media Services.

p. 438, adaptation by the author of an illustration by Alex Raymond from *Flash Gordon,* © King Features Syndicate, Inc. Reprinted with special permission of King Features Syndicate.

p. 440, montage by the author of illustrations from various Italian books

p. 442, lyrics by Bixio Cherubini, "La famiglia canterina" ("The Singing Family"), Milan: Edizioni Bixio, 1929. Lyrics reproduced by kind permission of IDM Music, Ltd. All rights reserved.

p. 443, adaptation by the author of an illustration by Lyman Young from *La misteriosa fiamma della Regina Loana* (*The Mysterious Flame of Queen Loana*), Florence: Nerbini, 1935, © King Features Syndicate, Inc. Reprinted with special permission of King Features Syndicate.

p. 445, adaptation by the author of an anonymous holy card